BEING
WOAKE

JON CROSS

Cover illustration: Mark Reeve
Editing and proofreading: Craig Smith (CRS Editorial)
Book design: SWATT Books Ltd

Printed in the United Kingdom
First Printed 2022

ISBN: 978-1-7396830-0-9 (Paperback)
ISBN: 978-1-7396830-1-6 (eBook)

Alsatian Publishing
Guildford, Surrey

www.alsatian-publishing.co.uk

This book is dedicated to all public servants, elected or unelected, regardless of whatever service they provide, endeavour to provide and, occasionally, fail to provide.

One

FEBRUARY 2016

It was seven o'clock in the evening and the Cabinet of Gretford District Council was in turmoil.

Earlier that morning, Gerald Gallagher (Leader of the Council) had become temporarily incapacitated, thereby allowing friends and rivals in the local Conservative Association and on the Cabinet to deselect him and rule him unfit for leadership.

Not that this was necessarily known by every member of the Cabinet, thought William Foster (Lead Councillor for Finance and Deputy Leader), who hoped to be shortly appointed his successor.

Foster addressed the Cabinet.

'As you may well be aware, Gerald has today left the Council,' he said.

'That's a bloody understatement. The old soak had a stroke. Drank himself into his hospital bed,' commented Reg Swaden (Lead Councillor for Parks, Leisure and Rural Affairs) as he looked towards the one empty chair, which had previously belonged to Gallagher. 'A lifetime of single malt, Sauvignon Blanc and womanising has succeeded where the Irish, the Argentines and the staff of GDC collectively failed.'

As Councillor Gerald Gallagher (sixty-four years old, formerly King's Royal Hussars) walked out of the shower, he was, without warning, struck by a stroke and fell to the ground with as much dignity as his sixteen stone could muster.

After a somewhat delayed but perhaps understandable response by the long-suffering Mrs Gallagher, an ambulance was called and he was taken directly to hospital where the prognosis was that he would remain in a medically induced coma for the foreseeable future.

All of which was entirely academic to the Cabinet of Gretford District Council. The Leader was incapable of leading, but he was still Leader.

Which meant a power vacuum.

'Thank you, Reg, for your input,' Foster responded. 'The question now, is what do we do?'

Within minutes of hearing the news from the Council's Managing Director (the Council's leading civil servant), the ever politically ambitious (though not necessarily the most politically competent) Foster had sensed his time had come and immediately sprang into action.

Foster, knowing that the extremely competent but domineering Gallagher was hated by his Conservative Party Sub-Association, persuaded the Association's Management Committee to deselect Gallagher as Councillor within hours on the basis he could no longer fulfil his municipal duty.

'I've already received notice from Gerald's Party Association that they will trigger a by-election for his seat, due to ill-health, as soon as decency allows,' said Foster, deciding to omit the full extent of his influence on their decision. 'So we now need to choose a new Leader.'

'Who, I am sure, we all agree must be one of us,' said Mark Skelding, the fat and balding Lead Councillor for Licensing Enforcement and Civil Protection whose barely concealed ambition imagined himself replacing Gallagher.

'Indeed, it must be. I think we all agree on that one,' said Craig Overton. In his mid-thirties, he was already Lead Councillor for Green Development, Sustainable Projects and Governance, as well as Deputy Chairman of the Gretford Conservative Association. His ambition to one day be sitting in the House of Commons had earned him the nickname "The Careerist" from Council staff.

The fact he was a homosexual would only be seen as a benefit by the Party's equality officers. 'It is imperative that we continue with our own agendas with as much of a smooth transition of leadership as we can manage.'

By that he meant it was imperative that they all keep their portfolios.

'But which one of us will stand?' asked Swaden. 'Hopefully someone who won't be pulled over for drink driving,' he added.

'The first time Gallagher blamed his conviction on the stress of his mother's death was one thing, but the third time the excuse was used was definitely a stretch.'

'Mr Deputy Chairman,' Skelding interrupted, 'as a longstanding member not only of the Council but also the Cabinet, I believe I am in a powerful position to present a viable alternative as Leader of the Conservative Group.'

'Unfortunately you don't have the support amongst the backbenchers,' Overton said, who was also the Secretary of the Conservative Group, the dominant political group on the Council.

Such was the dominance of the Conservative Group at Gretford, its leader would be an automatic choice for Leader of the Council.

'And who does?' Skelding asked, not a little piqued.

'The reality is,' said the extremely politically astute Overton, 'is that there is a danger that another faction within the Group will put forward their own candidate. We must therefore put forward the strongest possible candidate. I am too young. Reg, I don't think you want it?'

'You could say that. You could also say that the wife doesn't want me to do it. She already thinks that I spend too much time with you lot.'

'Serena, you have a full-time job and so don't have the time,' Overton said. Serena Kildare (Lead Councillor for Health and Community) was a surgeon at Gretford Royal Infirmary. Not only was she the only female councillor under the age of 40, she was the only woman on the Cabinet; testament to Gallagher's presence in the equality and diversity training session which the Council's Managing Director had insisted on sending him to.

'And Simon,' Overton concluded, 'you have already been Leader. Such a move to appoint you would be seen as a step backwards.'

'Which leaves Will,' Simon Newton said.

'I'd be honoured to put my name forward,' Foster said with smug satisfaction, to agreement from a Cabinet split between those who harboured an ambition for the top job, and those who were equally relieved not to have been asked to consider it.

Out of the previous three leaders, one was currently residing in hospital because of alcoholism, another was promoted rapidly to Alderman (Gretford's version of the House of Lords) having been seen talking to an imaginary resident in Gretford high street, whilst the third was divorced by his wife of thirty years on grounds of infidelity after only three years as Leader.

The look on Mrs Newton's solicitor's face when the allegations were first made was nothing compared to the judge's when he learnt that the third person was an entire council district of one hundred and fifty thousand people. It was after only listening to the wronged woman for five minutes that the learned judge was only too happy to grant the decree absolute before escaping to a dry sherry and a fortifying lunch.

'And if you were to become Leader, Will, who will take over the Finance portfolio and deputy leadership?' Kildare asked.

'I shall put my name forward for the deputy leadership,' Overton said, who had spent as much time in recent years as Foster had in charming and intimidating the Conservative backbenchers.

'And I don't see why I cannot continue with the Finance portfolio and be Leader,' said Foster. Being in charge of Gretford District Council's £250m annual budget was the most important portfolio available to a councillor; second only to the Leader.

'Not sure that the great Gretford public would look favourably on that Will; could be seen to be a bit of a power-grab,' said Skelding (not a natural ally of Foster) to murmurings of agreement.

'It is perhaps too onerous a task to have both the leadership and the Finance portfolio,' Foster said reluctantly. 'I do also have to work.'

'So who'll get finance?' asked Kildare again.

'Question is, who wants it?' asked Swaden.

It is despite the best intentions of Labour and the suspicions of the Liberal Democrats, that without a sound finance strategy, such things as community projects, bin collections, council housing, meals on wheels and low council tax are mere fantasy.

However, the main issue with finance is the officers' reports. Purposefully written to confuse the minds of councillors, bore the local press and baffle residents, the reports are totally impenetrable to all but the keenest financial minds.

Indeed, the principal reason that the aforementioned independent backbencher was seen talking to his invisible friend might have been explained by his holding the Finance portfolio for six years before becoming Leader.

'Dadswell?' asked Skelding.

'No, he's a banker in the City. He'll want to commercialise this Council,' answered Foster.

In the age of central Government cutbacks, it has become vital that councils like Gretford find ever more inventive ways to generate income. Otherwise, council tax would need to rise or the weekly bin collection would need to change to fortnightly. Both of which would be electoral disasters.

The main issue with commercialisation is that officers lack the private sector instinct of entrepreneurialism and the more commercially astute councillors lack the patience to properly explain business to them.

'Before we know it, we'll have another North Sussex Housing on our hands,' said Overton. North Sussex Housing represented Gretford District Council's first foray into the world of business.

'How about Jeremy Pakeman?' asked Kildare.

'God no, he's a bloody accountant. He might actually understand the officers' reports,' replied Overton, airing what all Cabinet members feared. Being an accountant, Jeremy Pakeman might just investigate Council spending, and he might just discover an uncomfortable truth.

Having been authorised to invest £600,000 in property, four senior officers demonstrated a commercial experience that can only come with a combined 120 years in the public sector and brought three two-bedroom flats to the centre of Gretford.

Unfortunately for Gretford, the company's business case failed to predict that the Council would be unable to rent the three flats. Whilst there may have been a market for one-bedroom flats, very few locals neither wanted nor could afford the rent of a two-bedroom flat without subletting the second bedroom; a restriction incorporated into the tenancy agreement because of the in-house legal team's insistence that it was a standard term.

In short, the Council had invested in property it could not rent out, and had now been forced to pay council tax alongside upkeep and running costs.

North Sussex Housing was GDC's inaugural move into private finance and, senior officers and councillors hoped, its last.

'Well, who else is there?' asked Skelding.

'Councillor Elliot?' asked Foster.

'She's in her eighties,' replied Overton. 'We've just dealt with one health emergency, please not another.'

'Bob Richardson?' asked Swaden.

'His voice sounds like a cross between an undertaker and Roy Hodgson,' replied Foster.

'Sounds perfect for the state of our finances,' said Swaden.

For the next five minutes, the Cabinet considered all the Conservative Group members who were, one by one, discounted for being too old, too extremist, too grey and too Welsh.

One name remained which had not been discussed.

'How about Sebastian Woake?' asked Kildare.

'What about him?' asked Overton.

'He could be perfect,' Kildare answered. 'He's a criminal barrister, so we're guaranteed half-decent speeches on budget night and he'll have no idea about public finance.'

'He sounds overqualified,' said Swaden.

'He's also an ardent Brexiteer, so he obviously has no political ambition, national or local,' Overton said.

Gretford was ardent Remain.

'Will,' Skelding interrupted, holding up his right hand. 'I would advise most strongly against promoting Woake to anywhere near the Cabinet. Let's not forget his behaviour on election day and Purple Flag. The man's an embarrassment.'

'And you think he'll agree to it?' asked Foster, ignoring Skelding, realising that they were out of other viable options.

'He's newly elected, so at least he'll be easy to control,' said Overton. 'I'll speak to him about it tomorrow.'

And so it was that with no finance experience and very little political knowledge, Councillor Sebastian Woake found himself promoted from lowly backbencher to member of the Cabinet.

The meeting was concluded shortly afterwards.

'Didn't take you long to replace Gerald, did it?' Newton commented as everyone was leaving. Newton remembered Foster's role in his own political downfall and the immediate rise of Gallagher.

Two

'The Sussex market town of Gretford is an old town, although its history is neither turbulent nor spectacular.' So reads the opening line of the Gretford entry in *The Shell Guide to England* and is a statement the residents of Gretford are duly proud of.

Located to the north of the South Downs, gentrified Gretford straddles the River Ford valley.

Starting life as a crossing point across the river, the town's unspectacular history only really started in the years following the Norman Conquest, when a Norman king chose the crossing as an ideal location for a castle. The local town quickly grew from a settlement of only a couple of hundred villagers into a town of a few thousand, all providing services to the royal household.

Unfortunately for the castle, Gretford was neither spectacular nor turbulent enough for the Plantagenets who, preferring to fight the French (and themselves), soon moved out. This left the ever-growing town with a castle which quickly fell into a state of disrepair in which "medieval ruin" would be a better description.

Gretford maintained its gradual growth over the centuries, reaching the point in the eighteenth century when it became one of the most important market towns in Sussex, complete with its own diocese. Due to its location, Gretford quickly became a staging post between London and the naval port at Portsmouth, guaranteeing a healthy trade of Royal Navy officers and Government officials desperate for a night in a warm bed and the night-time services of the locals as they journeyed back and forth.

Unfortunately, this idyll was to be shattered by the two major events of the twentieth century, both of which have left their mark on the town.

World War I marked the first occasion in which central Government noticed the ever-expanding market town.

It was a paradoxical consequence of the War that, whilst a previously unimagined number of local men had been killed in only four years, towns across the south-east were ordered to build homes for thousands of survivors forced to migrate south from their native Midlands due to the behaviour of unscrupulous landlords and modernising factory owners.

To say that this sent the then Gretford District Council into a panic would be an understatement. Its population was only 40,000 in 1919 and it was suddenly asked to provide homes for a further 20,000. Like many towns, Gretford had also accumulated its own war debt. It simply lacked the ability to build and the finances to buy the land required.

Thankfully, help from an unexpected source was at hand.

In an even worse financial position than local Councils, the British Government did what Governments through the centuries have always done when in need of money; they took from the perceived wealthy. Lloyd George, with all the venom of a liberal from the Welsh valleys, declared a new war on the English landowner, who soon needed to pay duties on inheritance and land which their incomes could no longer honour.

The Earl of Whittom (Gretford's local landowner) was no exception.

With typical upper-class disdain towards middle-class liberals, the Earl donated 10,000 acres of his land away to the Council rather than pay a single shilling to Lloyd George.

However, such a compromise presented yet another difficulty; it was potentially terrible PR for both parties.

The Council could not be seen to be so financially desperate that it would be eager to accept a gift from a tax dodger, a label that the Earl of Whittom was obviously more than eager to avoid.

Displaying a level of spin-doctoring genius not seen again until New Labour, the Council reached a solution.

So it was that in 1920, the Earl of Whittom (in an act of total selflessness) granted Gretford District Council a gift of 10,000 acres to the south of Gretford, with the express aim of building 20,000 homes for the returning heroes, on the southern side of the River Ford valley. With no small consideration to his legacy and with generations of self-publicity in his veins, he named the gift Whittom Village.

It was unfortunate for the residents of the newly built Whittom Village that the Countess of Whittom was a militant abstinent and prohibited the building of even a single pub to service the new homes. A hundred years later, there is still no pub in Whittom Village.

As Gretford's heroes were predominately residing in small plots of Belgium soil which would be forever Gretford, those few that did return found a surplus of dead comrades' houses on the property market. Gretford was therefore made to take in wounded servicemen from across England who were unable to work.

By 1925, Gretford was firmly on the commuter belt into London and the District Council was encompassed by the market town itself in the centre, with suburbia to the north and south, and quiet country villages to the east and west.

Within a couple of years, Whittom Village had become a slum and introduced Gretford to the dawn of the welfare state. With the prosperous northern side and the poor southern side, Gretford quickly became the tale of two towns.

It was at this time that the modern geography of Gretford emerged. With the River Ford winding its way at the bottom of the valley, the cobbled high street runs along the northern slope, reaching the residential suburbs of Wellington, Ferndown and Pentridge at the top of the valley.

Georgian shops, a Jacobean guildhall, medieval churches and a marketplace with a Corinthian-style entrance adorn the high street. Towards the southern end of the high street lies the Gretford gyratory system; a convoluted system of bus lanes, pedestrian crossings, traffic signals, dual carriageways and two road bridges across the River Ford, all intended to guarantee gridlocked traffic no matter what time of day.

The northern boundary of Gretford is marked by the A32 dual carriageway, providing the primary route from London to the south coast.

The population explosion of the 1920s brought about a hitherto unknown ambition amongst district councillors, who began to make decisions based upon legacy, economic development and the future. Gretford had arrived, and to mark its arrival the District Council began its most ambitious project to date; the building of a new cathedral.

Work began in 1930 on a site chosen so that Gretford Cathedral could be seen for miles around; a man-made hill fifty metres high on the southern side of the town. The cathedral was completed in 1939 and was consecrated just as the German tanks began their advance on Warsaw. Built with limestone in the neoclassical style, many consider Gretford Cathedral to be the ugliest building in the south-east.

Unwittingly, Gretford soon became vital to the nation's survival during its darkest hour. The town suffered during the Blitz, surprising as it had absolutely nothing of value to the war effort.

What it did have, in the shape of its new cathedral, was the largest homing beacon south of London.

Having missed their primary objective and not wanting to return to France with a full bombload, German aircrews quickly searched for easier secondary targets.

Failing to believe that such a large stone monstrosity could be such a sacred place of worship, German aircrews became convinced that the sprawling mass was of some importance to British survival.

So started a little-known game played out by German squadrons who competed to be the first to hit the cathedral, with a case of looted Veuve Clicquot as the main prize.

Night after night, Gretford burned as the cathedral remained a peaceful oasis during the firestorm of war as German bombers diverted precious bombs away from other targets of considerably greater value in order to be the first crew to hit the jackpot.

To the bewilderment of many Luftwaffe airmen and to the amazement of residents (who believed that a minor miracle was occurring) not one German bomb hit the cathedral.

That the cathedral survived the War unscathed is perhaps testament to the fact German precision bombing was not quite as precise as Nazi propaganda believed.

World War II also introduced Gretford to the Italians.

As Italian division after Italian division surrendered, the Government struggled to cope with hundreds of thousands of Italian immigrants. Gretford, like many provincial towns, played host to an Italian Prisoner of War camp. It only took the War Office a few months to realise a major benefit to Italian PoW camps not apparent in their German counterparts; very few guards, if any, were needed.

Unlike their German comrades, who were always eager to further the Axis war effort by whatever means possible, the Italians adopted a more serene philosophy to their incarceration and were more than happy to see out the War (to whatever conclusion) in more peaceful surroundings. To the War Office's delight, only a very few members of the Gretford Home Guard were ever needed on guard duty.

However, what pleased the War Office caused utter dismay amongst the Gretford men, many of whom were away fighting.

Starved of beddable male folk, the women of Gretford quickly found solace in their new Italian friends.

For once, Gretford set the trend. The post-War baby boom was merely a larger replication of a phenomenon which affected Gretford after 1941.

Indeed, it was many a Gretford man who despaired at what should have been the most joyous occasion of his life when presented with a new arrival with a curious tint to the skin which could never belong in Sussex. For many men serving on the front line, it was simply not worth calculating when they had last slept with their wives when notified that they were now proud fathers.

To be labelled "well-tanned" during a hot summer would remain in the Gretford vernacular for many years.

Traumatised by the bombings and relieved when the Italians were reluctantly sent home, Gretford District Council quickly retreated into the radical conservatism which had defined it before 1914.

Conservatism became a byword for sound governance, and the divisions between north and south Gretford became evermore pronounced. Its population was a healthy mix of townies longing to live in the countryside, suburban dwellers who believed they lived in the countryside and country dwellers who actually did.

The population of the district reached one hundred and fifty thousand by 2015 and the 2015 local election was typical of all local elections since 1945. Out of the fifty-six Council seats available, the electorate returned thirty-eight Conservatives (all in the more affluent north, east and west), ten Liberal Democrats and three Labour (unsurprisingly in the south).

The only storm cloud on the horizon of Gretford's pursuit in remaining neither turbulent nor spectacular came from central Government. Faced with a national housing shortage bordering on a crisis, orders were issued forcing every local authority to begin a programme of property building. Every authority was ordered to publish their own Local Plan to demonstrate how this was to be achieved.

The policymakers at Gretford had identified three potential sites, all with the space for two thousand homes. Unfortunately for the Council, all three sites were located in the more affluent areas. The locals fully accepted that Gretford needed to build, just not near them.

In anticipation for the impending Local Plan, a group of Gretford residents took matters into their hands and formed their own political party with the aims of delaying the implementation of the Local Plan, protecting the countryside and objecting to the three strategic sites. The new party was called the Gretford Guardians, led by seasoned battle-axe Patricia Lafontaine.

They were returned in 2015 with the remaining five seats.

It was into this political dogfight that newly elected Councillor Sebastian Woake was soon to find himself.

Three

FEBRUARY 2015

It was not through any grand design that Sebastian Woake became a councillor. It was certainly not through any political ambition, nor was it through any burning desire to represent the people of Gretford. Woake spent every working day representing the guilty, the oppressed and the occasional innocent, and he certainly had no intention of pursuing a pastime which mirrored his job.

It was, as he explained to his Head of Chambers, the result of trying to prove himself to an incredibly difficult former mother-in-law.

'Ah Woake, good of you to come in,' said Richard Myers as Woake entered his study. Myers was Head of Griffin Court Chambers, a small set of one QC, twenty barristers, two clerks and one pupil located in the Inner Temple.

It was a dark and wet February evening and Woake had just returned from a trial at Blackfriars Crown Court.

'No problem Richard, Louise passed on your message that you wanted to see me.' Louise was Woake's clerk.

'How's your customs case?' asked Myers.

'Pretty good, actually. The trial involves the personal chef to the Archbishop of Westminster. He's currently standing trial for attempting to smuggle in three offensive weapons from Romania.'

'Which are?'

'A pair of nunchucks and a stun gun. His defence is that he didn't realise that the nunchucks are banned and that he thought that the stun gun was a torch to help him in the Archbishop's kitchen.'

'Confident?'

'After today, definitely. He pleaded to the nunchucks when advised that ignorance is no defence, and the torch story is total bollocks.'

'Doesn't the Archbishop's kitchen have lights?'

'You would have thought that, Richard, but I do have some sympathy with the defence's case. The defendant is so fat he probably blocks the light when he's rummaging in the cupboards. What he failed to consider was that "Warning 40,000-volt stun gun" was plastered all over the stun gun's packaging.'

'So he's been convicted?' Myers asked.

'Unfortunately no, the case was adjourned until the morning and I've just returned from St Thomas's Hospital.'

'Christ, what happened?'

'Defence counsel asked the officer in the case to take the stun gun out of the packaging to show that it could be confused with a torch. It's a long thin object with two metal teeth sticking out of one end. My opponent asked the officer to turn on the gun and a small light did indeed come on between the teeth.'

'And that was it?'

'I'm afraid not. The officer must have kept his finger on the button for too long, or it's ultrasensitive, as an electric charge came flying out of the gun and attached itself to the stenographer, who promptly did what anybody would do when hit with 40,000 volts. The poor woman collapsed on the floor with a seizure and temporary paralysis.'

'She survived?'

'Yes, we rushed her to A&E but to be honest I don't know who was most distressed, apart from her. The officer who suffered his own paralysis as he was unable to move when the enormity of what he had done hit him, my opponent who realised that his defence was totally shot to pieces, or the defendant who I should imagine is currently enjoying gorging his way through his last night of freedom. Frankly, I couldn't have done a better job myself.'

'Well, I'm glad to see that there are some benefits out of another person's misfortune.'

'Indeed, but I'm sure that you didn't call me in to discuss the case of Fatty Fatty Boom Boom and the stun gun.'

'Completely correct, dear boy,' Myers said. 'I have heard some rumour which is currently going around Chambers that you've decided to become the next Tony Blair.'

'Not quite, Richard. I've just applied to become a councillor at Gretford.'

'What utter madness made you do that?'

'The utter madness of speaking to Sarah when pissed.'

'The ex-fiancée?' Myers asked.

'Yes. We last spoke a couple of weeks ago after I had moved to my new place in Gretford. She's still in her flat at Hampstead. She said that her decision was correct. That she needed someone of a bit more culture and who would give more time to public service. Her father was once CEO of some refugee charity. According to her over-the-top domineering mother, the criminal bar isn't virtuous enough.'

'So why be a councillor? I thought you had to be seventy and deranged to be one.'

'I was throwing away that day's junk mail whilst arguing with her. One letter was from the local Conservative Party inviting applications for the forthcoming elections. I thought this would be a good idea to prove her mother wrong. Unfortunately, whoever processed the application could read my drunken handwriting and I have my first selection meeting tonight.'

'So you're going to see this madness through?'

'You know me, Richard, never one not to see something through.'

'Except your recent engagement,' Myers said.

So Woake found himself going through the Conservative Party application process for prospective candidates.

He passed the interview stage with flying colours. The Association was only too happy to accept someone who wasn't past middle-aged, fat, bald and with an obsession for different shades of beige clothing.

The next stage was slightly more problematic. He had to find a seat. This involved half a dozen evenings spent in various district wards answering questions from local members. As these were all safe seats, successful candidates were either currently sitting councillors or long-term Party members. Woake quickly realised that, as the latest recruit, he must start at the bottom and work his way up. In politics, that means standing in a safe opponent's seat where your performance is marked by how well you lose.

Safe seat after safe picked their current councillor. Feeling dejected after congratulating yet another retired man on reselection to a safe seat, Woake was just leaving his latest (and last) selection meeting when he was approached by a thin, narrow-shouldered man in his late twenties.

'Hi Sebastian, I'm Craig Overton. Deputy Chairman of the Gretford Conservative Association and Councillor for Wellington ward,' the stranger said, holding out a limp hand for Woake to shake.

'Hi Craig, nice to meet you,' Woake said, under the impression that Wellington was in New Zealand and not Gretford.

'It's such a shame, Sebastian, that so far you have been so unsuccessful in finding a seat. We could do with a bit of young talent on the Council.'

'Thanks, but I think that the Association is determined to stick with the devils it knows,' Woake said.

'I might be able to help you with that. There is a ward available which returns three councillors. We have one candidate already but are having difficulty finding another two. Would you consider standing?'

Sounds like a bloody hospital pass, Woake thought. 'Why not. Put me down,' he said.

So Woake became a candidate for Whittom Village, a staunch Liberal Democrat ward. His two running mates were also no-hopers.

However, he was determined to prove Myers, amongst many others, wrong and so for three evenings a week and two hours every Saturday after rowing, prospective Councillor Woake knocked on doors, introduced himself to his would-be constituents and tried to convince them to lend him their vote.

Surprisingly, his canvassing awoke a hitherto unknown political talent. Woake was actually a very good campaigner.

With absolutely no shame at all, he could garner political support by telling the residents of Whittom Village exactly what they wanted to hear. He would promise Mrs Jones at No 1 Addison Road that he would reintroduce the No 42 bus (cancelled 10 years previously by the bus company); Mr Handley at No 3 that he would fill in the potholes; agree with young Miss Carole at No 5 that he would campaign to end student fees; Mrs Brown at No 7 was told that he would ensure that no homes would be built in the greenbelt; whilst Mr Wilson at No 9 was assured that Woake would help ease traffic congestion in the town centre by reducing the number of buses operating in Gretford.

It was normal for Woake, after canvassing an entire road, to have made up to a dozen (often contradictory) promises. His defence was that he was sure that he never be elected (Whittom had never returned a Conservative) and so would never have to fulfil them. Besides, he adopted the hope of all politicians through the ages. On the off-chance that he would be elected, he doubted that any residents would be able to remember him after a couple of months anyway.

Election day came and Woake, at seven o'clock that morning, was sitting in the briefing room of the Gretford Conservative headquarters, alongside the other fifty-five Conservative candidates.

Craig Overton, as the Association's campaign coordinator, stood up to give the briefing.

'Good morning all, and well done for an excellent campaign to date. Our polling suggests that we're in for a very successful day.' Woake sat in his chair, allowing his mind to fall asleep as Overton continued his briefing.

'You first-timers may not be aware, but the crucial element for today is getting our vote out. There's little point in all that canvassing if nobody actually bothers to vote. Thankfully, today is also a General Election and we're expecting a high turnout.

'So what will be happening is that our army of volunteers are recording the electoral numbers of everyone who has voted. That will enable us, the candidates, to knock up our supporters who have yet to vote.'

'I'm sorry Craig, do what to our voters?' Woake asked, interrupting the briefing. All fifty-five candidates turned towards Woake, the majority annoyed at the unveiled threat towards their own self-importance. A few were quietly bemused.

'Knock up, Sebastian,' Overton responded with some annoyance. He was not used to being interrupted. 'We call it knocking up because we knock on doors. It's what the Party calls encouraging our supporters to vote.'

'Should imagine it depends who's doing the knocking up.'

'It's a key part to any electoral campaign,' Overton continued 'for political parties to knock up their supporters on polling day. In fact, entire articles have been written about how election days have been lost by the party which has failed to do enough knocking.'

Shortly after lunch, Woake was sent out with the names and addresses of supporters who were yet to cast their vote.

His first attempt at knocking up was hardly a success.

He rang the doorbell to find an elderly Mrs Campbell standing in front of him.

'Good morning Mrs Campbell,' Woake said. 'I am here on behalf of the Conservative Party to knock you up.' It hardly surprised him when the door was slammed in his face, nor when he received a phone call a short while later from Overton.

'I'm afraid, Sebastian, that we're going to have to pull you back to HQ.'

'That seems very unfair Craig, may I ask why?'

'Sebastian, I think you probably know. We have been receiving several complaints about a Party representative walking around Whittom Village, informing its residents that he is there to have sex with them.'

'But that's what you sent me out to do, Craig,' Woake responded.

'You know exactly what the problem is. Do I need to remind you that we want to win today?'

Election day ended at ten o'clock, with fifty-five Conservative candidates collapsing in chairs at headquarters as the adrenaline that had fortified them all day wore off and they were all overcome with physical and emotional exhaustion from the campaign.

All that is except for Woake, who spent a very easy afternoon reading the following week's case papers accompanied by a never-ending supply of sandwiches and tea.

The following day was the count.

Woake stood with the other thirteen candidates for Whittom Village, surrounding a table in the basement of the local leisure centre, the somewhat needlessly named "Prism". Hundreds of people – candidates, their agents, supporters, party members and the local press – all congregated in the huge sports hall, eager for the results.

The ballot boxes were opened and the votes for Whittom began to be counted. The Conservatives were only fifty votes behind the Liberal Democrats after the block votes had been counted. These were ballot papers in which the voter had voted for all three candidates from the same party.

The individual votes were counted next. With a growing sense of excitement, Woake saw his number of personal votes soon become the largest pile. As Overton had said during his briefing, local opinion polls were indicating a Conservative landslide and for once they were correct, and Whittom Village was no exception.

With absolutely no regard for his Party's manifesto and by telling every resident exactly what they had wanted to hear, Woake had pulled off a minor political miracle and had thrown down a bastion of liberalism.

'Are you a councillor yet?' a bellowing voice called behind him. Woake turned round to face a tall thin man in his late fifties, wearing glasses and an army tie.

'Yes,' Woake said. 'You could say that.'

'Reg Swaden, I'm one of your Conservative colleagues,' the man said, extending his hand out, ignoring the question. 'Just been voted in for another four years at the madhouse. You?'

'Standing in Whittom. Looks like I'll be joining you.'

'Oh, well done. Aren't you that bloke who was knocking up his residents yesterday?'

By the end of the day, the result was confirmed.

The ward of Whittom Village had returned Liam Perkins and Simon Booth (both Lib Dems with 1,576 and 1,320 votes respectively) and Sebastian Woake (Conservative, 1,134) as its three councillors for 2015 to 2019.

Later that evening, Woake received an email from Myers. *Well done Woake, I didn't know that you had 1,134 friends.*

Four

OCTOBER 2015

The first six months were very uneventful for Councillor Woake, who was appointed to the district's Planning Committee and the Overview and Scrutiny Committee, a committee which met bi-monthly and scrutinised the decisions taken by the Council.

Considering that members of the said committee had directly voted on the decisions made by the Council on meetings passed, its focus was more on over-viewing than scrutinising.

Apart from the additional meetings of Full Council (which met six times a year) there was as little or as much work as a councillor wished for.

In Woake's case, this was very little.

Feeling just as shocked that a Conservative had been elected in their Liberal heartland as the rest of the Council, the more politically active (and therefore Liberal Democrat) residents favoured his two ward colleagues rather than Woake, if they required any help.

On the rare occasions that he did receive a cry for help from a resident (usually involving a planning application or an email detailing concern about the latest building development), Woake's colleagues were more than happy to take the lead in resolving the particular issue.

In addition to the homes set up for the Great War heroes, Whittom Village ward had three important assets: the cathedral; the University of South-East England (a former polytechnic which had attained university status in the 1970s); and Gretford Crematorium.

Gretford Conservative Association was also easily dealt with. Woake ignored it.

By the time that he was called to a meeting with Gerald

Gallagher, the Leader of the Council, seven months on from the election, Woake had settled into life as a backbencher. This involved attending the monthly Conservative Group meeting, listening to the Cabinet members justify their existence and voting the correct way at Full Council meetings.

This was something that not all backbenchers adhered to, much to the chagrin of the Cabinet.

The Cabinet.

The pinnacle of a councillor's career. Many aspired, conspired and plotted to gain a portfolio of their own. The gift of a seat on the Cabinet rested with Gallagher, as Leader.

The Cabinet was of very little interest to Woake, who had already achieved his own somewhat limited political ambition.

However, what he was more interested in was Councillor Serena Kildare, the young and pretty portfolio holder for Health and Community.

Woake had listened to a ten-minute presentation by Kildare on Inspire to Aspire, a key part to her portfolio which centred on providing career opportunities for the most underprivileged children in Gretford.

Her passion and emotion had allowed all the men in the room to stare at her without interruption.

The straight ones, anyway.

Woake had already discovered that there was not much else to do during Group meetings.

Woake walked into the leadership suite at Fordhouse, the head office of Gretford District Council.

A large building with decades' worth of additions since the first foundation stone was laid in 1922, Fordhouse sits next to the River Ford, at the bottom of Gretford high street. Inside were the offices for the Council's planning and licensing teams, social care, economic development and any other project which the senior management spent taxpayers' money on.

Fordhouse was solely for administrative staff.

All manual workers and machinery, including dustcarts and road sweepers, were kept at a separate location on the outskirts of Gretford.

The leadership suite was on the first floor, comprising half a dozen offices surrounding a central pool of three personal assistants. Five of the offices belonged to each of the five directors, the most senior offices at the Council. The sixth office was the largest; a long rectangular room belonging to the Leader and Deputy Leader.

A large oval desk, much like the Downing Street Cabinet table, dominated the office. Gerald Gallagher sat on one side of the table. Sitting next to him was William Foster, Gallagher's 5ft 6" overweight Deputy, with a small tubby face and hair swept from a side-parting.

In contrast, Gallagher was perfectly presented in his double-breasted blazer, sky-blue trousers and tasselled slip-on shoes. Although a heavy man with the face of a drinker, Gallagher exerted the cool authority that could only be expected from a former army officer.

The two men rose to greet Woake, who shook hands with both.

Gallagher invited Woake to sit.

'Thank you, Sebastian, for seeing Will and I today,' Gallagher said.

'That's fine Gerald, always a pleasure to see you both,' Woake replied. The suspicion of a questioning look flickered across Gallagher's eyes, lasting for only a brief second.

'As I'm sure you're aware, I am obliged by our Group rules to meet with all Group members once a year. This is essentially an opportunity for us to chat about the Council, see if we have any issues which need to be resolved and to check that you're happy. Nothing sinister.' Gallagher gave a faint hint of a smile.

'That's fine Gerald, there is absolutely nothing to report.'

'I usually hold these meetings in the early summer,' Gallagher continued. 'But considering the May elections, I thought it would be better to delay them whilst you newbies found your feet. How have you found the last seven months?'

'Fine thanks,' Woake answered. His experience of the last seven months was that minimal communication was key. It was invariably those that spoke too much and too often who found themselves with greater responsibility.

'You're on the Planning Committee and on Overview and Scrutiny, I understand?' Gallagher asked.

'That's correct.'

'And are you enjoying the experience?' Foster asked, wondering how such reticence could come from a criminal barrister.

'Overview and Scrutiny is as ineffective as it is, but I should imagine that you chaps are happy with that,' Woake responded. 'But the Planning Committee's training was a joke. We had two separate lectures at seven thirty in the evening, which consisted only of planning law, enforcement procedure and planning regulations. We're then thrust onto a quasi-judicial committee and asked to pass judgement on planning applications with no idea on what to judge or how to judge it.'

'You think the training could be better?' Gallagher asked.

'Of course. Although I suspect that the training is deliberately poor.'

'In what way?' Foster asked.

'Well, it doesn't take too much to work out,' Woake responded. 'The training is given by the officers, whose advice forms the basis of our decisions. Why would they want a councillor to question their opinion?'

'You're a criminal barrister? Are you having any difficulty in balancing the pressures on your time?' Gallagher asked, moving the conversation on.

'It's fine thanks. I'm able to ensure that my political life doesn't impinge at all on my professional life.' *Or personal life*, Woake thought.

'That's good to know. And how are you finding Whittom Village? You are, of course, a Conservative in a formerly safe Liberal area.'

'Quiet. Only issues seem to be potholes, lack of pub, bin collections and planning decisions.'

'Your ward colleagues?' Foster asked.

'They seem to be decent blokes. They're more than happy to do most of the workload, in light of the fact they've represented the ward for years and so know how the Council works.'

'It is worth remembering, Sebastian, that the Conservatives have been working hard for a seat in Whittom for a while now. It would be good to know that you're doing what you can to secure our future there.' Foster said, forever trying to sound politically competent.

Realising that Woake would not respond, Gallagher continued.

'Obviously the draft Local Plan will affect Whittom, not to mention the redevelopment of the crematorium.'

'Indeed.' That was the first Woake had heard of any planned

redevelopment of the crematorium.

'You're still quite young, aren't you?'

'I turned thirty-seven in March.'

'Which makes you the same age as Serena. There are currently three councillors under the age of forty; all except for you are on the Cabinet.'

'I really don't have time to take on a portfolio.'

'I wasn't asking if you wanted to be on the Cabinet yet,' Gallagher responded. 'You're far too inexperienced. I have, however, identified that there are about seven backbenchers capable of being on the Cabinet. I have decided that each Cabinet member should have at least one Deputy. This will help share the load, but more importantly, give councillors greater authority over the officers.'

'In short,' Foster interjected, 'we need to ensure that there are as many Group members at every meeting to discuss major policy or projects, so we can force through our vision for Gretford in the face of officer reluctance.'

'And you're young and presentable, Sebastian, as well as having some natural authority to you,' Gallagher continued. 'Officers will be more inclined to follow you than some of our more sedate colleagues. They will also believe that you are politically ambitious, even if you're not. I would like you to be a Deputy.'

'Is there any portfolio you're interested in?' Foster asked.

Woake was determined that if he was going to be a Deputy, then it would be as Deputy to Kildare.

'Well, Gerald, I'm not overly interested in the financial or planning side of the Council,' he said. 'I got involved in the Council to help make a real difference to people's lives, and you only have to drive through parts of my ward to see the deprivation. If I am going to be a Deputy, then I want to be a Deputy in a portfolio where I can really get my hands on the issues that matter. I am also, as I am sure you know, a rower and a cricketer. So I would be a natural fit for the Sports portfolio. I should very much like to join Serena in the Health and Community portfolio.'

'Indeed,' Gallagher replied. He fell silent for a second, staring intently at Woake. 'I think I'll put you with Mark at Licensing.'

'Thank you,' Woake answered.

***

'It surprised me, Sebastian, to learn that you were to be my deputy.'
Woake and Skelding sat in the Britannia, a pub located just 200
metres from Fordhouse and frequented by councillors and junior
officers sent by their superiors to eavesdrop on the councillors.
Senior officers suspected (and were correct) that whilst they would
be recognised by councillors, junior officers often went ignored.

'Frankly, I'm not sure why he chose you anyway,' Skelding
mused.

'I think it was to keep me away from Serena.'

'Uhm, very sensible. The Group can just about survive with
having one member with Gerald's reputation, let alone two.'

'And what is Gerald's reputation?' Woake asked.

'You really don't know?' Skelding asked.

'Appreciate it's a bit of a shocker, but I didn't follow local politics
much before May.'

'So why did you stand?'

'Because I was pissed.'

'Christ, the similarities between the pair of you are really stacking
up. Gerald has been arrested three times for drink driving, all within
the past four years.'

'Bet that went down well with the voters.'

'You'd be surprised. The rag sheets always make a big thing of
drink and drugs amongst the political class, but on the whole, the
electorate don't really care. Frankly, I don't think they care what
politicians get up to, as long as it's not fraud. Financial or electoral.
He's also involved romantically with an ex-Councillor called Kim
Colston. She got him into quite a bit of trouble last year. Got herself
into trouble as well, actually.'

'Love child?' Woake asked.

'Not that type of trouble. She's claimed throughout her
professional life to be a chartered surveyor. Unfortunately for her,
she upset a rather unpleasant backbencher who investigated her
claims. Found out that she was never a surveyor and had attained
career enhancement on the back of the fraud.'

'What happened to her? The Royal Institute of Chartered
Surveyors takes a rather dim view of that.'

'Colston was prosecuted for attaining funds by deception.
She pleaded guilty at the Crown Court and received a suspended
sentence. In fairness to Gerald, he stood by her. She's now his

business partner and his mistress.'

'What do they do?' Woake asked.

'They have a recruitment agency. Gerald runs the networking side, Colston does CV writing. What do you know about my portfolio?' Skelding asked.

'To be honest, not much. I know that a publican needs a personal licence and a pub needs a premises licence, but that's about it.'

'Did you do the licensing training when you became a councillor?'

'No, I'm not on the Licensing Committee so decided not to bother with the training.'

'That's not overly useful Sebastian. What was to happen if you were asked to be a substitute for a committee member?'

'Wasn't planning on saying yes.'

'I see. Let me buy you a drink and I'll tell you about licensing.' Skelding returned from the bar five minutes later.

'Thanks,' Woake said, taking a sip from his mineral water. 'As lead for Licensing Enforcement and Civil Protection, I essentially have to wear three hats. With my Licensing hat on, I have to make sure that we deal with all licensing applications within the statutory time limit, approve all officers' recommendations on each application and ensure that any enforcement issues are dealt with fairly and expeditiously.

'With my Civil Protection hat on I help set policy which ensures continual enforcement of any infringements, which also affects all our residents and guests to the town. I also have to ensure that all nightclubs, licensed sex trade venues and all events adhere to our strict health and safety policies.

'I also have to wear a third hat. My politician's hat. It's important that we keep the electorate on side by being tough but fair, but we must not isolate them or appear to be too draconian. Otherwise, they are more likely to vote for a political party which is a bit more lenient.'

'Such as the Lib Dems?' Woake asked.

'You are joking. They are the most draconian of the lot. No, I was referring to Labour.'

'So what hat will you require me to wear?' Woake asked.

'Uhm, that very much depends.' Skelding replied.

This question was actually a lot more taxing than it first appeared. As his deputy, Woake was a threat to Skelding, whether or not

Woake intended to be. If he gave Woake something important to manage, then there was a risk that Woake could be successful, and Gallagher was already hinting at a potential successor at any Cabinet reshuffle.

Why else appoint a deputy?

On the other hand, if he failed to give Woake a meaningful project, then he could appear to be fearful of Woake and therefore weak.

'You have limited knowledge of licensing, so why don't we stick you in Civil Protection? That legal experience of yours could come in useful. The Council is applying for the Purple Flag award, why don't we get you running that application?'

'Sounds great,' Woake said. 'What's Purple Flag?'

Five

OCTOBER 2015

'Councillor Skelding has asked me to brief you on Purple Flag,' explained Jill Boxall, a middle-ranking officer at GDC. A meeting had been organised between officers and Woake in order to discuss Purple Flag. Boxall was accompanied by two of her junior assistants, Vicky Walsh and Tony Hourahane.

'Good. I had a meeting with Mark last week. He said that it would be better if you explained it to me,' Woake responded.

The meeting was taking place in a windowless, airless room. Bright neon lights shone from the ceiling, reflecting off the white walls.

'Purple Flag,' Boxall continued 'is an accredited award given to towns and cities who have surpassed the standard of excellence in managing the night-time economy. It helps members of the public to identify towns that offer entertaining, diverse, safe and enjoyable nights out.'

'And who awards the accreditation?' Woake asked.

'Town Management Authority,' Hourahane answered.

'Who?' Woake asked.

'Town Management Authority,' repeated Hourahane. 'TMA is a not-for-profit organisation with members that come from the public, private and third sectors. They include key stakeholders and thought leaders who develop and implement shared visions, strategies and action plans for town and city centres throughout the UK.'

'Thought leaders? Stakeholders? I'm sorry, but can I have this translated into English?'

'The key thing is, Sebastian,' Boxall interjected, desperate to progress the conversation, 'is that Purple Flag has been shown to actively improve the local economy of successful cities and towns.'

'Has it?'

'Yes, it's much like the Green Flags for parks and Blue Flags for beaches.'

'We now have flags for parks and beaches as well?'

'Yes, we do, Councillor,' answered Walsh, getting frustrated not only with the questions but also with the fact that Woake had requested a meeting at six thirty in the evening, a full hour beyond which she was contractually obliged to stay at Fordhouse.

'Is there a problem, Sebastian?' Boxall asked. Woake had already identified her as one of the more sincere officers. Occasionally, this sincerity led her to ask somewhat unfortunate questions.

'Not really a problem. Just a slight concern that this is a total waste of our time. Having had countless nights out across England, not once have I asked what colour flag the town centre flies.'

'We don't actually get any purple flags, Councillor,' Walsh answered. 'We just get a logo we can place on all our literature, website and signs.'

'I didn't think for one minute that we get actual flags. My point is that the vast majority of those coming into Gretford for a night out will do so regardless of whether we have been accredited with a purple flag, blue flag, red flag or indeed pink flag status.'

'The LGBTQ+ community might, Councillor,' Walsh said, who apart from being Boxall's Deputy, also fronted the Council's pink agenda. 'Flags are an integral part of the campaign and struggle that this section of community faces.'

'How did we get onto the subject of the gay community? We're talking about Purple Flag.'

'It's not just the gay community, I should remind you Councillor, it's also the bisexual, trans, queer, questioning and others.'

'Others? How can there be "others" left after that list? And what the Hell does "questioning" mean?'

'The purpose of "questioning",' Walsh answered, taking the tone as if she was talking to an idiot 'is to help facilitate the identification of an individual's true self. An individual who is still undergoing the process of reflection before identifying themselves as a particular sexuality.'

'My point is,' Woake continued 'is that, regardless of what a lesbian or queer may think, the colour of the flag is extremely unimportant to most people.'

'So you have identified me as a subgroup of an oppressed minority and have used that as an offensive term of language?' Walsh asked.

'What?' Woake asked in wonder. 'I merely used the words "lesbian" and "queer" as an example as it was part of your LGBT1Q-H criteria.'

'It's actually LGBTQ+, Councillor,' Hourahane said.

'So I, as a woman, cannot be queer?' Walsh asked.

'Surely wouldn't that make you a lesbian?' Woake asked in ignorance.

'A woman has as much right to be a queer as a man, and indeed can also be described as a homosexual.'

'But a gay man cannot be described as a lesbian?' Woake asked. Walsh nodded. 'Not very inclusive of you lot.'

'Us lot?' Walsh asked.

'Sebastian, the Cabinet agreed to submit the application six months ago,' Boxall interjected again, desperate to keep some semblance of order to the meeting. 'The TMA has just contacted us to confirm their visit.'

'OK Jill, so what happens next?' Woake asked.

'The TMA will send down the delegation on Saturday 17th October, which is next week. We have drafted the night's itinerary for you to read.' She handed Woake the draft itinerary. 'Could you please read this and get back to me with any comments? The visit will start at five o'clock that afternoon and will finish at five o'clock the following morning. We would like you to be present.'

'Doesn't look like I have a choice. Will Mark be present?'

'No, he said that you will be adequate representation.'

No wonder he gave this to me, Woake thought.

'OK, I'll take a look at this for you and will get back to you with my opinion. Quick question: how much has this cost, not including officers' time?'

Boxall answered. 'The application has cost £2,000, plus expenses amounting to another £2,000. But it's not just the monetary value of the application we need to remember Sebastian. You have to remember that it's impossible to calculate the total number of man hours this Council and our associated stakeholders have put into this. From cleaning the streets, to briefing local companies, to inspecting destinations on the tour, to erecting suitable street lights, making sure that emergency services and the Street Angels are briefed on the application.'

'What a complete waste of time and money,' Woake said under his breath.

Woake read the itinerary later that evening. Even to his somewhat cynical eye, Woake had to accept that the Civil Protection team had done a first-class job in drafting an itinerary for the TMA delegation.

A team of five delegates would arrive at Gretford train station at five o'clock and would be met by representatives from Gretford District Council, including Woake. They would be escorted to the Lamb Hotel in the centre of the high street; chosen because of its central location as much as it being Gretford's only five-star hotel.

At six o'clock, the delegation would begin its tour of Gretford's night-time economy, starting with the three central theatres, followed by its pubs and restaurants. A table had been booked for dinner at a Sardinian restaurant at seven thirty.

At nine o'clock, the delegation would visit the nightclubs and bars at the bottom of the high street, where they would remain until midnight. At midnight, the delegation would tour the town, inspecting the many takeaway restaurants, paying particular attention to the level of homelessness, the behaviour of the club goers (in particular their interaction with each other and with the police) and the level of litter and damage caused by the takeaway trade.

Time had been allocated to allow the delegation to question the "night-time visitors", as the itinerary had named them. At two o'clock, the delegation would speak to the Street Angels and the police, including a tour of the police station. Particular attention would be paid to the vulnerability of young women, whether in a group or alone. The final event would be a last inspection of the town centre, to examine the results of a night-time's worth of revelry.

It would be an exhausted delegation that would finally return to their hotel beds at five o'clock in the morning. As good an itinerary as could be made, Woake concluded. He only had three minor issues with it.

***

The following day, Woake phoned Boxall during his lunchtime adjournment.

'Hi Jill, I looked at the Purple Flag itinerary. Looks fine to me, just got a couple of things to discuss. I understand the visit is the evening before the Gretford Agricultural Show. Is that a problem?'

'Shouldn't be. Why do you ask?'

'Only interested if Gretford has an increase in visitor numbers throughout the entire weekend. I should imagine that it's in everyone's interest to keep visitor numbers down to a minimum,' Woake explained.

Boxall answered. 'From my experience of the agricultural show, visitor numbers only increase on the day that the show is held.'

'OK Jill, understood. Second point, is it really a good idea that members of the delegation speak to the public early on the Sunday morning?' Woake asked.

'In what way?'

'From my experience of walking around town centres after midnight, the "visitors" tend to be pissed. We're trying to portray Gretford as a safe, vibrant town. I'm not sure that an official delegation speaking to a group of inebriated students is a good way of doing that. Sounds like tempting fate.'

'Unfortunately, Sebastian, the TMA insists upon it. Our ability to safeguard vulnerable visitors is a key part to the application.'

'Nothing vulnerable about a group of inebriated students. Last point before I let you leave. We're taking the delegation on a tour of our night-time venues, so why are we leaving out *Brazil's*?'

'Unfortunately, *Brazil's* has failed to abide by our own stringent health and safety policies in recent months and has subsequently been placed in special measures.'

'But won't the TMA think that there is something odd about us leaving out Gretford's largest nightclub from the tour?'

'That can't be helped. *Brazil's* has so far failed to demonstrate that it is willing to abide by the special measures, and so it looks like it will be closed down.'

'So why not include it and give the management one last warning?'

'Civil Protection will be very reluctant to agree to that. The Council's relationship with Pedro Brazil has hit an all-time low.'

'Then let's improve it and include the nightclub in the tour.'

'OK Sebastian, I'll see what I can do.'

It was an angry Councillor Skelding who, later that day, walked into the leadership suite. Gallagher was at his desk, immaculately groomed as always.

'Hello Mark. How are you?' Gallagher asked.

'I've just come from a meeting dealing with the effects of that idiot that you thrust upon me.'

'Ah yes, how is our criminal barrister getting on?'

'I have just discovered that he had a meeting last night with the Purple Flag team. It transpired Gerald that not only did he question the entire purpose of the application, he described it as a waste of money and even attempted to insult the homosexual community.'

'In fairness, Mark, Sebastian asked the same questions that I did back in April and frankly, he is probably correct that this is nothing more than a vanity project. As for his comments on homosexuality, I understand he did nothing more than question the colour of the flags.'

'That's not how Vicky Walsh describes it,' Skelding replied, wondering how Gallagher already had such an in-depth knowledge of the meeting.

'Oh yes, Ms Walsh. Can't imagine that she'll ever lose the "Ms". Can't imagine any man ever wanting her to lose the "Ms".'

'Can't imagine she's that into men either, Gerald. I do believe that she's a lesbian.'

'Indeed? In which case Woake should perhaps have been warned about her well-known political activism.'

'So it's my fault, is it?'

'No Mark, it isn't,' Gallagher replied, already tiring of the conversation. In truth, he was tired of Skelding. Unfortunately, Skelding was too powerful on the local Association for Gallagher to fire him. Skelding was Deputy Chairman (Membership) of Gretford Conservative Association in addition to his role as councillor.

'And to make matters worse, he's insisted that the TMA delegation visits *Brazil's* during the town's assessment,' Skelding continued.

'Indeed, that is most unfortunate,' Gallagher said, raising an eyebrow. 'Doesn't he have any idea about the history of *Brazil's*?'

'To be honest, Gerald, I'm doubting that Sebastian has much of a clue about the history of anything. It is my opinion Gerald, not only as a member of the Cabinet but also as a member of the

Conservative Group, that young Woake should be relieved as my Deputy immediately.'

'Why don't you ignore his suggestion about *Brazil's*?'

'Because Civil Protection has already phoned Pedro Brazil to tell him the news. We'll look bloody ridiculous if we phone him up again today to tell him that on second thoughts, we won't be requiring his services.'

Gallagher leant back into his chair, both index fingers gently tapping the top of his desk. 'Whilst I do not necessarily approve of how Woake spoke to the officers last night, I think we should give him a bit more time to see what he can achieve. Let's leave him with Purple Flag. You never know, you might be pleasantly surprised.'

'I bloody doubt it,' Skelding replied, walking away from the leadership suite.

A thin smile formed on the mouth of Gerald Gallagher. It was very good to see Skelding nearly as rattled as the officers.

Pedro Brazil stood in a cubicle in the ladies' lavatory of his nightclub. Even he had to admit that it was utterly repulsive. For Brazil, the merits of welfare came a distant second to the pursuit of money, and whilst *Brazil's* nightclub was famous amongst countless University of South-East England students as a reliable source for one-night stands, it was a nightclub never synonymous with hygiene.

But even for *Brazil's*, what faced its owner was shocking. It was a mistake brought about only by laziness. But then, Pedro Brazil was hardly a man to inspire confidence in personal hygiene.

To say that Pedro Brazil was of gypsy stock would be wrong.

Pedro Brazil was gypsy.

Born into a well-known local gypsy clan, Peter Brazil did not leave school at the age of 16; he never went to school.

Not for Peter Brazil the drudgery of reading, writing and arithmetic.

Peter Brazil became a trader of any stock (legitimate or otherwise) during his teenage years and was a millionaire by his thirtieth birthday. Not for Brazil the flash cars and one-bedroom caravan which were the trademarks of his forefathers, Peter broke generations of gypsy tradition and invested in static property.

By this stage, Brazil saw himself as a man who had graduated from businessman to property developer, a natural progression for all those who have obtained their wealth from rather dubious means. In 1991, Brazil grabbed the opportunity to cement his reputation within Gretford for generations to come. He purchased a rundown warehouse in the centre of the gyratory which defined the gridlocked southern end of the high street.

To provide him with even greater legitimacy, he converted the unit into Gretford's principal nightclub.

Drawing inspiration from his surname, he gave the nightclub a distinctive Latin America theme. In betrayal to the fact that none of his ancestors had ever set foot in the country, and ignoring that he owed his surname to his grandfather (who, when asked his surname by the police, quickly thought of the winner of the previous football world cup), Peter Brazil changed his Christian name (Peter Brazil was a devout Christian) to the more Latin sounding Pedro.

To complete Gretford's new South American influence, the nightclub was given the unoriginal name of *Brazil's*.

By 2000, the abandoned units around *Brazil's* had all been transformed into bars, clubs and well-known chains of cheap pubs until the bottom of the high street became the epicentre of Gretford's night-time economy.

Thus started his rather tempestuous relationship with Gretford District Council, which never appreciated that a man of such low stock as Pedro Brazil could apparently make such a success of his life.

When Pedro Brazil purchased land to the south of Gretford in order to build his dream home, the Council's planning department took him all the way to the Court of Appeal to stop him. Upon completion, the Council's planning inspector reviewed every measurement of his eight-bedroom mansion. When the Council's Civil Protection team served him an enforcement notice over noise complaints from his nightclub, Pedro Brazil opened a lap-dancing club in its basement.

When the Council ordered the lap-dancing club to close, Brazil built an extension to his house without planning permission. Planning enforcement ordered the extension to be demolished. Pedro Brazil refused, forcing the Council into legal proceedings. A matter currently being dealt with in the Court of Appeal.

However, Pedro Brazil was currently facing his biggest challenge.

In late September, an alarmed (or sober) club goer had reported the state of a cubicle in the ladies' lavatory to the Council, which was followed by an immediate inspection by the Council's Health and Safety team. Too immediate in Pedro Brazil's opinion.

Despite three children signifying the contrary, Pedro Brazil had never previously felt the compulsion to investigate the ladies' lavatories, secretly preferring the company of men.

What faced him, his management and the inspection team that Monday morning resulted from decades' worth of poor cleaning, cheap drinks and lax enforcement of the club's anti-drug policies.

Years of human waste, vomit, spilt drinks and drugs had given birth to mould around the toilet pan, which had now spread with alarming rapidity to the soil pipe and from the soil pipe up the wall with a speed of conquest not seen since the days of the Mongols. The mould itself had started its life as a translucent colour, and had then graduated to yellow, then green, and finally purple.

Unfortunately for the concerned club goer, she had not realised that the cubicle was known for being the drug den, ensuring that very few women ever cared about the state of the toilet.

The assembled audience stood in the doorway, hands over mouths. Even Pedro Brazil was shocked.

Tony Hourahane (temporarily unable to speak lest he vomited) handed an appalled Brazil an enforcement notice ordering the temporary closure of the club, pointing to the relevant condition stating that *Brazil's* had a month to make improvements or it would be closed permanently. He then barged through the group of weakening colleagues, limped downstairs and then collapsed in the fresh air outside the main entrance.

Pedro Brazil remained in the cubicle's doorway, mesmerised by the universe of creation which he had unwittingly created.

He eventually pulled himself away from the spectacle and looked down at the enforcement notice. *Brazil's* was to be closed for a month to allow the offending article to be rectified.

Or napalmed in Pedro Brazil's opinion.

It would only be opened again if it passed a second inspection four weeks later.

Three weeks and one cleaning team later (the original cleaning team had quit), the cubicle was still a haven of parasitic life.

However, the Wednesday before the TMA visit, Brazil had received a surprise phone call from Tony Hourahane, who explained that the TMA would visit a reopened *Brazil's* on Saturday night. If

Brazil failed to comply, then his nightclub faced permanent closure.

In surprising haste, Brazil visited the Gretford branch of B&Q where he purchased an all-in-one biohazard polythene suit, safety specs and dust mask. At the Gretford branch of HGS cleaning wholesalers, he bought a barrel of biohazard chemical cleaning solution. For the rest of the Wednesday and throughout the following Thursday, Brazil shut himself in the cubicle.

Wearing his tight new suit, which clung to his short and fat frame so that he resembled a bulging white sausage rather than a human, Brazil firstly scraped as much of the mould off the wall, soil pipe and toilet as he could with a metal brush. He then filled half a dozen buckets with diluted but still highly flammable biohazard cleaner, which he then threw over the remaining mould. Fighting his own urge to vomit, Brazil manically applied the wire brush, fighting back the tears from the fumes pulsating his nostrils.

By Thursday evening, Brazil was confident that he had removed as much of the mould as could reasonably be expected. Allowing the solution to dry, Brazil purchased a tin of white emulsion, which he applied liberally over the remaining mould, ignoring the advice of leaving four hours between applying coats.

It was a tentative Tony Hourahane who pushed open the cubicle door late on the Friday afternoon. As he pushed back the door, Hourahane was hit by the fumes of emulsion paint mixed with cleaning product. Rather than an entire ecosystem, Hourahane faced a shiny white cubicle, apparently spotless.

Shocked by the miraculous transformation, Hourahane handed Brazil a second enforcement notice, rescinding the closure order.

Brazil's was back in business.

Six

It was half-past four on Saturday 17th October and the sky had darkened as Councillor Woake approached Gretford train station, a masterpiece of Victorian gothic located in the centre of the Ford valley and south-west of the high street.

The Gretford District Council team of Boxall, Hourahane and Walsh were already waiting in the main entrance of the station. Woake walked up and greeted them.

Walsh could barely acknowledge him.

'Hello chaps, everything ready?' he asked.

'Good afternoon, Sebastian, thanks for joining us,' Boxall answered. 'Everything is as ready as it can be, thanks to Tony. *Brazil's* has been included at your insistence, despite an earlier complication.'

'Excellent, well done Tony. Anything to be concerned about?' Woake asked.

'Just a minor concern regarding the facilities in the nightclub, which has been rectified,' Hourahane answered.

An uneasy silence descended upon the group. Woake had noticed that such a silence usually descended when councillors and officers met outside a formal meeting. For officers, there was a general reluctance to say too much in case an unguarded comment would spark further questioning about their workload. For councillors, there was a general reluctance to say too much in case they destroyed the closely veiled secret that they were merely enthusiastic amateurs with little more than a basic understanding of their portfolios.

'At least it's not raining,' Woake added, looking up at the cloudless sky.

Woake wore pink chinos, suede brown shoes and a tight blue and white striped shirt underneath a navy blue Hugo Boss jumper.

He held a blue sports jacket over his shoulder. In comparison, the three officers each wore black trainers with black trousers and a dark shirt. Each officer wore a non-descript jacket.

'Any plans for the weekend, other than this?' he asked, not so much to make conversation but more to irritate Hourahane and Walsh by appearing to be as charming as he could.

'No, not really,' Boxall answered 'it's the agricultural show tomorrow, so I may go to that depending on how tonight goes.'

'Yes, I'm supposed to be going to that too, but like you, it depends on tonight. It's been a while since I've pulled an all-nighter.'

The uneasy silence descended again. Boxall and Woake looked at each other and the surrounding station forecourt, Hourahane looked intently at the platforms, Walsh looked down at her feet.

'I understand that you're a criminal barrister, Sebastian?' Boxall asked, attempting to fill the silence.

'Yes, that's right. I was Called back in 2009. Just about to start a trial down at Canterbury Crown Court on Tuesday involving a young Latvian accused of smuggling in cocaine with the bulk value of about £250,000. I'm afraid that you won't be seeing too much of me after this evening, not that you chaps will be that upset by that.'

'They're here,' Hourahane said, saving Boxall from having to attempt further conversation.

Woake turned around, and sure enough saw a group of three men and two women walk through the station foyer, all suited and carrying overnight holdalls. All five wore a TMA badge on their jacket lapels.

Boxall led the Gretford team towards the delegation and held out her hand to the leading man. 'Good evening and welcome to Gretford,' she said. 'I trust you had a pleasant journey down? I'm Jill Boxall and I have been leading our Purple Flag application. May I please introduce the other members of the team?'

Woake was duly introduced to Stuart Townsend, a man of medium height, bald and in his fifties who led the TMA delegation; Vijah Singh, a turbaned gentleman of Indian descent; a short and plump lady in her late forties called Eileen French; a taller woman in her early forties called Veronica Abbott; and the most junior member of the team, a short, fat man in his mid-twenties called Simon Delling.

Boxall led the combined groups away from the train station and towards Gretford high street.

'You've all seen our application, and our itinerary for tonight. We've booked you into the Lamb Hotel, chosen because of its central location in the town. That means that you have ample opportunity to explore Gretford throughout the whole of tomorrow if you so wish.'

'Thank you very much, though I am sure that most of us will leave shortly after lunch,' Townsend replied.

The combined delegation made it to the Lamb Hotel. The Gretford representatives sat in the Georgian hotel's reception area as the TMA delegation checked into their rooms.

The three officers shared a sofa. Woake sat in an armchair. The three officers stared silently at the wall opposite. Woake read a copy of *The Field* which had been left on the central table. Presently, the TMA delegation made its way downstairs, all five with a clipboard and pen in hand.

And so the tour of Gretford began.

'We're very lucky to have three theatres in Gretford,' Boxall explained on the walk. 'We'll take you to the most modern first, which was built ten years ago at a cost of £180 million. It's located at the top of the high street, so it's a good place to start as we'll walk down the hill.'

The tour made it to the theatre, a glass and steel monstrosity of design which, the architect explained to the Council, lent itself to the post-Blairite contemporary thought. It was very much one of GDC's more brash planning decisions.

'As you can see, the theatre has its own restaurant and two bars, plus the Thai and Chinese restaurants opposite put on a special pre-theatre menu.' The delegation studied the theatre, paying attention to the couples and groups eating in the restaurant, positioned at the front of the building in order to make the theatre appear to be busier than it actually was.

'What is the capacity of the theatre?' Townsend asked.

'I believe approximately 1,800, with productions ranging from classical to contemporary concerts to productions for children as well as adults.'

'What is the name of the theatre?' Delling asked, eager to impress his seniors with his enthusiasm.

'G-On,' Boxall answered. A contemporary name, Woake thought, just as meaningless as the architect's inspiration of design.

'G-On?' Delling naively asked. 'What does the "G" stand for?'

'Were you not concerned about the connotations of that name?' French asked, ignoring Delling's question.

'What possible connotations could there be?' Woake asked, deciding he should take a lead.

'The sexual connotations of using the letter "G" in such a manner,' French replied.

'You know, that never came up. Which I'm surprised about,' said Walsh, ever ready to crusade on behalf of women, the gay community and the seemingly oppressed.

'Should hope lots of things come up when dealing with the letter "G",' Woake said. 'In any case, I hope that the directions on G-On's website are easy to follow.'

'Why's that?' French asked.

'Well, no man will ever be able to find it.'

'I think that we should probably move on down to the other two theatres,' Boxall quickly interjected.

The Purple Flag delegation continued its tour down the high street, Boxall leading alongside Townsend. The four other TMA delegates followed, with Walsh and Hourahane behind them. A very bored Woake trailed in last.

As the tour progressed, Boxall commented on every feature of Gretford's night-time economy from the number of restaurants and wide range of food available, to the selection of takeaway outlets, the number of Deliveroo drivers on duty, to the taxi companies and the number of visitors (of various ages) to the town.

Occasionally, the tour would stop as the delegates inspected a particular feature, commented upon the standard of cleanliness of the high street, or wrote some note onto their clipboards.

The delegates were taken to the two other theatres, where they were introduced to the managers, having both been well briefed by Hourahane in advance. The delegates asked about disabled access, health and safety procedures, the variety of the performances shown and the annual footfall of visitors.

The questions were easily answered, and the delegates left both theatres appearing to be happy.

'Jill,' Veronica Abbott said as the tour was making its way to dinner, 'in order to attain Purple Flag status, a successful applicant must demonstrate that it can provide a safe environment. Not only does this include emergency services, but a critical part is how you manage taxi companies.'

'I agree,' Boxall replied. 'I would refer you to our application, where we set out in detail how taxi companies and drivers apply for a licence in order to trade. As well as our strict enforcement procedures should there be a transgression.'

'Yes, I was most interested in that,' Abbott said. 'May we please visit one?' she asked.

Boxall had been expecting such a request and so directed the tour to the offices of Gretford Taxis, chosen not just because of its professionalism but also because its staff were all English and (officially at least) not criminals.

The tour left the offices ten minutes later, satisfied that women and the vulnerable of Gretford could be escorted home safely.

'A most professional company, Jill,' Abbott said. Woake had already identified her as typical public sector worker; an individual of middling professional competence with an air of seriousness far exceeding the importance of her role.

'Although Jill,' Abbott continued. 'It just isn't the professional firms that are important to Purple Flag. Vulnerable individuals, especially intoxicated women, are more likely to choose a taxi company due to its locality rather than reputation. *That* taxi company, for example,' she said, pointing to a small taxi sign hanging above an outdoor staircase attached to the side of a kebab house.

Half of the neon bulbs in the sign were no longer working and even Woake could see that this was a taxi company which did not extol confidence in an ability to get the client into the office safely, let alone home.

Somewhat unoriginally, this taxi firm was also called Gretford Taxis.

Abbott marched straight up the stairs, expertly avoiding the remains of kebabs, food wrappers, cigarettes, and an assortment of rubbish not worth thinking about. The rest of the group followed sheepishly behind, with Woake trailing into the office last. He walked into a room with two large moth-eaten cigarette-burn encrusted sofas, a carpet covered in chewing gum and dank windows covered in dust.

The room stank of kebabs, body odour and stale alcohol.

Much like his sixth-form study at boarding school.

Abbott marched towards a timid looking middle-aged man of Pakistani origin, sitting at a desk covered with a line of telephones, an intercom and a notebook and pen. A bulging filing cabinet was located to the right of the desk. A limp evergreen plant 6ft high was the only attempt at office decoration.

'Good evening. Taxi for nine?' he asked in a thick Pakistani accent. It was unfortunate for Rehan Khan that his position within the taxi firm was front of house; a position chosen for him because it was believed by the firm's management that, as the oldest member of staff, he would be considered to be trustworthy by the firm's often inebriated clients.

The fact he only had a basic grasp of English was not considered to be a hinderance to his job.

'No thank you,' Abbott answered. 'We're here on behalf of Town Management Authority.'

'Who? You want taxi for nine?' Khan asked again.

'No thank you,' Abbott replied patiently. 'We're here to ask you a few questions about your company's practices.'

'You Government?' Khan asked. A look of abject panic appeared on his face. 'All company practices fully above-board, madam.'

Abbott smiled down at the panicking man. 'No, we're not the Government, we're a quango.'

'Kango?'

'No, I am not a pneumatic hammer used to drill through concrete. I represent a quango. A quasi-autonomous non-Government organisation.' The panic on Khan's face slowly turned to one of confusion. For Woake, it was satisfying to finally meet someone in Gretford who knew even less about what she was talking about than him.

'May I ask your name?' Abbott asked.

'My name is Mr Khan,' he responded proudly. There was much note-taking in the audience.

Abbott continued to talk patiently. 'We are here to assess Gretford District Council's application for Purple Flag status.'

'Purple flags! Very pretty,' Khan responded.

'Indeed, but in order for the application to be a success, we need to ask you a few questions about your relationship with the Council.'

'Relationship very good madam, all drivers fully licensed.'

'That is good to know, Mr Khan, but may I ask what safeguarding measures you have in place?'

'Safe guarding?' Khan asked, bewildered.

'Yes, safeguarding measures.'

'No need for a guard for the safe madam, company's safe is very well hidden.'

'No not "safe guarding" Mr Khan, "safeguarding measures".' Accepting that Khan's open mouth was the only response she was going to receive, Abbott tried another approach. 'What policies do you have in place to protect your clients?' she asked.

'Police!' Khan shrieked in panic. 'No need to call police madam, Gretford Taxis very law-abiding taxi firm.'

'No, not "police" Mr Khan. "Policy". How do you protect your clients?'

'Very good, madam. All cars have central locking. Client safe from outside and anyone trying to break in.'

'But how do you know that the client is safe from the driver?'

'All drivers fully trustworthy, all drivers know not to hurt client.'

'But how do they know not to? Has the company told them not to?' Abbott asked.

'Would be terrible for business madam, clients would never come back if we hurt them.'

'And how do you ensure that your clients get home safely?' she asked.

'Insure? Gretford Taxis fully insured thank you, madam.'

'But how do you make sure your customers get to their destinations safely?'

'Because none of our taxis have ever had a crash, madam.'

'But how do you look after them once they leave the taxi?'

'Not the job of Gretford Taxis to be bodyguards, madam. Customer says where they want to go. We take them. Wouldn't be in business long if we took them to the wrong address.'

'How can you be called Gretford Taxis? We've just come from another taxi firm called Gretford Taxis,' Woake said.

'We're taxi firm, sir, and we're in Gretford, so we're Gretford Taxis,' Khan replied. Woake had to accept that there was a logic there.

'But how do you make sure that your clients get home safely, Mr

Khan? What have you got in place to make sure that the client has been dropped off at the correct address?'

'Easy, madam, every car has satnav. Taxi goes straight to address given by client!'

'I don't think that we're making much progress here, Veronica,' Boxall said. 'Perhaps Tony could look into this for us on Monday and we'll get back to you with all the relevant information.'

'Not necessary, madam, Gretford Taxis fully legitimate. Owned by Mr Akram. Lovely man,' Khan said.

'And where is Mr Akram? Can we speak to him?' Abbott asked.

'Not possible, I'm afraid. He lives in Pakistan.'

'Perhaps we should go to dinner?' Woake said.

Seven

The Gretford Agricultural Show is the highlight of the annual farming calendar, held on Wellington Park, a 100-acre area of meadow in the centre of Gretford town. For one weekend in mid-October, members of the farming community invade Gretford from across the south-east.

Thousands flock to the show to stare in wonder at the livestock, watch the two rings dedicated to showjumping and hoping to tire their children at the large carnival. Hundreds congregate in the shopping, food and exhibition marquees, whilst thousands more wander the seemingly never-ending lines of shops.

Aristocratic landlords, gypsies, middle-class professionals and working-class tradesmen all mingle happily together for one day.

Farmers spend weeks preparing their prized bull, favourite boar and pedigree ram in anticipation for the judges' verdict, knowing that a favourable result would propel the breeding value of their animals.

It is said that the sun always shines on Gretford during the agricultural show.

The marquees were erected in the weeks leading up to the show and farmers and their livestock all arrived on the Saturday before. The farmers camped with their animals, staying up late to apply the final touches to their prized possessions.

One such prized possession was Boris, the Highland bull. Weighing in at 840kg, with a height of 140cm, Boris was the pride of his owner's herd. A champion of several shows, father to dozens of calves, Boris was favourite to win Best Bull in Show award. Rival farmers looked on in envy, as the sun shone off the mop of blond hair which hung lazily between the bull's two horns. Where the blonde hair came from would forever remain a mystery, but it ensured that the sun also reflected off the bull's crown just as the presiding judge was going to give judgement.

Two unfortunate events were going to unfold for Boris the Highland bull on the night of Saturday 17th October. The first was that his owner, Jock Stewart, could not attend owing to an untimely dose of the Tangier trots. Boris, and the reputation of the Stewart farm, was left in the care of Jock's eldest son Andrew, a prodigious talent in the Sussex Young Farmers Association.

Andrew followed his father's strict instructions; shampooing, brushing, drying and coifing Boris' magnificent coat, using only Pantene Pro-V, followed by talcum powder, in order to give Boris' coat an unearthly complexion.

By six o'clock on Saturday evening, Boris looked magnificent, his coat glistening under the artificial light.

However, Andrew Stewart was not a prodigious talent in the Sussex Young Farmers Association because of any natural farming talent or attention to detail, but rather his talent for consuming scrumpy.

Andrew, having checked in with his father over the phone at five minutes past six that evening, began consuming his first pint of cider at a quarter-past. It was unfortunate for Boris that his handler's attention to detail was not what it should have been.

The Gretford Purple Flag tour made it to the restaurant, a Sardinian restaurant of excellent reputation. The party of nine was directed to its table. In deference to his position as head of the TMA delegation, Stuart Townsend sat at the head of the table.

Woake sat at the far end, opposite Simon Delling; who, as the most junior delegate, instinctively knew his position amongst the public sector staff.

The waitress took the drinks order, starting with Townsend and ending with Woake. The waitress received eight orders for soft drinks, until she reached Woake.

'May I have a Peroni please?' he ordered.

'Small or large sir?' the waitress asked.

'Large please.' Woake ignored the looks he received from the others.

'Will you need the wine list?' the waitress asked the group, addressing no one in particular.

'Yes please,' Woake answered on behalf of the group.

The table settled into small talk whilst it deliberated its order. Woake ensured that the table also ordered a starter. By the time the starter arrived (calamari for Woake), he was onto his second Peroni; by the time the starter was cleared, Woake had ensured that the table had an excellent Barolo Fenocchio Piemonte DOCG ordered.

The rest of the party refused Woake's offer of wine, attributing the tour on the need to remain sober.

'We have got a long night ahead of us, Sebastian,' Boxall, who was sitting next to Townsend, reminded Woake.

'Exactly Jill, it's a Saturday night, and there is nothing in our Purple Flag application that says I cannot enjoy myself. Would you like a glass of wine Simon?' he asked Delling, who looked sheepishly down to the table.

For Woake, the dinner continued in its dull predictability, culminating with a dire inevitability to its tedious conclusion. The only two saving graces were that GDC was paying for it, and no one dared question his drinking again.

Whilst not inebriated, it would be fair to say that by the end of the meal and keeping the wine to himself (despite his many offers to share it), Woake was rather merry.

Over the starters, Stuart Townsend explained to the table that the TMA had recently launched 'a one-day process for local areas as part of the national strategy to tackle serious youth violence. We use a broad-brush set of interviews and focus groups with frontline practitioners to gather information, knowledge and perception whilst building a qualitative picture of the key issues and drivers around the county lines drug trade, gangs, youth violence and vulnerability.'

'A one-day course?' Woake asked.

'No, a one-day process,' Townsend answered.

'But it lasts one day?'

'Yes,' Townsend answered with more than a hint of annoyance.

'And who will take part in the course?'

'It is a process, Councillor, not a course. And it will be open to every stakeholder with an interest in youth violence.'

'So the police, youth workers, criminal lawyers and local authorities?' Woake asked.

'Primarily them, yes.'

'Interesting. Don't you think these stakeholders may already know more than you can tell them in only one day?'

The main course arrived (Woake had ordered a calzone). Eileen French explained to the table a new communication initiative that the TMA was about to launch. 'It is called Everest,' she said, 'and will improve the way dialogue is facilitated amongst our members. Everest will allow cross-peer real-time networking anywhere in the UK. Members who join the scheme will be able to talk to other members at any time, all based upon our partnership model.'

'That sounds fascinating. What's stopping everyone picking up a phone instead?' Woake asked. Vijah Singh jumped to French's rescue.

'The key challenge facing TMA is convincing our members about the importance of diversity.'

'That's such a coincidence,' explained Walsh. 'I have been challenging the Council at Cabinet level to embrace diversity.'

'Yes Vicky, but it's not just diversity amongst different subsections of the population,' Singh continued, 'which is important, but also the combined diversity amongst the night-time attractions to encourage all the subgroups of the diverse elements of modern society to feel safe, entertained and welcomed. That remains our greatest challenge,' he concluded.

'Surely the greatest challenge facing TMA is convincing members of the public that you actually exist?' Woake asked.

'In what way?' Singh retorted.

'Well, the reality is Vijah is that until last week, I had never heard of you. Should imagine that it's probably the same for at least ninety per cent of the population. In fact, how do you end up working for TMA? I should imagine that it doesn't come up that often in schools career fairs. "What would you like to do when you grow up?" "I would like to work for Town Management Authority!"'

'It's now nine o'clock,' Boxall said. 'Shall we get the bill and continue with the tour?'

If Woake's evening was progressing with uneventful tedium, then the same could not be said for Boris the Highland bull. As fate would have it, Boris had been placed in a pen at one end of the cattle enclosure, at the closest point to Greenbanks Road, a residential street marking a boundary to the show.

At half-past nine that evening, Boris woke from a deep slumber with the hunger pains that any 840kg bull would feel when woken. Lazily, Boris walked towards his hay net, which Andrew Stewart had tied to one of the metal railings which formed Boris' pen.

Boris began munching on the hay net, head firmly encased within the netting. As he pulled on yet another mouthful of hay, his left horn caught on the netting. With growing panic, Boris began to walk away from the net.

Unfortunately for Boris, he was soon to discover Andrew Stewart's carelessness for which he was infamous. Whilst the hay net had been tied securely to one of the metal railings, it could never be said that the pen that Stewart had constructed for Boris was a firm structure.

As Boris attempted to walk away from the hay net, the metal railing continued to follow him. It was at this point that Stewart's carelessness became apparent.

The feet at one end of the metal railing had not been placed in the concrete weight. As Boris pulled on the hay net, the metal railing tottered on the brink. It wobbled and it shook, until gravitational force became too much.

With one last desperate move, Boris yanked at the invisible force pulling at his head. The metal railing, not yet recovering from Boris' latest attempt at its structural integrity, followed the hay net.

It clattered to the ground, freeing the hay net from the horn.

Boris jumped back, launching his 840kg bulk into the air. He stood in the pen, shaking like a newborn calf. Minutes crept by and still he did not move.

Boris' break for freedom was a cautious affair. Eventually the hunger pains became too much. The scent of fresh grass from the neighbouring residential gardens wafted into his nostrils.

The temptation proved too strong.

Tentatively, he advanced towards the fallen railing, placing one hoof on the metal, followed by another. Summoning the courage which had hitherto escaped him, Boris walked out of his pen and with one last salute to his previous confinement, strode through the enclosure's flap.

Boris was gone, an escape only witnessed by fellow livestock. None of the camping farmers had yet returned from their various nights of joviality.

The Purple Flag team continued with its tour. By ten o'clock, it had reached a tapas bar in one of the town's many side streets.

'If it is ok with you Jill, I would like to take the opportunity to question some of Gretford's visitors,' Townsend said.

The group only had to wait a few minutes until a young couple left the tapas bar. Townsend strode up to them.

'Good evening. My name is Stuart Townsend and I was wondering if I could please have a few minutes of your time to ask you a few questions?' he asked.

'What do you want?' the woman asked. Despite being a relatively new Gretford resident, Woake could easily identify them as residents from the southern side.

'I am from the Town Management Authority,' Townsend replied.

'The what?' the boyfriend asked.

'The Town Management Authority,' Townsend answered.

'Never heard of it,' the man said.

'I think you'll find that they get that a lot,' Woake interjected, receiving a sharp look from Vicky Walsh. Townsend ignored him.

'May I please ask you about Gretford's night-time economy?' Townsend persisted.

'Night time economy?' the young woman asked 'are you saying that I'm a prostitute?'

'The correct phraseology is sex worker,' Walsh said.

'Whatever,' the lady said. 'Are you saying that's what I am?' she asked again.

'Not at all,' replied Townsend. 'I am just enquiring about your experiences of Gretford. If you enjoyed your night out, if you feel safe, if there's an area of Gretford at night that you would change.'

'What's it got to fucking do with you, mate?' the man said as the couple walked off.

For Boris, the night was slightly more successful. After leaving his pen, he walked up Greenbanks Road. When he arrived at the T-junction that marked the end of the road, he faced a stark choice. Turn left up Gretford's hill leading to middle-class suburbia or turn right down the high street.

The decision in the end was simple. He turned right and strode down the high street. With scant regard for pedestrians and cars alike, Boris started his own tour of Gretford. He walked past Greenbanks School for Girls, one of the country's leading independent girls' schools, past G-On and its surrounding restaurants, past startled diners and drivers and past the Gretford Grammar School, a leading independent boys' school despite having the word grammar in its name.

Boris entered the cobbled area of the high street and still he continued to walk, tail flapping happily behind him. However, Boris faced a problem.

No matter how pleasant the night-time walk was, it still had not settled his burning problem; food. It was only when he was halfway down the cobbled high street that salvation presented itself.

A gust of wind blew across the high street, taking with it the fragrancies of freshly planted shrubs. Boris lifted his head to the air, salivating at the thought of grass, his nostrils twitching in the night sky. With the toss of his head and a snort from his nose, Boris trotted in the direction of the scent.

Within minutes, the soft texture of lawn had replaced the hard surface of stone under Boris' hooves. He looked up. In front of him lay a public garden of paradise.

Illuminated by the uplighters and floodlights, light shone off the recently cut lawn, reflecting off the autumn-flowering verbenas and helleborus, emphasising the final flowering of that season's roses.

Boris had arrived in paradise. He was at Gretford Castle.

The emergency services received its first Boris-related call shortly after ten thirty.

'Police,' the female operator said to the caller.

'Yeah, hi,' the male caller said with the usual amount of trepidation a caller has when phoning 999, caught between wondering whether he was doing the right thing or if he could be arrested for prank calling. 'Uh, there's a cow walking down Gretford high street.'

'A cow, you say?'

'Yeah, a cow.'

'What type of cow?'

'A big brown one, with horns.'

'And you say it's walking down Gretford high street?' the operator asked.

'Yeah, I'm on a night out with a group of friends and we have just seen it walk down the high street.'

'OK sir, we'll take a look at it. May I have your name and address please?'

The report was logged as a drunken prank and ignored. By eleven o'clock, there were eighteen more incidents of a cow walking down Gretford high street. Concerned that there might actually be a cow wandering around Gretford, the phone operator spoke to her supervisor.

'So there's nineteen reports that have come in during the last thirty minutes about a cow in Gretford?' the supervisor asked.

'Yeah, that's correct. Apparently it's brown and big, with horns.'

'With four legs?'

'He didn't say sir.'

'Has it caused any damage yet?' the supervisor asked.

'No, apparently it's just walking down the high street.'

'OK, I'll speak to Gretford.'

The supervisor phoned Superintendent Jenkins of Gretford Police Station and explained the nineteen reports of an escaped Boris.

'You're telling me that you have nineteen reports of a cow walking down Gretford high street?' Jenkins asked.

'That's right. The operator thought it might be a prank at first, but nineteen reports gives some credence to the story.'

'A cow walking down Gretford high street?' Jenkins asked, his voice growing louder. 'Do you have any idea what the Hell is going on in Gretford?'

'I appreciate that there has been quite a bit of traffic in Gretford tonight,' the supervisor responded.

'Quite a bit of traffic?' Jenkins shouted 'We've got a major fucking incident unfolding in Gretford, and all you can say is that there is a cow walking down the high street? It's the Gretford Agricultural Show tomorrow, so those nineteen reports are probably the young farmers out on the piss,' he said, hanging up.

Eight

The young farmers of Sussex were not the only ones getting drunk that night.

Brazil's nightclub had reopened.

Hundreds of University of South-East England students and hundreds of twenty-something locals flooded *Brazil's* and its orbiting bars. The management had said that it had closed for refurbishment, though what that refurbishment entailed was never fully disclosed.

And with the special promotion on beer, spirits and shots that *Brazil's* was running that night, none of the cliental were ever sober enough to notice, let alone care.

At nine o'clock, *Brazil's* and its locality were busy. An hour later, that part of Gretford was heaving, with traffic struggling to drive through the crowds on the Gretford gyratory system. A squad of police officers, stationed outside *Brazil's* in anticipation of the night ahead, struggled to cope with the bustling crowds.

Kelly Holloway made it into *Brazil's* at nine o'clock. A first-year University of South-East England student, she had preloaded with alcohol at the union bar before taking a very crowded and noisy bus into Gretford.

Her friends and she had queued for half an hour before entering *Brazil's*. Inside, it was everything that her previous drunken nights half remembered.

Loud thumping music from the overfilled dance floor, queues outside the (limited number of) lavatories, cheap alcohol at the drink-spilled bar, and plenty of opportunities to hook up with someone, hiding the reality of a drunken mistake until both parties woke up next to each other the following lunchtime.

By ten thirty, Holloway had added to her preloading with a shot of tequila and two double vodka and cokes, the last one paid for by a fellow University of South-East England student who she had already identified as a potential suitor for the night's post-club entertainment.

However, the alcohol and the near certainty of a one-night stand could not dispel the gagging urge of her additional vice, smoking.

Like Boris earlier, Kelly Holloway faced a choice. Leave the nightclub for a cigarette, but then have to queue again, with longer queues and losing her friends (and her new companion) or staying indoors, and risk being thrown out?

In the end, the potential risk of indoors won out.

Signalling to her new friend (she had not yet caught his name), Holloway made her way upstairs to the women's lavatory.

Despite a couple of cubicles being free, she still had to wait. There was only one cubicle she wanted to use; the cubicle two to the left. One by one, Holloway waved through any other girl wishing to use the facilities.

Eventually, her chosen cubicle became free. Entering quickly, she locked the door behind her and, pulling the toilet lid shut, sat down. She reached into her handbag and took out a packet of cigarettes and lighter. Kelly lit the cigarette and took a long drag.

She began to panic. Was she in the right cubicle? She was sure that she had gone to the correct one, but the cubicle seemed different, markedly so. Gone was the mould, and as she sat there, the smell of disinfectant and paint swelled her nostrils. That was it. Despite the alcohol she had made it to the correct cubicle, it was just that it had been cleaned!

She closed her eyes, savouring the nicotine shot. She wasn't worried about being caught; the lavatories did not have any attendants (it was not that type of nightclub) and experience had proven that you can stand under the fire alarm with a lighter and it still would not go off.

Legend said that the cubicle had gained its notoriety owing to an enterprising university student deactivating the alarm, in order to allow smokers to fuel their habit once the smoking ban came into effect.

It had not taken long for smoking to lead to drug abuse and other activities in that cubicle.

Kelly sat on the toilet, enjoying the cigarette for as long as possible. With one last drag, Kelly rose from the seat, knees still bent over the toilet, and lifted the toilet lid.

With the tip of the cigarette butt still burning, Kelly threw it into the toilet pan and went to replace the lid.

Had Kelly stood up, lifted the toilet lid and threw the cigarette butt into the water at the bottom of the toilet pan, subsequent events may never have occurred. As it was, laziness won and rather than land in the water, the cigarette butt became lodged in the top rim of the basin, an area of particular focus of Pedro Brazil's attempt at cleaning.

Before she could move her hand to the toilet handle, Kelly noticed a powerful force shoot up from the toilet. The flaming cigarette butt had made contact with the industrial strength (and highly flammable) detergent Brazil had used to soak the cubicle.

The toilet basin erupted into a miniature volcano, an eruption powerful enough to blow the toilet seat off its hinges.

The toilet seat smashed straight into Kelly's squatting nether regions and lifted her off her feet. The sound of a toilet exploding was enough to perforate her eardrums, and the eardrums of the other women using the lavatory.

By now in mid-flight, Kelly was catapulted up through the air, straight through the cubicle door which fell off its hinges due to the pressure, knocking over two other women and finally landing unconscious on the soaking lavatory ground.

The combination of an enormous bang, an explosion, prone bodies and the consumption of copious amounts of alcohol resulted in the only possible illogical next step.

'Bomb!' a woman shouted, causing panic amongst the nearby clubbers, who blindly rushed towards the exit.

Drunken club goers, failing to understand the cause of the panic, screamed, the music was halted and the club's full lighting switched on. What started as minor drunken panic turned into mass hysteria without seconds. Hundreds of club goers stampeded towards the exit, knocking each other over in the rush to leave *Brazil's*.

The police section outside failed to contain the stampede, and called for immediate back-up.

The club's security staff phoned the emergency services. At the report of a bomb, the police phoned for an Armed Response Unit. Within minutes, the entire emergency services of Gretford and surrounding towns congregated on the Gretford gyratory system.

The Purple Flag tour watched the young man and his girlfriend walk away from them in disgust. 'Shall we continue with the tour?' Boxall said. Within seconds, the calm and peaceful night sky was rudely disturbed as the sound of numerous sirens heralded the arrival of police cars, ambulances and fire engines at *Brazil's*.

'Sounds like something is kicking off at the bottom of the high street,' Woake said.

'Sounds like it's coming from the direction of *Brazil's*,' Hourahane said. Boxall looked angrily towards Hourahane.

Hourahane should have known better than to mention *Brazil's*. Boxall still hoped to avoid *Brazil's*, if she could.

'What is *Brazil's*?' Singh asked.

'Gretford's biggest nightclub,' Woake answered, not caring if he should have answered or not.

'In which case, why don't we have a look at what all the fuss is about?' French asked.

The tour walked down the high street towards *Brazil's* with the sound of the sirens growing ever louder. The tour reached the bottom of the high street and turned right onto the gyratory system and stood transfixed at the chaos as they beheld *Brazil's*.

Police cars blocked the gyratory system at all four entrances, bringing the traffic of Gretford to gridlock. The cars already on the gyratory system when it was closed lay abandoned as their occupants were forced to flee in fear of another explosion.

Armed police officers patrolled the vicinity, submachine guns strapped across their chests. Unarmed police officers corralled drunken revellers into groups, interviewing potential witnesses. Paramedics tended to anyone who had suffered injury from the stampede, or were already far too drunk to get home unaided.

Stretchers could be seen being loaded onto ambulances, the injured being taken to hospital.

The Purple Flag tour tentatively walked towards the nearest police officer, standing guard with his forefinger stretched straight out across the trigger guard of his submachine gun. His eyes were alert for any potential threats.

'Police incident! Back off!' he shouted to the group when they were only ten metres away.

'We're from the Town Management Authority, and we're here to inspect Gretford,' Townsend shouted back.

'I don't care who you are,' Sergeant Owen shouted. 'You're not to come any closer!'

'I'm a senior officer at Gretford District Council,' Boxall shouted. 'What's going on?'

'Suspected terrorist incident. Gretford is now in lockdown. Please leave the area.'

The group looked on as a heavily bandaged Kelly Holloway left the nightclub on a stretcher, escorted by two armed police officers.

If being thrown from a toilet cubicle was not bad enough, Kelly's night took a dramatic turn for the worse when she woke heavily concussed, suffering from two broken arms and a pair of heavily bruised buttocks, to see two armed police officers standing over her, arresting her for terrorism.

Not that Kelly would have much of an idea then about the terrorism charges she faced.

'Perhaps we could see a bit more of Gretford,' Woake said.

'Not sure there's a huge amount more point now that Gretford is in lockdown,' Veronica Abbott said.

'Nonsense,' Woake replied, taking over the lead from the shell-shocked Council officers. 'If you would like to follow me.' Woake led the tour back up the high street. 'What that brief episode has perhaps demonstrated is how safe visitors to Gretford are.'

'Safe?' Townsend asked. 'That police officer just said that a bomb went off.'

'He actually said that there had only been a suspected incident,' Woake answered. 'But just look at the response of the emergency services. As you can see, it's now eleven thirty at night, and all the roads and paths in the town are completely safe. If we could just cut in through here.' Woake led them to the boundary of Gretford Castle. 'As you can see, we're by the castle grounds, and not fifteen metres away from us is the Royal Feathers pub, a very popular bar and restaurant. Perhaps we should take a closer look at the castle, which I think you'll agree is looking majestic in the floodlights.'

Woake led the group into the castle grounds. 'It is a shame that we're seeing the gardens at night, as they really are quite wonderful and have actually won quite a few regional awards. I understand that it's a very popular place to sit. Bollocks!' he exclaimed suddenly.

'What's wrong?' Boxall asked.

'Nothing Jill, but I think I've just stepped in something rather unpleasant.'

'Dog walkers. Should be ashamed of themselves,' said Delling.

'I don't think it's dog, Simon,' Woake said, using the torch on his phone. 'What the Hell happened here?' he asked, looking towards the illuminated remains of the once award-winning castle gardens. Hoof prints had turned the once manicured lawn into a quagmire, the remains of flowers lay mangled and trodden in the once beautifully tended flowerbeds.

Suddenly, the silence was disturbed again as loud explosions ruptured the night sky, startling the more nervous members of the group.

'Oh God, it's gunfire!' shouted a panicking Eileen French.

'It's fireworks, you stupid woman,' Woake said.

The fireworks display would be the second unfortunate event for Boris the Highland bull that evening. Castle Gate is a residential road of six large Victorian villas which borders the grounds of Gretford Castle, and is considered by many (primarily by those living there) to be the premier road in the whole of Gretford.

That evening, one of the residents, Peter Lo, was hosting a party for one hundred of his wife's closest friends on the occasion of her fiftieth birthday. A successful city trader, Lo had approached the party in the way that only a city trader can. Brashly.

'And so I said to the Council, when they told me I couldn't have fireworks, "bollocks to you!"' he shouted at the conclusion of his speech. He leapt off a raised platform in his garden and signalled to the fireworks team to start the display.

A neighbour had seen the fireworks van parked outside his house the previous day and, aggrieved that he had not been invited, reported the matter to the Council claiming noise nuisance.

Fearful that the fireworks would interfere with Purple Flag, the Council had issued a prohibition order.

The fireworks team started the display. Sky hawks, preceded by skull rockets, followed halos, war hawks and graveyards, culminating with a demon lighting up the Gretford sky. Lo stood with his guests, staring in total wonder at the display.

The Purple Flag tour was not to have such an enjoyable time.

To say that Boris was startled at the first sky hawk would be an understatement. Crying out a wail of terror, 840kg of bull jumped up to its hindlegs, its forelegs crashed back down to earth, shuddering the castle gardens under his hooves.

The continuation of the sky hawks drove him into a frenzy, and forgetting the paradise which he had been previously enjoying, his one thought was of peace away from the explosions. As his forelegs shuddered underneath him, he charged.

The first the Purple Flag tour knew of him was the feeling of tremors shaking the ground away from them. The group stood nervously as the fireworks exploded over their hands, deafening them from all other sounds.

A halo exploded in the sky, casting light on the whole of the castle garden, and on Boris, who was charging straight towards them, only fifteen metres away. A second halo showed he was only a few metres away when Woake shouted, 'Move!'

The group parted as Boris charged straight through them, knocking them all to the ground. Woake landed straight into the remains of a flower bed.

Singh had been at the back of the group and so had not noticed Boris until it was too late. He made to turn and offered his back to Boris, who, with his head bowed, lifted Singh off the ground when his right horn became attached to the seam of Singh's trousers.

Arms flailing, back stretched outright against the pain, Singh's turban worked itself loose in the ensuing panic. It caught on Boris' left horn and hung lazily on Boris' blonde hair.

Singh screamed in agonising pain as the bull's horn sliced through his right buttock. Not wanting to be encumbered by the additional weight in his flight from the fireworks, Boris flung Singh from his horn with nothing more than a gentle shake of his head.

Singh landed whimpering in the flower bed, as Boris continued his flight out of the garden and back onto the cobbled high street. Boris instinctively turned left back down the hill, down the high street and towards *Brazil's*, picking up speed in his blind panic which would not have disgraced a Chieftain tank.

French called for an ambulance, whilst Woake and the others raced onto the high street after Boris.

***

Sergeant Owen remained on station. Behind him, the last of the injured were being tended to, but dozens of club goers remained to be questioned and the surrounding buildings had still not been cleared of any further bombs.

He could see fireworks towards the top of the town. *At least one bastard's enjoying himself tonight,* he thought grudgingly.

The sirens had been turned off, though the lights were still on, reducing Gretford to eerie silence save for the sound of the fireworks display.

A low clip-clop sound could be heard coming from the high street, growing louder by the second. 'What the fuck's that, Sarge?' Officer Brown asked, appearing next to Owen.

'Buggered if I know.'

'Look Sarge, it's a bloody bull.'

Boris appeared from around the corner, taking the bend on his two right legs.

'Is that a turban on his head?' Owen asked.

'It's a fucking raghead, Sarge. What do we do? Shoot it?' Brown asked.

'I'm not shooting a bloody cow,' Owen replied, Boris approaching them with alarming speed. Owen stood transfixed.

'It's coming straight at us, Sarge,' and indeed Boris was. Whilst the noise of the fireworks might have faded, the memory had not. Boris' panic, encouraged by his momentum running down the hill, was now exacerbated by the flashing lights from the police car. Blinded as well as deafened, Boris had the unstoppable urge to destroy the lights.

He charged the car by which Owen and Brown stood. With the deft fleet of foot one would normally expect to see on a ballerina, Boris jumped on top of the police car, landing spread-eagled on the car roof, destroying the lights and denting the roof as it buckled under nearly a ton of cow.

Owen and Brown cowered by the side, shocked by the momentum. A police search light was shone on Boris, whose forward momentum carried him off the destroyed police car.

With escape from the beam the only thing on his mind and with the road still littered with cars, Boris chose to run up the pavement.

'Don't shoot!' Owen cried. 'Civilians in the way.'

He could only look on in horror as Whittom Bridge recreated its own Pamplona bull run. Boris charged the bridge, forcing drunken revellers to hide behind cars. Others were less fortunate, and were forced to jump for safety into the River Ford below, where at least they quickly sobered up.

Boris made it across the bridge and ran onto the roundabout at the far end. Unfortunately for Boris, a bus was turning right at the roundabout. Boris slammed straight into the side of the bus, the vehicle shuddering under the impact, his horns locking into the vehicle's framework.

Boris gingerly removed himself from the bus, took a couple of uneasy steps and fell to the ground. By the time Sergeant Owen and the rest of the Armed Response Unit appeared, Boris was fast asleep on the tarmac.

'Now what do we do, Sarge?' Brown asked.

'Find a way to move that lump off the road. And you had better contact the RNLI or Search and Rescue for that lot,' he said, looking down at the formerly drunken revellers emerging from the River Ford.

Unlike the other members of the Purple Flag tour, Woake did not follow Boris but witnessed the disaster unfold from the top of the high street.

He looked at his watch. It was now firmly past midnight. With one last look at the scene below him, he turned and walked home to his bed.

Later that day was the Gretford Agricultural Show. Woake did not attend; he had already seen enough livestock.

Nine

Four days later, Woake was sitting in the advocates' robing room of Canterbury Crown Court during the lunchtime adjournment when his mobile phone rang.

'Hello,' he answered.

'Hello Sebastian, it's Gerald.'

'Gerald who?'

'Gerald Gallagher from GDC,' was the exasperated answer. 'Do you have a couple of minutes to talk about Saturday night?' he asked.

'I'm due back into court in twenty minutes. But sure, fire away,' Woake answered.

'I'm sure you know that our Purple Flag application was unsuccessful.'

'That was quick. I didn't realise that the TMA was that efficient.'

'We found out on Saturday night,' Gallagher answered. 'Apparently they didn't think that a night-time economy of a rampaging bull and a terrorist attack qualified for their high standard.'

'Was it terrorism?' Woake asked.

'No, thankfully. A girl blew up a toilet from underneath her whilst smoking in a cubicle. She's just been released from hospital, suffering from severe concussion and two broken arms.'

'How did it happen?'

'Investigators are of the mind that the cubicle had been recently cleaned and redecorated with several flammable objects of industrial strength.'

'Any other casualties?'

'A few broken limbs, a couple of traumatised club goers. Nothing serious, thank God.'

'What happened to Brazil?'

'Scarpered. Would have been tipped off by a member of the

management before the police went knocking. He's got a place in Spain, so I should imagine that's the last we'll be seeing of him. Unfortunately, Sebastian, this whole episode has left you with a bit of a problem.'

'In what way, Gerald?' Woake asked.

'Getting pissed at dinner, insulting the delegation, acting unprofessionally throughout the evening,' Gallagher answered.

'Wasn't pissed and all I did was ask the delegation a couple of questions. It wasn't my fault there was a deranged bull on the loose and the local nightclub owner blew his own premises up. In fact, you could argue that I nearly rescued the evening given what went on at *Brazil's*.'

'I appreciate all that, and in all honestly, I agree with you over these quangos. I don't think that anybody can really blame you for Saturday. But it was Mark's application.'

'Then he should have been there instead of me,' Woake interrupted.

'I agree, but see it from his perspective. He needed to give you something from his portfolio, we had a strong application which he had organised and he would have taken the glory had it been granted, regardless of whether he was there or not. And unfortunately, you have denied him of that.'

'And now he wants me gone?' Woake asked.

'In a word, yes. He's insisting that you go or he'll resign from the Cabinet.'

'And you believe him?'

'Not prepared to find out,' Gallagher answered. 'You're back to the backbenches Sebastian. But you have an additional problem. The local press has got hold of this and the Overview and Scrutiny Committee have called it in.'

'Meaning what exactly?'

'Meaning that on Thursday night, when Overview and Scrutiny will next meet, they will ask the Purple Flag team a number of questions.'

'And do they have any powers of reprimand?' Woake asked.

'Of course they don't. I deliberately fixed it so that, as a committee, they can only ask questions. Nevertheless, it could lead to a formal investigation if the senior management deem that one is appropriate, either because of the answers the team gives or if the public wants one. Plus, it could be negative publicity. Barbara Mason is on the warpath, so be warned.'

'Thanks Gerald,' Woake said.

'Aren't you on Overview and Scrutiny?' Gallagher asked.

'Yes,' Woake answered.

'Then at least you'll be the only member in Gretford history to have scrutinised himself.'

'Depends on what your definition of member is,' Woake said.

'And that's another thing. I'm sending you off onto an equality and diversity training course.'

Nineteen-year-old Georgs Auza met Alberts Prusack, a man not only twenty years his senior but a man at least eight stone heavier, in a Turkish bath in the Latvian city of Jelgava. With absolutely no hint that their relationship was nothing more than platonic, Auza agreed to accompany Prusack on a tour of western Europe 24 hours later.

Together, they left Jelgava on Wednesday 1st April and flew to Dublin, where Prusack bought a fifteen-year-old Mercedes C-Class saloon later that same day. Prusack drove the car, with Auza in the passenger seat, to Belfast, where they boarded the ferry to Holyhead.

From Holyhead, they drove to Dover, crossed the Channel to Calais and arrived in Amsterdam 48 hours after leaving Jelgava.

In Amsterdam, Prusack and Auza went their separate ways for the Easter weekend, and met up again on the morning of Easter Monday. Prusack then drove the Mercedes and Auza back to France, where they re-crossed the Channel at Le Havre. Their intention was to drive from Portsmouth, back to Holyhead, then drive back to Dublin before flying home to Jelgava.

Unfortunately for Prusack and Auza, they never made it past Portsmouth.

The first hint that they were in trouble was as they drove off the ferry's ramp and were directed away from the other passengers by a suspicious team of officers in the UK Border Agency.

Faced with a pair of Latvians whose grasp of the English language was insufficient to explain why they had left and re-entered the UK via two different ports on single tickets, the focus of the officers' attention turned to the car, which they began to tear apart with alarming efficiency.

It was only a matter of minutes before five kilos of cocaine was discovered hidden in the front wheel arches, with a bulk value of £250,000.

Prusack and Auza were both duly arrested.

Initially maintaining his innocence, Prusack reconsidered as the severity of the situation in which he found himself was brought home when he was remanded in custody. When it was explained to him that he could receive a discount of up to a third off his custodial sentence if he pleaded guilty, Prusack admitted his guilt at the first available opportunity.

To ensure that the sentencing judge look as favourably on him as possible, Prusack fully cooperated with the authorities, even giving evidence that Auza had no knowledge of the drugs, a state of affairs that Auza himself maintained.

For Woake, the trial had so far gone well. As prosecutor, he put his case first and the customs officers and the unidentified police officer from Special Branch had said as eloquently as they could the route taken by Prusack and Auza, why they became suspicious of the vehicle and its passengers, and how the drugs were found.

Furthermore, and unlike a number of other trials Woake had been involved with, the correct procedure had been followed, meaning that all of the prosecution evidence was admissible.

Woake had concluded his case on the Wednesday afternoon. Thursday morning saw the start of the defence case, and it was an understandably nervous Auza who took to the witness box.

In faltering English, Auza explained how he came to be in the car on 1st April and Woake quickly realised that his opponent had played a blinder. By claiming that his client's understanding of English was sufficient to ensure a full understanding of the trial, Auza had refused the services of an interpreter.

Any difficulty in answering a question from the prosecution could be excused as a reasonable lack of understanding of the English language.

By ten to one in the afternoon, Auza had finished giving his evidence, and it was to everyone's relief that Judge Williams adjourned the trial until after lunch. Auza would face his cross-examination by Woake at two o'clock.

At two o'clock, Woake rose to his feet. 'Thank you, Mr Auza, for your evidence earlier,' he said. 'As I am sure you understand, I am going to ask you some questions.'

'OK,' Auza responded nervously.

'I am interested in how you met Mr Prusack. You say that you met Mr Prusack in a Turkish bath in Jelgava. Is that correct?'

'Yes.'

'And you had never met him before?'

'No, I hadn't.'

'How long were you at the baths for?'

'A couple of hours.'

'And how long did you speak to Mr Prusack for?'

'I'm not sure what you mean.'

'What I mean, Mr Auza, is how long did any conversation between you and Mr Prusack last?'

'I think about half an hour.'

'I see. And you met this man in a Turkish bath and within half an hour or so of meeting him, you agreed to travel with him?'

'Yes,' Auza answered. Woake knew that the secret to a good cross-examination was to keep the witness to simple yes/no answers and to agree with the questions being put, and then to draw them into a trap.

'You have a girlfriend back in Latvia, so there was never any hint that this was nothing but a friendship with Prusack?'

'I have a girlfriend and I am not gay.'

'I didn't for one moment suggest that you are. You said that it was Prusack's suggestion that you go with him to the UK?'

'Yes.'

'He must have told you what was planned?'

'He said that we would be driving through the UK.'

'So this was a sightseeing holiday then?'

'Yes, that's correct.'

'Are you often in the habit of accompanying men you have only just met in a Turkish bath, on holiday?'

'No, this was the first time.'

'So what changed now?'

'I wanted a holiday.'

'You can't have that many ties to Latvia that you can give everything up with only a few hours' notice?'

Auza looked nervously at the judge. 'I don't understand,' he stammered.

'Let me rephrase it then. Do you have a job?'

'No.'

'But you needed a holiday?'

'Yes.'

'How were you going to pay for it?'

'I had some savings.'

'Surely better to keep the savings and try to get a job?'

Auza didn't answer.

'How did your girlfriend react when you told her you were going on holiday with a man you had only just met in a Turkish bath?'

'She didn't say anything.'

'You're a very lucky man, Mr Auza. Your girlfriend is considerably more understanding than many of the women I know,' Woake said. 'So you arrived in Dublin on 1ˢᵗ April and you travelled to Belfast immediately, and boarded the ferry within twelve hours?'

'Yes.'

'See much of Dublin?'

'Not much. Mr Prusack bought a car as soon as we got there.'

'Go to the Guinness brewery? See a game of Gaelic football at Croke Park? Visit Dublin Castle?'

'No.'

'Didn't it strike you as odd that Mr Prusack bought a car rather than insist you take public transport to Belfast? Especially as the two cities are in two separate countries?'

'Mr Prusack said it was cheaper than hiring a car, as he could resell it in the UK afterwards.'

'You're saying that Mr Prusack's plan was to sell a foreign car in the UK, after adding yet more hundreds of miles on the clock and hope to save more money than simply buying two train tickets?'

Auza shrugged. 'It was his money.'

'And at no time did you question why you flew to Dublin, when you saw nothing of any interest in the city?'

'No, Mr Prusack was in charge.'

'OK Mr Auza, let's move on. You drove to Belfast where, on the same day, you got the ferry to Wales?'

'Yes.'

'You obviously didn't have time to see much of Belfast?'

'No.'

'You must have been disappointed. You were on a holiday, but you hadn't actually seen much of what the UK had to offer?'

'I knew we were coming back.'

'Oh, did you? But I thought you said that you were going to sell the car in the UK?'

'Belfast is in the UK.'

'Of course it is, Mr Auza, my mistake. So you arrived in Holyhead in the early hours of 2nd April and within twelve hours had boarded a ferry out of Dover?'

'Yes.'

'See much of the UK did you in that twelve hours?'

'I don't understand.'

'Did you see much of the UK on your drive? You know, Stonehenge? Oxford University? Shakespeare's Stratford? The Tower of London?'

'No.'

'Did you see anything?'

'No, we were driving.'

'How was the conversation with Mr Prusack by this point? You must have been running out of things to say?'

'We didn't talk much.'

'Did you ask him why you weren't stopping off at any of the attractions along the way to Dover?'

'No. Mr Prusack was driving, so what was the point?'

'The point is, Mr Auza, is that on a supposed sightseeing tour of the UK, you saw absolutely nothing. And what is more, Mr Auza, is that not only did you not see any sights, you also do not seem to be very disappointed about it.'

'I saw quite a lot from the car window.'

'That must have been a very interesting holiday for you, Mr Auza. A holiday with a man who you barely knew, who you barely spoke to, seeing Ireland, Wales and England via motorway and then you landed in France.'

The cross examination continued, with Mr Auza maintaining his story and asserting that he had visited friends from Latvia during the two days they were in Amsterdam, enjoying "The Russian Egg Festival".

'Or, as we call it, Mr Auza, Easter. Did you question why you were to return to England via a different port?'

'No.'

'And you were found to have tickets in your possession for a ferry from Holyhead back to Belfast later that same day?'

'What are the names of your Latvian friends?'

'Janis Berzins and Edgars Jansons.'

'And are they giving evidence that you saw them?'

'No, I didn't want to disturb them.'

'And what do they do in Amsterdam?'

'They work in a plant nursery.'

'What did you do together?'

'We went out for dinner.'

'And Mr Prusack? Did you know what he did?'

'No.'

'You didn't ask?'

'No.'

'Should imagine that would have been a perfectly normal conversation on the way back, especially as you hadn't seen each other for a few days and you had a long drive ahead of you.'

Mr Auza remained silent.

'So another quick trip through England was planned on the way back, following the same motorways?'

'Yes.'

'How is Mr Prusack's English?'

'Not good.'

'Not good, he needs an interpreter to speak English, does he not?'

'Yes.'

'And we have already heard that it was you who spoke to the UK Border Agency officers when the car was inspected. Is that correct?'

'Yes.'

'I put it to you, Mr Auza, that your entire story is fabrication. We have established the nonsense of the car purchase, that you couldn't possibly have time to see any of the UK, that you barely knew Mr Prusack and that you apparently have friends in Amsterdam, which we're going to have to take your word on. But the reality is that Mr Prusack needed you to help with the drugs, that you were needed as an interpreter and navigator. You knew about the drugs didn't you,

Mr Auza?'

'No, none of that is true.'

'No further questions, Your Honour,' Woake said and sat down.

Woake was driving back home when his phone rang. It was Myers, his Head of Chambers. He answered.

'Woake, dear boy, how is your trial going?' Myers asked.

Woake gave him a brief summary of the progress. 'Think you've got him?' Myers asked.

'Difficult to say. His cover is obviously total nonsense, but the problem is that his accomplice, who was actually driving the car, will give evidence tomorrow saying that the defendant had no knowledge of the drugs,' Woake answered.

'Bad luck. Juries always accept the supporting testimony of a co-defendant who has already pleaded. How old is your man?'

'Nineteen.'

'You have no chance. The jury is bound to give him the benefit of the doubt. They always believe in the naivety of youth, especially if you have a calculating senior.'

'Thanks.'

'So how will you play this one?'

'I'll ask him how he was planning to drive through several countries without speaking a word of the language. Anyway, what can I do you for?' Woake asked.

'I've just been asked to give an opinion on the likely success of a prosecution brought by the Department of Work and Pensions and I was wondering if you would like to be my Junior, if it progresses?' As a QC, Myers would need a Junior (a non-QC) to assist him through the trial.

'Sure, why not?' Woake answered.

'Excellent, it will be like old times.'

'What, me carrying your robes and papers behind you? Can't wait.' Woake could hear Myers laughing.

'How's your pro bono?' Myers asked.

'Brilliant. I'm on my way now to a Council meeting. Overview and Scrutiny is tonight's enjoyment.' Woake thought it policy not to tell Myers that he was the subject of one of tonight's topics.

'Have fun. I'll have Louise email you over what we have and she'll get the meeting in your diary.'

All the Gretford District Council meetings start at seven o'clock, a reluctant acknowledgement from Council staff that some councillors were required to work for a living. There was the added benefit that catering was available for councillors in attendance. At a cost of £25,000 per year to the Gretford taxpayer, councillors could gorge themselves before every meeting on a feast of stale sandwiches, stodgy canapes, mild cheese, soggy miniature sausage rolls and maturing pork pies.

The meetings were all held in the Council Chamber; a room dominated by a raised dais (for the use of the district's Managing Director, the Mayor, the Leader and Deputy Leader of the Council and the district's legal advisor) at one end and the public gallery (rows of moveable chairs) at the other.

In between were rows of mobile desks, where the councillors sit according to seniority; Cabinet members in the front row, members of the opposition parties towards the rear.

During Full Council meetings, Woake sat firmly in the middle.

Tonight's meeting was a committee, so the moveable desks had been positioned into a rectangular shape. Barbara Mason, Leader of the Liberal Democrats and Chairperson of the Overview and Scrutiny Committee, sat at the head of the table, with the committee members sitting on the three sides around her.

Woake walked into Council Chamber on the dot of seven o'clock, carrying a plate of sandwiches from the buffet. He had showered and changed before walking down towards Fordhouse. He had not had time for dinner; that would have to wait.

Woake sat down in his appointed chair and nodded to Mason, who acknowledged his presence by starting the meeting. Unsurprisingly, he was the last member of the committee to arrive.

'Good evening, and welcome to tonight's Overview and Scrutiny Committee. We have a full agenda tonight, so moving onto agenda item number one, minutes from the last meeting, are they agreed?' she asked the committee.

'Agreed,' came the somewhat unenergetic response. Woake sat eating the sandwiches, reading his notes and case papers from the

Auza trial, writing possible questions for Prusack tomorrow and writing his closing speech.

'Item number two,' Mason continued 'disclosure of any pecuniary interests. I would like to remind members that they should declare any disclosable interests and should leave the room whilst the relevant agenda item is being discussed. Are there any?'

Woake turned on his microphone. 'Yes, Mrs Chairman,' Woake deliberately used the proper terminology rather than the modern creation "Chairperson". It was always gratifying to see the flinching by the politically correct. 'I should disclose that I have an interest in relation to the Purple Flag application, in as much as I am the relevant councillor to be scrutinised. I shall therefore leave the room when this item comes up, only to return immediately for you to question me.'

'Thank you, Councillor Woake,' Mason said, 'it shall not be necessary for you to leave the Chamber.'

Woake had already noticed Jill Boxall, Tony Hourahane and Vicky Walsh sitting amongst the other Council officers. He smiled at them in greeting. The always affable Boxall smiled sheepishly back, Hourahane looked straight past him in embarrassment, Walsh looked at him with pure resentment.

Woake failed to recognise the other officers, but he saw that Craig Overton and William Foster were in attendance.

The meeting continued. Overton and his team were questioned on the latest decision taken to help alleviate the daily gridlocked rush hour along the Gretford gyratory system; the closing of one end of a neighbouring road as the residents had complained about it being used as a rat run and the establishment of a new public transport network, christened a 'sustainability corridor', which went through the gyratory.

Unfortunately, the mandatory lack of foresight, which is always a part of the Council's decision-making process, had failed to predict that the new sustainability corridor would grind to a stop within minutes as the hundreds of motorists who used the rat run would instead be diverted straight into the new road system.

As Lead Councillor for Sustainable Projects, Overton had been responsible for this disaster.

'The most challenging situation,' he explained to the committee 'that currently faces the transportation network in the town centre is educating stakeholders and commuters that there is a sustainable alternative to the car. I call that "model shift", a shift away from the current model of car ownership and usage and into a new model of public transportation, using the corridor of bike rental, buses, trains and boats along the River Ford. As the public authority, it is vital that we, as policymakers, re-educate our residents not in the long-term, but very much in the short-term.'

After half an hour, the committee had had enough of sustainable model shift and instead turned its attention to the Finance department's decision to invest £3 million into a fund for the possible redevelopment of Gretford Museum, a decision that every member was keen to support as it would help secure their own future legacies as councillors.

It was quarter-past eight when the Purple Flag application was called on. Woake noticed that Foster and Overton had remained, no doubt hoping to witness the evening's main sport.

'We now move onto tonight's remaining item,' Mason said, 'the recent Purple Flag application. I have added this to tonight's agenda as several of us thought that this was a matter which required our attention. As Councillor Woake has already told the committee, he was the councillor responsible, so perhaps you would like to start,' she said, turning to Woake.

'Thank you very much Mrs Chairman,' Woake said, 'but it is perhaps worth mentioning that I came to this matter very late in the process, after the decision had been made by the Cabinet. As the application was submitted by the Civil Protection team, I feel that the officers might present the report before I comment on it.'

With reluctance, Mason turned to the three officers. 'Perhaps you would like to explain what happened?' she asked with a smile.

Boxall described the Purple Flag application, from its initial inception through to making the application, the work undertaken by the Council in the weeks leading up to the tour, Woake's involvement and finally the events of the night itself. The committee sat in silence, every member listening to what was said.

After fifteen minutes, Boxall was finally concluding. 'And considering the events of 17th October, we were notified immediately that our application was unsuccessful.'

'How much did our application cost?' Mason asked.

'The application itself cost £2,500,' Boxall answered.

'And that money is not refundable?' Mason asked.

'Of course it's not,' Woake answered. 'Do you honestly think that the TMA would refund the money of a failed application?'

'Thank you, Councillor Woake. Perhaps you would like to explain your involvement in the application?' Mason asked.

'With pleasure, although I'm not sure that there is much for me to explain. I came to the matter a week before the delegation visited Gretford.'

'Apparently you made a homophobic comment at your first meeting with the officers,' Councillor Mann said. Mann was a Conservative, and one of Skelding's ward colleagues.

'What comment was that?'

'You apparently questioned the definition of LGBTQ+. That could be defined as homophobic.'

'No, all I did was make a comment about the colour of flags. The issue of LGBTQ+ was brought up by a Council officer,' Woake said, looking at Walsh. 'All I asked was the definition of "questioning" and that is really not homophobic.'

'I think in fairness to Councillor Woake, he may not realise that it is not so much what is said that can be defined as homophobic, but the way it is said,' Walsh told the committee.

'I think in fairness to Vicky Walsh, she may not fully understand the law around homophobic comments. If she would like me to, I'd be more than happy to discuss this with her further, but perhaps this is not the correct time, Mrs Chairman. It is also worth mentioning that we are not bound by parliamentary privilege, so is there anybody here brave enough to say it was homophobic, or do we all accept my explanation that it was just a misunderstanding?' There was no response. 'No? Good. Does anyone have any further questions?'

'But you questioned the relevance of Purple Flag status?' Mason asked.

'Yes, I thought it was £2,500 better spent on something else.'

'So you wanted it to fail?'

'No, I agreed to take it on after a brief explanation from Skelding, and I turned up for the delegation tour, scheduled to last all night. Which is more than what any other councillor did.'

'We understand you got drunk at the dinner with the TMA?' the Liberal Democrat Adrian Philips asked.

'Did I?' Woake responded.

'Apparently you drank two large beers and a bottle of wine. That would have got me drunk,' Philips said. 'You then asked a series of awkward questions to our guests, which bordered on the insulting.'

'I didn't drink the entire bottle and I didn't get drunk.'

'Well, it would have got me drunk,' Philips said.

'But you could have a low tolerance for alcohol. If asking how somebody can end up working for an organisation nobody has ever heard of can be construed as insulting, then frankly they should see a bit more of the world.

'The reason the application failed,' Woake continued 'was because of an incident in a nightclub and an injury caused by a demented bull, both of which were nothing to do with me.'

'It was you who insisted that *Brazil's* would be part of the tour?' Mason asked.

'Yes. It makes sense to include the town's principal nightclub in any application which involves the night-time economy.'

'But didn't you think it would be risky to include *Brazil's*, especially given the history with the proprietor?'

'Not necessarily. I was unaware of the history, especially as nobody bothered to tell me,' Woake said. 'Also, my decision could not reasonably have influenced an explosion at the venue.'

'The officers say that the delegation was met with some hostility from members of the public,' Councillor Norton (Conservative) said. 'Did you attempt to defend them?'

'Saw little point. The delegation comprised three grown men and two women who had just brought terror to a Pakistani taxi driver. It wasn't my fault that they interviewed the public, using terminology that nobody outside the public sector could ever understand.'

'But you described a member of the delegation as a "stupid woman"?' Mason asked.

'Yes,' Woake answered.

'Would you like to explain?'

'We heard fireworks. The noises were obviously fireworks and a cursory glance to the sky would also have told her that. Therefore, what she said was stupid. And Eileen French is also a woman, so the expression "stupid woman" was quite apt.'

'And you can tell the difference between gunfire and fireworks, can you?' Mason asked.

'Yes,' Woake replied.

'How?'

'Because before reading for the Bar, I spent three and a half years in the army.'

With a surprising honesty not always to be expected in a Council meeting, the committee meeting was concluded.

Thus ended Woake's first foray into frontline politics. He was relegated back to the depths of the backbenches, with no further action taken. The local paper, *The Gretford Gazette*, ran a story on Purple Flag, but the details were lost amongst the more interesting incidents of that night. Within days, the Council's Purple Flag application had been forgotten.

Not that the majority of the Council's one hundred and fifty thousand residents ever had any idea that it had been made.

A verdict was returned in the case of Mr Auza.

Much to Woake's annoyance, frustration and surprise at the gullibility of the jury system, the jury accepted Auza's account that he was an innocent bystander and Prusack's evidence that he alone was responsible for importing the drugs. No doubt they also felt sorry for Auza due to his age.

As Myers said, Woake never really stood a chance.

Woake continued with his backbench career as Auza returned to Latvia, seeing more of England than he ever intended.

Ten

Woake sat in one of the meeting rooms at Fordhouse, alone save for a large woman who sat opposite him. An unfolded flip chart stood by her side. *Equality and Diversity in the Modern Workplace* was written at the top of the front page.

A power point projected a paused film onto a large white screen.

The woman had introduced herself as Marianna McGillip, an equality and diversity training coordinator. With her short purple hair, skin complexion which reminded Woake of an upside-down plimsole, and with a tattoo on her fattened arm comprising a skull smoking a cigarette and wearing a top hat, Woake assumed she was a lesbian.

However, the look in her eye as she eyed Woake cast a slither of doubt in his mind.

'Good evening, Councillor. Welcome to this special training session on equality and diversity.'

'Please, call me Sebastian,' Woake said, smiling.

'I have been asked to provide this session, Councillor,' McGillip said, ignoring Woake, 'as I understand that you have recently struggled with the concept of accepting full diversity in the public sector. I note that you failed to attend my training session provided to all new councillors earlier this year. Why was that?'

'Probably because I was busy doing something slightly more worthwhile, like working,' Woake answered.

'Indeed, then perhaps had you attended then you may have accepted homosexuality within the Council.'

'Who said that I rejected it?'

'The questioning of the symbol of same-sex campaigning can in itself constitute a rejection of the acceptance of same-sex relationship.'

'Of course it can.'

'Good, then acceptance of your ignorance is the first step in rectifying it,' McGillip said, failing to grasp the irony in Woake's statement. 'With my guidance and tuition, I am sure that you will throw off the shackles of ignorance and embrace the freedom of acceptance. You will become what we call "woke".'

'Excuse me?' Woake asked.

'You will become woke.'

'But I am Woake.'

'You most certainly are not,' McGillip insisted.

'I most certainly am. I am Sebastian Woake.'

'That is merely your name. I am talking about the spiritual rebirth you will experience which will enable you to become a valued member of the twenty-first century. Think of Prince Harry.'

'What? A member of the upper-class who has grown a ridiculous beard, has an unhealthy obsession with beads and walks around barefoot everywhere like a hobbit? No thanks.'

'No, a drunken youth leading a life of pleasure and hedonism with little thought to the more important things, who needs to be educated so that his mental well-being can embrace the challenges of modern life.'

'Can't wait.'

'We shall start with a short film, which we shall then talk about. We will then walk through a role-playing scenario together. You shall be provided with a certificate at the conclusion of our ninety-minute-long session.'

'Ninety minutes to understand equality and a role play?' Woake asked.

McGillip hit the play button, ignoring Woake.

Woake sat in his chair, watching a fifteen-minute film comprising a never-ending sequence of actors from different colour, race, religion, sexuality, disability and gender (including reassignment) holding messages written on whiteboards explaining exactly what equality in the workplace means for them.

There was the single mother complaining of a boss who failed to understand childcare, an attractive woman saying that she could never be taken seriously because of her looks, a homosexual saying how he had to fight for acceptance, and a Muslim saying that she would never be trusted because of her religious beliefs.

A white middle-class male complained of the struggles with the work-life balance, whilst an Asian woman was left depressed as she was unable to understand another language.

The video was completely silent, whilst a fat white woman in the corner of the screen translated the video into sign language. No doubt in order not to insult the illiterate deaf.

McGillip turned round to face Woake when it finished.

'What did you make of that?' she asked.

'Not much,' Woake answered truthfully.

'What do you mean?' McGillip asked, unable to deal with the rarest of things; someone being honest with her.

'Well, for a start,' Woake answered 'whoever produced that film was obviously discriminatory against the blind for the obvious reason that there was no sound. Secondly, the person who wrote the messages must have been absent from school the day basic grammar was taught. The message which read "Its the awkwardness when I get mistaken for someone else of the same ethnicity" needed an apostrophe in the word "Its".

'Furthermore, I would have some sympathy for the message held by two women which read "People make the assumption we come from the same part of the world" if the board was actually held by two women of the same ethnicity. As it was, one woman was an Arab, the other was Chinese and the only thing they had in common was that their hair was black. That's assuming that the Arab woman had black hair. It was impossible to tell because of the hijab. It could have been green for all we know.

'And as for the schizophrenic, I have little sympathy for him. Who the Hell wants to be served by a schizophrenic barista?'

'Let us go back to the Muslim woman wearing the traditional form of Arab dress,' McGillip said.

'You mean the hijab?' Woake asked.

'Yes, the hijab. The fact you have highlighted it is an obvious demonstration of your out-of-date beliefs. You have used it as an excuse to attack the poor woman.'

'No, I'm stating a fact. The hijab was designed and is worn in order to protect a woman's modesty in front of men other than a husband or immediate relative. It is therefore impossible to know what is underneath it,' Woake said. 'The fact you are questioning whether a Muslim woman can have anything but dark hair is in itself a demonstration of indirect discrimination on your part.'

'You can't say that,' McGillip spluttered.

'Yes I can, because it is a fact. Like many people, you assume she is adhering to a strict code of modest conduct. Perhaps she is wild in her private life with a penchant for Ann Summers lingerie? She may even have a tattoo.

'And as for them coming from the same part of the world, the deaf dumb and blind kid could see that's an impossibility.'

'So now you're mocking disabled children?' McGillip asked, hoping this would let her regain the initiative.

'No, I'm quoting from a song, from an era which you probably disapprove of.'

'Shall we now do some role play?' McGillip asked.

'Always my favourite way to spend the evening,' Woake said with a smile.

'I am going to play you a short clip,' McGillip said in a way as if she was addressing a moron 'and I want you to express the feelings of the main protagonist.' McGillip clicked a button on her laptop, projecting a cartoon slide of the outside of a restaurant. A lesbian couple and a mixed-race heterosexual couple sat at two tables.

A narrator provided the commentary. 'You are Darren,' the estuary English male voice said. A cartoon figure, presumably Darren, appeared on the screen. Darren was white, with gelled blonde hair set in a quiff and an ear piercing. Combined with a stance more akin to a dancer, Woake made the assumption his character was gay.

'And you have applied for a job as a waiter. Unfortunately, the manager of the restaurant only wants a heterosexual male applicant for the job.' The manager of the restaurant appeared on the screen; a big-breasted woman wearing a tight-fitting corset straining under the pressure of what it was attempting to withhold.

'Bloody hell!' Woake exclaimed 'looks more like a French madam than a restaurant manager.'

The cartoon of an obviously straight black male now appeared on the screen next to Darren.

'You have therefore had your application rejected,' the narrator continued regardless, 'which is an example of direct discrimination. You now have to discuss with your equality and diversity training coordinator how you feel about this rejection.'

'So, Councillor,' McGillip said 'what are your feelings?'

'About what?' Woake asked.

'About your job application being rejected,' McGillip continued.

'Not much,' Woake answered.

'You don't feel a sense of unfairness, that your sexual orientation was an unwarranted hinderance on your job prospects, an anger that the job went to another man whose success was owed solely because he wasn't gay?' McGillip urged.

'Not really,' Woake answered.

'Can you please elaborate?' McGillip asked.

'If I have to,' Woake said with resignation. 'I wouldn't feel any of those emotions because I feel a job should only be given to an applicant who matches the criteria set. In this case, the successful applicant just so happened to be straight. And who says that Darren was unsuccessful because he was gay?'

'But why should any of this matter?'

'Exactly. None of this does. Your very example is utter bollocks. I've been to plenty of restaurants and have been served by plenty of gay men. Who has ever heard of a gay man being denied a job in a restaurant?'

'So you deliberately notice such things, do you?' McGillip asked.

'Of course, who doesn't?'

'Well, I don't,' McGillip answered.

'Of course, you wouldn't, but those of us in the real world notice such things. Mainly that, on the whole, gay men act differently, talk differently, walk differently, and in fact are completely different to straight men. Hence why they are gay.'

'Don't you think there's something disgusting about what you're saying?'

'Not really, and as for your example just now, I could ask if the black man who got the job was better qualified? Did he have more relevant experience? Perhaps Darren is a total wanker and the black bloke is actually a nice guy, and on that basis was awarded the job. Not that that would be such a concern to you, would it?' McGillip sat silently, staring at Woake.

'I should imagine that you're the type of woman who hates it when a man opens the door for you, aren't you?'

'I consider it to be a particular form of patronising behaviour,' McGillip answered.

'Why is that?' Woake asked.

'Because it confirms the stereotype that laid down erroneously over centuries that women need the assistance of men, that they are somehow inferior.'

'Bollocks it does. It's actually a mark of good manners and a decent upbringing.'

'You mean an upper-class upbringing?'

'No, manners are universal, regardless of class, sexual orientation, race or religion. But the fact you have mentioned the upper-class in such a disparaging way, and have therefore labelled me as such, demonstrates your own form of prejudice. For you, the perception of upper-class is a social immorality.'

'Not necessarily. All I said was that women believe that having the door opened for them is patronising.'

'No, that's what you think. Possibly out of jealously for other women. I would argue, and I believe I'm correct, is that most women appreciate what is called gentlemanly, even gallant, behaviour.'

'Such as help to put on a jacket or "women and children first".'

'And do you know where the "women and children first" came from?' McGillip failed to answer. 'HMS Birkenhead was a frigate used as a troop vessel at the start of the Crimean War, and in 1852 it sank off the Western Cape. Knowing there were not enough lifeboats for the six hundred and forty odd souls on board, the cry of "women and children first" went out. There were only one hundred and ninety-three survivors.

'Many of the men who perished were common sailors and soldiers. The upper-class concept you are so derisive of was born out of working-class heroism, and you are telling me that, in a similar situation, you would not take advantage?' McGillip continued to sit in silence.

'Thought not,' Woake said. 'And the sad reality for you is that the vast majority of people are not racist or homophobic or misogynistic, but your kind have created this feeling that there is inequality or discrimination wherever you go. I would like to say that's probably in order to provide you with an income, but the sad reality is that's probably more to do with making up for your own lack of confidence or shortcomings.'

'Have you quite finished?'

'On the basis that it is now half-past eight, the time this session is due to end, yes I am.' Woake stood up to leave. 'Many thanks for your time Maz. It has been most interesting.'

'Councillor, you are forgetting your certificate,' McGillip said, handing him his certificate of attendance. Thankfully for Woake, Gallagher had had the foresight to organise a session in which attendance was the only requirement to passing.

'Many thanks,' Woake said as he accepted the certificate. He left Fordhouse and headed towards his car.

Woake threw the certificate into a bin as he left.

Eleven

FEBRUARY 2016

It was four months later when Myers led Woake into the London headquarters of the Department for Work and Pensions, a large monolithic monstrosity of concrete and glass. A triumph of the 1960s, it is rivalled only by the National Theatre and the Southbank Centre for ugliness.

Woake followed Myers through the front lobby. The double-fronted glass doors opened into a spacious reception area. Beige tiles were on the floor, dull cream paint was on the walls.

The equally bland receptionist directed Myers and Woake onto the fourth floor, with directions to wait in meeting room 4.3.

Myers and Woake walked the full length of Level 4, passing rows of civil servants sitting at their desks. The room was flanked by meeting rooms and offices (reserved for more senior civil servants) on either side. Despite it being only eleven thirty in the morning, strip lighting on the ceiling provided the only source of light.

Faded grey carpet covered the whole of the floor, adding to the sense of despondency.

They found room 4.3, which held nothing but six desks laid out in a square. Eight chairs were tucked in under the desks. Two fading sailing prints were hung on the dirty cream walls. Scum had congealed between the glass sheets of the double-glazed windows, the only source of fresh air being the ageing air conditioning system.

Dank paint peeled off the walls.

Myers looked around the room. 'What a fucking shithole,' he said. Myers studied the window, attempting to find the window lock. 'It would appear, dear boy, that the window won't open.' He turned back towards Woake. 'Probably to stop the poor bastards who work here from topping themselves.'

'Who are we here to meet, Richard?' Woake asked, laying out the case papers.

'Marla Rajeesce, the case officer and Jennifer Worsford, the DWP lawyer,' Myers answered.

'Any idea if they'll proceed with the prosecution?' Woake asked.

'Should do. The bloody woman is as guilty as Hell,' Myers answered.

"The bloody woman" in question was Tiffany Westbrook, an unemployed forty-three-year-old mother of two in receipt of jobseeker's allowance as well as housing benefit for the period of June 2012 to November 2015. Whilst the legitimacy of her claim for jobseeker's allowance was never questioned, it was her housing benefit claim which was.

Unfortunately for Ms Westbrook, the DWP caseworker assigned to her claim became aware that her children were no longer living with her. In other words, the caseworker had been informed by a vindictive neighbour back in July 2015 that the children had moved back in with their estranged father, himself a benefit claimant.

Not wishing to be denied a substantial source of her income and displaying the entrepreneurial spirit which is a hallmark of the professional claimant (Ms Westbrook had never had a job), she let out her now two vacant bedrooms for cash.

Following (what Myers assumed to be) an in-depth investigation into the allegation, Marla Rajeesce had ascertained that the children were indeed living with their father.

An unforeseen, but perhaps unsurprising, result of her children moving back in with their father was that the father could now apply for additional housing benefit.

Not even the entrepreneurial spirit of a professional claimant could explain how two children could live in two separate addresses ten miles apart, at the same time.

A quick calculation by Marla Rajeesce had deduced that Ms Westbrook had claimed up to £90,000 in benefits which she was otherwise ineligible for.

'But?' Woake asked, sensing hesitation in Myers's voice.

'The "but" Woake,' Myers answered 'is that this is the DWP, and the issue is whether they want to prosecute.'

'Adverse publicity?'

'Indeed, they'll be concerned about being portrayed as bullying an unemployed single mother.'

Myers was leaning back against a wall, his arms folded as he stood staring through the window of the door.

'Christ, could you imagine working in this dump?' Myers asked. Woake walked towards him, also staring through the window. The rows of civil servants faced them. 'I mean, look at them. They're sitting there, in front of their computers. They bend down towards the postbag to their left, pick out an envelope with their left hand, open it, enter whatever they need to enter into their computers, file the letter, then it's back to the postbag.

'And the amazing thing is, is that they do this for eight hours, five days a week. And that's their life. And you know what the depressing thing is, don't you?' Myers asked.

'What?' Woake asked forlornly.

'Is that this is only one floor in one office of the civil service. Just imagine how many more there are, across the country. All doing work like this, not providing any discernible service to the public, costing the taxpayer hundreds of millions each year. And the truly amazing thing is, is that nowadays communication is said to be easier, but did you know that at the height of the Empire, the Foreign Office only had a dozen civil servants? Should imagine this is reminiscent of the Council,' Myers added.

'You could say that,' Woake answered. 'You quickly learn that there is more to a local authority than emptying bins. It's parks, meals on wheels, social care, planning; there seems to be an officer for just about everything. And you can't help but feel that many of the officers' jobs could be condensed. Did you know that the starting salary of a junior officer in the HR department is £25,000 a year?'

'Bloody hell,' Myers responded.

'And it gets better. The top five officers are all on a greater annual salary than the Prime Minister, and GDC's salaries are considered to be relatively modest. And imagine this, Richard; there are twelve district councils in Sussex plus the County Councils. That therefore means that there are potentially fifty public sector workers in Sussex on more money than the Prime Minister, with only a fraction of the responsibility and stress.'

'Didn't you have some incident in Gretford a few months ago?'

'There was a minor explosion in a nightclub at the same time as a bull went on the rampage,' Woake answered, deciding against telling

Myers the full extent of his participation.

Woake could see two women walking towards the door. He went back to the case papers.

'What amazes me, Richard, is how bloody serious the officers all are. It's not so much that they're politically correct, it's more the fact they can never be impolite and always have to be smiling at each other. Christ knows how they'd survive in the real world.'

The door opened as the two women walked into the room.

'Sorry for being late,' the first woman said. In her early forties, she was short and thin, with shoulder-length blonde hair. 'Jennifer Worsford, the DWP lawyer assigned to this case,' she said as she introduced herself, holding out her hand.

Behind her walked an older stouter woman, with short dyed-brown hair, being what older Gretford residents would describe as having "well-tanned skin". 'Hi, I'm Marla Rajeesce, case officer,' she said.

The two women sat opposite Myers and Woake.

'Richard Myers, and this chap next to me is Sebastian Woake, he'll be acting as my Junior for the duration of this case,' Myers said.

'What does that mean?' Rajeesce asked.

'It means that he is a barrister in my Chambers who will act as my assistant in this matter,' Myers answered. 'Thank you for seeing us this morning. I hope you have read my opinion?' he asked.

'Yes, I have. Thank you,' Worsford answered. 'I have to say, you seem very confident that we should bring charges against Ms Westbrook.' Woake began taking minutes; his role in the meeting would be note-taking, looking up any point of law or fact in the case papers and publicly agreeing with Myers at every opportunity.

'I certainly am,' Myers responded. 'As I'm sure we all know, the test whether we should press charges is, first, is there a reasonable chance that the prosecution against Westbrook will succeed? And second, is it in the public interest? The answer to both is yes.'

'But how do we know there is a reasonable chance of success?' Rajeesce asked. With a sigh, Myers answered.

'Perhaps we should look at the case papers,' he said.

For the next hour, Myers led Worsford and Rajeesce through the evidence. Westbrook's benefits applications, as well as that of her estranged partner, were analysed. As were her utility bills, bank statements, Gumtree advert advertising the two bedrooms, and the statements of the principal witnesses, her neighbour and landlord.

'As far as I can see,' Myers summarised, 'the only difficulty is proving that the children were not living with her throughout the whole three years. We have a couple of witnesses; yourself Marla, her landlord and her neighbour, who all say that the children were not living with her. And we have the father's own benefit application. But are these witnesses sufficient so that the jury will be sure that the children were not there?'

'What's the problem with that?' Rajeesce asked.

'The problem,' Myers answered, 'is that the one statement may not guarantee conviction as there could be too many holes in it. How can you be sure that there were no children living at the address? How many times in the three years did you go to the defendant's address? Did you ever set foot inside the property? Did Westbrook and the neighbour have a falling out? Is the neighbour ignoring all the times when she saw the children? Those are the questions that I would ask in order to cause doubt to the prosecution's case.'

'So you're saying that we should ditch the case?' Worsford asked. *Perhaps too readily*, Woake thought.

'No, I'm saying, let's proceed. If nothing else, being in the dock for the first time in her life will probably drive the fear of God into her and she'll end up pleading in any event.'

'We also have a slight problem with the landlord,' Rajeesce said.

'What's that?' Myers asked.

'He's unwilling to give evidence,' Rajeesce answered.

'I'm sorry?'

'He's unwilling to give evidence,' Rajeesce repeated.

'And why's that?' Myers asked.

'Apparently he has several properties which are rented out to benefit claimants. He says that he is unwilling to give evidence in court against Ms Westbrook because he doesn't want to get a poor reputation amongst his tenants.'

'Well, there's an easy way to deal with that,' Myers said.

'And what's that?' Worsford asked.

'Arrest him for wasting police time, stick him in the cells for twenty-four hours and then ask him how he wants to proceed.'

Woake finished writing his notes during the subsequent silence.

'Perhaps there is other evidence we could use?' he asked.

'I have conducted surveillance on Ms Westbrook's property,' Rajeesce answered.

'Fantastic,' Woake said. 'What surveillance would that be?'

'I have video footage on four separate days during the hours in which the children would go to and coming home from school,' she said.

'During how long a time span?' Myers asked.

Rajeesce looked at her notes. 'About six weeks, between November and December 2015.'

'So in addition to her application, her ex-partner's, a couple of witnesses and now video surveillance, I'd say we have more than a reasonable chance of success,' Myers said.

'But the remaining issue Richard is, is this in the public interest to proceed?' Worsford asked.

'Well, we're dealing with a woman who is suspected to have cheated the taxpayer out of £90,000, so yes, I'd say there is a public interest,' Myers said.

'But there is the concern that we are dealing with a single mother,' Worsford responded.

'Whose children do not live with her,' Myers retorted.

'There is still the fact that we could be prosecuting a single unemployed woman,' Worsford said.

'How do we know she is single? And why does it matter if she's a woman?' Myers asked. 'There is robust evidence to suggest that this woman has committed a serious crime and she should be prosecuted like any other suspected criminal.'

'Thank you to both of you,' Worsford said. 'If you could please give me some time to discuss this with my line manager, we'll get back to you shortly with our decision.'

Myers led Woake back to Chambers. They had left the austere surroundings of the Department for Work and Pensions and were walking down Chancery Lane towards Fleet Street and the Middle Temple. The Victorian gothic of the Royal Courts of Justice lay majestically to their right.

'Have you ever met a more pathetic, cowardly group of jobsworths than those bloody bastards in that office?' Myers asked.

As a matter of fact, yes, Woake thought, though he remained silent.

'What a group of knit your own yoghurt pots, *Guardian* reading, oak-stripped front door, sandal-wearing bloody morons,' he added. Woake's phone vibrated in his jacket pocket as they walked into Griffin Court. He dug it out of his pocket and noticed it was Craig Overton phoning him.

'Richard, do you mind if I answer this?' he asked. 'I'll see you back in Chambers.'

'Sebastian Woake,' he answered as Myers walked through the door of Griffin Court Chambers.

'Hi Sebastian, it's Craig from the Council. May I have a moment of your time please?'

Twelve

Woake sat with Foster and Overton in the Britannia later that evening. The Planning Committee had just finished and the three councillors had ensured that they had left the Council Chamber with as little attention as possible, lest a fourth councillor felt tempted to join what was planned to be a private discussion.

Woake bought the drinks at the bar as Foster and Overton found a table. They were engaged in small talk as Woake brought the drinks over; a gin and tonic for Foster and a glass of Sauvignon Blanc for Overton.

As a couple, Foster and Overton could not be more different. Foster was short and fat, with lanky straight hair and cracked veins indicating the start of drinkers' nose. Overton, however, was tall and thin, and whilst considered to be good looking, suffered from an arrogance, snobbishness and an air of disdain which could only belong to a man who wishes that his parents sent him to boarding school rather than the local comprehensive.

Foster and Overton were, however, totally inseparable. To the point that if it wasn't for the twenty-year age gap and that Foster was married (to a woman), Woake would guess that they were lovers.

Overton looked disappointingly at Woake's drink, a pint of lemonade. 'Not a drinker?' he asked disapprovingly.

'I think we all know the answer to that after Purple Flag,' Woake responded. 'Anyway, I'm training for a couple of events later in the summer, so I'm cutting back on alcohol during the week.'

'We heard that you're a rower,' Foster said.

'Have been since school and have tried to keep it going ever since. I've entered a couple of long-distance races in September. Anyway, Craig mentioned you wanted a word with me.'

'Yes we do,' Foster answered. 'I take it you've heard about Gerald?'

'Heard he had a stroke a couple of days ago. Any news on how he's doing?'

'He's in a medically induced coma, but it's obviously too early to determine what the long-term effects will be.'

'Which leaves us with a problem,' Overton said. 'Gerald is obviously the Leader, but it is equally obvious that he is unfortunately incapable of leading. The Cabinet was placed in the difficult position of having to decide, which it reluctantly had to.'

'What you mean, Craig,' Woake said 'is that Gerald's stroke will mean he has to retire from the Council, providing the opportunity for a Cabinet member with ambition to take over.'

Woake noticed Foster and Overton looking at each other. Foster drew a breath as he answered Woake.

'The Cabinet decided that with the challenges facing the Council at the moment, namely the upcoming Local Plan, that a continuity candidate replace Gerald as soon as is practicable.'

'And that candidate has been chosen?' Woake asked.

'Yes,' Foster answered. 'It has.'

'And who will that candidate be?'

'It will be me,' Foster answered. 'Once the Group has chosen its new Leader at the special Group meeting next week, an extraordinary Council meeting will be held to select the new Leader of the Council and his new Cabinet. As the most dominant Group on the Council, it's a foregone conclusion that our new leader will be selected Leader.'

'To be honest, Will, I'm not sure why you're telling me this. I think it's well known that I have only a limited interest in the Council and I've never actively sought the friendship of any Conservative members, so I'm not a member of the various factions within the Group which I'm sure exist.'

'We're telling you this Sebastian, because there will soon be an opening in the Cabinet,' Foster said.

'You know, Sebastian, that it will be too big a portfolio for an individual to have both Finance and the leadership,' Overton said, somewhat patronisingly.

'And Will is currently Lead Councillor for Finance, which he'll have to relinquish when he becomes Leader in two weeks.'

'You're assuming that Will will indeed become the new Leader. I had thought that was a decision left to the Group?'

'Of course you're right, Sebastian,' Foster answered. 'There must be seen to be a proper selection to choose the next Group Leader, but we understand that any other nominated candidate will not have any real chance of success.'

'What you mean, is that you will fix it so that any other candidate will only have the support of a couple of Group members,' Woake said. 'Which leads me back to my question. Why are you telling me all this? I can assure you that I will not be putting my name forward for the leadership. I can think of nothing worse.'

'Don't worry, Sebastian, we know it will not be you,' Overton said.

'But we would like you to consider taking over the Finance portfolio.'

'You want me to have Finance?' Woake said, laughing. When he saw that Foster and Overton remained silent, the full enormity of the horror unfolded on him. 'Why me? I know nothing about finance, barely have the time as it is for Council work, and let's face it, I think given the fall out of when I was Skelding's Deputy, people will think you're mad having me in the Cabinet.'

'I wouldn't worry too much about Purple Flag, everyone knows that that was only Mark looking out for himself,' Overton said.

'And as you said earlier, you're not a member of any faction within the Group so nobody can accuse me of favouritism. Don't mind if I quickly pop to the loo, do you?' Foster said as he rose from his chair.

'And as for time, you'll find that you'll probably be less busy as you'll no longer be a member of Overview and Scrutiny,' Overton said as Foster walked towards the gents.

'Only because I'll be attending it as a lead councillor,' Woake interrupted.

'Even so,' Overton continued, as if with no interruption, 'the Finance portfolio is perhaps the least time-consuming Cabinet portfolio. There'll be a couple of reports to read and decisions to make, but very few meetings.'

'But I'm a criminal barrister, Craig. I have absolutely no experience or indeed even interest in finance, the subject will bore me to tears and Christ help me if I get asked any difficult questions in Council, because with my lack of knowledge, I'll be bloody massacred.'

'You needn't worry about your lack of experience with finance,'

Overton answered. 'The Finance team is incredibly competent. Have to be with some of the lead councillors they've been given. Anyway, they're criminally liable if the Council goes bankrupt. And don't forget, they've had Will for the last five years, and he only has a very limited knowledge of finance. Did you know that he's a tax inspector?'

Foster returned from the toilets.

Woake sat in silence whilst Foster and Overton looked questioningly at him. He went to open his mouth to refuse their offer, but was interrupted by Foster.

'At least meet the team before you refuse,' Foster said.

Woake walked into the leadership suite the following Monday. He had been defending a man charged with the criminal damage of a former employer's car in Gretford Magistrates Court.

Faced with irrefutable CCTV footage, the defendant had little option but to plead. Woake's task then became limiting the sentencing.

It was three o'clock on the Monday as he entered the central PA pool in the leadership suite. He introduced himself to the three PAs. They ranged from a woman in her late twenties (Holly Sampson) to the eldest, a woman Woake guessed to be in her late fifties called Jill Granger. The third was a woman in her early fifties called Frances Hallond.

'Hi Sebastian, it's great to see you up here,' a high-pitched voice called to him. Woake turned to face Giles Bane grinning at him, his right hand outstretched. Woake shook it, smiling back.

Giles Bane, a cross between Michael McIntyre and an Andrex puppy, was the Managing Director of the Council; a rather grandiose title denoting that he was the most senior officer in the Council.

Woake's only interaction with him up to this point was observing sitting at the dais at Full Council meetings.

'Thanks Giles, I'm here to see the Finance team.'

'So I heard,' Bane responded, ever grinning. 'I understand that you're the new Lead Councillor for Finance. Congratulations.'

'Thanks, though I've not yet accepted it.'

'No, but you will. The Finance team is in Charlotte's office. Let me show you.'

Bane led Woake through one of the doors leading from the leadership suite. He knocked once, opened it and motioned Woake to enter.

'Hi Charlotte, this is Sebastian. He's your new lead councillor,' he said as he left the office. He closed the door after him.

Charlotte Bateup stood up from the board table in her office. Two other officers sat at the table and they also rose to greet Woake. Bateup walked towards Woake, offering him her hand. She was about 5ft 10" tall, blonde and like Bane, at least two stone overweight.

Another victim to the Council's policy of providing free food at the start of every meeting.

Woake noticed that she was incredibly young for a Council director, being in her late thirties. Bateup was known to Woake, from his time on Overview and Scrutiny, in which Bateup was a frequent witness.

The two other officers were unknown to Woake. The first introduced herself as Jessica Greenwood, a much slimmer woman in her forties. The second officer was as tall as Woake, at least 6ft 4", but narrow-shouldered with a slight stoop and the beginnings of a little pot belly.

The measurable demeanour was finished by his slow monotonous voice.

'Hi Seb, I'm Tim Anderson. I'm in charge of our commercial services,' he said.

'Thanks Tim, nice to meet you,' Woake responded, not sure what the commercial services were.

'Would you like to take a seat, Seb?' Bateup asked, motioning Woake to an empty chair. 'Jennifer didn't tell you, but she's in charge of the Council's investments.'

'Fantastic, thank you very much to all of you for agreeing to see me,' Woake responded.

'Well thank you Seb for agreeing to be our new lead councillor,' Bateup said.

'I haven't actually agreed to take the job, I just promised Will that I would consider his offer.'

'Will?' Bateup asked. 'I wasn't aware that he was the one who could make offers.' Woake chose not to respond to this, sensing that he had perhaps already said too much.

Realising that Woake would not comment further, Bateup

continued with her own pre-prepared introduction.

'I'm not sure how much you know about our work in the Finance team, but essentially we're responsible for the collection and generation of the Council income and how that money is spent. I understand that you were not at last year's budget night?' she asked.

'No, that's correct. I had a sentencing at Kingston Crown Court during the day, and we didn't get on until shortly after three in the afternoon. I, unfortunately, could not get back in time.'

'That's what I thought, so I had the budget reports printed for you.' Bateup walked over to her desk and returned with three large bundles under her arm, each about four inches thick. She placed them in front of Woake. 'Just a little bedtime reading,' she added.

'Thanks,' was all Woake could say.

For the next hour, Woake was introduced to the complicated world of local authority finance.

'Finance, Seb, can be broken down into two parts; the General Fund and the HRA. The General Fund comprises the greater part of our budgetary cycle.' Woake sat and listened as the General Fund was broken down for him, essentially income generation and expenditure.

Council tax collection, business rates, parking fees and fees for services rendered all formed a substantial share of the General Fund income. Charlotte continued with her explanation.

'It is all essentially a balancing exercise for us. We need to keep the council tax at a high enough level that it generates an income but low enough that it isn't too punitive.

'What you have to remember, Seb, is that we as a council receive a tiny proportion of the council tax income that we generate. Out of every £100 of council tax we collect, we have to send £50 to the Government and £40 to the County Council.'

'So we keep only ten per cent of all council tax collected?' Woake asked.

'That's correct. And it's the same with business rates, we keep only thirty per cent of income generated, and even then we have to keep the rates as low as possible otherwise businesses will close.'

It was the Housing Revenue Account which provided the greatest challenge. 'The grim economic situation which faced the coalition in 2010 meant that the Government had to get imaginative with how they made money. The then Chancellor authorised a rather sublime policy. He ordered that all public housing landlords had to re-buy their housing stock.

'Unfortunately for Gretford, GDC is one of the largest public housing landlords in the county. Which meant that in order to keep it, we had to take out a public loan.'

'How much?' Woake asked.

'About £190 million.'

'How much?'

'About £190 million. It was actually a stroke of genius by the Government. Not only did they get instant cash from every Council in the country, but they also get the guaranteed income as the loan provider.

'So the income we generate from our housing stock is lost as we service the debt?'

'That is correct,' Bateup answered. 'But it's not our only debt.'

'Not our only debt?'

'No,' Bateup answered hesitatingly. 'Before that, the Council had a serviced deficit of £60 million.'

'Christ,' was Woake's response.

'Actually Seb, that's not too bad for local authorities. One midlands County Council had debts of over £250 million. Ours is in line with what can be expected by local authorities.'

'So how do we make money to service our debt and provide the services the taxpayer pays for?' Woake asked.

'That's where I come in,' Greenwood answered. 'Apart from the money we generate from the General Fund, which is still quite substantial, we currently have £100 million in investments to provide an income.'

'One bedrock of the Finance team philosophy is that all our investments have to be safe but still generate income, rather than generate a large income from high-risk investments,' Bateup added.

'We currently have investments in five separate investment streams. Four are doing well, one less so.'

'What happened there?' Woake asked.

'Will, unfortunately, followed the advice of Hargreaves Lansdown, our advisors, rather than us. The investment dropped in value dramatically after only two months and has been recovering modestly ever since. It's currently in the third year of its six-year cycle, so we're confident that it will recover to its starting value by year six.'

'And am I correct in assuming that like many investments, we can't withdraw the investments until the end of their respective lifespans, unless we incur a penalty?' Woake asked.

'That's correct,' Greenwood answered. 'But you should also know the opposition, primarily the Gretford Guardians, is questioning where the money is invested.'

'Meaning?'

'That they're accusing us of investing in unethical companies.'

'Such as?'

'One company benefitting from our investment is BP.'

'What's wrong with that? BP is one of our major companies. Anyone with a pension would have money in it,' Woake said.

'Oil spill, climate change, carbon emissions,' Greenwood answered. 'Another company we have invested in is BAE Weapons Systems.'

'Yes,' Woake said 'I can see how that can be an issue.' Woake sat in silence for a moment before adding, 'So, as a local authority, we're broke,' he said, not as a question but more as a statement of fact.

'Well not quite, Seb. Bankruptcy is the inability to pay outgoings because of an insufficient generation of income. We're not quite at that yet.'

'But we're getting there?'

'I'm afraid so, Seb,' Bateup answered. 'We're going to have to make some rather drastic changes if we're going to continue providing the services we need to. Parks, social care, meals on wheels, officers' salaries, bin collections and planning and licensing could all go if we're not careful.'

'Can't we increase council tax?' Woake asked.

'No,' Bateup answered. 'Not only will that be punitive but you politicians risk losing your seats at the next election if we raise it too high. The same with business rates as an increase could drive businesses out of the district. We also can't raise parking fees as it may stop people from visiting Gretford.'

'Having been stuck in the gyratory system for an hour yesterday, that may not be such a bad thing,' Woake responded.

'And it's not just the services that will suffer, it's the major projects we need to finance,' Bateup said, ignoring Woake.

'So we're going to have to generate income like a business then, aren't we?' Woake suggested.

'We already do Sebastian,' said the dull tones of Tim Anderson. 'We have the Sir John Gielgud Theatre, G-On, the Prism and the crematorium, which are all major money earners.'

'But they also have their challenges,' Bateup said.

'Such as?'

'I'll let Tim answer.'

'Thanks Charlotte. G-On is unfortunately too small to attract a major booking, so even if we have a full house, the income will never be what was projected when it was built. Plus, we have a management company in situ, but I'll explain to you on another occasion the problem with them.'

'Why was it not bigger?'

'I did recommend that when it was first designed, but unfortunately the Council were worried about upsetting residents in a firmly Conservative neighbourhood in the run up to the then election. The Sir John Gielgud generates the Council £360,000 per year.'

'Fantastic,' Woake said.

'Yes,' Anderson answered. 'It would be were it not for the fact that the Council is liable for the upkeep of it rather than the tenants. Unfortunately the then councillor who authorised that agreement was very culture-minded.'

'How much does it cost us?'

'About £300,000 per year.'

'Jesus. Any other issues?' Woake asked despairingly.

'We have the Prism leisure centre, which attracts over a million visitors per year. Unfortunately, it's now thirty years old and is coming to the end of its lifespan. Frankly, it was badly designed and badly built, and we need to knock it down and rebuild.'

'And does it cost us anything?'

'Yes, despite us planning on knocking it down in a couple of years, we have to spend money on keeping the roof intact and the ice-rink from melting.'

'I'm sorry?'

'The roof leaks.'

'Bloody hell. So it costs us money?'

'Yes.'

'Anything else?' Woake asked, hoping the answer would be no.

'The crematorium is a major money earner for us. Unfortunately that too is approaching the end of its life. Ironically, when you come to think of it. It was built in the 1950s and we're just about to put in a planning application to knock it down and build a new one.'

'So my duties will be presenting reports to the Council, authorising decisions and trying to ensure that we don't go bankrupt whilst ensuring that we can still provide basic services?'

'Yes Seb, and don't forget the major projects. I've prepared this document for you,' Bateup said handing him a smaller bundle 'which will explain all the projects which this Council hopes to undertake in the next few years.'

The meeting broke up. It was five o'clock. The PAs and the Managing Director had all gone home.

The current Leader was still in his medically induced coma, a state of affairs not dissimilar to the Council's finances.

After dinner, Woake sat in the study of his Victorian home. He had bought the property when his relationship with his then fiancée had finally reached its disastrous climax. A climax that both parties were quite happy to have reached before making the even more disastrous mistake of actually marrying.

After the meeting with the leading members of the Finance team, Woake had gone for a 10k run around Gretford, an exercise he undertook four times a week. It was not just the physical challenge that appealed to him; it was the opportunity that the runs gave him to clear his head. No one could ever disturb him.

In front of him lay his case papers for the following day; the sentencing of a dangerous offender down in Winchester, which had been adjourned for the probation report following his trial for armed robbery.

But it was the Finance team that he now turned his attention to, and he began to write down a number of questions he had formulated during his run. He would ask them at the follow-up meeting he promised to have with Bateup, Greenwood and Anderson at the end of the week.

***

Woake was not the only Gretford district councillor who sat in his study considering his political future.

Mark Skelding sat in the fading light, whisky in his hand. A man in his early sixties, he cared little for medical guidelines. The gin and tonic before dinner, the wine with dinner and now the whisky attested to that. Approaching the end of his professional life, his political career became his principal concern.

A man whose ambition far exceeded his ability, he was naturally disappointed that the Cabinet had chosen Foster to be its nomination for the leadership.

There was no doubt in Skelding's mind that Foster would be voted Leader at next week's Group meeting, as there was no doubt that Foster would appoint that young careerist Overton as his Deputy over men who had vastly more experience.

Like all politicians (local and national), Skelding's thoughts turned to his legacy, and he had been working on another project ever since the Purple Flag debacle had unfolded.

He had told Foster so much that very night; that his support of Foster's candidature for the leadership was conditional on Foster supporting Skelding's latest project.

Soon, Skelding hoped, he would launch the Joint Enforcement Team into Gretford, and he knew exactly which officer would be ideally suited to help.

Thirteen

Woake phoned William Foster the following week to tell him his decision.

'Right, Will,' he said. 'I'll do it but only on the following basis. First, it's temporary only for six months. If my work is suffering at the end of the six months, I'm off. Second, my work takes precedence. I do not want there to be any briefings against me if I'm unable to attend a meeting at short notice. Third, you and I will have a chat about the state of the Council's finances.'

'Thanks Sebastian,' Foster responded, 'but remember that the position is also subject to me becoming Group Leader tonight.'

'Of course, I'll see you later,' Woake said and rang off.

Woake's second call during his lunch break was with Charlotte Bateup.

'Hi Charlotte, I just wanted to let you know that I have accepted Foster's offer of Lead Councillor for Finance.'

'Oh, that's great Seb,' Bateup responded.

'Thanks Charlotte,' Woake said, suspecting that Bateup would have said that to whoever had accepted the post. 'I've accepted subject to certain stipulations.' Woake repeated the first two he had told Foster, but added a couple more for Bateup.

'Third,' he continued, 'all our meetings are to be held at my convenience, not at the convenience of officers. I'm afraid that may mean some later finishes. Fourth, we need a meeting ASAP to discuss our finances, or the lack thereof. We need to make money and start thinking like a commercial entity, and I have a few ideas.'

'OK, Sebastian,' Bateup said slowly, obviously thinking of a suitable response to what was effectively her new minister. 'I think we can do most of that.'

'Excellent,' Woake responded. 'I already have a few ideas that I want put into immediate effect. And don't panic about the ramifications. I'm the Lead Councillor, so therefore the enthusiastic amateur. I appreciate that this is your job and your living, so I'll always face the consequences.'

'OK, Sebastian, would you like to tell me what you would like done?' Bateup asked, already fearing the possible ramifications.

Woake told her.

Within minutes of Woake's conversation with Bateup, Foster's own mobile phone rang. It was Giles Bane.

'Hi Giles,' Foster said as he answered.

'Hi Will, how are you?' the ever-cheerful Andrex puppy asked.

'Fine thanks, prepping for tonight's Group meeting.'

'Oh, of course, it's your big selection meeting for the Conservative Group. Anyone standing against you?'

'There is one other candidate, the backbencher John Foreman.'

'You'll be a dead cert, the Group will never choose a backbencher with no experience.'

'Thanks,' Foster responded, thinking that John Foreman's selection as Group Leader (and therefore Council Leader) was Bane's preferred choice; an inexperienced Leader totally dependent on senior Council staff. 'What can I do for you?' Foster asked.

'I've just spoken to Charlotte; it would appear that our new Lead Councillor for Finance has been on the phone to her.'

'Any problems?' Foster asked.

'Only a list of demands that were the prerequisite of his accepting the position.'

Foster smiled. 'Yes, he's already told me about them. To be honest, I don't think that they're too unreasonable considering he works.'

'And the one demanding that GDC becomes more commercial?'

'What?' Foster asked, jumping up from his chair. 'Has nobody informed him of North Sussex Housing?'

'Not yet, he's having another meeting with Charlotte and the team next week. We'll explain to him our own finance strategy. But that's not our only problem. He's also given Charlotte a list of policies to be actioned immediately.'

'Such as?' Foster asked, a tone of resignation in his voice. Bane told him. Foster sat in silence for a few seconds, the full horror at the consequences playing through his mind. 'Christ, and Charlotte didn't try stopping him?' he asked.

'How can she? Sebastian's her new lead councillor.'

'And didn't he know that it's the Group meeting tonight?'

'I don't think that such things are important to him,' Bane said cheerfully 'Good luck with tonight Will,' he added before ending the call.

In the end, Foster did not have to worry about the selection. John Foreman had been encouraged to stand as a candidate by an ally of Craig Overton; a fellow backbencher who had been ordered to act as Foreman's friend in return for being appointed Overton's Deputy.

The attention had flattered John Foreman, his fantasy not being matched by his intelligence nor common sense. But for Foster and Overton, it was important that democracy was seen to be done, and John Foreman had proved to be an unwitting accomplice in the advancement of both their careers.

Foster and Foreman were required to address the Group and outline their vision for the future of the Council. Foster went first; an unspectacular but safe speech centring on building on the legacy of Gerald Gallagher.

Unsurprisingly, John Foreman tried a riskier approach, promising to return power away from the strong leader model and back to the collective members of the Group. Unfortunately for Foreman, he wasn't counting on Cathy Fulcher-Wells; a small thin woman in her late forties with a high-pitched squeaky voice. Being about 5ft 2", she had the misfortune of suffering from duck's disease. Indeed, her arse looked like it needed a bra of its own; a sort of jock strap but in reverse.

In one question, interrupting Foreman mid-sentence, Fulcher-Wells asked how he intended to do this, considering that there was no ability to do so in the confines of the current Council rules.

John Foreman sputtered and stammered a reply, unable to answer the question. The rest of his five-minute speech became a disaster of stammering, mumbling and rambling.

Unbeknown to Foreman, Cathy Fulcher-Wells had been told to ask this question by Overton, who had been briefed on Foreman's speech by the encouraging backbencher. In return for this service,

Fulcher-Wells had been promised a post on the new Cabinet.

Foster was elected Group Leader by thirty-one votes to four, the four being John Foreman and three other councillors who felt sorry for him.

Woake voted for Foster.

Foster addressed the Group once the results had been announced, a dejected John Foreman taking his place with the other group members.

'I just want to thank John for tonight and to send him my deepest commiserations. It was important that we, as a Group, had a good debate about our future,' he said, a smirk on his thin lips as he looked towards Foreman. He continued, 'I should imagine that you are all bored with hearing from me tonight, so I shall keep the rest of the meeting brief. I will take on the Planning Policy portfolio in conjunction with being Leader. We shall have a Group away day in a couple of weeks to discuss the Local Plan.

'The only other announcement I wish to make at this point concerns the Cabinet. There will be changes, and I am happy to confirm two of them. Craig will become Deputy Leader and Sebastian Woake will join the Cabinet as Lead Councillor for Finance.'

Whereas a triumphant smile found its way onto Overton's lips, Woake remained completely passive, leaning back in his chair as he surveyed the Group. Four members were under the age of forty, a possible further three were under fifty. The rest ranged between fifty and possibly seventy-five, a mixture of the retired and semi-retired.

'Craig, would you like to address the Group?' Foster asked.

'Yes, thank you Will and congratulations. A new administration provides us the opportunity to really get to grips with the outstanding projects within the district. As Lead Councillor for Sustainable Projects, I look forward to coordinating our efforts. The major projects we will concentrate on are the new crematorium and the redevelopment of a former industrial suburb into potentially one thousand new homes.

'Like Will, I recommend we discuss this all properly at the Group away day in a couple of weeks.'

'Thanks Craig. Sebastian, would you like to say anything to the Group?' Foster asked with a certain amount of trepidation.

'Not really, Will,' Woake responded 'bearing in mind that the time is now half eight, I should imagine that we all want to go home.

So I'll be quick. I had a meeting with the Finance team last week, and I am afraid that we are broke. We have debts totalling £250 million and an income that can barely service it, let alone provide the services we need to provide by law.'

'When you say broke, what do you mean?' asked Simon Newton, a seventy-plus councillor and Cabinet member for Housing and a former Leader.

'That we have no money, Simon. I have today ordered a series of measures to help with our financial problems. There will be no more complimentary food before Council meetings. The food bill is £25,000 per year, which wouldn't be quite so bad if we actually ate the food, but you only have to look at the canteen at the end of any Council meeting to see that most of it gets chucked in the bin.'

'But we've always had food,' protested Newton.

'Appreciate that, but we won't any more. The second measure I have implemented is a halt on all projects.'

'You've done what?' Overton interrupted.

'Put a halt on all projects, Craig. From now on, every project will need a business case proposing how we can pay for it and how it will generate an income,' Woake said, addressing the Group.

'And the final measure is a commercialisation of the Council's services. There are plenty of business opportunities out there, and I intend for the Council to make some money.'

'I have to say Sebastian, that I am finding this all a bit drastic,' said Helen Turton, a seventy-year-old representative from the district's eastern villages. Turton's whole life had been dedicated to service, having married a rising star of the diplomatic corps at a young age, who had retired ten years previously with a knighthood along with his generous pension. Now a member of the nobility, the former secretary subsequently became a bastion for tradition, joining the Conservative Party not out of any great political conviction but because she considered it is what people like her would be expected to do.

As she herself had once said in her adopted soft diplomatic voice, 'it is important that those of us with the ability to represent others do so, because there are many within Gretford who lack the ability to do so themselves, and I believe it is the duty of those who can to do so for them.'

She now turned her duty onto Woake. 'When you say

commercialisation, what do you intend?'

'That we start our own businesses on certain services which we provide, which we therefore sell to other authorities, such as waste collection, gardening services and car park fee collections.'

'I didn't think that we were allowed to do that?' she asked.

'Thankfully the coalition Government changed the law. We also have a housing company, so I have asked the Finance team to look at potential investments, as well as commercial space.'

'But how can we pay for that?' asked Newton.

'We can borrow the money cheaply from the Public Works Loan Board and the income generated will be enough to service the debt and provide us with an income from our investments.'

'I don't like this, Sebastian,' Lady Turton continued, with a sly smile breaking out across her lips. 'I don't think that our residents would appreciate us turning their Council into a shady property developer.'

'I don't think that they would appreciate having their council tax increased or their bin collection reduced to fortnightly cycles. Or indeed you Helen, at the next election when you're voted out,' Woake responded.

'And the food, that's only £25,000 per year,' she said.

'Indeed it is, but it's still a waste of money.'

'But can't the leftovers be donated to a local charity or food bank?' Newton asked.

'Can't do that, health and safety as well as food hygiene regulations prevent that,' Overton said.

'I take some sandwiches home for my dogs,' Reg Swaden interjected. 'Although I have to say, I no longer give them the sausage rolls. Jenny has never forgiven me for the mess we woke up to the following morning.'

'I just don't think you appreciate, Sebastian, how necessary it is for those of us who are busy to have food provided for us,' Turton said, ignoring Swaden.

'You are retired, Helen,' Woake responded, 'so you can eat before the meetings. It is worth noting that the only councillors to complain about the food are those who are retired.'

'Very good idea, Sebastian,' Swaden said. 'It might concentrate councillors' minds if they have not eaten before the meetings. Hopefully the meetings will be a lot quicker from now on.'

Fourteen

Swaden did not have to wait long to test his theory. Full Council took place the following week. Woake was walking up the steps towards the front foyer of Fordhouse when he was accosted by Swaden.

'Wouldn't go towards the members' room if I was you, dear boy,' Swaden said 'you're not exactly flavour of the month in there. In fact, you could say there aren't any flavours at all, which is the problem.'

The members' room was the personal domain of the councillors, including the private canteen, now sitting resplendently redundant.

'They haven't taken the withdrawal of food very well?' Woake asked.

'Could say that. You're here early, you rarely bother to arrive until after the meetings have started.' The time was six thirty.

'New position, new mentality.' Woake could see the scepticism in Swaden's eyes. 'Have a meeting before Full Council with Overton and Foster, better go.'

Woake left Swaden on the steps and made his way up to the leadership suite. He waved to Charlotte Bateup in her office, walked through the empty PAs pen and entered the leaders' room.

Foster and Overton were at their respective desks, Foster sitting at Gallagher's old desk, Overton occupying what was formerly Foster's. Woake sat down on the Cabinet desk, facing the Leader and Deputy Leader. Both were eating M&S salads.

'Hi chaps,' he said.

'Hiya Sebastian,' Foster said, not looking up from his computer. 'You alright?'

'Fine, thanks,' he responded. 'You wanted to see me?'

'You know, Sebastian, I would have appreciated you speaking to me before speaking to the officers about the major projects,' Overton said.

'Had nothing to do with you, Craig,' Woake responded. 'The financial implications of the projects are my responsibility, and it's the responsibility of the relevant officer in charge of the projects to ensure that they have a strong business case before the draft plans are submitted to you for approval.'

'But you've called a halt to major projects vital for the future viability of the district, such as the crematorium.'

'Exactly, we already have one which works, so there's no rush to replace it.'

'Look Sebastian,' Foster broke in, 'nobody is having a go at your decisions, especially as you've just become a Lead Councillor. And if you can make a success of commercialisation, then great, but please be cautious about upsetting too many people, especially as a lot of hard work has already gone into the crem.'

'OK Will, understood. But please be aware that the Council is in extreme financial problems, not helped by previous lead councillors failing to grasp the problems. If you're not careful Will, you'll be the Leader of a bankrupt council and all these projects which are so important to you will be dead in the water.'

Woake stood up, 'Right chaps, I'll see you in Full Council.'

Woake's new position was in the middle of the front row of desks in the Council Chamber, as befit a member of the Cabinet. He was now the third most senior councillor after the Leader and Deputy Leader.

The backbench Conservatives and the opposition Liberal Democrat, Labour and Gretford Guardian councillors sat in the rows behind the Cabinet.

Woake took his seat, acknowledging the councillors nearby. He ignored the few jealous glances which were thrown his way by the backbench Conservatives, mainly from the accountant Jeremy Pakeman.

The other Cabinet members took their places either side of him; Skelding, Swaden, Kildare, Newton and the newly promoted Cathy Fulcher-Wells, Lead for Culture, Arts and Heritage.

'Welcome to the team, Sebastian,' Skelding said grudgingly to his right.

'Thanks Mark,' Woake replied 'let's hope we have no repeat of

Purple Flag.'

'A bloody sandwich would be good.'

'Hi Sebastian,' Fulcher-Wells squeaked to Woake's left, 'we need to talk about the development of the museum and Edgeborough Farm.'

'How much will the new museum cost?' Woake asked.

'About £3 million,' she answered.

'No chance.'

The Mayor interrupted Fulcher-Wells before she could respond and called the meeting to order.

'Good evening, councillors,' the ageing Mayor said. Woake estimated that he was at least seventy-five years old. 'Before we start tonight's meeting, I would first like to send all our best wishes to Councillor Gerald Gallagher, whom I am delighted to say has today come out of his induced coma.' A murmur of sympathetic agreement could be heard from the Council benches. Gallagher was feared, respected and disliked in equal measure. Perhaps testament to his success as a Leader, it could never be said that he was liked.

'Tonight's extraordinary meeting has been called in response to Councillor Gallagher's resignation from the Council.'

'Point of order, Mr Mayor,' Patricia Lafontaine, Leader of the Gretford Guardians interrupted, 'how can a man who has been in a coma since his stroke, be capable of resigning?'

A stunned Mayor turned in panic to Bane, who whispered calmly in his ear.

'Councillor Gallagher's resignation was submitted as per Regulation 12.3 paragraph 2 of the Council's constitution, which enables the indirect resignation of the Council Leader if he or she becomes otherwise indisposed,' Mayor Joplin answered.

'Mr Mayor,' Lafontaine said, taking her opportunity in mock exasperation. 'I note that this is nothing more than a power grab by members of the Cabinet to unseat the current Leader and take his place.'

'Mr Mayor, this is an absurd statement,' Foster said loudly, feigning his own anger towards an opponent. 'The Cabinet held an emergency meeting on the advice of the Council officers as we faced the real prospect of an indefinite length of time without strong leadership.'

'So what will be different?' Lafontaine asked.

'Councillor Lafontaine,' Bane interjected, solely out of his own self-preservation as the integrity of the Council officers had been questioned. 'It is worth noting that this was a perfectly lawful procedure. Unfortunately, there was little reason to believe that Councillor Gallagher would ever make a full recovery, or indeed would want to remain Leader. We had a crisis, which needed to be dealt with as expeditiously as it could, to the great misfortune of another. Mayor Joplin.'

'Ah, yes, thank you, Mr Bane. This meeting has been called in order to elect the new Leader of Gretford District Council. There is only one candidate, William Foster, Leader of the Conservative Group. Could all those in favour please raise their hands?'

In one movement, all the Conservatives raised their right hands.

'And those against?' The opposition members all raised their right hands as the Conservatives lowered theirs.

'I can confirm that William Foster has been elected as the new Leader.'

All the councillors watched as Foster, closely followed by his Deputy Overton, took his seat on the dais next to Bane.

'Thank you, Mr Mayor, and thank you to all for their trust in me,' Foster said with a satisfied grin.

The meeting was concluded shortly afterwards. Having lasted only thirty minutes, it was one of the shortest Council meetings in Gretford's history.

No doubt because many of the councillors wished to return home for dinner.

William Foster was driving home later that evening, but where his concentration should have been on the dual carriageway leading to his hometown of Plaistow, his mind was far too concerned with Sebastian Woake.

It was not so much his decision to promote Woake which concerned him. Woake's youth, relative lack of experience in local authorities and political naivety still made him a more pliable Cabinet member than someone like Jeremy Pakeman. What concerned Foster was that Woake was seriously heeding the advice of the officers; that the district was effectively broke.

Like many politicians, Foster was little concerned with the

financial impact of decisions, confident in the knowledge the next generation of councillor would deal with all the consequences of his decisions.

As with all newly appointed leaders, Foster held grandiose plans for his own legacy as political Leader; a vision for the future of Gretford, a vision for the projects he wished to see complete, a vision for what he would leave future generations.

Visions which all required one thing; money. Not something which had worried Foster up to this point, as the Finance team had always found the money. By borrowing.

Now, Woake had effectively shut that particular stream of revenue.

Now all his plans for the future were at stake.

Gretford needed money. Foster needed money. And the money was needed immediately.

Fifteen

Woake signed into the advocates' register in the robing room of the Inner London Crown Court and checked the name of his opponent, a Miss Melanie Shone. He was the prosecutor in a homophobic hate crime.

Woake looked around the robing room, which was filling with both male and female barristers before the morning sessions began.

Woake noticed Shone standing in a group of young barristers, her back to him. She had removed her suit jacket in order to tie her bands around her neck, displaying a crisp white shirt hanging tightly to her figure underneath. Her curly auburn hair fell down to her shoulders.

Woake placed his sports bag down on a table and silently crept up behind Shone, who was too engrossed in her conversation with the three other barristers to take any notice. Woake stuck out his hands as he approached her. Shone spoke.

'The interesting thing about the Blair Government was that... Argh!' she cried, spinning round to face the person who had tickled her underneath her ribs. 'You bastard,' she said when she saw Woake, her smile hiding her anger and embarrassment.

'Still ticklish are we then, Mel?' Woake asked as he leant forward to hug her. Woake ignored the disparaging looks from the older barristers and the embarrassment of Shone's younger colleagues. As a barrister, Woake was supposed to remain professional at all times, to the point that even shaking hands between barristers was frowned upon.

'So what was the interesting thing about the Blair Government?' Woake asked, retrieving his sports bag and placing it next to Shone's holdall.

'Doesn't matter. I'll explain later. What are you doing today?' she asked.

'Prosecuting some idiot, you?' he asked, removing his suit jacket.

'Defending a man wrongfully prosecuted for committing a homophobic act. Still using that old bag?' she asked, throwing on her gown.

'Very insulting thing to say. This sports bag is a lot healthier than those holdalls you and the rest of the Bar insist on using,' he replied, fishing out his bands and stiff collar.

Barristers are expected to wear soft collars and ties when not in court; another minor rule Woake broke. As he once told Myers, the benefits of being self-employed meant he could form his own dress code.

Woake looked in the mirror as he attached his stiff collar to his shirt.

'In what way?' Shone asked. Like most barristers, she pulled a holdall which contained her practice books, case papers and court dress.

'Because those things become so bloody heavy, they put too much pressure on your backs, meaning that you're guaranteed a bad back by the time you're fifty.' Woake finished tying his bands. He took out his gown, wig and case papers and stuck them under his arm.

'Who's your opponent?' Woake asked.

'Haven't checked yet. Anyone here in the case of Daniel Brown?' she called out to the robing room. The blank stares answered the question for her. Shone walked towards the advocates' register.

Woake had already reached the door when Shone looked towards him. 'Hilarious,' she said, smiling.

'Come on, Mel, I'll buy you a coffee,' he said. He held the door open for her as she led him to the advocates' canteen.

'Any chance of the CPS chucking this?' Shone asked as Woake placed their drinks on their table; a white decaf coffee for her, a black tea for him.

'Not a chance. And why should they?' he asked.

'Because the defendant is homosexual.'

'What's that got to do with anything?'

'Please be serious for just a moment. How can the defendant be guilty of homophobia when he's gay?'

'Quite easily, Mel,' Woake answered. 'Because the law concerning hate crimes centres around perception; namely is there somebody in the vicinity who can take offence? The fact the defendant is gay doesn't mean anything.'

'I know that Sebastian. Why has the CPS taken the stance it has?'

'Simple, Mel,' Woake said, sipping his tea 'because of policy.'

'What?' Shone asked. Woake and Shone had been friends since university. Woake was six years older than Shone, having joined the University of Exeter at twenty-four after serving a short-term commission in the army.

After university, they had both joined the same law school to read for the Bar and, as members of the Inner Temple, had been called to the Bar at the same call night.

However, their careers had then taken a divergence. Woake had secured his pupillage straight away; his age and life experiences giving him a slight edge over younger applicants.

Being a few years younger, Shone had to spend the next couple of years paralegalling her way through an overdraft before securing a much-coveted pupillage.

Despite sharing the same call year, Woake was much more experienced than Shone, who had always looked to Woake for advice and guidance, which was always freely given.

'What you have to remember Mel,' Woake said, 'is that the CPS is guided just as much by policy as it is by the law, or indeed by the individual case. Now, you and I know that your man is gay, and it therefore is reasonable to suppose he cannot be homophobic, especially given the alleged crime. The problem is Mel, is that the CPS must follow Government guidelines that all reports of a supposed hate crime must go to court, regardless of individual circumstances.'

'Which means we're going to trial?' she asked.

'I'll have a word with the CPS now for you, but why won't your man plead?'

'Says he didn't commit a crime,' Shone answered.

'But why did it make it to the Crown Court? This case could easily have been dealt with in the Magistrates. All he did was shout out the word "poof".'

'Because he chose trial by jury,' Shone answered.

Over ninety per cent of criminal cases were dealt with in the Magistrates Court. Only the most serious cases were sent to the Crown Court, or in the very rare cases, when a defendant opted for the jury system.

'Christ. Really?' Woake asked. 'In which case I recommend you speak to your client and explain the law to him and try to get him to plead. I'll go to the CPS and see if we can drop the case. Hopefully we can get this trial cracked.'

A cracked trial provided the advocate with half a trial fee; half the pay for doing not even a quarter of the work.

Woake finished his tea. Shone was looking at him. 'Do you really drink that without milk?' she asked.

'Old school tradition, Mel,' he answered. Woake could see the questioning look on her face. 'Each House was entitled to a daily ration of milk for us to make tea with. Unfortunately, there was only ever enough for the sixth form. So by the time I was House Captain I already had four years of milk-free tea, and frankly hated the taste of milk.'

'Didn't you have milk at home?'

'I was a boarder.' Woake stood up. 'Right, I'll see if I can sort this mess out for you. Meet you outside the courtroom in half an hour?'

Woake walked towards the CPS room. Every Crown Court has a CPS room, an office for the employed barristers of the CPS and the case officers who oversaw each day's busy caseload.

Woake had to be careful with what he was going to say. As a self-employed barrister who undertook a substantial amount of prosecution work, he could not afford to alienate the organisation with the sole responsibility of providing a sizeable chunk of his income.

However, it was also his duty to see that justice was done, including for the defendant just as much as for the complainant.

As he approached the opened door, Woake could see that the CPS room was a hive of activity. Robed barristers were receiving last-minute instructions from their relevant case officer, other officers were leaving for their respective courtrooms, large bundles of papers under each arm. Three High Court Advocates sat at their desks.

High Court Advocates were an invention of the Blair

Government. They were former CPS lawyers or caseworkers who had undergone a couple of weeks of advocacy training in return for the same rights of audience as barristers who had spent years attaining the same privilege.

HCAs are also employed, a betrayal of the Blair Government's motivation for their introduction. A self-employed professional is impossible to govern; a CPS full of employed advocates could be easily managed and therefore controlled.

Suffice it to say, deep animosity exists between barristers and HCAs.

Woake positioned himself against a wall, waiting for an officer to become available. Patience was a virtue learnt early at the Bar; most of a barrister's time is spent waiting.

A High Court Advocate looked up from his desk; a tall, thin middle-aged man with glasses and mousy brown hair Woake recognised from previous visits to Inner London.

'May I help you?' the HCA asked. Woake walked towards him.

'I hope you can,' he said, hoping he sounded charming. 'I'm prosecuting the case of Daniel Brown and was wondering if I could have some last-minute instructions.'

'What's the fact of the case?' the HCA asked, searching through the prosecution files for the relevant papers.

'The defendant was out for a night with his boyfriend. They had an argument, probably both drunk. They argued, and the defendant called his boyfriend "a bloody poof". Unfortunately, this was outside a gay nightclub in Vauxhall and someone in the queue to the club took offence and reported it to a police officer.'

'Any previous?' the HCA asked.

'Nothing at all. Good job in London, still lives with his boyfriend. In fact, his boyfriend is listed as a prosecution witness, so there's a possibility he could turn hostile.'

'It wasn't the boyfriend who took offence?'

'Nope.'

'Are the defendant and the boyfriend still together?'

'I believe so.'

'Then you're going to have to get him to give evidence that the defendant committed the act and then treat him as hostile as and when it happens. Any other problems with that?' the HCA asked, returning to his computer.

'Don't have a problem with it, per se,' Woake said, trying not to sound as exasperated as he felt. 'I was just wondering that in the circumstances if we would like to reconsider this?'

'But why?' the HCA asked.

'Because the defendant is gay, his intended recipient of his outburst took no offence and is it really in the public interest to prosecute?'

'I'm afraid that the defendant's sexuality has nothing to do with it. As I'm sure you know, a hate crime such as this has nothing to do with what the intended victim felt, just enough if there was somebody nearby who could have taken offence. We must always prosecute so called hate crimes. He should have been more careful,' the HCA said, still looking at his computer.

'I fully appreciate what the law is,' Woake said. 'So you would still like me to prosecute?'

'Yes,' the HCA responded without bothering to look up.

Woake left the CPS room without bothering to respond.

There was one more duty to undertake before going to the courtroom. Woake reported to Witness Services to ask if his two witnesses had appeared; the boyfriend and the complainant.

'Oh yes, Mr Woake,' the earnest volunteer who worked for Witness Services said. 'They're both here. Would you like to speak to them?' she asked.

'Not desperately,' Woake answered. Noticing confusion on the woman's face, Woake softened his statement with a smile. 'Of course, may I see the complainant first, please?' The volunteer led Woake through the security door which cordoned off the large room set aside for the court's witnesses.

Worried women sat with children, men sat with wives and gowned barristers sat next to witnesses appearing to be more sincere than they otherwise felt.

Woake was led to a thin man under 6ft tall, wearing beige trousers, a green t-shirt and a brown corduroy cardigan. Three days' worth of stubble hid deep acne scars. 'Mr Willets,' the volunteer said, taking a seat next to Willets. She subtly leant her head as she sat next to Willets, crossing her legs towards him, looking like she was evaluating every word Woake was going to say.

'Hello, Mr Willets,' Woake said, remaining standing. He did not offer to shake the man's hand. 'I'm Seb Woake, and I'm prosecuting in your case. Now there's not much to worry about.'

'That's easy for you to say. You weren't the one assaulted,' Willets said. Woake decided against arguing over the finer points of English law.

'No, I should imagine that it was a very disturbing incident to have been involved in. Have you got your witness statement?' Willets waved a piece of paper. 'Excellent, I would study that if I were you. There is a chance that the defendant will plead, so you won't have to give evidence,' Willets looked disappointed, 'but that's just a chance. What you're about to go through is a deeply distressing thing for most people. In fact, you would have to be drunk or mad in order to enjoy it. I'm going to call you, ask you some questions and the other side will ask you some questions too. Afterwards, you'll be able to watch the rest of the proceedings. Should only take a few hours for the entire event. OK, Mr Willets? Excellent, see you in court,' Woake said, not allowing Willets enough time to answer.

'There's another witness for you to meet,' the woman said. 'A Justin Clark,' she added, leading Woake towards another man; a large, round individual wearing a suit.

'Hello, Mr Clark,' Woake said. 'I understand that you're the defendant's partner.'

'Yes, that is correct,' the well-spoken Clark said.

'Probably better that we don't speak,' Woake said. He turned towards the woman. 'Thank you very much for your time.'

Woake walked towards Court 4. Shone was sitting in one of the chairs outside the courtroom. A suited young man in his twenties was hovering nervously nearby. The defendant, Woake assumed. Shone stood up as Woake approached.

'Any joy?' she asked.

'Afraid not, you?' Woake placed his court papers on the chair next to Shone as he put his wig and gown on.

'My client will not plead.'

'So it's a trial then,' Woake responded. He used the reflective plastic covering the courtroom noticeboard as a mirror to check his wig was on straight. 'Your man?' he asked, pointing with his head.

'Yes,' Shone answered.

'Excellent. The witnesses are all here, so why don't we go in and see if we can get this over with?'

Woake held the door open as Shone led her client through to Court 4.

The jury was chosen. As defence counsel, Shone sat nearest to the jury. Woake noticed she was making a note of each juror's name. If the case was more important, Woake would have followed suit. As it was, Woake was struggling to sustain any interest in the case.

'Yes, Mr Woake,' His Honour Judge Williams called down from the bench.

'Thank you, Your Honour,' Woake replied, rising from the benches. He addressed the jury. 'Members of the jury, I represent the prosecution. My learned friend Miss Shone represents the defendant. This will be one of the simplest cases you will have to deal with during your two weeks as jurors and it involves a homophobic hate crime.

'As prosecutor, I will put it to you that the defendant shouted "bloody poof" outside a busy gay nightclub at midnight in order to cause offence. My learned friend will put it to you that this was a statement taken out of context. Your Honour, may we please call the first witness?'

Woake remained standing as the first witness was called in, the complainant who had reported Daniel Brown to the police.

Under Woake's questioning, Shane Willets explained how he had been queuing outside a Vauxhall nightclub when he had heard the defendant shout "bloody poof". Willets had explained how upsetting he found this, especially as the comment was directed straight at him.

'The man sitting in the dock was looking straight at me as he shouted "bloody poof". He was so angry his whole body was shaking. I felt very vulnerable and was relieved to see a group of police officers nearby.'

Shone stood up to begin her cross-examination.

'I understand, Mr Willets, that a velvet rope segregated the queue off from the pavement,' she said.

'Yes, that's correct.'

'And the defendant approached you from behind, didn't he?'

'Steady now Mel,' Woake said so quietly that only Shone could hear him.

'Yes, I think that's correct.'

'And you were facing away from him?'

'I think that's how they usually do it,' Woake said.

'Yes,' Willets answered.

'So, just so I'm sure in my mind, he was walking up to you from behind where you were standing?'

'Yes.'

'You, therefore, did not know that he was approaching you until he was up against you?'

'Please Mel, your man's not here for rape.'

'No, that's not quite true, there was a lot of shouting between two men.'

'Was there? Like an argument?'

'Yes, two men seemed furious with each other.'

'So your attention was drawn to the defendant solely because of the argument, not, as you earlier said, because the defendant was shouting directly at you?'

Willets looked sheepishly at the judge. 'Yes, that's correct,' he said.

'Therefore, it would be perfectly reasonable to assume that the statement "you bloody poof" was said as part of the argument?'

'But how was I to know that?' Willets retorted. 'I am a gay man, outside a gay nightclub, and someone shouted a homophobic comment straight towards me.'

'You do know, Mr Willets, that the defendant is gay?' she asked.

'Is he?'

'Yes he is, and he was having an argument with his boyfriend.'

'I didn't know that.'

'Yes, and that he was calling his boyfriend "a poof".'

'Well, he still shouldn't have done.'

Shone's cross-examination continued. She could not move him from his entrenched position that the behaviour deeply insulted him. Eventually, she sat down.

Woake called his second witness, the defendant's boyfriend

Justin Clark.

Clark explained how he and Brown had been out for dinner and then drinks with friends when they had argued over a comment which Clark had made about the date when they were planning on moving in together. A silly argument aggravated by alcohol.

'So he called you a "bloody poof"?' Woake asked.

'Yes, Dan did.'

'That must have been deeply upsetting?' Woake asked, hoping that he sounded more sincere than he felt.

'Not really,' Clark answered.

'I'm sorry?'

'It wasn't that upsetting.'

'Well I would have thought it would be,' Woake said.

'Are you gay?' Clark asked.

'No, I'm not actually. But that isn't important.'

'It is actually, because how would you know if I was supposed to take offence to it?'

Woake was now in a very difficult position. The witness had, unsurprisingly, turned hostile. This was always going to be the risk with this case. If he continued with the questioning, then he could undermine his case. If he sat down, then he could appear to have made little effort in the trial.

Clark was making the decision for Woake.

'The thing is,' Clark continued, 'you wouldn't know this because you're not gay, but members of the gay community call each other "poof" all the time.'

'Really?' Woake asked.

'Yes, we always call each other names you would think are homophobic. "Poof, queen, queer, fairy," it's all fair game. And if it's a gay man saying it, what's the issue? Plenty of black men use racist language, and they're never done for racism. So how can my boyfriend be accused of being anti-gay?'

'Thank you, Your Honour, no further questions.'

Shone stood up.

'I just have one question for you, Mr Clark. Are you absolutely sure that it was you who the defendant called a "bloody poof"?'

'Absolutely, no doubt about it.'

Shone stood down.

Woake called the arresting officer to explain the arrest and the subsequent police interview with Brown and then concluded the prosecution's case. Shone stood up.

'Your Honour, before I open the defence case, I would like to make an application.'

The jury was ushered out of court. Shone applied for no case to answer, hoping that the judge would throw the trial out at the halfway mark. Her application was based upon the prosecution's evidence as offered by Clark and the defendant's sexuality.

She spoke well, confidently and fluidly, blaming the CPS for an unhealthy addiction to policy and a failure to grasp the subtleties of the twenty-first century.

Judge Williams looked down sympathetically at her as he called for Woake's response.

'Thank you, Your Honour,' Woake said, 'and I congratulate my learned friend for her passionate application on behalf of her client. I must say that I have some sympathy and I am sure that I would have made such an application if I had been in a similar position.

'But we are unfortunately where we are with this. The law doesn't take into account the defendant's own circumstances, nor the feelings of the intended recipient but only that there was somebody close by who could be insulted. And unfortunately for the defendant, Mr Willets was quite certain about how he felt.

'On that basis, Your Honour, and notwithstanding the defendant's own sexuality, there is a case to answer.'

'Mr Woake, I am extremely disappointed. Anybody with only a simple grasp of English law would know that prosecuting a homosexual for homophobia is not in the public interest.'

'There is very little, Your Honour, that I can say to that. I enquired if the prosecution wished to proceed, but unfortunately policy dictates that we must prosecute a hate crime.'

'I by no means hold you responsible, Mr Woake, as I know that you would have come to this case very late. I am just incredibly frustrated that policy dictates common sense in such a way.'

'There is nothing I can add to that, Your Honour, save to say that Shakespeare was wrong. In this case it is not the law but Government policy which is the farm animal.'

Shone's application duly failed.

The defendant gave evidence; explaining that it was a drunken stupid mistake, that he was not homophobic and that he was incredibly sorry for any offence caused. Woake's cross-examination centred on the remark itself, that regardless of the intended recipient of the comment, that the term "poof" could only be construed as being homophobic.

Under the stress and pressure of the occasion, the defendant reluctantly agreed.

His evidence complete, the defendant was led back to the dock.

That concluded the defence case.

Judge Williams looked down upon Woake and Shone. 'Yes Mr Woake,' he said 'would you like to make your closing speech?'

Woake rose. 'Thank you, Your Honour.' He turned to the jury, one hand in a trouser pocket, striving for as much pomposity as this particular trial warranted. He spoke without notes.

'Members of the jury, you should be honoured, for today you have been allowed to take part in a truly momentous day in the history of English jurisprudence. What we at the Bar would call a precedent.

'For today, you are tasked with deciding whether a homosexual man can be homophobic. You have heard the evidence of three witnesses, including the defendant, as well as that of a police officer. It is not in doubt that the defendant uttered the words "you bloody poof" nor can it be doubted the distress this caused Mr Willets.

'The complainant has bravely given evidence before you all, strong and compelling evidence we should accept at face value.

'The issue before you now is to consider the meaning of the word "poof", a derogatory term used throughout the last 100 years to describe members of the gay community. And the use of the word "bloody" only aggravates the offence further.

'I am confident that His Honour will explain to you the full intricacies of the relevant law, but,' Woake raising his voice whilst increasing the clarity of his speech 'remember this when you will shortly deliberate on your verdict. The law is not concerned with the defendant's circumstances. Nor is it concerned with the opinions of the intended recipient. It does not care if the defendant is homosexual and neither should you.

'The *only* thing,' Woake rose the forefinger of his right hand for emphasis 'you need be concerned with is this. Is the term "bloody poof" homophobic and was there someone nearby who could take offence?' Woake lowered his voice.

'I am sure that we all have sympathy for the defendant. But in this case members of the jury, you have no choice *but* to find this defendant guilty.' Woake sat down.

Shone rose to present her closing speech, which mirrored her comments in the defence's midpoint application.

Judge Williams summed up the basic legal points and summarised the trial for the jury, who were then led out of the courtroom by the usher to deliberate. Judge Williams then addressed Woake, who rose.

'Mr Woake, it is now one o'clock. I propose that the jury be released for lunch and that they be asked to reappear at two. I don't propose that you or Miss Shone be here at two to check if the jury has returned. I'd be happy to do that myself if you are willing to agree.'

'Thank you, Your Honour. I have no issue with that and I don't suppose my learned friend does either.' Shone rose from her feet.

'None, Your Honour,' she said.

'Excellent, then I look forward to seeing you both here, hopefully as soon as possible after lunch.'

Woake followed Shone and Brown out of the courtroom. Shone led her client into an interview room for a debrief. Woake walked to the advocates' canteen and bought himself lunch. He removed his gown, wig and bands as he wrote his case notes; a brief paragraph summarising the trial. The only thing missing from the notes was the verdict and sentence, if any.

It would allow the relevant case officer to enter the result into the CPS system when he returned the file post-trial; and by doing it now, he wouldn't have to worry about doing it post-trial.

His phone buzzed as he finished writing. It was a text message from Craig Overton.

Are you still coming to the meeting at the crem tonight? it read. Woake responded with a simple *Yes.* Thirty seconds later, his phone buzzed again.

Excellent Sebastian, we all look forward to seeing you at seven. It really is important to get this project going ASAP.

Woake smiled. A meeting had been organised at Gretford Crematorium within days of Woake temporarily cancelling every major project. He had a meeting later on in the week with Cathy Fulcher-Wells to discuss the proposed selling of Edgeborough Farm, located just outside Gretford.

It was a meeting he was not looking forward to. He asked to have a briefing from Charlotte Bateup to discuss the sale prior to the meeting. Bateup's answers were not encouraging when asked what they were. 'It's a farm and it's in Edgeborough.'

Woake finished his lunch, bought another tea and walked back towards the robing room.

He did not bother to respond to Overton.

Shone was eating her packed lunch with the three young barristers she had been speaking to that morning. She was facing the door and waved at Woake as he walked into the robing room.

He placed his court dress and case papers in his sports bag, removed his briefing notes on the proposed crematorium development, and sat down to read the document.

He ignored the small talk in the robing room.

As two o'clock approached, cases began to be called on and the robing room quietened down as the barristers returned to court.

By two thirty, Woake and Shone were on their own save for two other barristers who had returned from court; their jury was also out considering its verdict.

Shone approached Woake and sat down next to him.

'How do you think it went?' she asked.

'I'm afraid that your man is buggered, Mel, which could be, depending upon your viewpoint, somewhat unfortunate or deeply lucky.'

'Thanks,' Shone responded.

'Thing is, I have an enormous amount of sympathy for him.'

'Oh, you do?' Shone asked.

'Of course, Brown is one of those unfortunate but rising class of person. An otherwise law-abiding individual who our politically correct world is turning into a criminal for nothing more than a stupid mistake. Take these chaps,' Woake said, turning to the other two barristers. 'What are you chaps here for?'

'Trial for armed robbery,' one of them said, pulling up a chair next to Woake and Shone. 'Jury's gone out.'

'And is he guilty?'

'Of course he is,' was the response.

'And he's for the defence,' the other barrister said.

'Which is my point exactly,' Woake said. 'We all know that well over ninety per cent of those who go through the criminal system are guilty of something, it's our job to determine exactly what. We've got a trial where a homosexual is accused of being homophobic just because the CPS is obsessed with hate crime.'

'It's the same with domestic abuse,' the barrister who sat down said. 'I was in Richmond Magistrates Court last week prosecuting in the trial of a man accused of abusing his wife. On the face of it, he was guilty. But the incident took place during a very heated and drunken argument where the wife gave as good as she got.'

'What happened?' Woake asked.

'The wife broke down in tears and begged me to stop prosecuting her husband. Said I was breaking up the family as her husband, who was on bail, was banned from residing in the family home as part of his bail condition as per the law.

'The trial had to be adjourned whilst I took further instructions from the CPS as she refused to give evidence. They insisted that I continue and treat her as a hostile witness. All because their policy dictates that an alleged incident of domestic abuse has to be prosecuted, regardless of the wishes of the complainant.'

'And we all know what the results of that will be,' Woake said.

'What's that?' Shone asked.

'That particular victim will go home and explain her traumatic experiences to her friends and family, who will tell their friends. The court experience will be misunderstood as the story is told again and again by others who had no part in it until it reaches another victim of domestic abuse who will hear that the courts and justice are not on her side, and the victim will be even more unwilling to go to the police.'

'And that's what happened with you guys just now?' the barrister who remained standing asked.

'Yes,' Woake answered. 'He shouted "bloody poof" to his boyfriend outside a gay nightclub late at night and some idiot took offence. Now he's more than likely going to be a criminal for the rest of his life for nothing more than an idiotic mistake.'

'But it is a hate crime, Sebastian,' Shone said.

'Exactly, a hate crime, one of the most ridiculous expressions of this century. Every crime is hate, that's the very definition of it. I was listening to the radio on the drive in this morning. A campaigner from Stonewall was being interviewed.

'Apparently someone was stabbed in Liverpool overnight and the attacker apparently shouted something homophobic to the victim.' Woake could see the look on Shone's face as he explained his point. 'Now, I fully appreciate that a stabbing is one of the most appalling acts and I am not disputing that.

'But this chap from Stonewall then said that the homophobic comment propelled this act into a hate crime. Since when has stabbing someone ever been anything but a hate crime? I appreciate that in France you have crimes of passion, but how many times have you heard of someone saying to their victim "I really love you, so I'm going to stab you"?'

'Unless you're gay,' the other prosecutor said.

The court tannoy system called all parties in the case of Brown back to Court 4.

'Excellent Mel,' Woake said, raising from his chair. He began to put on his court dress. 'I think that must be a verdict.'

'Guilty,' the foreman of the jury returned the verdict.

A cry of anguish came from the dock. Justin Clark broke down in tears in the public gallery.

Judge Williams addressed the courtroom. 'I shall now move to sentencing,' he said, ignoring Clark.

Woake rose. 'Your Honour, there is nothing further for me to say. The facts in the case are as you have heard them in the trial and I can confirm that the defendant is of good character. If I cannot assist you any further?' Woake asked. Judge Williams motioned for him to sit down. Woake sat as Shone rose.

Shone presented her mitigation, an attempt to lower the sentencing as much as she could by emphasising his previous good character, his good career and the limited severity of the incident.

The judge asked to see evidence of the defendant's financial history. Daniel Brown received a £500 fine and a 100 hours' community order.

The jury was discharged.

Judge Williams addressed Woake and Shone, who rose in anticipation. 'A sorry business,' the judge said.

'Indeed it is, Your Honour,' Woake responded.

Judge Williams rose from the bench and bowed to the court. Woake and Shone bowed in return as the judge left.

Woake approached Shone as she was collecting her case papers. 'You did well on an awful case,' he said.

He held the door open as Shone led her client and his boyfriend out of the courtroom.

'I am very sorry for that, Mr Brown. Just put this behind you as much as you can and try to move on as quickly as possible.'

'Thanks,' was all a dejected Brown could say.

Shone held the door open into an interview room as Brown and Clark filed in. She smiled to Woake as she followed them in.

Woake dropped the purple cardboard file containing the case papers off in the CPS room. Only one case officer sat at her desk. The rest were in court.

'These are the papers in the case of Brown,' Woake said to the black officer.

'Thank you,' she said as she took the file from him. 'The homophobic case. How did it go?'

'Guilty.'

'Oh, that's excellent. Well done,' she said.

'Thanks,' was all Woake could say as he left the room.

'An early bath, Mel,' Woake said as he de-robed.

'Indeed, and without you, Sebastian,' Shone said.

'Back to Chambers?'

'Yep, and you?' Shone asked.

'Home,' Woake said, as he picked up his bag. He followed Shone out of the robing room and out of the court building. 'Got to get back to Gretford ASAP, I have a meeting this evening at the local crematorium.'

'Really? That's a bit premature now isn't it?'

'Believe it or not, but I'm a politician now.'

'Christ, really?'

'Yes, really.' They reached the foyer of the court building. 'Fancy a lift back to Chambers? I've parked just around the corner.'

She went to hug him. 'No thanks, Woake, I'll get public transport.'

'Peasant.'

Sixteen

Woake drove onto the main drive of Gretford Crematorium shortly after five o'clock that Tuesday evening. He had arrived home an hour earlier and had showered and changed. Thinking it would only take ten minutes to drive the two miles from his house to the crematorium, he failed to consider the impact of the Gretford gyratory system.

Woake parked his Discovery in the half-empty car park and made his way to the entrance of the main building on the complex, the chapel.

Built in the 1950s, Gretford Crematorium was a grey-stone monolith, with dull-brown window panes and an indoor decoration scheme based around varying shades of beige and cream.

A cemetery bordered the main buildings on two sides, while a car park and an extensive field bordered the other two sides.

Faded roses in dire need of dead-heading sat in the central roundabout outside the chapel's front doors, providing the space for each funeral procession to swing round at the start of each service.

The chimney of the crematorium's cremator stood proudly behind the chapel, a thin wisp of smoke escaping through the slits at the top of the thin tall tower.

The overcast sky provided the perfect backdrop as Woake approached the team from GDC. Despite being in the centre of Gretford, a peaceful serenity rested on the 25-acre complex.

Woake shook hands with the officers and councillors. The officers were represented by Bane (with his ever-present smile), Charlotte Bateup and the effete Philip de Lusignon, the surprisingly heterosexual director in charge of sustainable projects, and therefore the proposed redevelopment.

Four junior officers who Woake did not recognise accompanied the directors. Two were from the Finance team, the others from Sustainable Projects.

Foster, Fulcher-Wells, Swaden and Overton represented the councillors. Out of all those present, Overton provided the limpest handshake.

'Apologies for being late,' Woake told the group 'bloody one-way system was blocked.' Woake turned to Bane. 'You know, Giles, it really is time that you lot sorted that mess out.'

'Thank you, Sebastian,' Overton interrupted 'that is a separate project that will come up in next week's Group away day. Now we're all here, shall we start?' He held his thin arm out to the group, pointing towards the field opposite the chapel. Overton waited for the group to walk past as he shepherded them forward.

'Think you've pulled off the undertaker look there, Craig,' Woake said as he passed by.

Woake and Bane were towards the back of the group.

'Been in court today?' Bane asked.

'Yes, I have Giles,' Woake answered. 'Been dealing with a trial centred around homophobic crime.' Woake could see the interest grow on Bane's face. 'The defendant went rampaging round a queue outside a gay nightclub in London shouting "you bloody poofs".'

'Was he guilty?' Bane asked. Woake remained poker-faced at Bane's innocence. As a layman, he naturally presumed that people could be innocent.

'Certainly was,' Woake answered. 'Which is all the more amazing as he himself was gay.'

The group stopped at the front field to be met by a petite, well-tanned (betraying her Italian ancestry) 5ft 2" tall woman dressed in a black skirt suit, black tights and white shirt.

'Apparently, it happened outside the Pink Elephant nightclub in Vauxhall. Do you know that one Craig?' Woake asked.

'Oh no,' Overton stumbled, embarrassment blushing across his thin face. 'I don't think so. I mean, how would I know of it?' he said, regaining his composure. Embarrassment swept across the group; it was the worst-kept secret at the Council that Overton was gay.

'May I introduce Angelina Burbridge, who is the manager here,' Bane said, introducing the small woman to the group.

'Angelina, would you like to start?' Bane asked after everyone had introduced themselves to Burbridge. As her name and tan suggested, her father had been an Italian visitor to Gretford during the War.

'Thank you, Giles, and thank you to all for coming here this evening. This tour will show how we operate and, I hope, demonstrate why it is of the utmost importance that Gretford has a modern crematorium in the near future.

'Before we go in, I would just like to point out that this is where the new crem will be built.'

'Right here?' Foster asked.

'Yes, Councillor. This area is used as an overflow car park during the larger funeral services. Our plan is to build the new crem here, whilst still using the old one. When the new one is built, we'll demolish the old one and turn it into the car park.'

'And is that to ensure we maintain our income from the existing crem?' Fulcher-Wells asked. As a trained economist, she was vexed that she had been overlooked for the Finance portfolio and wasted little opportunity to demonstrate her financial acumen to Foster.

'Yes, that is correct,' Burbridge responded. 'The current crematorium is a massive moneymaker for the Council as it currently provides an annual income to the Council of £5 million. The running costs of the crem are currently circa £1.5 million, which is a very healthy profit.

'Our main issue is capacity. As I'll show you in a bit, we're currently only running at eighty per cent capacity, so precious income is bypassing us. The new crem will allow us to tap into this income.'

'Well done Charlotte,' Woake said. Bateup looked at him questioningly. 'Well done for providing a first-class set of instructions for Ms Burbridge.'

'Why here?' Swaden asked.

'Because of regulations. We're unable to build a crematorium within two hundred yards of residential dwellings and we're not allowed to build over and disturb existing cemeteries. Unless we knock the old crem down, we have no choice but to build here.'

'Which we can't do because of the business case,' Bateup put in.

'Indeed. The new crem will take about a year to build, so we'll be out of action for most of that time. Not only will this impact our finances for that year, we'll also run the risk that repeat business will disappear.'

'Repeat business?' Woake asked. 'This is a crematorium. How many times does someone need to be burned?'

'I think what Angelina means, Sebastian,' Overton answered for Burbridge, 'is repeat business from local funeral directors.'

'Really, Craig?'

'Yes, Sebastian. There is a serious concern that funeral directors will go to our competitors. Leatherhead, Woking, Guildford and Horsham all have their own crematoriums.'

'Craig,' Woake responded, 'those crematoria that you have mentioned range in distance from ten miles to thirty miles from Gretford. Who the Hell is going to have the funeral service of loved ones thirty miles away from where they lived? Also, what undertaker is going to recommend that to a customer once this thing has been built. They'll be so relieved that they wouldn't have to travel that distance they'll be recommending us to everyone.'

The tour progressed into the chapel. Burbridge continued with her commentary. 'The crematorium was built in the 1950s, and as you can see, it's really showing its age.' Woake looked up. The filthy beige wallpaper was peeling off in the corners of the walls. Cobwebs hung from the rafters in the roof.

The skylight windows were now so encrusted by dirt that it was impossible for light to shine through, despite the overcast clouds outside.

'Despite owning the building, the Council has failed to invest any substantial money on the public face of the building since then. The only thing that they did invest in was the new sound system.' As Woake looked up, he noticed a Bose speaker jutting out of the wall; the only modern addition to the ageing 1950s backdrop.

'It's important to remember that this just isn't about the finance,' Burbridge said. 'Just as important is the emotional side to this project. The current building just isn't fit for purpose. It was built at a time of different views and attitudes, as well as different faiths. This chapel is a Christian chapel.'

'Well, we are a Christian country, Angelina,' Woake said.

'Yes, but we're also a country of many faiths. And the overtly Christian nature of this chapel is off-putting for non-Christians. Humanists, for example, and Muslims.'

'I thought they all lived in Woking,' Swaden said.

'What we need,' Burbridge continued, 'is a non-faith specific chapel, open to all, of every and no faith.'

'Tell us more about the dignity aspect?' Overton asked.

'We currently have one entry point and one exit, as well as only one point for the funeral processions to park. Unfortunately, that means we often have overcrowding outside as the services overrun. Sometimes, we have a queue of funeral parties back out of the main gate. To compound the issue, as there are no suitable waiting rooms, the funeral parties can intermingle amongst themselves.

'Those who arrive early often join the wrong service, whilst the bereaved relatives of the previous service have to walk past relatives for the next.'

'What do you mean by only working to eighty per cent capacity?' Woake asked.

'If it's ok Councillor, I'll answer that in a minute.'

Burbridge led them past the dais in the chapel where the deceased's coffin is laid to rest during the service. A door was located opposite the gurney.

'Have you ever wondered what happens when the curtains are pulled during the farewell?' Burbridge asked.

'Not desperately,' Swaden answered.

'As each service concludes, Robbie walks through the door here with a gurney and collects the coffin. He then pushes the coffin through to the room on the opposite side of the door.'

'Who's Robbie?' Bane asked.

'Robbie Cole,' Burbridge answered. 'He's our operations manager. He's in charge of what happens in this room.'

'How many people does he manage?' Woake asked.

'Only one. Himself.'

Burbridge led the group through the door and into the back end of the crematorium.

The room was divided into three sections.

The first section measured five metres by three, a cramped space comprising two rows of plastic chairs facing through a viewing window and into the second section. 'I should ask if anyone here is of a squeamish disposition?' Burbridge said. Everyone present shook their heads.

'This is our viewing area,' Burbridge said.

'Viewing area?' the high-pitched squeal from Fulcher-Wells asked.

'It's important for several faiths to see their deceased relative embark upon their last journey. This viewing room allows the relative to watch in quiet dignity.'

'Quiet dignity?' Swaden asked. 'Looks like the execution chamber from the Deep South.'

Through the viewing window, the group could see the cremator in all its glory.

Two shiny round metal doors were hung on one wall, and each door had its own control panel to the right of it. The cremator, as well as the viewing room, was painted in its entirety in shiny white paint. The immaculate floors were just as white.

Three gurneys were lined up outside the two doors. Each carried a coffin.

The group walked through to the cremator.

'And this is where the operations side of the crematorium is carried out,' Burbridge said.

'You mean this is where the coffins are burned,' Woake said, staring at the two doors.

'Yes. Behind each door is an oven. As soon as the oven has reached optimal temperature, the coffin is placed in the oven.'

'How long does it take for the coffin to burn?' Woake asked in morbid fascination.

'Depends on the size of the coffin, but usually a couple of hours.'

'You mean the fatter you are, the longer it takes to burn,' Woake said.

'Surely these can't be coffins left over from today?' Swaden asked, bent over one coffin, reading the nameplate.

'Unfortunately, we cannot process every coffin because of capacity and efficiency.'

'You mean to say that you leave a coffin here unattended overnight?' Swaden asked.

'Unfortunately, we have nowhere else to store them,' Burbridge answered. 'There was a lack of appreciation when the crematorium was built at just how popular the service we provide would become.'

'I understand that we have, by law, seventy-two hours in order to burn each coffin,' Woake said, sensing that the besieged Burbridge could do with some assistance.

'We, unfortunately, don't have a choice,' Burbridge said. 'This is exactly what I mean by failing to work at full capacity. Except for the Bose sound system, this equipment is the only thing that the Council has spent money on. But it is also fifteen years old and approaching the end of its life. It is so inefficient for us to process a coffin, and therefore time-consuming that we're limited to how many coffins we can burn each day.'

'Inefficient?' Foster asked.

'Environmentally, this cremator is one of the biggest pollutants in the district.'

'Jesus,' Woake said under his breath.

'I think this place is trying to get rid of that chap,' Swaden said.

'What are you limited to?' Overton asked.

'We need to conduct up to eight services a day to maintain our level of income,' Burbridge answered, looking at Bateup. 'Unfortunately, we can only process six coffins a day maximum.'

'So some coffins can take up to two days to be burned?' Woake asked. The question went unanswered.

'What happens if you have relatives who want to watch?' Swaden asked.

'Thankfully, that hasn't been a contingency we have had to deal with recently. Most Gretford residents are either Christian or atheist.'

'How would a new crem deal with this?' Overton asked.

'Easily, we'll have a brand-new layout, new equipment, new everything. That will enable us to cut down the waiting list, process more services and thereby increase the income generated.'

'Waiting list?' Bane asked.

'How long it takes to book a service.'

'Which is how long?' Bateup asked.

'About three weeks, unless we get a cancellation.'

'A cancellation?' Woake asked.

'Yes, sometimes we get cancellations.'

'Who the Hell cancels a funeral service?' Woake asked. 'You can imagine the phone call, can't you? "Bit embarrassing, but it turns out that my beloved relative isn't actually dead. Bit of a shock for the undertaker when he heard screaming from the coffin. In fact, if the slot is still available, you may need it for the undertaker, who dropped dead out of fright.'"

'You'd be surprised,' Burbridge added, sighing.

'Bet the undertakers were too.'

Burbridge led the group through to the third section of the room. They walked past the two long ovens and into a cramped five-by-three-metre windowless room. A large square object took up a third of the room. A second third was taken up by shelves full of empty urns. The final third provided space for the operator.

Angelina Burbridge entered the room and deliberately stood in front of a bucket which had been placed on top of a large, oven-like object.

'I do apologise. This is a bit cramped,' she said to the group, which was lined up along the side of the ovens. Only Woake and Swaden had made it into the room. They stood opposite Burbridge.

'This is where the remains of the deceased are processed. Once the coffin has been sufficiently burned, the oven is cooled down. Once the oven is sufficiently cool, Robbie then removes the remains and places them in this compactor,' she pointed to the object behind her 'where the remains are then powered down into ash.

'Between the oven and the compactor, the remains are examined to ensure that no metallic objects go in the compactor.'

'Such as?' Swaden asked.

'Knee replacements, hip replacements. That sort of thing. A compactor has to be used because there are always parts to a human's remains which won't have sufficiently burned down into ashes. Bones and teeth are good examples.'

She motioned for the group to leave. 'Perhaps we should now go outside?'

Swaden stopped her.

'What's that in the bucket?' he asked. Burbridge remained rooted to the spot.

'Nothing,' she said.

'No, there is definitely something in it,' Swaden said. Being a tall man, he could peer over Burbridge's shoulder.

Woake also took a look.

'Bloody hell, Reg, I'll let you deal with this.'

Woake followed the rest of the group back into the chapel. He left Swaden berating the poor Burbridge.

'What was all that about?' Overton asked.

'Nothing Craig, don't worry about it.'

As Woake had looked over Burbridge's shoulder and into the bucket, he saw a femur bone and the top half of a human skull staring back at him. A couple of minutes later, a pale Burbridge and a puce Swaden joined the rest of the group.

'Let's go outside,' she said. She led the group through the exit in the chapel and began to regain her composure. The group reached a set of cloisters. Flowers from that day's services still littered each memorial. 'At the end of each service, the mourners are led out to here to review the flower display. I think we should visit the Room of Remembrance.'

She took the group to a small octagonal building with a pitched roof. Four of the walls were French windows. As with the skylights in the chapel, dirt encrusted the French windows.

Inside the building was an octagonal wooden cabinet, a book of remembrance taking pride of place. Shelves were attached to the four walls.

The building was completely dominated by flowers in various stages of life. Brand-new cut flowers with their bright vibrant colours lay next to older flowers whose colours were beginning to wain next to plants displaying the far extremes of floral rigor mortis, requiring an oven of their own.

'One of the most obvious differences between a cremation and a burial can be a lack of permanent memorial for those cremated,' Burbridge said. 'This building of remembrance provides the bereaved with exactly that, a place to remember.'

'What do you do with the flowers?' Bane asked.

'Unlike the funeral flowers, we always keep the plants here that have been placed here until they have died back. Once a fortnight, we purge them.'

'What do you do to the funeral flowers?' Woake asked.

'We always used to donate them to the local hospital. We stopped doing that when flowers were banned by the NHS.'

'Really?'

'Yes, a lot of crems did that.'

'Bet that must have been a jolly conversation,' Woake said. '"Poor old Mrs Jones is laying in her hospital bed and asks the doctors her chances. The doctor says 'very good Mrs Jones and just to cheer you up, we brought you these' and he then hands her a bouquet of flowers reading 'In Memoriam'".'

'I think I'll take you into the office before touring the cemetery. We work until about six thirty every evening, and the six of us in the office handle everything, from booking services to building and grounds maintenance, to fulfilling our legal obligations regarding body transportation and disposal of remains.'

The group entered the admin office. Five workers were sitting at their desks. Angelina Burbridge introduced them to the group.

'This is also where members of the public can come and collect their relatives' ashes,' she said.

'What's the procedure for that?' Fulcher-Wells asked.

'Very simple, all you need is to arrive with a form of identity.'

'A form of identity?' Foster asked.

'Yes, we have to ensure by law that the ashes of the deceased are returned to the rightful family rather than those who steal the ashes.'

'Who steals ashes?' Foster asked.

'Usually family members who are in dispute with each other. If we're not careful, we could grant the ashes to family members who would then hold the urn as emotional blackmail against other family members.'

'That's very good to know,' Woake said to the group. 'If we inadvertently gave the ashes away to arguing family members, they could sue us.'

'Exactly,' said Burbridge, 'we need to ensure that due diligence is always done.'

'You'd have thought that conflicting relatives could open the urn and take a handful of ashes each,' Swaden said.

The tour concluded with a visit to the cemetery. The two junior officers from the Council's Sustainable Projects team had by then produced detailed plans of the proposed redevelopment of the crematorium.

Woake and Swaden held back from the others. 'Did you see what was in the fucking bucket?' Swaden asked.

'What, the skull and crossbones?'

'It's fucking serious Sebastian, that was someone's remains in that bucket. I tell you Seb, it's fucking typical of the public sector. "Five o'clock, I'm off home. Bollocks to the fact that I've got to deal with some poor bugger's ashes in a dignified manner, I'm not paid past five, so I'm off!'"

They followed the others back to the front of the chapel. Angelina Burbridge was summarising the key points of the tour. 'I would like to thank you for all coming here today. I think you would agree that we need a brand-new crem, one that will be centred around fulfilling capacity, a sound business case, open to every faith and flows better than this one in order to provide the deceased and the family greater dignity than this one does. I am sure that we can deliver a truly special environment here.'

'A crème de la crème, eh Angelina?' Overton quipped. Woake ignored Overton's pitiful attempt at a pre-prepared joke.

'You still haven't explained how we can afford a new one?' he asked. Foster leapt to Burbridge's defence.

'I think we can discuss this in the next couple of days,' he said. 'I'm sure that you and Charlotte can discuss it during your meeting tomorrow and we'll discuss it at the next ManCab,' he added with a smirk.

The tour concluded and the individual members made their way back to their cars. Bateup approached Woake.

'Are you still OK, Sebastian, for our meeting tomorrow?' she asked.

'Yes Charlotte. I'm working from home tomorrow so I'm still available.'

'Excellent, I'll see you at two then,' she said as she walked towards her car.

Seventeen

Woake woke up at six thirty the following morning. His three and a half years spent in the army ensured he would always be an early riser. He undertook two hundred sit-ups and one hundred press-ups before showering. As well as his running and rowing, these daily exercises meant that he never had to join a gym.

He showered and dressed, but did not shave. Woake only ever shaved in the evening after work; he found that perspiration from exercise irritated his skin. As he was working from home that day, he would make sure that he would go for a run that evening.

Summer had finally hit England on a hot mid-May day, so Woake dressed in grey-blue shorts, moccasins and a pink polo shirt and made his way downstairs.

Woake owned a three-bedroomed Victorian townhouse, bought with money he had received from an inheritance. Situated in a cul-de-sac at the top of Gretford high street, his house was one of only six in his road. All six houses had been built in the sand-coloured bricks unique to Gretford. Being incredibly quiet, the road provided a calm oasis in the heart of a busy town.

Woake cooked his breakfast in the kitchen, which led to a large wooden conservatory, which in-turn led to the small rear garden.

Though small, the garden had two terraces; the lower attracted the morning sunshine whilst the higher terrace would bask in the sunshine from lunchtime to sunset.

Woake placed his breakfast, which he still referred to as "brekker" from his school days, on a tray accompanied by a pot of tea, a jug of orange juice and that morning's work, and sat down outside. He read his first set of solicitors' instructions as he ate his two poached eggs, ham and toast.

While predominately a criminal barrister, his accountant occasionally requested Woake to boost his income by undertaking civil work; namely representing one party in a dispute over a road traffic accident.

He had four sets of papers to work through that day; two opinion pieces and two Particulars of Claim to draft.

Technically, Woake should have gone to Chambers. Despite being self-employed, there was still an expectation at the Bar for barristers to work in Chambers on days when not in court. However, freedom from the drudgery of a morning commute, the tedium of office small talk and being his own boss was why he became a barrister rather than a solicitor.

Furthermore, a high peak-time train fare into London and the cost of lunch were unnecessary expenses which would have eaten into the £350 per paper he was going to earn that day; a sum already diminished by Chambers' rent, clerk fees and taxes.

Woake read the first set of instructions with the sense of quiet disdain which he always reserved for RTAs. With predictable inevitability, Woake read how the claimant had been involved in a rear-end shunt at thirty miles per hour, resulting in whiplash for three months and six months' worth of travel anxiety.

The claimant had received a doctor's report, confirming the mental as well as physical trauma of the minor incident.

The claimant's solicitors had received an offer from the defendant (the insurer of the other driver), offering to settle the claim at £1,500 plus expenses for personal injury and had asked Woake's opinion if the offer should be accepted.

Woake wrote his first opinion, a resounding yes.

The second set of instructions requested Woake to value a potential claim. The facts were nearly identical to the first, except that the physical injuries lasted for four months and the mental trauma for eight.

Woake wrote his second opinion, valuing the claim at £1,800, plus expenses.

To Woake, these two cases epitomised the avarice of the human condition encouraged by an American influence on English law since the 1990s. The two cases centred around two individuals involved in the most minor of incidents, with minimal damage to their cars, but who were now going to benefit to the best part of £2,000 solely based on a ten-minute appointment at their local doctor.

The whiplash was diagnosed following an examination by touch on the claimants' backs, whilst the claimants had never seen a psychiatrist, let alone been diagnosed by one.

Instead, their insurance companies had dangled the promise of easy money in front of them, and they had accepted, regardless of the truth. Woake never ceased to be amazed at how far people were prepared to lie for money, especially as these otherwise law-abiding citizens were committing perjury, an incredibly serious crime.

Just ask a Conservative MP.

The result? The continual transfer of cash between insurance companies and the inevitable increase in insurance premiums.

At the start of his career, Woake had gone so far as to accuse a claimant of exaggerating the anxiety, by asking if she had continued driving during her six months of anxiety. Until the judge had reminded him that the level of cynicism he was entitled to display was lower in the civil courts than in the criminal courts.

These two cases were in sharp contrast to Woake's third. A woman had become trapped in an upside-down car whilst fully conscious for two hours, with the smell of leaking petrol from her car. If that was not bad enough, the claimant was also five months into her second pregnancy. The first had been a miscarriage.

For Woake, this was a genuine mental trauma, one that demanded every possible sympathy. Woake was halfway through writing the Particulars of Claim when his mobile phone rang. It was Richard Myers.

He answered.

'Woake, why are you not in Chambers?' Myers asked.

'Why are you not either?' Woake responded.

'How do you know that I'm not either?'

'Because, Richard, it is eleven thirty in the morning and you should be in court. I can't hear any traffic, so you're not driving. As it's such a lovely morning, and you have two young children, I should imagine that you're working at home, with them.'

'Smart-arse.' Having been his pupil-master, Myers had also defended Woake's more than occasional absence from Chambers and insistence of working from home, from other members of Chambers for whom rules and convention were there to be followed.

'Anyway, I've got four cases to draft and I have the case papers as well as access to our online resources, so what would I gain by coming into town?' Woake asked.

'Couldn't care less. I understand from your clerk that you won yesterday, well done.' Myers said.

'Thanks, we knocked it out in a day, so all's good. What can I do for you?'

'Believe it or not Woake, but the DWP have just grown a pair of balls and have decided to prosecute Westbrook.' It took Woake a couple of seconds to remember that Westbrook was the female benefits cheat. Like all barristers, Woake had terrible short-term memory, remembering only the facts of the current case. The trial of Daniel Brown was already a fading memory.

'Fantastic,' Woake responded 'did the landlord agree to give evidence?'

'How the fuck should I know?' Myers responded. 'With typical DWP efficiency, they have only just told us, and Westbrook's first court appearance is tomorrow at Aldershot Mags. I want you there to handle it.'

'Can't, I've got a plea and case management hearing at Kingston on a trial I've got coming up.'

'You can, and you will, I'm afraid. I've organised cover for your PCMH.'

'Why couldn't one of their in-house lawyers deal with the first appearance?' Considering the sum involved, Westbrook would be transferred to the Crown Court automatically. Tomorrow was nothing more than a formality.

'Look, don't bloody argue, will you?' Myers said, growing more than frustrated. 'I need you as my representative and to report anything the defence will say to you. You're going and that's it.'

Woake had little choice but to agree. As Myers's Junior, it was his role to do the less glamorous hearings. His one consolation was that at least tomorrow would be an easy day.

Woake disconnected the call and finished writing. At twelve thirty, he started on his way to Fordhouse. The fourth case could wait until after he returned.

It was one o'clock by the time Woake reached the leadership suite. He had bought lunch in the Council's canteen, which he took upstairs with him.

The leadership suite was quiet; it was lunchtime and it is the right of every public sector worker to not only have an hour off every day, but to ensure that the full hour is taken.

Charlotte Bateup and Philip de Lusignon were out for lunch, Sharon Hughes (the Director for Planning) was at yet another Local Plan meeting, and Peter West (the taciturn Director for the Environment) was also out. No doubt reviewing the latest addition to the fleet of dustcarts.

Neither Foster nor Overton were at their desks, though Woake could hear movement from Bane's office.

Frances was the only PA at her desk.

'Hi Frances,' Woake greeted her, 'pretty dead in here.'

'I know,' she responded with a sigh. 'Everyone seems to be out at the moment and the other two are both off sick,' she said, motioning to the two empty PA desks.

'Why are you not at lunch?' Woake asked.

'Not allowed to,' Frances answered 'practice states that there must always be a PA on duty, so I'm stuck here.'

'What absolute rubbish. It's only Bane you're PA to, nobody important.'

'I can hear you, Sebastian!' Bane shouted from his office.

'Then you'll know I'm saying it with a smile on my face,' Woake responded. 'Tell you what Frances, take some lunch and I'll cover for you.'

'What, you'll do my job for me?' Woake nodded. 'You're the first councillor to ever offer. I won't be long,' she said, raising from her feet.

'Be as long as you want. What do I need to do?' he asked.

'Only answer the phone and take messages. I'll deal with the rest when I'm back,' she said, walking out.

Bane walked into the PA area. He saw Woake sitting at Frances's desk.

'Ah Sebastian, that's very sweet of you.'

'Thanks Giles, though it is worth pointing out that at least I'm helping Frances. Rather than ignoring her, like you.'

'I know Sebastian,' Bane said, in a simpering mock-caring tone 'that's why we all love you.' Woake swivelled the chair to face Bane.

'Speaking of which, where are our leaders?' Woake asked.

'Will's going to be here in a bit and Craig's at work,' Bane responded.

'Craig has a job?' Woake asked in genuine wonder. 'I didn't know that. I thought he was a career politician.'

'How do you know that's our nickname for him?' Bane asked.

'What, "Career Politician"?'

'No,' Bane responded, '"The Careerist".'

'I didn't, but thanks for the info.'

'Oh well, sure it doesn't matter. Craig works for the family business.'

'But three days out of five he's in here,' Woake said.

'Exactly.'

'Oh great,' Woake said, 'so his parents pretend to employ him in order to provide him with an income whilst he does his best to arse-lick his way into the Commons?'

'Quite, and he's already mastered one of the first tricks of being a politician. Just because he's got a thousand votes beside his name, he thinks he knows everything,' he said as he walked back into his office. Being an overweight man put on a permanent diet by his wife, Bane ate his salad lunch in his office.

Woake returned to his lunch. For the next hour he sat at Frances's desk, but the PA god looked favourably upon Woake, for the phone rang only once.

Woake looked at the phone as it rang. The information display identified William Foster as the caller. He adopted his best Essex-girl accent as he answered.

'Hiya,' he said 'Gretford District Cancul, Giles Bane's PAaah.'

'Oh, hello, uh, yes,' was Foster's startled response. 'Hi, is Giles there please?'

'Giles who my lurve?' Woake the PA asked.

'Uh, Giles Bane,' said a still startled Foster.

'He's not here, my lurve.'

'OK, uh fine. Can I leave a message?' Foster asked.

'Yes, my lurve.'

'OK, thanks. Um. Can you tell him that I'm running late?'

'OK, my lurve. And who are yoo?'

'I'm William Foster, the Leader of the Council,' Foster answered pompously.

'William who?'

'Foster.'

'Fostah? And how do you spell Fostah?'

'Oh Christ,' Foster said, startlement making way for impatience. 'F-O-S-T-E-R.'

'OK Mr Fostah. And who are yoo?'

'What do you mean "who am I?"'

'What do you do, my lurve?'

'I'm the Leader of the bloody Council,' Foster said, raising his voice.

'Leada of the Cancul? Which Cancul?'

'Which one do you bloody think?' Foster asked angrily, deciding that the ability to think was one thing which this particular PA could not do.

'I don't know my lurve.'

'Bloody Gretford.'

'You Leada of the Cancul? Is that like Prime Minista?'

'Well, actually yes, it is,' Foster said. Whilst he was obviously dealing with an idiot, at least it was an idiot who appreciated his position.

'And you want me to tell who that you're coming late?'

'Giles fucking Bane!'

'OK my lurve, I'll tell Mr Bane that the Prime Minista of the Cancul is late fucking him.'

'Thank you,' Foster said. At least she had grasped the essence of the message. 'Are you new?' Foster asked, hoping to God that she wasn't.

'The agency sent me my lurve as cuffer. All the PAaahs are currently ill.'

'Thank fuck,' Foster said as he disconnected the call.

'What the Hell was that about?' Bane asked from his office.

'That was Foster,' Woake responded. 'He's running late for you.'

Woake sat opposite Charlotte Bateup at the board table in her office.

'Thanks very much,' Woake said, 'for the briefing notes on Edgeborough Farm. Do we really own them?'

'Afraid so Sebastian.'

Edgeborough Farm constituted a former farming complex in the tiny hamlet of Edgeborough, to the south of Gretford. The Council became the proud owners of the dilapidated buildings twenty years previously in a fit of enthusiasm for culture and heritage, to the lasting regret of the Finance team. The farm was of historical importance to the district as it was not only thought to comprise the oldest farm buildings in the county of Sussex, but archaeological evidence had suggested that the ditch running parallel to the northern boundary of the farm may well have once been the latrines for a hunting lodge which was thought to have existed on the site back when Gretford Castle was a royal residence.

Having spent a minimal sum on renovating the complex, the Council passed over day-to-day running of the buildings to the local Parish Council, which became the tenants. From that moment on, the farm became the wedding venue of choice for couples who wished to celebrate their nuptials in an idyllic, if rustic, setting.

Rustic was very much the theme of the weddings, as the guests sat under a high beamed roof with its ceiling proving a battleground for bats, sparrowhawks, songbirds and the occasional owl, all of which jostled for power in an avian dogfight.

For the Parish Council, the beauty of the deal was that all it required them to do was demonstrate to their landlord that the farm was generating an income. The level of income was never stipulated, such was the district's determination to own this cultural gem.

As is typical of most parish Councils, the Edgeborough Parish Council's primary aim was to limit the number of visitors to the parish. The farm was therefore limited to only six weddings per year.

Unfortunately for the Parish Council, the twenty-year agreement was due for renewal in little under six months' time.

'But as landlord, we're responsible for the upkeep, maintenance, preservation and the running costs of the buildings,' Woake said.

'Indeed, we are,' Bateup said in agreement.

'And the farm costs us about £100,000 per year in those costs alone?'

'Indeed, it does,' Bateup agreed.

'And the local Parish Council keeps all income generated?'

'Indeed, it does,' Bateup agreed, again.

'And you have just passed me a report from one of our surveyors which states that unless we spend about £250,000, the farm will fall down. Which will leave us not only in breach of our contractual obligations to the Parish Council but also to English Heritage as the farm is Grade I listed property?'

'Indeed, I have,' Bateup answered.

'So we have what someone has optimistically described as "an asset" in your briefing notes, which is in fact a total liability?'

'Indeed, it is,' Bateup answered.

'And which idiot handles this mess?' Woake asked.

Bateup looked over Woake's shoulder, thinking of the diplomatic and political answer. She couldn't find one.

'One of your predecessors,' she answered slowly 'in the Finance portfolio, who was a well-known supporter of the arts and culture. He died not too long ago.'

'Shame,' Woake said. 'I'd have appreciated a chat with him. So our choice is either to spend the money and renew the lease, or...?' Woake asked.

'We sell the farm,' Bateup answered for him.

'Excellent Charlotte, now you know what your instructions are,' Woake said, raising from his chair.

'But the decision lies with you and Cathy as councillors and Peter as the relevant director, not with the Finance team,' Bateup said, with growing panic.

'Charlotte. You and I are responsible for the financial well-being of this Council. Of course the decision lies with us. If we say that selling the farm is in the best interests of our residents, we sell the bloody thing. No matter what pisspot some king might have pissed in.' Woake reached the door.

'But this is culture, Sebastian. Cathy is bound to remind your Cabinet colleagues that Edgeborough always votes Conservative in elections.'

'Don't worry, Charlotte,' Woake said, breaking into a soft smile. 'As I said to you before, you're my team. Any fallout will be on me, and I'll say that this is solely my decision to sell.' He opened the door. 'I'll catch you later, Charlotte,' he said, and walked straight back into the leadership suite.

Despite it being only two thirty in the afternoon, William Foster was already wearing a dinner jacket. He drove his Mini Cooper into the Council car park, parking in the space reserved solely for his use.

A small man, Foster was typical of his breed in attempting to overcompensate his lack of stature with a more forthright personality. 'The twat suffers from little man syndrome,' Bane once complained to his wife.

Foster exited his car, breathing in and tucking his shirt into his fully stretched trousers as he did so. Having always struggled with his weight, even Foster was shocked about the availability of free food a councillor became accustomed to.

Even if his wife cared, she would not have complained about his growing weight. A sly grin appeared when he thought that for his wife, a Ukrainian, a successful man was overweight. Only a successful man could overeat in the former USSR.

Foster breathed in and buttoned up his dinner jacket as he walked through to the leadership suite.

Frances was at her desk, the only PA present.

'I thought you were all ill, Frances?' he asked by way of saying hello.

'No, only Louise and Sam,' she answered, barely able to hide her contempt for Foster.

'But I spoke to a PA who said she was covering for you lot,' Foster responded.

'Not sure who you spoke to, Will, but I assure you that I'm the only one on duty here,' she said and returned to her work.

Bane appeared from his office, to rescue Foster as much as he needed to rescue Frances.

'Hiya Will, good to see you. Off to the University of South-East England event tonight?' he asked.

'You know I am Giles, you're going to be there too,' he said. 'Have you come across another PA today?'

Bane caught the look from Frances. 'No, Will,' he said.

At that moment, Charlotte Bateup's door opened and Foster turned to look as Woake walked through.

For Foster, Woake was everything he hated. Tall, slim with an athletic build, Woake carried with him the quiet confidence that could only be gained from boarding school. The fact his eyes quietly scanned the three individuals present gave testament to his first career.

'Hi Will, how are things?' he asked, his eyes flicking up and down Foster's late middle-aged physique. Perspiration was already breaking out across Foster's forehead, despite the air conditioning in the leadership suite.

Foster broke out into a smile, pretending to be friendly.

Hopefully Woake would be foolish enough to fall for it. 'I'm fine, thanks Sebastian. Good to see you. We must catch up for a coffee soon.'

'Would love to. Frances, catch you later,' he said as he walked out of the leadership suite. Foster caught Frances smiling as he walked into Bane's study. 'Giles, I understand the Guardians are planning on...' he said, closing the door on Frances.

Woake was sitting on the upper terrace in his garden. He dialled a number on his mobile. His call was answered on the seventh ring.

'Hello,' the voice on the other end said.

'Oh hi,' Woake said as informally as he could. 'Is that Edgeborough Farm?'

'Yes,' the female voice on the other end answered.

'Oh, that's great. My name's Craig Overton and I've just got engaged and my fiancé and I were wondering if we could have a tour around the farm. One of our friends went to a wedding there last year and told us how special the location is.'

'I'm afraid that all our dates next year are already fully booked,' the woman said.

'But it's only May?' Woake asked 'and we're looking for something for next year.'

'I'm very sorry to have to say this, but we're a very small venue and have very small resources available to us. We don't consider bookings for the following year until at least the autumn.'

'But most people want to book their weddings at least a year in advance,' Woake said.

'That's as maybe, but unfortunately, we're a very small parish and so we must manage traffic flow along with other considerations. Is there anything else I can help you with?' she asked.

'Yes, just one thing. What's the maximum capacity of the venue?'

'Sixty people,' she answered.

'Sixty people, is that all?' Woake asked.

'Yes, it is,' she said curtly. 'As I said, we're a very small parish, and so we're restricted to the number of people we can have visit us. Is there anything else?'

'Don't worry,' Woake said, looking at the briefing notes. 'You've already been more than useful,' he said and hung up the phone.

Foster's day was going from bad to worse. His tight-fitting dinner suit, which had started the day as an irritant, had now graduated into being downright uncomfortable.

But Foster's annoyance just wasn't restricted to his ill-fitting suit. It was what the ill-fitting suit represented.

His weight gain had not been a quick process, but had rather been a gradual progression. Not requiring a dinner jacket in order to investigate the tax liabilities of the self-employed, the fact he had not noticed that his dinner suit no longer fitted only told him a very inconvenient truth; for the six years that he had been a councillor, Foster had never been required to wear it. He had simply not been important enough to be invited to a black-tie event.

Having been made Leader solely due to the misfortune of his predecessor, Foster would never feel that he had attained high office out of his own political successes.

This sense of potential fraud had been heightened as he dressed. A proper leader would have checked that his suit still fitted. As his disinterested wife had said, 'breathe in darling' as she left the house for the gym.

Not that Tehri's disinterest was a new thing. The poor woman had been disinterested in Foster since he was first elected, complaining like most spouses that their councillor husbands much prefer playing politics than playing with them.

Not that Tehri's disinterest in Foster was limited solely to him being a councillor; it had rather more to do with the highly toned personal trainer at Gretford Prism who was closer to her age than the older Foster.

By the time that Foster had entered Bane's office, Foster felt like a fraud.

It was obvious that he was the victim of a practical joke, and it was more than obvious that the Managing Director was covering up. Not that Foster believed Bane to be the perpetrator; as Managing Director, Bane would be too scared to make such a public show of disrespect.

Even the PA had covered for the perpetrator.

What angered Foster was that nobody would have dared to have done the same to Gerald Gallagher: who combined the perfect mix of fear and respect found in all good leaders which Foster simply lacked.

That someone dared do that to him only emphasised that he could never sit comfortably as Leader.

Unfortunately, Foster's paranoia that he didn't belong was only to be further acerbated by that evening's entertainment.

Foster was invited to the University of South-East England's annual technology awards night. Despite being located in Gretford, the university is considered to be one of the UK's leading experts in electrical engineering, satellite technology and space exploration.

As Leader of the Council, Foster was sitting on the top table.

To his left sat the vice-chancellor, Sam Tong. Officially, Tong had been appointed as he was one of the world's leading experts in nanotechnology, but unofficially, because he was Chinese. Born in the small-sized Chinese town of Binzhou (population of over two million at the last census) on the Korean peninsula, Tong trained as a chemical engineer in a town which owed its wealth solely to the oil deposits that were discovered in the town in the dying days of World War II.

That Binzhou is culturally more Korean, to the point that dog is a mainstay on all domestic and commercial menus, was an inconvenient fact conveniently overlooked by the university.

The simple fact was that the university's finances were in an even more perilous position than the Council's and it was hoped that Tong's appointment would provide a guaranteed income stream for years to come.

'Ah Will, congratulations on being made Leader,' Tong said as he greeted Foster as if they were long-lost friends. They had never previously met.

'Thank you, Sam, and thank you for inviting me tonight. It's a pleasure being here,' he responded, breathing in.

Unable to bear the pain of the trouser button sticking into his ample stomach, he subtly undid the button when he sat down. He just hoped that he wasn't required to stand up unexpectedly without being able to do it back up again.

'That was quite a coup against Gallagher,' a strong South African voice said to Foster's right. Foster turned round to see a middle-sized, stocky, grey-haired man in his fifties facing him.

'I'm sorry?' Foster stuttered.

'That was quite a coup against Gallagher. He was a good man. How is he doing?' the South African asked.

'Uh, I'm not sure,' Foster stammered, picking up on the implication that whoever this South African was, he didn't consider Foster to be a good man. 'The last I heard, he was awake.'

'Sounds like you guys couldn't wait to get rid of him,' the South African said. Foster sat in silence, embarrassment at the stranger's astute observation rendering him temporarily speechless.

'I think what Will means to say, Nick,' the soft voice of Serena Kildare said as she stroked the South African's right hand 'is that with great reluctance, it was considered that Gerald found himself incapable of guiding the Council through the many challenges that the Council finds itself in. Wouldn't you say that, Will?'

'Uh, yes, well, quite,' Foster said, trying to turn his gaze from Kildare's low-cut dress.

'Will,' Kildare said, ignoring Foster's downward gaze, 'have you met Nick Churchouse, chief executive at the university?'

'Uh no, sorry, I haven't,' Foster answered with some mild irritation. Churchouse had turned around and had blocked his view of Kildare's ample cleavage.

'Good to meet you Will,' Churchouse said, taking Foster's hand in a vice-like grip, with a tone of voice that it was anything but good to meet Foster.

Churchouse was well known for his disdain for councillors' pretentiousness.

The evening progressed with conversations about the importance of nanotechnology in medical research, the breakthroughs of sustainable energy in the future of space exploration and the increase in life expectancy of satellites caused by the greater potential orbit of the Earth.

To say that Foster struggled to understand a word of it would be as much an understatement as to say that he spent most of the three-course dinner (complete with a selection of chocolates with after-dinner coffee) staring at Kildare's barely concealed breasts.

As she leant forward towards her soup, Foster was amazed that she didn't spill out, and it was a silent prayer of thanks he said when she leant backwards. Not so much out of embarrassment for her, but more to spare his own blushes as he was distinctly aware that his trouser button was still undone.

The conversation ebbed and flowed across the table, with Foster barely able to contribute beyond the occasional exclamation of agreement and approval. Even Kildare could talk about the university's role in Gretford becoming the central hub of computer gaming in the UK.

And she was a surgeon.

Gallagher, he was sure, would have been able to hold more than his own against these academics. And he wouldn't have needed to undo his trouser button.

'Wouldn't you say, Will?' Kildare asked, breaking him out of the trance he had found himself in.

'Uh, what would that be?' he asked in response, barely able to keep himself from her chest as she leant forward to get his attention. She certainly had it now.

'That the priority of a council should be to provide social care and services to its most vulnerable, rather than vanity projects all in the name of culture?'

'Uh, absolutely. Yes, you're quite right,' Foster said.

'Then you're saying that no money should be spent on anything to do with the arts? Like the new outdoor opera venue just outside Gretford, which brings untold joy to our residents and helps advertise Gretford within the wider region?' Churchouse asked with more than a hint of irony.

'Well, there is that I suppose,' Foster said, now totally confused as to what to say. Gallagher would never have sounded so inept.

'But can we afford to, Will?' Kildare asked, Foster wishing that she hadn't.

'Well, that depends on who you speak to.'

'In what way?' Churchouse asked.

'Well, if you speak to my Lead for Culture, then we can. If you speak to my Lead for Finance, then we can't.'

'And what do you think?' Churchouse asked to an ever-increasingly uncomfortable Foster.

'Well, I think we need to balance our budget in as responsible a manner as possible, bearing in mind the needs of all the people we serve,' Foster, ever the politician, said.

'Well, Sebastian thinks we can't,' Kildare said.

'Sebastian who?' Churchouse asked.

'Sebastian Woake. He's our new Lead for Finance. He's put a block on all major projects. He's even cancelled councillors' food before meetings.'

'Has he now?' Churchouse asked, laughing. He slapped Foster on the back of the shoulders. 'At least that means you chaps will lose some weight.'

'But it means that my funding for Inspire to Aspire is now in jeopardy,' Kildare said, bending forward ever so slightly more.

'What is Inspire to Aspire?' asked the ever-smiling Tong, his eyes fixed firmly on Kildare's.

'My initiative for helping to improve the lives of some of Gretford's most vulnerable residents. I'm hoping that we will be able to educate teenagers that they do have a future by providing them with the employment opportunities that are currently denied to them.' She stroked Churchouse's hand again. 'And that means I would like some meaningful work experience offers from you, Nick.'

'Are you worried that it may not be funded?' Tong asked.

'Depends on Will,' Kildare said, leaning forward even further. Churchouse's back slapping and the view available had placed Foster in a rather hard predicament. If it wasn't for his napkin, Foster would be concerned that the waitress serving their table would receive a view she would not forget in a hurry.

'Uh, you'd better speak to Sebastian,' Foster mumbled, and returned to his coffee, hoping the coffee cup would hide his blushes.

'Are you struggling at the moment, Will?' Tong asked.

'I'm sorry?' Foster replied, hoping to heaven that Tong hadn't noticed his below the table predicament.

'Are you in a hard position?'

Tong noticed the blank look Foster was giving him. 'Your finances? Are they that bad?'

'It's fair to say, Sam, that we're currently facing unprecedented financial challenges. Our income has been withdrawn from central Government and we're forced to take on even more services. And it's not helped that every lead councillor wants yet more funding.'

'I might be able to help you,' Tong said.

'How?' Foster said, trying not to sound as desperate as he felt.

'I'm friends with my hometown's city government. I know that they are keen to further their relations with a similar council in the UK. Perhaps we should discuss this further at a later date?'

Foster's evening was beginning to take a turn for the better.

Eighteen

Woake waited to be directed through the security gates at Aldershot Magistrates Court. Every criminal court throughout the country now has a security entrance reminiscent of airport security checks.

A sad state of affairs, Woake mused, indicative of the broken society where now even courts could not be safe havens from violence.

Woake waited patiently in the line along with the other lawyers, defendants and witnesses as they waited to gain access to the court. Overweight and officious security guards waved visitors through the security gate one at a time, inspecting every crevice of every bag that a visitor wishes to bring with them. Once deemed safe, the visitor would be directed through the security gate.

If the alarm was activated, the visitor would be directed to one side as a security wand was waved over them.

Only then would the visitor be deemed safe and allowed in.

Throughout his time as a barrister, Woake had never seen anyone attempt to bring in a banned substance or item, least of all a knife. Indeed, it was only very rarely had he seen any form of unacceptable behaviour.

Even the most violent or intimidating of defendants tended to behave themselves in court. Being in the close confines of the dock did that to people.

Except for the mentally ill.

For Woake, the security checks were one of the greatest ironies of the legal system. The presumption of innocence was one cornerstone on which the criminal system was built. However, for the security guards on duty in every court, a visitor was guilty of attempting to bring in an offensive weapon until they had proved their innocence.

Not that many of them would have been useful in an altercation. For many of them, their only move would have been sitting on someone.

Even known lawyers halfway through a high-profile eighteen-month inquest would still be subject to the same degree of suspicion as members of the Little Hound Gang supporting their bruvver on an indictment for murder.

Eventually, Woake was waved through security. Much to the chagrin of the overweight, pale and blotchy faced security guard, Woake failed to set the alarm off.

Being a Magistrates Court, there was no robing room for Woake to escape into. Instead, he joined everyone else around a television screen hanging from the ceiling, waiting for the screen to flick on to the relevant display, telling him which courtroom Westbrook would appear in.

Eventually, the screen flicked to the listings for Court 4 and Woake made his way to court.

The Magistrates Court system remains an anomaly from an archaic legal system. Initially evolving from a medieval system into a nineteenth century means for the local squire to remove troublesome and occasionally criminal residents from his village, it became by the twenty-first century a mainstay of the criminal justice system.

Magistrates are unpaid legal amateurs who have to commit to twenty-eight half days of legal work a year. Such facts are made even more depressing because ninety per cent of criminal cases are dealt with solely in the Magistrates Court. Days are clogged up as three legal enthusiasts, with little legal training and even less legal understanding, struggle to work their way through the daily lists.

The actual power in the Magistrates Court lies with each courtroom's legal clerk, who in the Blairite era were renamed legal advisors, as clerk was considered belittling of their status.

Legally trained and with the experience that can only be gained by years spent trawling over legal procedure combined with a hatred for lawyers (they were always failed lawyers), the clerks' influence over the magistrates is unmatched. The first lesson Woake learnt in the Magistrates Court was never to argue with the clerk; their knowledge usually surpassed that of any QC.

An alienated clerk could spell disaster for your case, as their influence would be enough to sway the intimidated bench.

For Woake, the magistrates' system desperately needed reform, if not dissolution. In the incredibly unlikely event that he would be appointed Justice Secretary (the new Blairite name for Lord Chancellor), then he would disband the system and replace it with fully paid judges.

Whilst the benefit of a magistrate is that they are unpaid, and a judge would require a healthy salary, Woake was convinced that the salary would be more than compensated by working quickly through the time wasted by a bench of magistrates.

As Woake was fond of saying, a patient admitted to hospital would not be prepared to be operated on by an unpaid amateur doctor, so why should a defendant in a criminal trial be tried by a magistrate?

However, Woake would always add that being operated on by an amateur might be preferable to a surgeon.

Woake had studied clinical negligence.

Proponents of the magistrates' system always argued passionately that it guaranteed local justice. An argument slightly undone by the unprecedented number of court closures. Nowadays, a defendant could be tried miles away from their home.

Woake walked into Court 4 and joined a group of suited individuals who he assumed were the lawyers and casually dressed individuals who were their clients as they congregated around a harassed-looking robed court usher and the learned clerk sitting in her station in front of the empty bench.

Woake sat down in the public gallery, his papers resting on his lap, and waited as the court staff dealt with the numerous requests that faced them. Patience is a skill that every barrister learns soon in his career, and Woake had already learnt that the key to appearing in a Magistrates Court is never to annoy the staff for one very simple reason; they decided the order in which the cases would be heard.

Eventually, the group thinned out as lawyers and their clients either sat beside Woake and waited for the court session to start or left the courtroom for a conference. The usher, a petite brown-haired middle-aged woman, noticed Woake for the first time and approached him.

Woake stood up as she walked towards him with a clipboard.

'Good morning, may I help you?' she asked.

'Hiya,' Woake responded, 'hope you can. I'm appearing in the case of Westbrook. Please tell me I'm in the right courtroom.' Woake had already noticed the absence of a possible Westbrook or her solicitor.

'You are indeed,' the usher said with a faint smile 'and you are?' she asked.

'Sebastian Woake, of counsel,' Woake responded, denoting his status as a barrister. 'I'm representing the DWP.' The usher wrote his name down on her list.

'Are you here for Westbrook?' a loud woman's voice asked. Woake turned to see that it belonged to a large, short-haired, bespectacled ugly woman in her mid-fifties; the court clerk.

'That's right,' Woake said, walking towards her. 'It's her first appearance, and considering the value of the crime, this matter will no doubt be indicted to the Crown Court.'

'And what is the crime?' the clerk asked, opening the relevant court file, despite reading the file earlier that morning in her office and thereby knowing the answer.

'Benefit fraud,' Woake answered.

'And the value?'

'£90,000,' Woake answered.

'And is the defendant on bail?'

'I believe so. My instructions are not to oppose her bail.' The clerk continued to read the papers. 'Busy day?' Woake asked. The clerk looked up.

'Very, we have the remand list in from last night to deal with along with two trials and your matter.'

'Well, the good news is that at least my matter shouldn't take too long,' Woake said.

A smile appeared across the clerk's face, softening it for the first time. 'You don't know our bench, but I'll try to get you on this morning.'

'Thanks, much appreciated.' The remand list was the caseload which had formed overnight and consisted of the individuals who had been arrested over the past 24 hours and needed to be dealt with as priorities in case their custody time exceeded the 24-hour limit laid down by law.

Woake knew that the defendants in custody always took precedent over bailed defendants; a policy which he did not always agree with. As far as Woake was concerned, time spent in a cell was what many of the defendants needed. And it wasn't as if many of them had anything else to be doing with their day, so what difference would a few extra hours make sitting in a cell?

He approached the usher. 'Could you please tell me if my opponent and the defendant have turned up?' he asked.

The usher looked down at her clipboard. 'Yes, they're both here. Your opponent is a Mr Paul Adams.' She looked round the courtroom, but was interrupted by a loud knocking from the far end of the courtroom. 'Be upstanding for the bench!' the usher shouted.

Woake stood stiffly as the magistrates (two men and a woman) entered their courtroom and sat down on the dais.

'They're outside,' the usher whispered. Woake quietly thanked her and bowed to the bench as he left the court.

Woake looked up and down the busy corridor. Every seat in the waiting area was taken. Some visitors had even taken to sitting on the filthy tiled floor. Every court was now in session, so ushers appeared every few minutes, calling out the name of the next case to be heard.

A procession of lawyers, clients and family followed the ushers in.

'Anyone in the case of Westbrook?' Woake called. Fifty hostile faces turned in his direction, none answered. 'No?' Woake asked. Still no response. 'Thanks,' Woake said.

Woake walked round the court building, to occupy himself as much as an attempt to find his opponent.

There was one other person missing too; Marla Rajeesce. As officer in the case, Rajeesce was required to be present at every court appearance; as the investigating officer she (should) have the most in-depth knowledge of the case and should be at hand in case the defence or the magistrates (an unlikely event) asked a question Woake could not answer.

Woake found Rajeesce's office phone number in his papers and dialled the number. It answered on the sixth ring.

'Hello, Marla Rajeesce,' the voice answered.

'Hello Marla,' Woake said 'it's Sebastian Woake.'

'Sebastian who?' Rajeesce asked. Woake took a deep breath.

'Sebastian Woake, I'm Richard Myers's Junior in the case of Westbrook.'

There was silence at the other end. Woake had a faint feeling that he could hear the cogs in Rajeesce's head turning. 'Oh yes,' she said eventually, 'can I help you?'

'You can indeed,' Woake said, 'where are you?'

'I'm in my office. Why?' she asked.

'Because,' Woake responded, 'today is Westbrook's first appearance in court, and you're supposed to be here.'

'Am I?'

'Yes.'

'Where am I supposed to be?' she asked.

'At Aldershot Magistrates Court,' Woake said, in much the same tone as Foster had spoken to the fake PA the day before.

'But I've only ever been present at trials,' she said.

'What?' it was Woake's time to ask the questions.

'I only ever go to the trials. Why am I needed before then?'

'What happens if she pleads to the charges or the defence requests urgent information which only you know the answer to, which could cause the trial to be chucked out?'

'Could that happen?'

'Not at this point, but I'm going to look pretty bloody stupid not being able to answer questions because my OIC is not present.'

'OIC?' Rajeesce asked, reverting back to asking the questions.

'Officer in the case, i.e. you,' Woake said, tone rising. A tall slim man in a brown suit and black tie walked towards him.

'Well, what do you want me to do?' she asked.

'Get down here ASAP.' The man stopped opposite Woake. 'I've got to go,' he said and rang off the phone.

'Sebastian Woake?' the man asked. His long unkept hair was fine accompaniment to his white shirt which had started to turn cream. Woake nodded. 'Paul Adams. I'm representing Tiffany Westbrook,' he said as he held out his hand.

Reluctantly, Woake shook it. Not out of rudeness, but because it had been years since his hand had been shaken outside a courtroom. A solicitor, Woake decided.

'Good to meet you,' Woake said. 'Fancy a chat?' he asked.

Adams led Woake into a conference room he had commandeered. A large, short blonde-haired woman in her thirties sat at the table. She wore a pair of grey tracksuit bottoms along with a blue t-shirt, which hung tightly across her large frame. As she looked up, Woake noticed that she wore hardly any make-up.

'My client,' Adams said. He turned to Westbrook. 'Would it be possible for me and Mr Woake to have a quiet chat?' he asked.

As Westbrook left the room, Woake reflected on how she was the complete opposite to how he imagined her. She did not have the glary cheap jewellery, or flash clothes, or indeed the layers of make-up that many expect with benefit cheats.

Westbrook looked exactly like she was, a working-class woman attempting to scratch a meagre living on benefits before her inevitable retirement on a state pension.

'Any issues today?' Woake asked Adams.

'None, hopefully, a quick in-out,' Adams responded. 'Will you be opposing bail?' he asked.

'Those are not my instructions. And having met your client, albeit briefly, she doesn't look the type to skip the country.'

'You a barrister?' Adams asked.

'Afraid so,' Woake answered. He leant back in his chair, knowing that Adams would not have requested a conference unless there was an issue, and Woake certainly was not prepared to rush him. It was not as if there was much else for him to do that day.

'We may have one problem,' Adams said.

'Oh yes?' Woake asked.

'Yes,' Adams replied, looking through his papers. 'I don't think the amount fraudulently claimed has been properly calculated.'

Woake leant forward. Adams certainly had his attention now. 'In what way?' he asked.

'Her entire benefits for the three and a half years have been included in the alleged fraudulent amount. From my understanding, only her claim for the children is allegedly fraudulent. She was still entitled to claim housing benefit for herself as well as jobseeker's allowance.'

'Indeed,' Woake said. In one statement, Woake was placed in an extremely embarrassing situation; a simple calculation that, in truth, both he and Myers should have checked. Instructions should always be checked.

Woake had to stall for time. He smiled.

'I'm afraid that I have a rather embarrassing confession to make,' he said. 'My case officer has failed to appear. Unfortunately, she failed to realise that her presence was required. She'll be the one to check the prosecution's calculations.'

'Where is she?' Adams asked.

'She's on her way down now from London. But, given my dealings with her, I am not confident in her making it to Aldershot, she'll probably go to Addlestone instead. What do you value the case at?' Woake asked.

'About £50,000,' Adams answered.

'In which case,' Woake said, with some relief, 'the case will still be referred to the Crown Court.' Woake and Myers therefore had plenty of time to check.

'Quite, but could you still check this before our next court appearance, please?' Adams asked.

Woake phoned Marla Rajeesce outside the courtroom. Whilst he doubted that the value of the claim would become an immediate issue, it was better to get her looking into the calculations sooner rather than later.

This time, a man answered the call.

'Hi,' Woake said 'I'm trying to get through to Marla Rajeesce.'

'I am afraid that Marla is not around at the moment,' the voice at the other end said.

'May I ask where she is?' Woake asked.

'I am afraid that I cannot answer that,' the voice said.

'What I mean,' Woake said, 'is that she is due to meet me in court in Aldershot and I was merely wondering if she is on her way?'

'I am sorry, but I cannot tell you that.'

'Why not?' Woake asked.

'Security, we're not allowed to say where our colleagues are.'

'Security? You're the DWP. Look,' Woake said, attempting to sound more reasonable, 'my name is Sebastian Woake and I am a barrister instructed on one of her cases, and I need to speak to her urgently. Does she have a mobile?'

'I'm sure she does, sir, but I cannot provide you with that.'

'Why not?'

'Security and data protection. Not only would I be in trouble if you threatened her, but I could also be liable under data protection regulations.'

'So how am I going to contact her?' Woake asked.

'I can take a message for you and pass it on when she gets back in,' the voice said.

'But she's on her way to see me now.'

'In which case you can talk to her when she arrives,' the voice said.

'The issue,' Woake said, exasperation entering his voice 'is that we have an application which will only last five minutes, and we could be called on at any moment. I may not see her, and she could have wasted her time coming down.' Woake stopped, expecting the voice to answer. Silence descended on the conversation instead. 'Are you still there?' Woake eventually asked.

'Yes.'

'Then could you call her and ask her to call me as soon as possible?' Woake asked.

'I am afraid that I cannot do that.'

'Why not?'

'We're not allowed to call mobile numbers whilst at work.'

'But this is a work call,' Woake said.

'Doesn't matter, we're not allowed to call a colleague's mobile number whilst in the office unless it is an emergency.'

'But this is an emergency.'

'I am afraid that an emergency is defined as when the safety of the relevant officer or the public is at risk.'

'In which case, could you please ask her to call as soon as she can?'

'Of course, sir, may I take your name and telephone number?' Woake gave it to him. 'And may I ask you if you're happy for me to pass on your mobile number?'

'Of course I bloody am! Why wouldn't I be?' Woake asked.

'Data protection, we now have to ask anybody who leaves a message to confirm that they are happy for their details to be passed onto the recipient.'

At Woake's suggestion, he, Adams and Westbrook sat together in the public gallery of Court 4, knowing they stood a chance of being called on sooner if they remained in view of the clerk.

Adams and Westbrook watched as each remanded defendant was dealt with. Sentencing was given to those who pleaded, a next court appearance date was fixed for those who did not. The magistrates dealt with each case studiously and slowly.

Woake sat working on his GDC iPad, working through that week's emails. As always, most of his emails concerned planning matters, but now he was Lead for Finance, there were requests for funding as well as investment reports to read.

He still directed all ward matters to his two ward colleagues.

His attention was diverted from a request from Rowbarthon Parish Council for £2,000 to install benches in the public areas by the raised voice of a defence lawyer.

'But Your Worships, there is no need to adjourn the court to consider a bail application. No bail application has been made. The defendant has just pleaded not guilty to a charge of domestic violence and because the defendant has no other address, save the matrimonial home, in which he can stay pending the conclusion of these proceedings, you have no option but to remand the defendant in custody.'

'That's quite right, sir,' the clerk said, addressing the bench. 'The law is quite clear in this matter. The defendant cannot return to the family home until after his trial. If there is no other address that he can live at, then he must be remanded in custody.'

'Nevertheless,' the chairman of the bench addressed the court, 'my colleagues and I will still leave to consider this matter.'

'Please rise!' the usher shouted to the packed courtroom as the bench rose.

The court sat back down in silence after the bench left. Woake went back to his emails.

After twenty minutes, the bench had still not returned.

'This must drive you mad,' Woake said to the clerk. Everyone else in the court turned around to look at him.

'This is the third time this morning that they have adjourned the court,' the clerk responded.

'How many cases have they dealt with so far?' Woake asked.

'This is the third,' the clerk answered.

'And how many have you got today?' the defence lawyer dealing with the current case asked.

'Twenty this morning.' The time had now gone eleven thirty.

'What the bloody hell are they talking about in there?' Woake asked. 'They've spent twenty minutes considering a non-existent application that a lawyer and the learned legal advisor have advised doesn't exist, but they've still gone out to talk about it. I appreciate that these magistrates are getting on a bit, but if they need a comfort break, why don't they just bloody say so!'

'I'll go in there and check on them if they're not back in a few minutes,' the clerk said.

'The problem is,' Woake said 'is that they've taken over an hour and a half dealing with cases that, frankly, the village idiot with only one brain cell could do in a matter of minutes.'

'The problem is,' the defence lawyer said, 'is that they gain a sense of their own self-importance as soon as they sit up there. Plus, everybody in whatever walk of life is far too scared to actually make a decision without discussing it ad infinitum with everyone else.'

'Is your case ready?' the clerk asked Woake, attempting to break up the conversation. Whilst she secretly agreed with the two lawyers, like all members of a system, she could not be seen to be criticising it.

'Yep, we're ready to go as soon as you are,' Woake responded.

'In which case, we'll get you on next,' the clerk said, hoping to get rid of Woake before he caused more embarrassment to the magistrates' system in front of defendants.

The knock on the door announced the arrival of the bench.

'We have considered the defendant's bail application,' the chairman of the bench said when they had resumed their seats. 'And we are confident that the defendant has failed to meet the required test. And on that basis, the application has failed.'

There was a bustle as the two lawyers in front of the bench withdrew from the courts, to be replaced by Woake and Adams, who signalled for Westbrook to stand beside the dock as the preceding defendant was led down to the cells.

'Sir,' the clerk addressed the chairman of the bench, 'the next case is the case of Ms Westbrook. Please note that this is not listed on your remand list but is a first appearance on a matter to be indicted to the Crown Court.'

'Very good madam legal advisor.' The chairman looked to Woake, who was sitting in the prosecutor's chair.

'Your Worships,' Woake addressed the court, 'in this case I appear on behalf of the prosecution. My friend, Mr Adams, appears on behalf of the defence.' As a barrister, Woake was entitled to be addressed as learned. As a solicitor, Adams was not.

And Woake was not prepared to give the solicitor even that minor honour. Woake continued with his address.

'The defendant stands before you today in her first appearance on an indictment of an alleged fraudulent claim for benefits which the prosecution maintains that she was not entitled to make. There is an outstanding issue of the value of the fraudulent claim, which I am currently unable to answer, although my friend assures me that this is an issue which can be dealt with subsequent to today.

'Your Worships, there is nothing further for me to say but to request that this matter be sent to the Crown Court for a plea and case management hearing at the earliest available opportunity.' Woake sat down. The chairman of the bench turned to Adams, who stood.

'Thank you sir, I have nothing further to add to what my learned friend has said, save to request that my client is allowed to continue to enjoy her unconditional bail.' Adams sat down.

'Thank you,' the chairman of the bench said. 'Madam legal advisor, is this matter able to be dealt with here?' he asked.

'No sir,' the clerk answered 'this is an indictable only offence and on that basis, it has to be passed to the Crown Court.'

'So we cannot try the defendant?' the chairman asked.

'No sir, you cannot.' The clerk consulted her diary. 'And the first available date for the plea and case management hearing will be on 2nd August at Winchester Crown Court.'

'Any objections to unconditional bail, Mr Prosecutor?' the chairman asked, with the magistrate's typical inability to work out what was going on in his own courtroom.

'None, Your Worship,' Woake said, sitting down as quickly as he had stood up.

'In which case, this matter is passed to Winchester Crown Court,' the chairman said with some regret. 'Unconditional bail is granted.'

Woake smiled at the clerk as he followed Adams and Westbrook out of the courtroom.

'I'll look into that issue for you straight away, Paul,' he said to Adams and left the solicitor walking into a conference room with his client.

'See you in Winchester,' Adams said.

Woake phoned Marla Rajeesce's office as he walked back to his car, to warn her that the hearing was over. The phone line was engaged. He was unable to leave a message.

One man who was certainly not afraid to make a decision was Mark Skelding, who strode into meeting room 1 at Gretford District Council as purposefully as only a completely bald 5ft 10" tall and equally wide man totally confident in his own skin can manage.

Skelding was present for ManCab, a monthly meeting which acted as a liaison between the senior Council officers, namely the directors as the Council's Management (the Man) and the Council Cabinet (the Cab).

The choice of name had been the subject of a long debate between councillors and officers. For councillors, it was important that they exerted their control by demonstrating their elected authority and therefore have Cab before Man.

For officers, it was important that Man preceded Cab; whilst politicians and policies change, the officers of the Council will always remain permanent. And what better way than demonstrating their permanence by having Cab follow Man?

It was a debate which waged for an entire day between Gallagher and Bane, and was won by the officers as they were the ones who actually wrote CabMan's monthly agendas.

After appearing to agree with Gallagher, Bane showed the slight of hand which can only be found in a civil servant. He subsequently ordered the agenda to be printed with the title "ManCab".

By the time that an angry Gallagher found out, it was too late. Blaming an innocent typing error by one of the PAs (her identity was never revealed), Bane had already ordered that evening's twenty agenda items to be printed, and the Cab had to acknowledge defeat.

For Skelding, this evening's ManCab was of primary importance, as it marked the first stage in his attempt to re-establish his legacy, so badly undone by Purple Flag.

Skelding took his allotted space at the large, rectangular boardroom table, acknowledging the other members of that exclusive gathering. Where he was made to sit was a continual source of annoyance to him.

ManCab was a meeting whose position at the table was laid out strictly according to seniority.

At the head of the table sat Foster and Bane, as the two most senior members present. On either side of the table sat the Cab and the Man, sitting directly opposite each other, and never allowed to mingle.

The more senior a member, the closer they sat to Foster and Bane.

Skelding looked towards Woake with envy burning in his eyes; Woake was the third most senior councillor present and so sat next to Overton. Despite his years of loyal service on the Cabinet, Skelding had never sat any closer to the head of the table than where he sat presently; next to Cathy Fulcher-Wells who, as the most junior of the councillors, sat furthest away from Foster.

A situation Skelding was determined to change, starting that night.

At the stroke of seven o'clock, Foster started the meeting. 'Good evening everyone,' Foster said smugly 'there are only three items on tonight's agenda,' Foster continued 'so turning to the recently promoted Lead Councillor for Finance, may I ask Sebastian to introduce the first.'

'Thank you, Will,' Woake said 'this report before us tonight represents the start of the budget process for the forthcoming year.' Woake flicked through the report, making it look as though he was studying the report more than merely giving it a cursory glance. 'I am delighted that all major projects have been removed. So no more moving of the sewage works, railway level crossings, redevelopment of the eastern section of the town centre and the building of the bus station, until these projects can show that they can pay for themselves.

'But don't worry Craig, your sustainable corridor and the crematorium have survived the cut.

'The rest of the report is there for us to study, Mr Chairman, and I won't bother wasting our time quoting it. There are only two areas worth mentioning. The first is that this budget cycle now formalises this Council's commercialisation from an organisation with a sole focus on spending money, to an organisation which can also generate income. Another issue I have some concern about is spending £25,000 on Mr Raison, an application for expenditure which will not be successful.'

'What does that entail?' Foster asked.

'It is an application,' Woake answered 'for the budget confirmation for the employment of Mr Simon Raison, a twenty-two-year-old graduate who has just completed one of our three annual internships. His job will entail, and I quote straight from the application "The insurance of the high maintenance in standards of Gretford District Council's noticeboards located throughout the district, with particular emphasis on the maintenance of input of paid advertising, to help generate income for the benefit of the local population."

'In short, ladies and gentlemen, Simon Raison will be paid £25,000 per year to check that the eighty noticeboards owned and operated by GDC contain the correct advertising material.

'Frankly, I can think of a thousand better ways to spend £25,000 per year, such as sending the author of this report on a spelling and grammar course or paying the officer who granted this application to take a sanity test.' Woake noticed the name of the authorising officer stated clearly at the top of the application. 'Which I notice is Charlotte Bateup, and I also notice she is glaring straight at me.'

'But Sebastian, this figure is only £25,000,' Bane said.

'Exactly Giles. Only £25,000 per year. All we need is ten other similar applications, and that is £250,000 per year being spent on wasted projects.'

'But it isn't wasted,' Bane said.

'Giles, this individual will be tasked with checking that the noticeboards are not empty and for taking advertising bookings. That's hardly a full-time job and I'm sure that there is somebody already in our employ who has the necessary skills to do this.'

'Seb, Simon has already been promised this job and he'll be made redundant,' Bateup interjected.

'And I have every sympathy,' Woake said 'but he's still young and he has to learn that life isn't fair. Frankly, I think we're doing him a favour by forcing him to get a proper job.'

'Thanks, Sebastian,' Foster said, determined to move on. 'Is there anything else?'

'No, thank you, Will, apart from to say that the budget process will go through the usual scrutiny and Working Group stages, and I look forward to each stage as it progresses.'

'Thank you, Sebastian,' Foster said with relief as he turned to Mark Skelding. 'Mark, I believe that the next item is yours, the JETs.'

'Excuse me, Will, but I would like to voice an opinion,' Councillor Simon Newton said. A seventy-two-year-old former City solicitor, Newton had the ability to remain sufficiently silent enough in meetings for everyone else to think (and sometimes, hope) that he had silently died, only to gain a temporary fit of animation and talk for a sufficiently long enough time that his audience all wished that he actually had died, and not too quietly either.

'I commend your efforts Sebastian in attempting to improve the financial stability of this Council,' Newton continued, leaning forward so that he talked directly to Woake 'but as I said in a recent Group meeting, I have severe concerns about this so-called commercialisation of this Council's traded services.

'We are a service provider, a public service provider, and the officers, in all due respect to them, are not businessmen. Neither are you, and neither am I. Frankly, I do not think that our residents will appreciate us speculating with their money in order to buy office space and housing stock, especially as North Sussex Housing was such a disaster.

'I also foresee difficulty in progressing this through Overview and Scrutiny, and I foresee difficult questions at Full Council. This is a council, Sebastian, not a business.'

'Thank you, Simon, for your comments,' Woake responded. 'I am more than happy to discuss other ways in which we could reduce our budget deficit as well as continue to provide the services our residents are dependent upon. Perhaps we could increase our council tax? But then you'd struggle to be re-elected. Or we could increase parking charges and drive people out of the town centres? Or we could cut meals-on-wheels or reduce the waste collection?'

'Thanks, Sebastian,' Foster said before Newton could respond or indeed Woake could continue to insult Newton. 'Mark, perhaps you would like to talk about JETs? Hopefully that will be a bit less contentious,' he said, more in hope than expectation.

'Thank you, Mr Chairman,' Skelding said loudly, leaning confidently forward from his chair. 'This item concerns the formation of the Joint Enforcement Team for Gretford. As I am sure you all know, especially our new Lead for Finance, the Licence and Civil Protection team is the only department in the Council which currently makes a profit.'

'Only because you lot can't stop fining people,' Swaden interrupted.

'Thank you, Reg,' Skelding continued, as if he had not

interrupted. 'The Joint Enforcement Team is an exciting new proposition for Gretford and marks a collaboration between Sussex Police and Gretford District Council. Initially, we will have four officers who will be empowered to deal with matters including anti-social behaviour, anti-social parking including outside schools, dealing with traveller incursions, dog fouling, fly-posting and graffiti, fly-tipping and littering, street trading, abandoned vehicles, notices to clear waste on land and taxi licensing.

'But this just isn't about catching low-level offenders. They will also provide a visible presence to deter would-be offenders. This report in front of you is for the formation of the team and it is my intention that they should become operational within the next four weeks.

'The JETs will become part of the Civil Protection department, under the general direction of Peter West, as director, and myself, as lead councillor. However, the day-to-day leadership of the JETs will be provided by Vicky Walsh, who some of you may know from her work on Purple Flag.'

Skelding turned to Foster. 'Mr Chairman, those are my submissions and I commend this report to ManCab.'

'Thank you, Mark,' Foster said. He addressed ManCab. 'Any comments?' he asked.

'Yes, Will,' Woake answered. 'Just a couple. I'm more than slightly concerned by this. Firstly, from the financial side. I'm just looking at the financial implications of the report. It's going to take about £45,000 to kit out each officer, by the time we take into account their van, equipment, radio and comms, uniform and training. That's £225,000 for this entire project. That's a Hell of a lot of fines they have to make.'

'You have to remember, Sebastian, that this is a money earner for the Council and is projected to earn its cost within a couple of years,' Skelding said, not to be perturbed. Woake had already ruined Purple Flag, Skelding was determined that he would not ruin this.

'Mark, it will earn money from fining people, our residents. And let us not forget,' Woake said, addressing the group 'is that we would be essentially turning otherwise law-abiding citizens, our residents, into criminals.'

'Well, technically what they would be doing is against the law.'

'Yes Mark, and I appreciate these issues are nuisances ranging from the relatively minor, such as dog fouling and littering, to real problems such as fly-tipping and gypsies. But my primary issue is that of training. What training are they going to receive?

'The police spend months in police college, learning the law and how to use their judgement. You want the JETs operational in a month, so the training will be basic at best. Will they even know the law? What education will they need? The reality is that give people of less than high intelligence and a limited grasp of common sense a small amount of power, then they will abuse it. And before we know it, we'll be inundated with complaints from mothers who have received on-the-spot fines totalling £120 because they parked badly whilst dropping little Johnny off.'

'That's fine, Sebastian, and thank you for your comments,' Peter West said. Looking like a 1980s police officer himself, with broad shoulders supporting his square torso, West spoke with a calming manner, raising his hand to Woake as he spoke. 'I have taken on board your comments in relation to training and rest assured that the training will be provided by Sussex Police themselves and will only qualify each JET officer once they are satisfied that the officer in question has demonstrated the necessary skill and acumen to practise as a JET.'

'I also have some problems with this,' Swaden said, 'although mine are not quite the same as my learned friend's, though I agree with him. My concern is in the idea of our staff driving around the district in a van as if they were Judge Dredd, handing out fines when they want to.

'Also, how is an individual who is going to be kitted out in the way that this report says they will be, going to be a reassuring presence on our streets? There are only going to be four of them in a population of one hundred and fifty thousand. Not to mention the fact, none of the residents would have heard of them.'

'There will be a full press release to the local media outlets and a media launch at Fordhouse for the local press,' West answered.

'Which will no doubt be read by no one,' Swaden said.

'Anyone else?' Foster asked, hoping that the answer would be no. Granting the JETs had been the price of Skelding's support in the leadership election.

'I'm in favour of this,' Fulcher-Wells said. 'Many of our culture and heritage assets are located in rural or semi-rural areas which are at risk of the type of anti-social behaviour that the JETs want to tackle.'

'And as Lead for Health and Community,' Kildare said 'I agree with any attempt to improve the well-being of our residents, and whilst there might be some in this room who do not consider dog fouling to be a burning issue I, as a doctor, can assure you that there are serious health conditions associated with dog fouling.'

'Only if you're stupid enough to eat it,' Woake said.

'Whilst fly-tipping can have serious implications as there are often dangerous substances left as part of the waste. Farming waste and asbestos, for example. So I will support this,' Kildare concluded.

'Are we all agreed?' Foster asked.

'Agreed!' the meeting responded, minus Woake and Swaden.

'Our final meeting tonight concerns Gretford's twinning.' Foster turned to Overton. 'Craig, as the lead councillor responsible, would you like to introduce this item?'

'Yes, Will, and thank you very much for this opportunity,' Overton said to the meeting, straining for every facet of his self-importance, for the enormity of his announcement.

'As some of you may know,' he continued, 'the Council has recently been in contact with the Foreign Office. Most of us know that Gretford is currently twinned with Wurzburg in Germany, but what is not so well known is that we are also currently twinned with Bar-le-Duc in France. Our relationship with Wurzburg is considered excellent with our mutual councillor annual trips to both towns.'

Woake interrupted.

'Craig, what benefit do those trips actually bring Gretford?' he asked.

'In what way?' Overton countered.

'What I mean Craig, is what benefit do the people of Gretford gain from being twinned with a town in Germany that most of them couldn't point to on a map?'

'Well,' Overton stammered, 'there's a key exchange of policy. For example, during last year's visit, we encountered a new payment machine in the municipal car parks, which will be rolled out across the district next year.'

'Excellent Craig, I just wanted to make sure that these weren't annual jollies for lucky councillors.'

'No Sebastian, they're not, but are proper fact-finding missions.'

He turned back to the rest of the gathering. 'But our relationship with Bar-le-Duc isn't quite as strong.'

'Probably because the councillors don't realise they could get a free holiday out of it,' Woake interrupted.

'So the Foreign Office has suggested,' Overton ignored Woake 'that we replace Bar-le-Duc with Versailles?'

'Why?' Woake asked. Unfortunately, this time, Overton could not ignore Woake. Woake had merely asked what everyone else was thinking.

'Because both Gretford and Versailles have once been royal residences,' Overton answered.

'I'm making the assumption there is somebody at the Foreign Office with a sense of humour?' Swaden asked.

'Perhaps we should talk about Binzhou?' Foster asked, realising they were beginning to lose a very important debate.

'Ah, yes, quite,' Overton said, attempting to regain his composure. 'There is the possibility that Gretford could gain an important commercial partnership with Binzhou City Authority in China.'

'How?' Swaden asked.

'Through the University of South-East England. This is only at the preliminary stage. A report has been prepared for you which was sent to your home addresses this afternoon. Please read it, but be aware that a city delegation from Binzhou will visit Gretford in three months' time. And this relationship has the potential for being of the utmost financial importance to the district.'

'Thank you Craig for the report, something which I am sure we are all looking forward to reading.' Simon Newton looked around the meeting.

'Like everyone else here,' Newton continued 'I knew nothing about this before tonight. And I have to say Will, I have severe reservations about whether Gretford needs nor wants this potential business relationship. However, I appreciate that the evening is now getting late, and so will raise my particular objections at a later date.' Newton went silent, to everyone's great relief.

'Thank you, Simon,' Foster said. 'So are we in agreement for the proposed delegation in three months' time to proceed?' he asked.

'Agreed!'

'In which case, a full itinerary for the delegation's visit will be issued shortly. That concludes tonight's meeting and I wish you all goodnight.'

The meeting rose, with participants speaking and bidding farewell to their neighbours.

'Goodnight Craig,' Woake said to Overton. 'I enjoyed your bit about Bar-le-Duc, though to be honest,' Woake looked around the meeting and led Overton away from the board table, 'I was slightly concerned about the pronunciation. I had thought that Duc, as in Bar-le-Duc, was supposed to sound like duck. Still,' Woake said as he walked out of the room, 'I wouldn't have a clue, ça fait des années je ne parle pas couramment le francais.'

It's always great to pull pranks on the utterly pretentious, Woake thought as he reached his car.

'Sebastian, may I have a quick word please?' a voice asked. Woake turned. He saw the blonde-haired Kildare walk towards him.

Nineteen

It was mid-afternoon on the following Friday when Woake entered Myers's study in Griffin Court Chambers. Myers was sitting behind his desk, reading through a trial bundle, a fountain pen in his right hand. He looked up as Woake sat in a chair opposite his desk.

'So you've decided to remind us that you're a member of Chambers then, have you?' Myers asked.

'Why do you say that?' Woake responded.

'For the simple reason that people are beginning to talk that you're never here,' Myers answered.

'I collect my post and my case papers a couple of times a week. I attend court when required and my non-court work is always completed on time. So what's the issue if I decide not to work in Chambers on the days I'm not in court?'

'The issue Woake, is that tradition of the Bar dictates that barristers should always be in Chambers during working hours. It's Chambers policy that you check into Chambers for our late afternoon tea at three thirty in order that we might socialise in a convivial atmosphere. Apparently, you have attended only three afternoons in the past month, and only six in the month before that.'

'Richard, what is the point that if I'm appearing in Winchester in the morning, to traipsing up to London for a cup of tepid tea in the afternoon and listening to other barristers boring on about their clients for an hour and then driving back two-thirds of the way to Winchester an hour later, when I could be home working?'

Myers looked hard at Woake and removed his reading glasses, a trick Myers had learnt from many a judge, when wanting to emphasise a particular point to a Junior.

'Sebastian,' he said, 'when you became a tenant, I gave you some advice. Quite a bit of advice actually, which you have no doubt forgotten or ignored. One piece of advice was that you should always maintain an air of business about you. Come to Chambers, blow your trumpet to members about how busy your diary is and create an aura of success about you. The more successful you appear to be, the more work you'll get in.'

'I am busy, Richard, that's why I'm never here,' Woake responded.

'Quite,' Myers continued, undeterred, 'but busy people make time. There's another reason why you need to be in Chambers more often. The next stage of your professional development is applying for silk in a few years' time. For that, you need to network and you need friends to support your application. I should imagine that your attendance record at the Temple is worse than here. Start lunching in Temple more, start making friends. Otherwise you'll be my Junior for the rest of your life.'

'Thanks Richard, ever the pupil-master.'

'Which leads to another problem, Woake. Chambers has received a complaint about you.'

'Oh yes,' Woake responded 'don't tell me, it's the Bar Council complaining that I haven't attended one of their tea parties?'

'No need to be truculent Woake,' Myers said. 'The complaint is from the DWP. Apparently, you requested Rajeesce to attend the court, only for the hearing to have long since concluded before she had even left London. I understand Rajeesce took all morning getting to court, only to be told when she finally arrived that her case had been dealt with. It then took her a couple of hours to return to work. They're blaming you for the officer's wasted day.'

Woake laughed. 'Richard, Marla Rajeesce failed to turn up when she was required to. I told her to attend as I was being asked to answer questions I couldn't possibly know the answers to. I phoned her to tell her that she was no longer required, but I got through to a colleague unable to pass on a message because of data protection and security. I phoned her again, but the line was engaged and I could not leave a message.

'Besides, I'm sure that she has other concerns to worry about with the Westbrook case.'

'In what way?' Myers asked.

'In that she has potentially miscalculated the amount of money which the defendant has defrauded the DWP from.' Woake told Myers about his conversation with Westbrook's solicitor.

'I have emailed Rajeesce, asking her to check the amount. So far she hasn't got back to me and I'm going to chase her again on Monday.'

'By how much has she over-calculated?'

'Nothing definite, but the other side say by at least a third. Could even be half.'

'How the bloody hell did the stupid woman achieve that?'

'Because she apparently failed to consider that Westbrook was still entitled to legitimately claim some benefit. It would appear that Rajeesce included every benefit Westbrook received into her calculations.' Woake thought it would be politic not to mention that he and Myers should have checked the calculations themselves.

'Could you let me know when this has been resolved?'

'Of course. I've taken a day off in the next couple of weeks to work out a definite answer. But I warn you, you need a degree in aeronautical engineering to work out how the DWP calculates benefits.'

'That would probably explain why that idiot over-calculated,' Myers said as Woake left the study.

It was six o'clock when Woake walked into the leadership suite at Gretford District Council. Unsurprisingly, all the officers had gone home for the weekend. Only Peter West remained, and only then because he had a meeting with Woake and Cathy Fulcher-Wells, Gretford's Lead Councillor for Culture.

Woake walked into West's office, who rose from his small oval-shaped board table to shake Woake's hand. Woake was relieved to note that West gave a firm grip. Fulcher-Wells was sitting at the table. She didn't rise to greet Woake.

'Thanks, Sebastian, for coming this evening,' West said.

'My pleasure,' Woake responded, 'and thank you for staying late. I appreciate you want to get home. Hopefully this shouldn't take long. Hi Cathy, good to see you,' Woake said as he sat down.

'Hi,' was the monosyllabic response she could muster. Woake sensed that Fulcher-Wells knew exactly what the outcome of this meeting was going to be, and already hated Woake for it.

'It's probably a good idea if we start this meeting by allowing me to give a brief outline of the issues facing Edgeborough Farm and how we have arrived at the point we're currently at,' West said.

Woake didn't respond; for him a good start would have been a quick agreement that the farm had to be sold.

However, Woake had come to realise that every Council meeting needed at least a ten-minute introduction of "how we got here" before any meaningful discussion could take place.

He sat and relaxed as West explained the history of the farm; how it had started life as royal hunting lodges; that it had remained in the same family for five hundred years but had fallen into disrepair as the royals left Gretford; how its descent into dilapidation mirrored its increasing age and how it had taken the then owners over ten years to find a purchaser with the required level of romanticism combined with a near-endless amount of funds topped with the requisite lack of financial acumen.

Much to the growing desperation of the owners, such individuals are difficult to find in England's south-east.

Thankfully for them, and to Woake's current irritation, they had eventually found it in Gretford District Council. Out of a compulsion for an affection of a romanticised past which only exists in the minds of cultured councillors, a previous Lead for Finance had purchased the farm, intending to restore it into a learning centre highlighting Gretford's royal past.

Unfortunately for the project, the Council also had to demonstrate sound financial acumen. Caught between the need to restore the farm out of fear that it would finally succumb to age and the repulsion at the series of estimates as to how much the farm would cost, the lead councillor's dreams were never fulfilled.

So Edgeborough Farm was restored only to a standard forever demanding continual investment in the years to come. Twenty years later, GDC now found themselves in the same position as the previous owners.

'And that is unfortunately the crossroads which we have now reached,' West concluded. 'The Council passed over the day-to-day management of the farm to the local Parish Council for a fixed term of twenty years, which is now due for renewal. A matter made more complicated by the emergence of a potential purchaser, which has only recently been identified. It is for us to decide what to do. In fact, it's for you to make the decision,' he said.

'It seems to me,' Fulcher-Wells said in her high-pitched squeal 'that we have a choice of investing properly in the property and providing the local community with a real hub, or we sell it.'

'That is correct, Cathy,' West said, 'and is the choice I have outlined in my report.'

'I don't think that we have a choice,' Fulcher-Wells said. 'The farm is an important part of our heritage, it reflects the early history of our town. It should therefore remain firmly in public ownership and allow us to maintain a fine community asset.'

It had not been lost on Woake that Fulcher-Wells had started off with the hard sell. Knowing she was vulnerable, she had deliberately played her strongest hand. A mistake, Woake thought.

'Peter, I'm curious,' Woake said. 'How much will it cost to renovate the farm?'

'Our early estimates indicate at least £300,000,' West answered.

'And if we were to retain ownership of the farm, we would hand over day-to-day running of the complex to Edgeborough Parish Council?'

'That is correct.'

'I read the draft tenancy agreement last night, and I am curious that whilst we keep ownership, all income generated from the farm will be kept by the Parish Council.'

'But they would be the ones generating the income,' Fulcher-Wells interrupted.

'And whilst we as the landlord would gain zero per cent,' Woake said, ignoring Fulcher-Wells. 'We will still be liable for the ongoing costs of maintenance, rates and tax. So it will still cost us money?'

'Yes,' West said reluctantly.

'It currently costs us £100,000 to maintain. If we were to keep it, how much would the annual cost be once we have renovated it?'

'Projected to be about £20,000. Though, as we all know, that could rise.'

'So we would spend at least £300,000 in order to save £20,000 a year?' West nodded. 'What are our potential purchasers like?'

'They're property developers,' West answered. 'They would aim to create three luxurious barn conversions on the complex.'

'How much can we sell them for?' Woake asked. The answer, as he knew, was in West's report, but he still wanted Fulcher-Wells to hear the answer.

'The offer is in the region of £400,000.'

'Then Peter, we sell. Right chaps, as it's quarter to seven on a

Friday evening, I recommend we all go home,' Woake said and rose from his chair.

'But, Sebastian, this is our heritage, an asset of great local importance,' Fulcher-Wells said desperately.

'Cathy, it's a dilapidated farm of limited historical interest costing this Council a small fortune each year.'

'But it's of great interest to the local community.'

'Who have done nothing to promote it.'

'They have prepared a strategy to generate income. Because of our investment, the farm will become an events venue and will host a whole range of different functions, from weddings to parties, to wakes. They have drafted a strategy to develop a learning centre, where children can learn the important cultural heritage of their district.'

'Cathy, they do this already. I phoned them last week to book a wedding for next year, and they told me they weren't interested. There is nothing in the tenancy agreement to force them into adopting the strategy if they don't want to.' Woake picked up the Parish Council's strategy document. 'The Parish Council only submitted this croc of shite, which you are in love with, after Peter identified a potential purchaser. They don't want to use the farm, they want to prevent the farm from being developed.'

'You don't know that,' Fulcher-Wells said.

'I do. Otherwise they would have more than just the token number of six weddings a year.' Woake leant forward. 'They don't want hundreds of visitors to their village. They want it to remain a quiet utopia. Hence why they cobbled this rubbish together and hoped that we fall for it. We're selling it, just accept it.'

'But it's one of the oldest farms in the country,' Fulcher-Wells pleaded, using her one last argument.

'Cathy,' Woake said, as soothingly as he could. 'There are no doubt a dozen farms in Sussex which claim to be one of the oldest farms in the country. And there are no doubt hundreds throughout the country which also claim that honour. In the absence of hard proof, the answer is no. We're selling.'

Woake made his way to the door and turned around. 'I hope you both have a lovely weekend,' he said as he left.

***

Richard Myers was not the only one to wonder about Woake's attendance.

William Foster sat as the members of the Conservative Group of Gretford District Council filed into Burchetts Barn. A building located in the centre of Gretford, it is a renovated barn of more recent vintage than Edgeborough Farm. Its structural integrity and public ownership lent itself to being a perfect venue for any meeting whose participants wished to remain firmly off campus.

It was a quarter to ten on the following morning as Foster sat at the head table, with Overton sitting to his left, acknowledging each member of the Group as they entered.

As Group Secretary, Overton had spent his morning at a cash and carry, buying pastries, tea and coffee in bulk.

With the experience that can only be gained by attending countless Council meetings, the Group members congregated around the refreshments table. Foster looked at his watch and turned to Overton.

'Any absentees?' he asked.

Overton, who had been ticking off the name of every Group member as they entered, consulted his list. 'Only two. Serena.'

'No need to worry there,' Foster interrupted 'she's always late.'

'And Sebastian.'

'Did you remind him about today?' Foster asked.

'Of course I did,' Overton said with some little pique. As Deputy Leader of the Council, he prided himself on his efficiency. 'I sent him a message last night and phoned him this morning. Suffice to say he hasn't responded to either.'

'We've got ten minutes to go before we start. Better call him.'

Overton left the barn in order to make the call. Woake answered on the third attempt.

'Hi Craig,' Woake said, 'How are you doing?'

'I'm fine, Sebastian. Are you coming to the Group away day?' he asked. Ever-efficient, he did not see the need to have an extensive conversation.

'No,' Woake said, equally determined to have a brief conversation.

'Why not?'

'Because it's a Saturday and I'm driving back from rowing.'

'But your presence is required.'

'Why?'

'Because it's an away day for Group members to receive a briefing on the Local Plan.'

'Where's it being held?' Woake asked.

'In Gretford,' Overton answered.

'Not much of an away day, is it, if it's held in Gretford?'

'It's called an away day,' Overton responded, exasperated, 'because it is held away from the Council offices.'

'Really, Craig?'

'Are you coming or not?' Overton asked.

'As I said Craig, it's a Saturday and I am on the way back from rowing. You may want to spend your weekend playing politics, but I have a life to lead. Unless you want me in my rowing kit?' Despite secretly wishing that he could see that, Overton ended the call.

He looked at his watch. It was now five minutes past ten. The meeting was now running late. He noticed Kildare parking her car as he made his way back into the barn.

Overton stopped by the front door as Kildare walked towards him. Overton had one hand on the door. 'Come on Serena,' Overton said. 'We're all waiting for you and we're running late.'

Ever-efficient, he opened the door and walked back into the barn before Kildare, who hurriedly followed him.

'Good morning everyone,' Foster addressed the Group. 'I note that most of us are now here and that the time is after ten, so perhaps we should make a start.' He waited as the Group members took their seats.

'The reason we have organised this away day is to discuss the Local Plan. As you all know, this establishes our planning policy for the years 2017 to 2037. But much more importantly, it establishes the strategic sites which will enable us to meet our housing need.'

'You mean where we have to build a couple of thousand houses?'

'Thank you, Reg, that is correct. Now, I am sure that every single one of you would have noticed the bundles on your seats. That bundle,' Foster said with some small pride 'is our draft Local Plan. Inside it is every strategic site for potential development; from those which will hold just three houses, right up to major developments of about a thousand.

'Before we go through the sites, I would like to tell you all some exciting news which is hot off the press. Our strategic housing need has been assessed along with the neighbouring Councils of Waverley, Guildford and Woking.'

'That means how many houses we have to build,' Swaden said, appointing himself Group translator.

'Indeed,' Foster continued, undeterred. 'And it has been decided that Gretford's housing need is 537.'

'So am I correct in understanding that this means that we only have to build 537 homes?' Lady Turton asked.

'No,' Foster said nervously 'it means that we have to build 537 every year for the duration of the Local Plan.'

'And the duration is for how long, Will?'

'Twenty years.'

'So that means,' Swaden said, doing some quick calculations on his phone, 'that we have to build 10,740 houses by 2037?'

'Yes,' Foster said, to loud groans from the Group.

'And how did we get to that number?' Turton asked to the consternation of many of her colleagues, for whom listening to Turton's diatribes was an experience more akin to Chinese water torture. She continued expressing her own thoughts before Foster could cut her off by answering. She spoke as if she was speaking to an idiot, which in Foster's case, was exactly what she thought.

'I think I speak for many here Will,' she said, with a smile that she considered to be diplomatic but many concluded to be smug, 'that is a totally outrageous number. Gretford, as I am sure you know, Will, is a town which prides itself on being conservative. Not just in politics, but in policy; in particular, housing.

'Whilst we all agree that there is a housing shortage in this country, it seems to me that Gretford is taking more than its fair share of the housing quota. How many houses do our neighbouring authorities have to build? What challenge have you made as Leader of the Council to this number? Has there been any attempt to reduce the number? Can we appeal?

'I notice that you're fidgeting, Will, but this is a really important issue. There are many of us here who could well face a tough challenge at the next election. Just look at the rise of the Gretford Guardians. Let us not forget that Gretford grows at a slow and steady rate. You're simply telling us that Gretford needs to drastically grow, by potentially twenty to fifty thousand people.'

Having had to suffer the dull tones of Turton, it was with the resignation more often experienced by a condemned prisoner minutes before his execution that the Group had to listen to Simon Newton, who spoke before Foster could respond to Turton.

As Lead Councillor for Housing, the Local Plan was a passion for Newton.

'If I may say, Will, I have some sympathy for what Helen has said,' he said, 'but I think it is vital that we address the real issue which faces not only the district of Gretford, but the south-east and the country as a whole. And that Will, is housing, or the lack thereof, especially the lack of affordable housing.

'I really appreciate that there might be some resistance to the housing figure, but Gretford must accept that it has the responsibility to help meet a housing need.'

'Thank you, Simon,' Foster said as soon as Newton had stopped to draw breath. Newton actually had not finished speaking. Experience, however, had taught Foster the need to stop Newton before he got into full flow of his speech. Otherwise, the away day had the potential of turning into an away weekend.

And Foster was conscious that Overton had only brought enough refreshments for lunch.

'In answer to your questions, Helen, I understand the potential frustration that many of you will be feeling, and believe me when I say that I share your frustration. The Planning Inspectorate calculated the housing target, considering factors such as housing lists, public transport networks and the projected rise of population in the district over the next two decades.

'We can challenge the numbers, and Craig and I will do just that next week when we meet the Secretary of State for Housing.' Foster nodded to Overton, who bowed in supercilious acknowledgment.

'But I should warn you, that whilst we may be able to reduce the number, it will be by a very slight number. In terms of neighbouring authorities, Woking has to take 12,000 over the same period, Guildford 11,000 and Waverley 10,000. So roughly the same as us.'

'But Will,' the octogenarian Councillor Elizabeth Palmer interjected out of genuine passion for her point, rather than reminding the other councillors of her existence. Palmer rarely spoke in meetings, and even then it was usually a repetition of preceding speeches. 'How is Gretford going to cope?' she asked.

It was a question that Foster had been dreading. He deflected the answer. 'In what way?' he asked.

'Our transport network is on its knees. How is Gretford going to cope with all these extra people?' Helen Turton asked, sensing the opportunity to antagonise Foster.

'Craig, would you like to answer?' Foster asked. 'You are the Lead Councillor for Sustainable Projects,' he added.

'Oh, ah, yes, thank you, Will. Uh,' Overton stammered, unexpectedly having to answer. 'Well, we're going to invest, mainly through public grants, heavily in our transport network. Model shift has indicated that people will stop using their cars in favour of public transport in the next couple of years.'

'What the Hell is model shift?' the backbencher Fred Dadswell asked.

'I think I had a model shift this morning,' Swaden said.

'Are you feeling well, Reg?' Palmer asked.

'It's replacing a congested means of transport with another to make the first less congested.'

'Is it a medical condition?' the octogenarian, and rather deaf, Palmer asked. 'I tried a decongestion a while ago. The loss of control I experienced for days afterwards scarred me for life.'

'People will start to use the public transport on offer, which will obviously mean more buses and trains, but also public ferries along the River Ford,' Overton continued.

'Will they have facilities to cope with model shift?' Palmer asked. 'I hope we don't have a pandemic.'

'An improvement and expansion of our existing saturated road network on the outskirts of the town centre will ensure that we realise our ambition of making Gretford "a go-to town" rather than "a go-through town".'

'If there's saturation involved, then I should imagine there'll be plenty of going-through on the way to going-to,' Swaden said.

'It's not a medical condition!' Overton said.

'How are we going to have more buses and trains? And what about the hospital and the schools?' Lady Turton asked.

'We're going to build a new bus station and two new train stations. Each major development will have its own school and we will build cottage hospitals,' Overton answered.

Foster called for calm amongst the growing turmoil.

'I just want to remind you all,' he said, 'that we have to adopt a new

Local Plan. It will enable us to keep control over our planning policy. Otherwise, the Government will force us with every development going until we reach our allotted housing number.'

'But you haven't answered where the houses are going?' Turton said, to a growing murmur of agreement.

'In which case, let us look at the bundles,' Foster answered.

For the next half hour, the Group studied their bundles, three sets of documents of five hundred pages each, which outlined the appalling future which faced the Gretford councillors. Three large developments each of a thousand homes dominated the south, east and west of the district.

An expanded A32 dual carriageway was to dominate the north. In the town centre, pocket developments would spring up wherever there was a gap in car parks, gardens and parks.

Dissent which had started off merely as a quiet murmur erupted into uproar as councillors became the first to see the most major transformation of the district in recent history. Also, it had occurred to many of them that they now faced a very uncertain political future. There was very limited chance that their residents would support a Party which had such little regard for the conservatism of Gretford's past. Even the Conservative Party.

'But Will, you're going to bulldoze and tarmac over my entire ward,' backbencher and rural Councillor Bob Collins said.

'I will not have any green space left in my ward,' Charles Williams, a representative of a town centre ward, said.

'It appears to me, Will, that the town centre should bear the brunt of development and that we should protect the villages. That is why we have the greenbelt,' Lady Turton said.

'Nonsense,' Jeremy Pakeman said. 'There's no room left in the town centre. The road network can't cope as it is.'

The meeting descended into chaos as all pretence of party unity and cohesion disintegrated as that most important need of the politician emerged into the meeting; personal survival. Faced with a document that would all but seal their respective fates at the next local election, the choice between Group unity or saving their own political careers, all 36 Conservative councillors facing Foster and Overton erupted into angry protests.

'Why not build in the town?' competed with 'The town's full, it's time that the villages take their medicine,' was answered by 'Why not build high-rise blocks in the town if there's no room?' was cut off by 'And destroy the important historical nature of the town.'

The only voice to support the number of houses came from Simon Newton, who apart from stating again that Gretford needed the housing, was quickly silenced by his colleagues. Not that anyone was taking notice of him.

Sitting in the eye of this particular political hurricane, Foster and Overton could only answer meekly with the comments that Gretford District Council (like all local authorities) was bound by law to adopt a Local Plan. 'And these are proposals only,' Foster cried above the cacophony of noise directed at him.

'This is a two-year process for us to adopt the Local Plan.'

'You mean that this will be around when we next have to face the electorate?' Fulcher-Wells asked.

Foster ignored her. 'This draft Local Plan will go out to a three-month consultation next Wednesday, which by law we need to do in order to establish that we have followed due process and to avoid a judicial review.'

'You mean to say that the public gets to see this in all its glory?' Turton roared.

It was a rather dishevelled and stressed Foster who left the Group away day three hours later. Lunch had been forgotten amongst the maelstrom which was the Group's reaction to the Local Plan.

Overton had warned him about the likely reaction, but had also reassured him that (most of) the Group would "come on side" once they had studied the Plan and had realised that adoption of it would be the best form of limiting the affects. As councillors, they would have the final say on the Planning Committee as to each of the developments.

Besides, once the acute shortage of skilled labour had been factored in, there was little chance of Gretford reaching the Government's target of 10,740 homes in five decades, let alone two. Overton was confident that once the emotion had started to wear off and cold reason began to take over, the Group would see the advantages of adopting the Plan.

Foster was not quite so confident as he drove for an emergency gin and tonic.

***

Like the rest of Gretford, Councillor Sebastian Woake was totally unaware of the political earthquake that William Foster's Planning department was about to unleash on the district. Unlike Foster, Woake was markedly relaxed, having spent that sunny Saturday afternoon reading his case papers for the week ahead in his town garden.

That evening he bathed before walking down into the town centre to meet friends for dinner.

The following Monday, a Savills "For Sale" sign was erected outside Edgeborough Farm. The reaction in the parish of Edgeborough to this news was nothing compared to the reaction caused as the draft Local Plan was released for public consultation the following Wednesday.

Twenty

June 2016

Oliver Gabriel was one of life's most frustrated young men. He was frustrated by his physical appearance. At 6ft 6", Gabriel was exceedingly tall, but unfortunately his height was not matched by the rest of his physique.

His narrow sloping shoulders ensured that his clothes fell off him like ill-fitting bed linen, whilst his little pot belly had been an unwelcome feature since his late teens. No matter what diet he tried, what exercise he undertook, his paunch had become a permanent fixture by his early twenties.

To hide it, Gabriel had taken to leaning forward whilst walking, so by the time he had reached the age of twenty six, Gabriel was already walking with a premature stoop. But his frustration was not only limited to his physique, Gabriel was also frustrated with his greasy short hair, receding chin and prominent Adam's apple.

As more than one councillor had observed, when Gabriel sat on the dais of the Council Chamber, it was almost as if a turkey was looking down on them from on high.

Which led to his next frustration. Gabriel had always been frustrated that his girlfriends (there were not too many of these) were considerably plainer and fatter than the girlfriends of his friends (and there were not too many of these either).

But his primary frustration had been reserved for his career, or the lack of one.

He had dreamt of becoming a police officer since a young age, attracted to the strict adherence and forced obedience of the public to the law. For Gabriel, rules were rules, and always had to be obeyed.

Everything about Gabriel's education had been chosen by him to further his application to the Metropolitan Police. Gabriel had read a combined degree of psychology, sociology and political science. Armed with a first-class degree and a certainty in his knowledge of the human condition and political theory born by three years of strict adherence to study and little human interaction beyond the lecture theatres and university library, Gabriel applied for the Metropolitan Police's fast-track course.

He failed at the first hurdle; the online psychometric tests. For what was possibly a first in the public sector's reliance on these dubious tools, the test had correctly identified Gabriel's total lack of empathy for the shortcoming of human nature.

And so, he was rejected.

Not to be deterred, Gabriel applied to Sussex Police. Rather than shun his commitment to the rule of law, Sussex Police had allowed Gabriel to enrol as a police cadet.

Whilst disappointed that he would not end his career with the guaranteed rank of superintendent he would have had as a fast-tracker, Gabriel was at least happy that he was finally to become a police officer.

Unfortunately for him, the same could not be said for his instructors.

Having quickly identified that in his zest for justice, Gabriel lacked the qualities vital for any police officer; an understanding of and sympathy for the frailty of humanity.

Realising that Gabriel was more of a danger to the otherwise innocent Sussex public rather than the Sussex criminals, the instructors had failed him, albeit with the encouraging proviso that he could reapply once he had gained more life experience.

Frustrated that his dream had, at least for the time being, been shattered, Gabriel had found a job working for the only other public sector employer which would welcome his strict adherence to rules in Sussex; Gretford District Council.

Gabriel became the Planning Committee Secretary, which at least allowed his somewhat limited personality the chance to flourish in a strict environment.

As Committee Secretary, Gabriel was responsible for organising the committee's agenda, liaising with applicants, their opponents and their agents, organising site visits and ensuring that every meeting was correctly recorded. Never before had the committee's minutes ever been so detailed, or so long. A fact Gabriel prided himself on.

However, no matter how efficient a Committee Secretary he had become, Gabriel was forever frustrated that he had never fulfilled his dream.

Which led to his latest frustration, that he had to serve the latest crop of councillors.

As far as Gabriel was concerned, many of the councillors were nothing more than background noise, a voice for the people of Gretford but one which would ultimately agree with the officers' original decisions, which was always the correct decision.

What annoyed Gabriel was that he now had to serve two councillors of similar age to him. Despite being a second-term councillor, Craig Overton had never previously served on the Planning Committee, which also counted Sebastian Woake as a member.

What frustrated Gabriel was how Overton and Woake epitomised everything that he envied and highlighted his own shortcomings. Despite knowing that Overton had attended the local comprehensive (a fact he knew as he was two years below Overton at school), he envied Overton's bearing and his ability to better himself.

On the other hand, Gabriel hated Woake's cool arrogance, how his suit jacket hung perfectly from his shoulders, whilst the collarless tunic shirt underneath not only betrayed Woake's passion for fine tailoring, but also Woake's cavalier attitude.

All the while, Gabriel's own suit would hang limply from his shoulders above a shirt valiantly trying its best above his thin shoulders and tight paunch.

His frustration was further enhanced by Woake's impeccable manners towards him at the start and end of every meeting.

What Gabriel lacked was the wit and intellect to understand that Overton's bearing was born out of snobbish arrogance, while Woake's demeanour was actually the cool confidence of a man totally at ease with himself, and who cared little for someone's schooling.

However, Gabriel's frustration had recently been abated by the news that the Council had launched the JETs and was recruiting immediately.

Lacking the resources, time and commitment to properly screen applicants, the Council was impressed by Gabriel and recommended him to undertake JET training. Gabriel had thrived through the month-long training and whereas his three fellow recruits looked upon him with scepticism (they were all retired police officers supplementing their pensions), Gabriel had become the darling of the course and had found himself standing next to Mark Skelding and Peter West for the launch photograph.

Dressed in a new uniform, with a peak cap and radio on his chest and a high-visibility vest across his narrow shoulders, the photograph was the proudest moment of his life. He may not yet be a police officer, but he had become the closest thing to one and he was confident that he could re-apply to Sussex Police within a couple of years.

One of his fellow recruits had even told him so as the photograph was being taken.

Gabriel stood in front of his van. Whilst it was not a police car, the van was still decorated with the JETs' cap badge, and the words "Gretford Law Enforcement" were stencilled on both sides. It was a shame that there was a sign on the rear door stating that the van's speed was limited to 54 miles per hour, but that did not matter, as the van was his and no one else's.

For the first time in several years, Gabriel was feeling a lot less frustrated.

It took only a few weeks for Gabriel to establish himself as a legend within the JETs and a menace to the Gretford public. Whether it was dealing with fly-tipping, littering, encouraging mothers to move their cars along during school drop-off and collection, or asking the homeless to move into another part of town, Gabriel had earned the reputation as a most efficient operator. Indeed, the income generated from his fines alone supported Councillor Skelding's assertion that JETs would become a valuable investment for the district.

It came as a pleasant surprise to Gabriel that there were not the same level of safeguards applicable to the JETs as there were to the police. Not because they did not exist, but because GDC lacked the staff with sufficient understanding to make sure that they were adhered to.

There was also a hope that each JET officer would be able to display some judgement. In three out of the four officers, this was the case, being former police officers. Unfortunately for the district,

Gabriel's lack of judgement was matched only by his zest for public duty.

Dog walkers were a particular favourite for Gabriel, who patrolled the council-owned parks and countryside with a venom which left innocent dog walkers skulking behind bushes by his very presence.

Dog walkers not clearing up after their dogs were his particular forte.

'But we're in the middle of the countryside,' one flustered dog owner had said when Gabriel had started writing out her fine. She was walking her dog in council-owned woods. There were no other dog walkers.

'That doesn't matter, madam,' Gabriel had responded. 'This is still local authority-owned land, and as such you have to clear up after your animal as per the Anti-social Behaviour, Crime and Policing Act of 2014.'

'But if we were in a park, or on a street, or next to a children's play area, then I would understand. But we're on a bridleway in the middle of the countryside.'

'Exactly madam. You accept your dog has fouled council land, and you have failed to clear it. Do you have any idea the disgusting health implications of dog faeces?' Gabriel asked, handing her the fine.

'Only if someone is stupid enough to pick it up and smear it over their face and eyes.'

'It can cause a public nuisance if someone walks in it.'

'Not as much as a nuisance if they stand in that horse shit over there,' she said, pointing at a recent deposit of horse manure. 'Foxes, horses and other wildlife can shit and crap all over the bridleway, but you're fining me for something which will wash away in a couple of days. Did you fine that owner of that horse?'

'I would have done had I seen it.'

'So horse riders need to bring shovels with them now?'

'I am not here to answer your questions, madam. And I should warn you not to swear. I can further fine you for outraging public decency.'

'But no one else is here,' she protested.

'That doesn't matter. We're in public and I'm a member of the public and I have to say I'm finding your attitude most unacceptable.'

'Oh fuck off,' she said, walking off with her Highland terrier.

A moment of particular pride was when he pulled over a white-van driver.

It was a matter of some indecision for Gabriel as to whether he should wear his peak cap as he walked towards the van. Should he wear it and appear more authoritarian, or should he carry it under his arm and be less formal? He chose the more authoritarian approach.

He approached the driver's window, which remained firmly up. He motioned for the driver to lower the window.

'Who are you?' the driver asked, too aggressively for Gabriel's sensitivities.

'Sir, I am a member of the Gretford Joint Enforcement Team and...'

'What the fuck is that?' the driver asked, interrupting. Gabriel ignored the question.

'I noticed that you littered the public highway.'

'What was I supposed to have done?' the driver asked.

'I was driving behind you and approximately two minutes ago observed that you lowered your window, extended a hand and threw litter out of your van,' Gabriel answered as he removed his pad from his belt and wrote a fine.

'Did I fuck!' the driver said. 'It was an orange peel, you bloody idiot. 'ere's the orange,' he added, holding out an orange slice.

'What it was is immaterial, it is still litter and as a result...'

'It bloody well is, mate, that peel will degrade over time, so it can't be litter.'

'What it is does not matter. It is the fact that you attempted to throw away rubbish illegally. Hence, you were littering.' Gabriel handed him the fine. 'That will be £90 unless you decide to pay within fourteen days of today's date. In which case the fine is only £45,' he said as he walked back to his van.

It was mid-morning and Gabriel was driving through the village of Rowbarthon, responding to a reported breach of public decency.

The alleged breach had been reported by a seventy-six-year-old woman, who had recently moved into Rowbarthon, and was said to have been committed at a shed dealership. Gabriel drove towards The Shed Palace.

The Shed Palace covered four acres of land and was devoted to garden sheds from different shapes and sizes, storerooms, workshops, offices and a car park. Gabriel found the dealership easily, the row of sheds along the main road provided him with an indication that he had reached his destination.

'Bloody disgusting,' he said to himself as he drove past the offending article.

He parked in the car park and checked his uniform in his van window. He had worn his peak cap, hoping that the additional formality would enhance his authority. He was already perspiring under the hot summer sun.

Gabriel started walking towards the sales office. He walked past a squat, heavily muscled bald man in his late fifties, with a beer belly and darkened skin, wearing a tight black t-shirt and cycling shorts.

The man was talking loudly on his mobile phone. 'What the fuck is Duncan doing at that job in Oxshott? I did everyone's diary yesterday and deliberately put him with the other team in Esher. Why the fuck would I have three guys put up that six by four and only have you put up that ten by six for that pain in the arse American?' The man looked suspiciously at Gabriel as he walked past.

Gabriel made a mental note to have a word with the man when he had finished his business at The Shed Palace.

He walked into the sales office, an airy converted cabin with two desks. The office was empty, save for a sales assistant, who was a woman of indeterminate age who, owing to a sizeable amount of Botox, could have been anywhere between fifty-five and seventy years old.

Her worn fizzy hair indicated towards the upper end of the range, but her impressive cleavage (the result of medical assistance) hinted at the lower end. The work of a surgeon more interested in the value of his invoice rather than the value of any aesthetic beauty, it was to Gabriel's alarm that the final product was very much on display due to a low-cut, tight-fitting vest.

A name tag with the name "Lisa" was pinned onto her firm left breast.

She looked up as Gabriel approached, who tried to keep his eyes fixed firmly on her eyes rather than her breasts. He failed.

'Hello officer, how can I help you?' Whether it was because she referred to him as officer (not a regular occurrence for him), her breasts or her offer of assistance, Gabriel would never know whether it contributed to an unfortunate choice of words.

'I'm here about the free erections,' he said.

Not sure how to respond to a long-limbed beanpole in a cheap replication of a police officer's uniform, staring at her cleavage, a startled Lisa mumbled a response. 'Are you?' was all she could ask.

'Yes, you're advertising free erections,' Gabriel said. Lisa realised immediately what Gabriel was referring to, but she was not prepared to let him off the hook just yet.

'It's been a long time since I had to advertise for it,' Lisa responded. 'Besides, I've never been one whoever needed to be paid for it, or indeed pay for it.'

'We have received complaints,' Gabriel continued.

'Had no complaints in the past, most people seem only too pleased to get one up for free.'

'The complaint has come from a woman,' Gabriel added.

'Doesn't surprise me,' Lisa said. 'A lot of men seem to think it's very clever, but they don't tend to be the ones who have to face it, are they?'

'I can tell you I don't think it's very clever,' Gabriel said.

'No, I wouldn't think you do. It's not much fun being woken up at night to face a mounting problem, especially as you get older.'

'You get them up at night?' Gabriel asked.

'Primarily that's when it happens, but you can do it during the day. Though it's never quite so easy as it seems, and usually takes some effort.'

'If you go around the country getting them up at night, it's a wonder that your customers' neighbours haven't complained.'

'Some neighbours might like it,' Lisa said.

'The noise alone would be a public nuisance. There's laws against it you know?'

'No one's ever told me,' Lisa responded.

'So, are you going to remove the offending article?' Gabriel asked.

'Suppose we have to in the circumstances.'

They were interrupted by the man who Gabriel had seen talking on his mobile phone, who stormed into the office and took a seat next to Lisa, all the while showing a total lack of respect towards Gabriel by ignoring him.

'Just been on the phone to Seth,' the man said, talking to Lisa.

'Turns out that fucking idiot Craig took Duncan and Gary with him to Oxshott. That's after I spent most of yesterday afternoon sorting out the team rotas for today. Which means that Seth is on his own in Esher. So we've got one team that has already finished all its work for today, and the other one won't be finished until tonight. I've got the fucking hump, Lees.' The man turned to Gabriel. 'What does he want?' he asked.

'He apparently wants a free erection.'

'What are you talking about?' the man asked. Gabriel decided that the time had come for him to re-establish control.

'I am from Gretford District Council, and I am a member of JETs. We have received complaints from members of the public concerning the large banner you have displayed offering free erections.'

'What about it?'

'The banner you have displayed outside your showroom which reads,' Gabriel consulted his notebook '"Free Erections" has received complaints from people insulted by its vulgarity and has been judged to be in breach of public decency.'

'By who?' the man asked.

'By me. And as a result, I am hereby ordering you to remove it,' Gabriel said as he handed the man a copy of the enforcement action.

'But the banner has been up since 1998 and nobody has ever given a fuck about it before now,' the man said aggressively.

'That doesn't matter,' Gabriel responded, feeling somewhat threatened. 'Somebody has now. You have twenty-eight days to remove the offending item or you will face enforcement proceedings from the Council. You can appeal this decision, but you will find that to be costly. I will make a further inspection in twenty-eight days' time and I expect to see the banner removed.'

Gabriel had been edging nervously towards the door whilst delivering the enforcement action. His action now concluded, Gabriel left the office, his previous confidence in tackling the man's aggressiveness having now evaporated. It was with relief that he found himself safely locked in his van, and not the type of relief he would have wanted, having met Lisa that morning.

The following day, a rather innocent banner which had only received one complaint in twenty years of existence, but which provided light amusement to motorists in an otherwise dreary drive, was removed.

It was a victory for oversensitivity, and Gabriel's lack of judgement.

Robbie Cole was another man who took his job extremely seriously. Unlike Oliver Gabriel, Cole actually provided the people of Gretford with a service.

Cole worked at Gretford Crematorium and his job was perhaps the most vital one in the entire operation; Cole was the technician responsible for operating the crematorium's two cremators.

In other words, he was responsible for the burning of the coffins.

A little man, Cole barely stood at 5ft. Unfortunately for him, the doors into the two cremators and their respective control panels stood at 6ft. To negate this problem, Cole made use of an upside-down beer crate when operating the controls. A further problem for Cole was that he was also dwarfed by the coffins when they lay on their gurneys.

To operate a cremator, he would have to stand on his crate, open the door, step off the crate, walk to the side of the gurney, step back onto the crate, slide it towards the open door, slide the coffin in, pull the gurney back, then close the door whilst standing on the crate, step down, move to the side, then operate the control panel whilst standing on the crate.

Cole had worked at Gretford Crematorium for thirty years.

On her first day as the new manager, Angelina Burbridge had made a surprise visit to the cremator, and had been shocked to observe a coffin appear to make its final journey by its own will. Her feeling of amazement was further enhanced by seeing the other two gurneys move, seemingly without the help of man.

Burbridge had promptly fainted at the sight of the Hand of God at work in Gretford.

A woman of some faith beforehand, she had been a devout Christian ever since.

Cole was a man who prided himself on his work. He kept the machines polished and gleaming, the gas line to the ignitors secure, the quantity of water in the coolants to the correct level and ensured that he maintained the machines to the safety level every two months, as required by law.

Cole would only ever take a holiday when it was guaranteed that the crematorium had secured the temporary services of a technician with as much pride as him.

Just as importantly, Cole prided himself on ensuring that he collected as much of the remains after each burning as he could. Not for him any cross-contamination of remains in the urns. The relatives deserved to get their relatives back, and that was what he always tried to achieve.

Yes, there might be a backlog of coffins waiting to be burnt. But the relatives did not need to know that. Whoever wanted the urn immediately after the funeral?

Used to the cremators being his own private sanctuary, Cole had occasionally made it bad practice to leave the results of the day's work within easy reach for the following morning.

It was unfortunate that nobody had bothered to warn him of the councillors' tour. A lowly technician (in more ways than one), he had been overlooked by the managerial staff.

For the oversight of leaving a crate full of Mrs Duckworth's remains on full display, Cole had been reprimanded.

The four months since the councillors' visit had been amongst the most stressful of his life.

Firstly, he had been told that a councillor had reminded Burbridge that it was illegal to store mortal remains in such a way. Secondly, the whole crematorium had come under even more pressure to conduct more services in order to generate more income.

This meant more coffins for him to process and Cole was processing coffins solidly for twelve hours a day, six days a week.

Unfortunately, the ageing machinery could not even begin to keep up with the growing demand. It had forced Cole to reduce the operating temperature of both cremators, making them even less efficient than before. Instead of pumping out brown smoke from the chimney, the cremators started to give out a grey-coloured smoke as it mixed with several elements which should ideally have remained in the urn.

The increased demand in usage exacerbated yet another problem. The coolant system, which struggled under the former demand, now began to show signs of genuine alarm.

Luciana Green's coffin was fifteen minutes into its ninety-minute cycle when Cole first realised that something was going wrong.

He had recently collected the latest coffin from the chapel when the alarm for cremator 2 sounded. Rushing from the gurney, he collected his crate as he ran to the control panel. A loud alarm was ringing in his ear.

The cremator shook as smoke escaped from the door. With a growing sense of foreboding that the crematorium's alarm system would soon kick in, he reached up to the control panel and saw that the temperature warning light had turned red.

Faced with the impending disaster of an exploding cremator, Cole realised that the only thing he could do was to abort.

A large booming noise sounded from inside the cremator, and with the alarm ringing in his ear, Cole slapped the emergency override bottom.

Peace was restored almost immediately as the fire inside the cremator was extinguished. The alarm fell silent, and the vibrations stopped. Cole collapsed to the ground.

In the chapel, the mourners (who were halfway through O God, Our Help in Ages Past) were blissfully unaware of the fate which had recently fallen on another dearly departed's coffin. Nor were they aware of a large bang from within the bowels of the crematorium, closely followed by a large plume of ash escaping from the chimney.

It was only when the ashes had sufficiently cooled did Cole realise that for a sixteen-stone woman, Luciana Green had left surprisingly few ashes.

Twenty One

It was a warm sunny Friday afternoon as Debbie MacGahey pushed her daughter's pushchair along the River Ford beside Fordhouse Lock. Debbie and Emma had gone shopping on Gretford high street and she had decided that lunch would be a picnic along the riverbank.

About twenty other mothers and their children were also picnicking beside the Ford.

Debbie picked Emma out of the pushchair and she quickly rushed off to play with the other children. Debbie unrolled a blanket that she had packed specially for the picnic and unpacked their lunch.

Debbie attempted to talk to her two-year-old daughter, who was more interested in the ducks which had waddled up from the river towards them.

Finally accepting that her daughter would not talk, Debbie began to carefully collect their waste, which had accumulated on the blanket and packed it all into a plastic bag.

Debbie hated litterers.

Keeping an eye on her daughter, Debbie knelt beside the pushchair and took out an old baguette from her bag. 'Emma, baby, would you like to feed the ducks?' she asked.

Emma turned round to face her mother, her face breaking out into a wide grin which betrayed her enthusiasm.

'Yes please, mummy,' she answered.

'Come on, then. But you can only do so if you promise to hold my hand.' Emma offered her hand immediately.

'Don't worry, don't be shy,' she reassured her daughter. 'Here, take some bread, break a small piece off and throw it just in front of each one.' Emma did as she was directed, diligently making sure that every duck received its share of the baguette.

After a minute, the number of ducks had swelled to about a dozen.

'Excuse me, may I please ask you to refrain from feeding the ducks,' a male voice asked behind her. Debbie turned around, startled. So enraptured was Debbie that she failed to notice that a tall, thin young man dressed in what appeared to be a policeman's uniform had joined her.

'Pardon me?' she asked.

'Is that your daughter, madam?' Gabriel asked.

'What does it matter to you?' Debbie responded.

'It matters to me, madam, because you are encouraging her to litter and I have to ask you to stop.'

'But she's feeding the ducks,' Debbie said.

'Actually madam, she is throwing food waste onto the ground, which counts as littering.'

'But the ducks are eating the food.'

'That doesn't matter, madam. Besides, bread is very damaging for the duck's stomachs. It's the starch. Will you please ask her to refrain from doing so?'

'But she's enjoying herself.'

'Are you saying that you are refusing a request to stop your daughter from littering?'

'Who's that strange man, mummy?' Emma called.

'I am a JET,' Gabriel answered, reaching for his notebook. 'That stands for Joint Enforcement Team and I am part of Gretford Law Enforcement.' He started writing Debbie a fine.

'What are you doing?' Debbie asked.

'I am writing you a fine for littering, madam. You have been asked three times to stop littering and have refused to do so. May I please have your name and address? Failure to provide your correct personal details to me is a criminal charge and could make you liable to prosecution.'

Reluctantly, Debbie did so. 'Emma, baby, please stop feeding the ducks.'

'But I want to, mummy,' Emma responded.

'I know, but you're not allowed to,' Debbie responded.

'But you said I could,' Emma argued.

'I know, but this man has said we cannot,' Debbie pleaded. 'What about those children over there?' Debbie asked Gabriel.

'All in good time, madam. I will deal with their mothers presently. Your daughter is still littering.'

'Emma, I have told you to stop doing that,' Debbie said, voice raising in anger.

Emma continued to throw the bread onto the ground, ignoring her mother with all the stubbornness of a toddler. Debbie walked towards her and snatched the bread from Emma's hands, hating herself for the public show of anger which was not directed to her daughter but to the embodiment of local law enforcement determined to make any innocent pastime a criminal activity.

Emma burst into tears, wailing as her mother picked her up.

The other mothers watched as Debbie placed Emma back into the pushchair, rolled up her blanket and walked off, a perfect lunch ruined.

Gabriel stopped her.

'Don't forget your fine,' he said before moving onto the other children. Within half an hour, all the mothers had been scared into stopping their children from playing, feeding the ducks and having a picnic.

The mothers collected their children and left. The area around Fordhouse Lock lay in perfect silence, save for the sound of the hungry ducks quacking as they returned to the river.

Woake was sitting in Gretford Côte Brasserie, his back to the rear wall as he watched the front door. It was seven thirty that Friday evening and he had been at the restaurant since seven o'clock.

The restaurant was packed, full of couples from their twenties through to their seventies and large groups of friends enjoying the start to the weekend.

Woake was the only diner currently on his own, a half-drunk French lager in front of him. He was due to meet Serena Kildare for dinner, having arranged to meet in order to discuss the financial support for Inspire to Aspire.

Woake had arrived on time, but Kildare had sent him a text message a couple of minutes later explaining that she was running late.

Woake was just about to pay for his drink and leave when the door was flung open and Kildare entered the restaurant like a blonde hurricane. She immediately noticed Woake sitting on his own and left a trail of bemused waiters behind her as she walked straight towards him.

Woake stood up as she approached the table.

'I am so sorry I am late,' she said as she dropped her handbag by the side of the chair.

'No need to apologise,' Woake answered, smiling. Despite being irritated, it was impossible to argue with how gorgeous she looked in a close-fitting summer dress.

'I had only just got here when you messaged me,' he added.

'Liar,' Kildare replied. A waiter approached the table with a menu for Kildare. They ordered drinks; a gin and tonic for Kildare ('with no ice but lots and lots of fruit') and another beer for Woake.

'You know you're getting a reputation,' Kildare said as the waiter left.

'In what way?'

'In that the Cabinet thought they could control you when they promoted you. They never realised that you would actually do something quite so stunning as to try to control Council spending.'

'What were they expecting? As we all know, we don't have any money. What we do have are buildings which are supposed to be providing us with an income which are actually falling down, funding cuts from central Government, greater pressure to provide more public services, not to mention the fact that we can't do anything particularly useful like raise council tax or business rates because that could be politically damaging.'

'Wow, you really are taking this seriously, aren't you?' Kildare fell silent as the waiter appeared with their drinks. He placed a glass containing a measure of gin and a bottle of Fever Tree tonic water in front of Kildare. A rainforest of fruit from oranges to lemon, cherries and cucumber filled the glass.

The waiter began to pour Woake his beer until Woake asked him to stop. They ordered their food, calamari followed by seabass for Kildare, duck liver parfait and steak for Woake. Kildare raised an eyebrow quizzically as the waiter left.

'It annoys me in a restaurant how the waiters never tip the glass when pouring beer,' Woake said. 'It ensures that you have more head and less drink in your glass, so you therefore need to buy another one.'

Woake leant forward and picked up Kildare's tonic water. He stared at her as she picked up her gin glass and squashed the fruit with her straw.

She looked up as she realised his gaze. 'What?' she asked with an embarrassing smile. 'I'm sorry,' she added, blushing. 'I'm very strange, I like to make sure that the drink has as much fruit in it as possible.'

'Don't be,' Woake added, smiling. He poured the tonic water into her glass.

'Thank you,' Kildare said. She leant forward, breaking into a mischievous grin. 'So what did you tell her to make her cry?'

'Tell who?' Woake asked.

'You know full well, Sebastian.' Her voice broke into a high-pitched squeal. 'The Lead Councillor for Culture, Heritage and general sponging.'

'Oh, her!' Woake laughed. 'Just told her we're selling a dilapidated farm in the arse end of nowhere. Apparently, some old dinosaur of an archaeologist said years ago that some king might have ridden past back in 28BC and as a result we need to save it.' Woake fell silent for a moment. 'Did you say she cried?' he asked.

'So the rumours say,' Kildare answered. She leant further forward, voice quietened down. 'Louise the PA told me she was working late last Friday and had to put some papers in Peter's room for a Monday morning meeting. Allegedly she saw Peter embracing Cathy, who was in floods of tears.' She took a sip of her drink. She leant backwards into her chair. 'So well done on that one, always good to see her suffer.'

'You're not a fan of hers then?' Woake asked.

'Ghastly woman,' Kildare said, looking away. 'But you should be careful, you're not making many friends on the Cabinet,' she said as their starters arrived. She squeezed as much lemon as she could over her calamari. 'I think we have already established how much I love fruit,' she said, smiling.

'I didn't realise that I had to make friends with that lot,' Woake answered.

'But you need friends in the Party if you want to become an MP.'

'But I don't want to become an MP,' Woake said hurriedly.

'Then why are you doing this?' Kildare asked.

'It seemed like a good way to annoy my former mother-in-law,' he answered.

'You're kidding?'

'Wish I was. I filled out the application forms following a drunken argument and unfortunately my campaign gathered more momentum than I initially planned.'

'So why did you put so much work into it?'

'I'm very competitive.'

'Even when it's making a point to someone who no longer means anything?' Kildare asked. Woake did not answer, accepting the truth to something which he was too emotionally blind to see at the time. 'The best thing to do,' Kildare continued, 'is to spout policy which is so at odds with your electorate that they can't help but argue with you. That way, they hate you so much that the only thing they remember about you is not to vote for you.'

They ate in silence for a few seconds.

'And then you got your reputation for an inability to take anything seriously. Insult the gay community, insult a delegation from an important organisation, had fun at the tour of the crem.'

'I didn't insult the gay community, I merely questioned the phrase "questioning" which is apparently enough to brand you a homophobe.'

'Bet you enjoyed the equality and diversity training session.'

'Yes, I sat there for an hour and a half in mild amusement as this fat, ugly woman of questionable sexuality spoke to me in a language that I couldn't possibly understand. She said that I had finished our session and I would become woke. She couldn't understand the irony of that remark.'

'There's a reason that particular woman was chosen,' Kildare said.

'And that is?' Woake asked.

'Because Gallagher knew you were more likely to listen to a fat ugly woman than a pretty young one.'

'But I'm listening to you,' Woake said.

'Quite. But are you seriously telling me that had the tutor looked like me, you would have listened to her rather than lech?'

Woake remained silent.

'The reality is Sebastian, is that as a man you have no idea how difficult it is for an attractive woman to be taken seriously and gain the respect of her male colleagues. There is a reason successful female politicians tend to be ugly.'

'And that is?' Woake asked.

'Plainer and uglier women are more likely to be accepted by men. The reason being that they don't want to sleep with them. With prettier female colleagues, men tend, whether subconsciously or not, to want to sleep with them. If they succeed, the interests of the women are usually ignored. If they fail, then the men will do their best to prevent whatever it is the women want to achieve.'

'Bollocks they do.'

'Of course it's true. Contrary to whatever you might think, I actually haven't slept with any other councillor.'

'Despite coming to dinner dressed like that,' Woake commented.

'Actually, you're one of the better ones,' Kildare said. 'Unlike most of the other men, you look into my eyes.'

'Beautiful eyes.'

'Whereas most other councillors are too interested in my breasts.'

'Dressed like that, I'm not surprised.'

'Which is a vicious circle. I dress like this precisely in order to get what I want. As long as he can look down my top, Foster is pathetic enough to give me what I want.'

'On the basis you're dressed like that, what do you want from me?'

'Later.'

'Got my attention.'

'Not like that.'

'So according to you, all Cathy had to do was have a facelift, a nose job and breast enhancement, and I would have given her what she wanted?'

'No, I don't believe that would have worked. Anyway, according to rumour, you've become much more serious,' she smirked as their plates were removed.

'Would you like another drink?' Woake asked. He ordered her a sparkling water and a large glass of Cabernet Sauvignon for himself.

'What made you more serious?' Kildare asked.

'Christ, what's with all the questions?' Woake asked, shuffling uncomfortably in his chair.

'I'm sorry. Am I making you feel uncomfortable?' she asked. Woake remained silent. 'I'm sorry, just remember that you're making enemies on the Cabinet. By calling an end to many of our vanity projects, you've done your best to derail many of their careers. Will is desperate to remain Leader, Craig wants to become an MP, and Skelding wants to replace Will.'

'I couldn't care about any of that. They asked me to do a job, and I'll do it, even if it makes me unpopular.'

Their main courses arrived. Woake continued to speak as they ate. 'Look, I'm sorry for snapping at you,' he said. 'My experiences in the army ensured that it's very difficult to take any of this seriously. The pathetic nature of the backstabbing, the briefings, and the games they play. I see Overton and hate his naked ambition. Apart from working for the family company, what's he actually done to make him a worthy MP, except for arse-licking the local Party?'

'I heard you were in the army,' Kildare said.

'I was in for three and a half years. I joined Sandhurst straight out of school.'

'Which regiment?'

'I was a para.'

'Where did you serve?'

'Here and there.'

'Really?' Kildare asked, breaking into a mischievous grin. 'Bet you've got a couple of great war stories.'

Woake remained perfectly serious. 'A couple,' he eventually answered.

'I'm sorry, that was an idiotic thing to have said,' Kildare said. 'But you don't understand, do you? It's precisely the arse-licking which means that he will eventually become an MP.'

'And you?' Woake asked. 'What do you want to achieve politically?'

'Oh, I just want a seat in the House of Lords.' She picked at her food. 'So you are taking this more seriously?'

'The service we provide, yes. The people? No.'

'So you actually want to make a difference to some people in Gretford?'

'Depends, but generally, yes. If I can, I will, which is why I want to cut spending and bring the finances under control.'

'But you accept there's more to life than pounds, shilling and pence?'

'You should become a barrister, you're very good at asking leading questions and getting people to reluctantly answer.'

'I'm a doctor, it's our job to ask questions. Do you?'

'Do I what?'

'Do you want to make a difference?'

'What do you want?' Woake asked.

'I'm setting up a new initiative for the worst parts of Gretford. The wards of Burcombe and Rockbourne, which are some of the most deprived areas in the south-east. The problem is that the children who are born and brought up in these areas are taught not to have any aspiration from their school or from their families. That a life on benefits is the sum total of what they can achieve. Because many of them leave school with no qualifications, they find even finding the most menial job difficult to get.

'So they end up committing crime. My ambition is to change that. I'm setting up a project, called Inspire to Aspire, which will sponsor teenagers through apprenticeships, provide them with support to help them find work and improve their CVs. I've spoken to local employers and they're on board with my vision. But the problem is Sebastian, I need money to make all this happen.'

'What will the money be used for?' Woake asked.

'Advertising, tutors, venue hire and senior officer's time at Fordhouse.'

'How much?'

'250,' Kildare answered.

'250,' Woake said, raising an eyebrow. 'Total bargain, the money's yours.'

Kildare smiled. 'You know full well that I meant £250,000.' She leant down into her handbag and pulled out a file. 'Knowing that you're a barrister, I realise you like to read. So I had this prepared for you.' She handed him the file. 'It's a report into Inspire to Aspire. Please look at it and get back to me.'

'Of course.' Woake placed the file beside him on the table. They finished their meal, and the waiter removed the plates. He returned a couple of minutes later with the dessert menu. Woake placed his on the table, ignoring it. Kildare studied hers intently. 'I think I'll have the crème brûlée,' she said as she looked up and saw Woake looking at her. 'You're not having one?' she asked, looking alarmed.

'I'm not a pudding person,' he replied. 'But you have one.'

'I'm not going to have one on my own,' Kildare protested.

'Don't worry, I'll have another glass of wine.' He could see that she still wanted one, but would not eat alone. 'OK, fine,' Woake said smiling. 'I'll share one with you.'

'No way,' Kildare answered. 'I will not share my pudding with you.'

'Why not?'

'People would think we're on a date.'

'Everyone round here thinks we're on a date, anyway.'

'We might be seen,' Kildare said.

'By whom? Nobody outside Fordhouse knows who we are, and most of the officers don't know who we are either.'

'We're colleagues. It's inappropriate.'

The waiter came back.

'Can I tempt you to any dessert?' he asked.

'Yes, may we please have the crème brûlée to share? And I would also like another glass of wine, please. Councillor Kildare, would you like another drink?'

Kildare glared at him. 'Sparkling water.'

'And a glass of sparkling water, please. May I ask for no ice but plenty of fruit in it as well?' Woake said to the waiter.

'Hilarious,' Kildare said after the waiter had gone.

'Just demonstrating that nobody outside the confines of the Council knows who we are.'

The waiter returned with their drinks.

'There's one more thing you need to know,' Kildare told Woake.

'Oh yes?' Woake asked.

'This is serious.'

'Yes, of course it is.'

Kildare ignored him. 'You should know that there's a battle at the moment between the Cabinet and the officers. Will is trying to assert his influence and is failing to establish his leadership. The officers, if not actively ignoring him and Craig, are at the very least briefing against them and trying to follow their own agenda.'

'I've often wondered at that phrase "actively ignoring". How can you actively ignore something? Surely it should be "passively" ignoring something? It's a bit like that awful expression "so-called" as in "so-called Islamic State". If an organisation is called something, that is its name. We didn't fight the War against the "so-called" Nazi Party.'

Their dessert arrived with two spoons. Kildare started eating her half, Woake picked at his.

'Well anyway,' Kildare said, ignoring Woake. 'The point is, is that by suspending their vanity projects you are denying the leadership a chance to assert their authority and playing straight into the hands of the officers. Will you please be more careful in future?'

'Did either Foster or Overton ask you to say this?'

'No, I'm saying it as a friend.'

'Oh, we're friends now, are we? I thought we were colleagues.'

'Ha ha,' Kildare said slowly. 'What would your woke tutor think of you sharing a dessert with a colleague?'

'Would probably have a meltdown into her syrup-infused mocha coffee she's drinking with her group of equally sexually frustrated female friends.'

They finished the dessert. Woake had barely eaten a quarter of it.

'You weren't kidding, were you?' Kildare asked. 'You're really not a dessert person. It's a bit like not going to the Group away day. That just looked really petulant.'

'It's nobody's damn business how I spend my weekends, and I had already told that little twerp I couldn't make it.'

They got the bill.

'I'll pay my half,' Kildare said, leaning down towards her handbag. Woake had already placed a credit card on the table. 'No need,' he said.

'But this isn't a date,' she said, sitting straight up again.

'Of course it isn't,' Woake answered.

'It isn't,' Kildare persisted.

'I know that.' Woake paid, giving the staff a generous tip; he thought they had earned it with the amount of fruit Kildare had consumed.

Woake held the door open for Kildare as they left the restaurant.

'Where are you parked?' he asked.

'On the high street.'

'I'll walk you to your car.'

'You don't have to,' she said, despite walking in step next to him. She slipped her arm through his.

'Now we're definitely not just colleagues,' he said.

'Oh, I'm sorry. Don't you want me to put my arm around yours?' Woake smiled. 'I'm actually a very tactile person,' Kildare continued, 'which can occasionally be misinterpreted as flirting. I'm sorry about all the lectures.'

'No need to apologise.' They reached Kildare's car, a red-coloured Jaguar F-Pace.

'Thank you very much for agreeing to look into Inspire to Aspire for me,' she said as she opened the door. 'And thank you for dinner.'

'My pleasure. I would say that we should do it again, but I was told by the equality instructor that that can be construed as harassment in the workplace.'

Kildare smiled. 'Don't forget, I'm a happily married woman.'

'Of course you are.'

'Why do you say that?' Kildare asked, looking alarmed.

'No wedding ring.'

'I've been operating all day.'

'No one has seen your husband at any official events where other partners are involved.'

'He's away with work a lot.'

'You've rather spent a Friday night with me.'

'I'm at work.'

'You haven't mentioned him once.'

Kildare got in the car. 'See you at Full Council on Tuesday night.'

'See you on Tuesday night.' He closed the car door for her and watched as she drove off. He walked back up Gretford high street towards home.

Twenty Two

Another political meeting was taking place about five hundred metres from where Woake and Kildare had dined.

The main auditorium of Gretford Baptist Church was already packed full of town centre residents. It became standing room only, yet still more people were filing in.

Martin St John looked on in pride at the meeting that he had organised.

St John (a retired accountant) was chairman of the Wellington Residents Association, which according to its constitution was to represent the views of those who lived in the town centre ward of Wellington. In practice, the Association (like all resident groups and Parish Councils) represented the views of its committee.

St John had convened the meeting in response to the publication of the draft Local Plan and the impending Council vote on whether to submit it for public consultation.

Along with the other town centre association chairmen, St John had received his own copy of the draft and had sat appalled as he read the proposals for the town centre.

In response, he had contacted the chairmen of the other town centre associations and had organised the meeting, intending to form a new pressure group with the aim of representing the town.

If the countryside had the Gretford Guardians, then why should the town centre not have its own protectors?

It was with a growing sense of satisfaction that St John noticed several town centre councillors from all parties were present. He smiled as he saw Charles Williams and Jeremy Pakeman, his own councillors, sitting towards the back.

St John was sitting at a table on the stage, facing the auditorium. He was surrounded by the five other chairmen, representing St Joseph's, Rockbourne, Westdistrict, Ferndown and Whittom.

Behind the chairmen a large drop-down screen had been hung, ready for the PowerPoint presentation.

With five minutes to go, the queue for the auditorium quietened down.

At the stroke of seven o'clock, St John opened the meeting. He switched on his microphone and addressed the meeting, which numbered at least five hundred people.

'Good evening and thank you all for coming this evening. I have called this meeting in response to the actions of Gretford District Council. Before I continue, I would like to thank my fellow resident association chairmen for helping me organise tonight. It is perhaps a good idea if I introduce all of us sitting here.' St John introduced himself and his fellow chairmen, all six of them retired men in their seventies.

'As I am sure that you can all remember from the email invitation and the flyers posted around Gretford, the Council will soon vote on whether to open the draft Local Plan for public consultation. I will shortly hand over to my colleague Peter Murray from St Joseph's Residents Association, but before I do, I think it is worth briefly describing the key points to the Plan, and the impact it will have on us all.'

St John described in greater detail than his promise to be brief initially hinted at. The audience sat in much the same way as the Conservative Group; with mounting horror. Unfortunately for the Conservative Group, St John interpreted the proposals with all the conviction and biasness reserved by a man who adhered strictly to conservatism.

St John described how over 10,000 homes were to be built in Gretford. The fact these were proposals only, which were subject to legal challenge and that the homes were to be built across the whole of the district, not just in the town centre, were inconvenient facts he ignored.

He described how the road infrastructure would struggle against the increased traffic, how roadworks would cause years of disruption, and how the air quality standards would deteriorate because of the increase in pollution.

It had gone eight o'clock by the time St John finally passed over to Peter Murray, a large barrel-shaped man who dwarfed the five other chairmen. A retired surveyor, Murray was the meeting's self-appointed expert on planning policy.

'Thank you, Martin, and thank you for organising tonight's meeting. It's a pleasure to see so many of you here tonight. For those who do not know me, I am a retired chartered surveyor, with forty years of planning policy experience at Gerald Eve. Martin has asked me to go into more detail regarding the Council's proposals and their negative impact.'

For the next hour Murray described in minute detail the proposals. Slide after PowerPoint slide described the Local Plan. Every proposed development within the town was shown to the aghast audience. Those present were shown how gardens were to be sold by neighbours, how two houses were to be built next door, how new estates were to be built on land unused for generations, how an abandoned hotel was to be rebuilt into a primary school, how road junctions needing to be installed with traffic lights slowing down cars were needed to improve safety.

It mattered little that these were changes to be made gradually over the course of twenty years, and in some cases, never. As far as the town centre residents were concerned, these were changes to be made on the first day following the adoption of the Local Plan.

At the end of his hour, Murray passed back to St John.

'Thank you Peter for that fascinating, and dare I say, alarming presentation. The key question now for us to consider is how best to fight this Local Plan. But before we answer, it is worth us considering the next steps which will be taken by the district. In two months' time, the Council will vote on whether to submit the draft Local Plan for consultation. If passed, the public consultation will last for three months.

'At the end of three months, the Council will make any changes it deems necessary. There will be a second, shorter public consultation three months after that. Once that one concludes, the Council will then vote on whether to submit it to the planning inspector for approval.

'A public hearing will then be undertaken, in which the planning inspector will sit in quasi-judicial capacity and will decide whether the Local Plan is fit for purpose. If the answer is yes, then the Council will have one final vote on whether to adopt it.'

'So how long will this process take?' the chairman of the Ferndown Residents Association asked.

'We expect about eighteen months,' Murray answered.

'But we will have an opportunity to voice our protests against this disgrace?' the Chairman of Whittom asked.

'Indeed, we will,' St John answered. 'Every Gretford resident will have the opportunity to voice their opinion and in fairness to Gretford District Council, they are actively seeking public opinion.'

'So what are the options available to us?' the Ferndown chairman asked.

'Thankfully, there are many,' St John answered. 'We can object at every possible opportunity.' The murmur from the audience reflected the public attitude as to the likely merits of that working. 'I suspect the Council will just ignore every objection, so I therefore propose the following. That we establish an umbrella organisation encompassing every resident association. Every town centre resident will be eligible to apply for membership and will have full voting rights on every major decision. I stress that this new organisation will not replace the existing resident associations, which will all continue to operate just as they always have done.

'But what this new group will do is take advantage of all the strengths available to us, and with a larger membership will come greater access to funds.

'Our membership will encompass retired accountants, planning advisors and lawyers, with centuries of professional experience. With our knowledge and, dare I say, spare time, we will formulate our own strategic vision for the future of our town, which will help us meet the housing need which exists, whilst protecting the heritage and identity of our town.

'We can object, which we will do, but we can also advise the Council. And when the time comes, such as at the public hearings, our combined assets will enable us to instruct our legal team to challenge the Council's.

'Finally, the villages have the Gretford Guardians. Our new organisation will be the guardians of the town. We can have our own candidates in the elections and hold our demonstrations against development. Who here agrees with this?'

A show of hands emerged from the audience. All supported forming a new group, except for the district councillors, who sat witnessing the rumbles of a political revolution taking hold in the district.

'What will our new group be called?' a voice shouted from the second row.

'We propose calling it the Gretford Advisory Group,' Murray answered.

The Gretford Advisory Group was formed; the latest campaign group formed to fight what was considered to be the injustice of the Local Plan.

For the next hour, the Management Committee of GAG was constituted, comprising the six association chairmen and an additional volunteer from each of the six associations. St John was elected as chairman and Murray was voted chair of planning policy and strategic thinking. A treasurer and committee secretary were also appointed.

The newly formed committee fielded questions from the audience, ranging from the cost of membership, frequency of meetings and the formation of subcommittees to help formulate policy.

No questions or comments came from the councillors present, who were all reluctant to publicly state their views, lest it impacts on their future electoral chances.

In order to demonstrate that it was not just GDC which had a monopoly of long-winded meetings (in which a lot is said and not much is discussed) the first meeting of the newly formed GAG finally finished at eleven thirty.

Martin St John went home that night as the leader of the latest political group in Gretford.

Twenty Three

It was Tuesday night, a Full Council night, and Simon Newton sat on the front bench of the Council Chamber. He swivelled round in his chair, observing his Cabinet colleagues. Cathy Fulcher-Wells was staring straight ahead at the dais, Serena Kildare was characteristically late.

Newton smiled to himself; he had been told directly from Foster that Kildare had been warned about her repeated tardiness; that it failed to further the image of Cabinet professionalism which Foster was so keen to promote.

That Kildare was a surgeon, and that patients required medical assistance at times which were occasionally inconvenient to the timings of Gretford District Council, was a fact ignored by the ambitions of the leadership.

Newton watched as Woake spoke to one of his ward colleagues, a pleasant and earnest Welshman. Woake smiled as he bade his colleague goodbye and greeted both Newton and Fulcher-Wells as he sat down. Newton greeted Woake back. Fulcher-Wells ignored him.

A full house of councillors was present, save for Kildare and the Mayor.

Newton turned to face the dais. Foster and Overton were sitting in position, looking down on the Chamber in quiet superiority. Foster smiled at Newton. Newton smiled back. Newton's smile was born from the knowledge that if things went to plan, then he could well have struck a mortal blow against Foster's fledging leadership.

It was little remembered that Newton had once been the Leader of the Council. A retired partner at one of London's more senior shipping law firms, Newton became a councillor in the late 1990s as he approached retirement. His ability to negotiate and his humility with others ensured his speedy promotion to the Cabinet and he was a natural choice once the existing Leader retired after thirty years' service.

After five years as Leader, he feared the election to the Council of the younger and more charismatic former army officer. Hoping that promotion to the Cabinet would settle Gallagher's ambitions, he had failed to reckon on Gallagher.

It was with the unwitting help from Serena Kildare that Gallagher struck. Having only been a councillor for a year, her lack of timing was still a surprise to the Conservative Group, but caused Newton to make a rather unfortunate remark. 'Good evening Serena,' he greeted Kildare as she entered a Group meeting late 'and I must say my dear how lovely you're looking and it really is a pleasure having you with us this evening.'

With ruthless efficiency, Gallagher struck.

Encouraging his friends in the Group to propose a vote of no confidence in Newton, Gallagher highlighted the use of the phrase "my dear" had passed judgement on the physical appearance of a female colleague.

'The man's a dinosaur and needs replacing,' Gallagher said.

And as with all dinosaurs, extinction came quicker to Leader Newton than he wanted.

William Foster had just been elected in a by-election and as Gallagher's ward colleague, he had been the perfect choice as Gallagher's pawn. Giving testament to the mantra "he who wields the knife never wears the crown," Foster set to wielding the knife.

By the time the confidence vote was taken, Foster's bullying, bribing and charm had ensured that Newton would lose the vote by a two-thirds majority in favour of Gallagher.

Foster had been made Deputy Leader, partly as a reward for his work, partly because of his political resemblance to Rudolph Hess; a weak man who could never challenge a stronger leader. Unless that stronger leader became incapacitated.

As an act of contrition, Gallagher invited Newton to serve on his Cabinet. As the Council was his life, now that he had retired, Newton had accepted.

Newton never forgave Gallagher, nor did he ever forgive Foster.

His smile grew even wider as he remembered Foster's betrayal.

***

Woake took his seat as the meeting was due to start. He laid his copy of the meeting agenda out in front of him and opened his counsels notebook. He took out his fountain pen, an expensive pen from Mont Blanc which had been a present from his former fiancée.

It was one of the few things he kept from that relationship.

He took out his iPad and read through his case papers for the following morning. If anyone asked, he was working on the latest financial report.

Woake had come straight from court, sentencing on a prosecution case he had dealt with a fortnight earlier. As is normal at the Bar, Woake had a late night of work to look forward to. He was once told by Myers that the most important quality a barrister needed was stamina to deal with the long hours. The idea that a barrister had weeks to work on a new case was a fairy tale best suited to television.

'Please be upstanding for the Mayor!' the Council usher, who also doubled as the mayoral chauffeur, shouted to the councillors.

All councillors jumped to their feet as Mayor Joplin entered the Chamber, gold chains around his neck. Kildare entered just as the councillors stood up. Her place was between Newton and Fulcher-Wells. Much to Fulcher-Wells's annoyance, she sat next to Woake.

Mayor Joplin addressed the Chamber. 'Before I start this meeting, may I ask my chaplain to say a few words.'

Woake stood, his head dropping onto his chest. The start of Full Council always made Woake feel that he was back at school.

The meeting progressed. There was a three-item agenda. The first item belonged to Woake and concerned the start of the latest budget cycle, and involved asking for volunteers from the Council to sit on the Budget Working Group; a group of backbench councillors tasked with overseeing the Finance team and its work on bringing forward a balanced budget.

The required ten councillor volunteers were found. 'Thank you, Mr Mayor, and thank you to all the volunteers for their services in the task group. I look forward to working with them in the months ahead,' Woake said in his summing up.

The final two items concerned Overton as Lead for Governance. The first was the proposed formation of a new Governance Committee, to be chaired by the Leader of the Liberal Democrats,

Barbara Mason, and that it should replace the Overview and Scrutiny Committee.

It was the hope of the backbench councillors, to whom the committee's formation had been another promise Foster had made on the eve of his election, that it would have more teeth than its predecessor. Indeed, one of its new powers was the ability to call an official inquiry into the conduct of any councillor. That said, the only punishment it could give was ordering the guilty councillor to retake training.

As with all Council decisions, the overwhelming majority of the Conservative Group ensured that the proposal was passed without incident.

The second to concern Overton and the third item of the meeting was about the twinning partnership of GDC with the far reaches of the world.

'I now move to agenda item number three,' Mayor Joplin said. 'May I please ask the Deputy Leader, Councillor Craig Overton, as Lead Councillor for Green Development, Sustainable Projects and Governance, to introduce this item.'

Overton lent forward into his microphone. The clock which recorded every councillor's speech ticked down. Proposers of a motion had ten minutes, everyone else had five minutes. It was a matter of some pride for some councillors to ensure that their speech lasted the entire allotted time.

Woake was one of the rare councillors who ensured his speeches lasted for as short a time as possible.

Newton sat, listening to the Overton speech. A look of contented self-importance passed across Overton's face as he addressed the Council Chamber.

'Thank you Mr Mayor,' Overton began 'this is an agenda item which has come as a surprise to many of us on the Cabinet, and is no doubt a surprise to many non-Cabinet councillors as well as many Gretford residents.

'This item is essentially in two parts, but both halves concern the place in the world which Gretford would like to project for itself.

The first part is as a request from the Foreign Office and is to do with our twinnings. That is, the towns with which Gretford is twinned.

'I know that many of you are already fully aware that Gretford is currently twinned with the German city of Wurzburg, but many of you are unaware that Gretford is also twinned with the French town of Bar-le-Duck.'

Overton was unaware of the looks of confusion sweeping through the Council bench, save for Woake, who remained perfectly impassive as he continued to read his case papers.

'We obviously have the Wurzburg-Gretford Liaison Committee and I understand that our Council delegation will go out to Wurzburg as part of our bi-annual visitation, but we obviously have had no such liaison committee with the authorities from Bar-le-Duck for many decades.

'I can tell from many of the sniggers coming from your benches,' Overton said with a smile, attempting to sound jocular, aware that a soft wave of laughter was making its way up to the dais 'and I was just as surprised as many of you when I was told by the Foreign Office about our twinning with Bar-le-Duck. Apparently, our relationship with Bar-le-Duck goes back to this country's cooperation with France during World War II. Back then, the UK and French Governments were keen to cement their relationship with each other, and so many towns were twinned. They chose Gretford to be partnered with Bar-le-Duck.

'Unfortunately, our lack of relations with each other,' Overton said, satisfied that his soft joke was met with laughter, 'has come to the attention of the Foreign Office, and they have asked us to withdraw our twinning with Bar-le-Duck. Apparently, another English town would like to be twinned with Bar-le-Duck.

'In order to compensate us for our disappointment with this proposal, the Foreign Office has liaised with their French counterparts and would like us to become twinning partners with Versailles.' It was with satisfaction that Overton could hear a gasp of shock from the Council benches. 'That is, of course, the Versailles outside of Paris. I understand that we have been chosen due to our close location to our respective capital cities, as well as both towns been well-known royal residences.

'It is proposed that a GDC delegation visits Versailles next November, with a reciprocal visit from the Versailles authorities three months later.

'Proposal 1 of the motion is therefore maintaining Wurzburg as our twinning partner, cancelling our relationship with Bar-le-Duck and authorising a delegation to be sent to Versailles.

'The second part of the agenda item is something that is even more unexpected. As we all know, Sam Tong is the current vice-chancellor of the University of South-East England and we all know that Sam is Chinese. What we may not know is that Sam comes from the northern town of Binzhou.

'It would come as no surprise that the University of South-East England is establishing ever-greater links to the Binzhou municipal authority, with benefits ranging from investment to exchange visits for students. A delegation from Binzhou will visit the university in August.

'Sam has invited us to co-host the delegation visit with the university. The Binzhou delegation will be in Gretford for five days and Sam proposes that we host them for two of those five days. Proposal 2 of the motion proposes that we send an invitation of establishing a relationship with the Binzhou City Authority and invite them to visit us as part of their university trip.

'There are many advantages of such a relationship for us. Potential investment, opening of commercial relationships for our businesses and opportunities to learn how the Chinese provide the same level of services. I hope that this proposal is supported.'

'Thank you, Councillor Overton,' Mayor Joplin said. 'I have received no notifications of any councillors who wish to make a comment. Are there any?' A couple of hands shot up, including Newton's.

The first to speak was Patricia Lafontaine, the prissy leader of the Gretford Guardians and continual opponent of every proposal made by the Conservative Group. Even the ones she secretly agreed with.

'Thank you, Mr Mayor,' she said in her clipped tones. 'I have some serious *issues* with this. I have no *issues* at all with us maintaining our relationship with Wurzburg, and I agree with scrapping Bar-le-Duc. But to what point is there with Versailles? What do we have in common with Versailles? Do we want additional tourists in our little town of Gretford?' she asked with the typical Gretford suspicion towards foreigners.

'But it is with Binzhou with which I have serious problems. I cannot help but feel that if it was not for a university connection with the town, then this would not even be thought of. What is the expense of hosting the delegation? If we have nothing in common with Versailles, what could we achieve with a partnership with a city on the other side of the world? The Deputy Leader has said it could open markets to Gretford business, but do our businesses need markets opened to them in Binzhou, which is located in a notoriously closely protected country. If the USA is struggling with trade in China, what chance Gretford?'

'Mr Mayor, this is a waste of money and a distraction in the governance of this Council. I therefore say that we should not send this letter and my Group will vote against the motion.'

Barbara Mason, Leader of the Liberal Democrats, spoke in favour of the motion. For her, it was to do with opening opportunities for Gretford at a time when the UK was retreating from Europe, and had nothing to do with the fact that as leader of the second largest political group she was all but guaranteed a ticket on every foreign trip.

However, the Liberal Democrats were split between those who supported Mason and those who displayed the usual Lib Dem failure to understand commerce and entrepreneurialism.

Those who spoke from the Conservative Party were broadly in favour of the proposals. Sir John Carr-Jones highlighted the extreme offence that would be served on Binzhou if the Council retracted the letter, which had already been published. A former ambassador, Sir John rarely spoke in public, preferring private conversations to help influence those around him.

Whilst only a backbencher, the fact he had spent a lifetime dealing with Arab governments made him a valuable asset when dealing with fellow councillors who could not see much beyond the boundaries of their own ward.

The most uncomfortable moment prior to Simon Newton's speech came from Jeremy Pakeman. An accountant, Pakeman had resented being overlooked for the promotion to the Finance portfolio. In his mind, he was the perfect choice and he could not understand why Foster had never wanted to take advantage of his profession. As far as he was concerned, he was the only councillor who could grasp the complex financial regulations on local authority finance.

As is typical of most politicians, Pakeman lacked any sense of irony. It was precisely because he could understand finance that he would never have the financial portfolio.

'Mr Mayor,' Pakeman said with all the glee of a man who harboured plenty of resentment to the leadership, 'it was with great interest that I sat here listening to the Deputy Leader's speech. I agree we need to extend Gretford's reach across the globe, to help counter this country's decision to withdraw from it.

'I was even more interested to listen to our relationship, or the lack thereof, with France. Especially Bar-le-Duc. I am sure that the Duck of Normandy would have been especially upset to learn how his descendants failed to maintain a connection with the country he conquered,' Pakeman said with all the smugness of a man who considered himself to be firmly European.

He lent back into his chair, a smug smile etching out across his face. As he laughed to himself, a couple of other councillors who were known to also hate Overton's pretentious arrogance joined in.

Woake remained peacefully passive.

Overton, however, sat at the dais, his face turning furnace red. It was difficult to tell whether it was with embarrassment or fury.

Simon Newton was the last to make his speech.

'Thank you, Mr Mayor, and thank you to all the public speakers. I commend the efforts of the leadership on this important issue. I am glad that there has been much support tonight for our friendship with Wurzburg. As a member of the Wurzburg-Gretford Liaison Committee of many years standing and as someone who has enjoyed much hospitality from our German friends, it is with confidence that I can say how valuable the Wurzburg twinning is to Gretford. Mainly through a shared enthusiasm for culture and heritage.

'Like most, I was surprised with Bar-le-Duc, though perhaps not as surprised as the residents of the French town when they realise that someone has recently renamed their town.' Overton bristled at the furthering of his humiliation. Foster and most of the Cabinet sat up. It was not the done thing for Cabinet members to make fun of colleagues. Woake continued to read his case papers, seemingly unaware of Newton's speech.

'But Mr Mayor, it is the proposed partnership with Binzhou which I have serious concerns with. Perhaps unsurprisingly, I too have never heard of Binzhou and before the latest meeting of

ManCab, I would never have been able to point to it on the map. I dare say I still can't and it would not surprise me if many councillors would struggle too.

'So, as a former lawyer, I conducted some research on Binzhou and I have to say that I am disturbed by what I discovered.

'According to the latest census, Binzhou has a population of over two million and encompasses an administrative land mass of over three thousand square miles. The district of Gretford has only a population of just under one hundred and fifty thousand with a land mass of just over one hundred square miles.

'Not much of a similarity just yet.

'The differences I am afraid continue,' Newton said with relish. 'Binzhou's economy is based on petroleum, the manufacturing of rubber tyres, textiles, electronics and petrol chemistry. Gretford's is based upon light industry, the manufacturing of coach chassis and consumer services. Once again, not much of a similarity and I would be interested to know exactly how a business based in Gretford could take advantage of Binzhou's petroleum expertise, an industry of which we know nothing.

'I note that Binzhou is currently twinned with the Texan city of Midland, another city famed for petrol production. I am not sure what Gretford could offer Binzhou.

'Culturally, we are different. Binzhou sits within the bay of Korea and the influence is strongly Korean. To the point that dog is a firm favourite of many a Binzhou menu. I am not sure what the dog-loving population of Gretford would think of that. Binzhou was established in the 1980s only after a huge oil field was discovered nearby. Gretford's history dates back to the Anglo-Saxons.

'I believe that this represents a waste of money with people of different culture and different priorities. The benefits as spouted by the leadership cannot be realised and I urge all councillors to vote against Proposal 2.

'It is therefore with much sadness that I announce my immediate resignation from the Cabinet.'

Newton sat smugly, Foster and Overton sat visibly stunned. Kildare turned round and whispered to Newton. 'Oh Simon, please don't,' was all she could say.

Mayor Joplin turned to Giles Bane (who sat next to him) for advice, who advised the Mayor to end the meeting as quickly as possible.

'Thank you, uh, Councillor Newton,' the Mayor said 'is there, uh, any other councillor who wishes to make a speech?'

Woake finished reading his case papers and casually leant forward and turned on his microphone.

'Thank you, Mr Mayor,' he said quietly and calmly. 'I did not plan on making a speech about this tonight, but as the financial implications have been mentioned, I feel as though I should. I have no issue with Wurzburg or Bar-le-Duc, although I am always rather cynical as to why councillors wish to be on twinning committees. I am sure that it has nothing to do with the free trips abroad.

'I am rather amused by the Foreign Office's decision to propose twinning Gretford with Versailles. The only similarity seems to be that both have royal residences, though I am not sure what a UNESCO World Heritage Site which is Gretford Castle could teach a dilapidated ruin like the Palace of Versailles.

'Mr Mayor, much has been said tonight about the proposed relationship with Binzhou and I think that it is worth us spending some time studying the proposed letter, which can be found on page 259 of tonight's agenda.' Woake waited as the councillors found the correct page. 'The letter is approximately sixty-five words long, including the addresses of both authorities and the signatures of Giles Bane and William Foster. The main body of text states: *We, the district of Gretford, extend the warmest welcome to people of the municipality of Binzhou and wish to extend our invitation to the visiting city delegation to the district of Gretford in order to discuss a potential relationship between our two Councils.* That is all it says.

'At no stage does it propose any formal twinning or business relationship between the two Councils. This is merely an invitation to explore a potential relationship. There might not be any relationship for us to develop.

'Finally, I have little sympathy with the argument that the distance is too great or the culture too different. The world is getting smaller and so are the differences which separate us. It was not so long ago that our predecessors would have baulked at the idea of twinning with a German town, as the prejudices existed because of two world wars would have been enough to veto it. "We fought wars with the Germans, why do we want to be friends with them?" would have been the cry. Now, a friendship with Wurzburg is considered the norm.

'In relation to the costs of the visit, they are detailed on page 278 of the report and come to an estimated £3,000. I recommend that Councillor Lafontaine actually takes the time to read the reports before asking questions about them.

'Mr Mayor, the state of our finances is well known and I have not tried to hide them since becoming Lead for Finance. However, this Council has an ambitious budget and a potential portfolio of projects. The only way that this can be realised is through finding investment, whether it be from the Public Works Loan Board, i.e. the Government, or from a third party.

'Perhaps Binzhou could be our third party. I would warn the leadership, however, that the Chinese give nothing away for free. We as a Council need to be extremely careful when dealing with them. Otherwise we could be strung up like a duck in Chinatown.'

'Thank you, Councillor Woake,' Mayor Joplin said. 'Councillor Overton, as proposer, is there anything you wish to say?'

Overton was still visibly shaken from Newton's resignation. 'I would just like to thank every speaker for their time tonight. The itinerary for the proposed visit will be agreed at the next meeting of ManCab and will be published in due course. The relationship with Binzhou could open the way for some much-needed investment into our district and I hope it receives the support of this Council tonight.

'Thank you to Councillor Woake for his speech, all of which I agree with. What I would say about the differences in culture between us is that this visit is exactly why we want to host so we can discover what differentiates us but also what links us. Yes, they eat dog, but that is their culture, who are we to say that this is wrong?' he asked, to visible signs of disgust amongst not only the councillors but also the one local journalist sitting in the public gallery.

Overton was not a dog lover.

'This relationship could mark a major shift in the direction of this Council, and I urge everyone present here tonight to support it.'

The vote was taken and was passed by 37 votes to 11.

The Chinese were coming to Gretford District Council.

***

Woake was climbing into his car when he was stopped by Kildare. 'How about that second dinner you promised me last Friday?' she asked.

'Didn't realise that I did,' Woake said.

'Sure, don't you remember?' she asked, breaking into a mischievous grin. 'You invited me just as I got in the car. Don't you want dinner with me tonight?' she asked, looking serious again.

'Can't I'm afraid,' Woake answered. 'I have a fresh case tomorrow morning and I need to prepare.' He could see the disappointment in her face. 'How about dinner later this week?'

'Great,' she said, breaking into a mischievous grin once again. 'And this time I expect a war story. Call me,' she added as she walked to her car.

Woake was working in his study when his phone buzzed. It was Foster calling him. Woake ignored it and continued with his case papers. He finally got into bed at one o'clock. He had to be up at six. Before getting into bed he listened to Foster's voicemail, thanking him for his speech which derailed Newton's resignation.

Much to Newton's annoyance, the headline on that week's local newspaper, *The Gretford Gazette*, was not concerned with his resignation. Instead, *Councillor Condones Dog Eating* was the headline. For Overton, it was the beginning of several issues he was going to have with the Chinese.

Twenty Four

July 2016

It was the following week and the Conservative Group was beginning its monthly Group meeting.

The frequency of the meetings has always been a subject of some debate within the Group. Some members believed they should be a fortnightly occurrence as they provided an opportunity for all members to have their say on policy and decision.

Many agreed because the Council was their life. It provided a social life and a hobby for their retirement. Little did they mind that meetings would last for hours longer than needed, or that they were held with such frequency that they became mere repetitions. A meeting provided them with importance, and whether it was the Scrutiny Committee, Planning Committee, Licensing Committee or a Group meeting, a meeting was always important.

The second subgroup comprised councillors who believed that a Group meeting was a nuisance. Not because they believed in denying members a say in important decisions, but rather because the Council was not the sum total of their life. A meeting had to have a purpose, not provide an excuse to get out of the house. Woake believed that Group meetings should be held ideally once a year but at a push once every two months.

In fairness, Overton, who occasionally acted his 28 years of age, was also a member of this group. It was a running joke for him that his monthly written report to the Group had not changed for six months. Not a single member had noticed.

This subgroup was very much the minority.

Woake's latest trial had concluded that afternoon, so he had a day of working from home planned for the following day. He had sent in his monthly lead councillor's report to the Group, a requirement as he was now a Cabinet member. There was not much to report. The budget cycle had started, and he had detailed a list of commercial initiatives which had been launched. It was with some pride that he had said that an office block had been purchased complete with an eighty-year lease on the entire building taken by a well-established regional law firm. The Council had also had two offers accepted on two further industrial units, both with established long-term tenants.

Gretford had also secured the contract for waste disposal from two neighbouring authorities, bringing in a combined annual income of just under £500,000.

Slowly but surely, the state of the district finances was beginning to change.

At the stroke of seven o'clock, Foster started the meeting.

'Good evening and welcome. I'm hoping that tonight's meeting won't be a long one as thankfully all the Lead Councillors have sent in their reports and I note that no one has requested to ask questions.

'There are only a few things to discuss. The Binzhou Council has accepted our invitation, and we need to discuss the itinerary. But before that, we need to discuss the Local Plan. I appreciate that at the Group away day there was a lot of tension and that emotions ran high, but I hope that we now feel that the Local Plan can be supported.'

'I think, Will, that I speak for many,' said Beryl Hunwicks, Chairman of the Planning Committee, 'that the Local Plan is not perfect, but we need to help ease the housing crisis. We should not forget that this Plan represents the worst-case scenario and we need to adopt it in order to secure control of our planning policy.'

'Thank you, Beryl,' Foster said.

'I have read the whole document,' Sir John Carr-Jones said. 'I don't agree with the amount of housing requested and I think it will play havoc with our election chances, but we need to continue with the process. My understanding is that if we don't adopt it, then the Government can impose whatever housing numbers they see fit, and as was said at the away day, we have a lot of space which the planning inspector will find very appealing.'

'I was wondering, Will, what success you have had with appealing the housing figure?' Mark Skelding asked in typical bullish tone. It was a pre-prepared question Foster had asked Skelding to say.

'Yes Mark, we have. Craig and I met with the Cabinet minister responsible for Housing yesterday,' Foster answered, hoping that his Group would sound impressed by their meeting up at Westminster.

Many were.

Woake was not.

'James,' Foster continued, hoping that the use of the minister's Christian name would add even greater importance to him 'has agreed to have the planning inspector look into it. He is confident that the number will be lowered by about a thousand homes.'

'Well done to both of you,' Skelding continued sycophantically 'unfortunately, we need this Plan. As has been said, if we don't have it, the consequences will be dire. I agree that it may damage our re-election chances, but our duty is to the people of Gretford, not to our political careers,' he said, although he did not necessarily agree with it.

Many people nodded their agreement, despite certainly not agreeing with it. Including Foster and Overton.

'In which case, are we agreed that as a Group we will support taking this Plan through to public consultation at next month's Full Council?' Foster asked. The Group nodded their approval, except for Lady Turton.

'Will,' she said with the patronising smirk that she reserved for when she disagreed with someone. 'I find this quite amazing. We are still talking about developing our district to the tune of about nine thousand homes, including the necessary infrastructure implications which will forever change the face of Gretford. This Local Plan will provide a licence to every developer in the area. And I also note that one of the three major sites of over a thousand homes is in my ward. That will spell doom for the sleepy hamlet of Carterton, as well as bringing chaos to the surrounding countryside. There is no way I can support this Local Plan.'

'So the only way you would support it is if we scrap the Cobe Nursery development?' Woake asked. 'That would mean that the 1,200 homes to be built in your ward will need to be built somewhere else within the district.'

'But you have the Chalk Pit Farm development,' Turton replied to Woake. 'You should also be against the Local Plan. Those thousand homes will spell doom for your re-election and for your ward.'

'I think what we all need to remember,' Woake said 'is that there is no guarantee that any of these developments will ever be built. Just because they're designated as development sites, permission will only be granted if the application adheres to planning policy as per the Local Plan, which we control. Send it to the public for their thoughts and get on with it is my opinion.'

The Group agreed and the Local Plan was to be sent to the public.

'Will, may we have some thought as to GAG?' asked Grahame Mann, a retired grocer with a nasal voice suffering from chronic rhinitis. He was also a town centre councillor.

'GAG is a protest group set up to be the town centre's answer to the Gretford Guardians. They're going to fight the Local Plan but to be honest we were expecting some form of town centre protest,' Foster said with all the hubris of a political leader convinced by the strength of his own argument.

'Craig, you have a quick announcement,' Foster said, changing the subject.

'Yes, Will. Considering the improvement in the state of our finances, and many thanks to Sebastian for that, we have established a Major Projects portfolio group. The first meeting of this group will establish what projects we would like to push forward, but we hope that EARP will be at the top of the list.'

'EARP?' Woake asked.

'The Enton Area Regeneration Project. We're going to develop the industrial unit, including updating the water treatment works and the Council waste depot. We're also hoping to continue with developing the bus station in the town centre. But we also have some exciting news. The Ivy is coming to Gretford.'

'The Ivy?' Swaden asked.

'Yes, Reg, *The* Ivy,' Overton said with obvious excitement.

'Is it moving?' Woake asked.

'Is what moving?'

'The Ivy?'

'No,' Overton answered.

'Then how can it be coming to Gretford?' Woake asked.

'Because they're going to be opening another restaurant in Gretford. They're opening a chain of restaurants in desirable locations throughout the UK, and they have bought the lease in the dilapidated Marketgate quarter. They have said that they will spend up to £2 million to make Gretford's most prestigious restaurant. But what is important to know is that every other restaurant in the chain is part of the Ivy Experience. This is not part of the Ivy Experience, but *The* Ivy.'

'So The Ivy is moving from London?' Woake asked.

'No, it's staying in Covent Garden.'

'But how can it be *The* Ivy? Surely only *The* Ivy in London can be *The* Ivy?'

'I think we're straying off topic here,' Foster said 'the important thing is that The Ivy is opening a restaurant in Gretford, highlighting the growing perception of our importance in the south-east. Craig, do you have anything else to say?'

'No thanks, Will.'

'Excellent. That leaves us with the last remaining substantive issue. Binzhou. As we all know, the Binzhou delegation is coming over next month, and we're hosting them for two days. The itinerary for the two days will be decided at the next meeting of ManCab, but as members of the ruling group, do any of you have any suggestions as to what we should do with them?'

'Why not a tour of the cultural and heritage sites?' asked Mayor Joplin. 'I could take them for a drive in the mayoral car around the district, show them our beautiful countryside, take them for a pub lunch, followed by a trip to the Charles Lockton Gallery, a tour around John Buchan's home, up the cobbled high street and finish at the castle.' As with every past Mayor, Mayor Joplin had the use of a now somewhat dated Jaguar XJ, and whilst it lacked in the same security details, every Gretford Mayor was proud that he or she drove the same cars as Government ministers.

'Only issue with that is,' Foster replied, 'is that there will be eight Chinese in the delegation. We won't so much need a car, more of a minibus to take them around Gretford.'

'In which case, why not take them to the theatre in the evening?' the Mayor added, always willing to extend the virtues of culture.

'Excellent idea, Mr Mayor,' Foster replied. 'Craig, could you please check what is on at the G-On and the Sir John Gielgud?'

'Just doing that now, Will,' Overton answered, digging his mobile phone out of his jacket.

'Why not take them to a meeting of your New Projects portfolio group?' Mann asked. 'Won't that show our ambition for the district and show where any possible investment will be used?'

'Fair comment,' Skelding answered, meaning that it was anything but. 'The only issue we could have with that is that we may appear to be desperate for the money. No point in saying to a bunch of strangers what we want to do only then to be embarrassed when we then add that we can't do any of this as we don't have the money.'

'In which case, why not take them to the crem?' Woake asked.

'Very jolly, Sebastian,' Swaden said. 'I'm sure that they'd appreciate a tour of the cremators. Could be a great metaphor for the strength of our relationship with each other. Come to Gretford, and die!'

'No seriously,' Woake interjected. 'Why not? It's a major multi-million-pound project, which we're financing through a loan from the PWLB. Just. It would show our ambition for the district, as well as standing as good evidence of what we want to achieve going forward.'

'I think Sebastian is right,' Kildare said. 'The new crem could be a great idea.'

'Certainly a better idea than driving around our lovely countryside and showing them the areas we want to destroy by building new homes,' Lady Turton said, with a surprising lack of diplomacy.

'Certainly a better idea than taking them to the theatre that night,' Overton said. 'I have just checked the theatre listings for that night. G-On has a performance of the Dream Boys!'

'The what?' Swaden asked.

'The Dream Boys,' Overton answered. 'They appear to be a group of gay male strippers,' he added, hoping that he did not appear to have betrayed his knowledge of gay strippers by explaining it all too keenly.

'Are they related to the Dream Girls?' the octogenarian and rather deaf Elizabeth Palmer asked. 'How lovely, a bit of Motown will be sure to entertain our Binzhou visitors.'

'I'm sure that bloody filth will do more than entertain the Chinese,' Swaden cut in. 'Sure as Hell appal them, as it would any right-minded individual.'

'And the Sir John Gielgud?'

'They're launching a Chekov season that week, starting with a production of The Cherry Orchard in its original language.'

'So we have a choice of a group of naked homosexuals or an impenetrable play impossible to understand even if you can speak Russian. Wouldn't envy the delegation's translator explaining either of those options,' Woake said.

'I do fear that we may have to scrap the theatre that night,' Overton said, trying not to sound too disappointed. And it would not be for The Cherry Orchard.

'Will, why not the Full Council that night?' asked Matthew Smith, Lady Turton's ward colleague. A retired fast-tracked police officer who had risen to the rank of superintendent, Smith opposed the new Local Plan just as much as Turton. They had decided between them to keep that a secret, hoping to cause the leadership as much damage with that lack of knowledge as they could.

'I've just looked at my calendar,' Smith said, putting his phone away, 'and I note that the date of the delegation coincides with the Local Plan Full Council. What better way to demonstrate democracy in action than that?'

'Excellent idea, Matt,' Foster responded. 'So are we agreed that the crem, a tour of the district and a night at Full Council should be considered?' Nodding heads from the Group confirmed that. 'Excellent, that will also give us time to hold the necessary meetings with the delegations so we can hopefully build a new partnership with them.'

'Just two more things,' Foster added. 'May I please have volunteers for the Versailles trip? On the basis that places will obviously be limited, you will have to give reasons as to why you should be chosen. Craig and I will obviously go as Leader and Deputy Leader.'

'Will, as Mayor, I believe that I should be included as the district's leading citizen,' Mayor Joplin said.

'And as the Lead Councillor for Culture, Arts and Heritage, I would be invaluable in establishing the necessary links for two areas of great heritage importance,' Fulcher-Wells added, demonstrating she was just as capable of taking advantage of a free trip as the Mayor.

'Will, as Lead for Finance,' Woake said 'I do not want to be on this trip, unless members have to pay their own way. As the one in charge of monetary constraints, I do not believe that the Gretford taxpayer should have to pay for what will amount to a jolly.'

'The last thing is to say congratulations to Charles Williams,' Foster said. 'Charles is our new Lead for Housing, who replaces

Simon Newton following Simon's resignation last week.' The Group applauded Williams, the backbenchers clapping resentfully, jealous that they had been overlooked yet again in the latest promotion to the top table.

'Will, would you like to discuss my resignation?' Newton asked, reminding the Group of his presence.

'No Simon, I would not,' Foster answered. 'I hereby call an end to tonight's meeting, safe journey home everyone.' Foster made his exit, talking to colleagues as they left. The rest of the Group departed, leaving a seething Newton sitting furiously at the board table.

Twenty Five

Anjali Prasad lay dying, succumbing to the lung cancer she had been fighting for the last two years. She knew it. The medical staff treating her knew it. The nursing staff caring for her in Ford View Nursing Home knew it. And her only surviving child, Vinod, knew it.

That did not mean that there had been a warming of relations between mother and son, with both of them determined not to make up for years of a strained relationship.

Anjali Prasad had always disapproved of her son; she disapproved of his perceived failings in his education, disapproved of his career, disapproved of his choice of wife, disapproved that her son had moved out of Hounslow and to the country town of Gretford, and she disapproved of the fact that since his sister had died tragically in a car crash thirty years previously, he was her only surviving child.

That Vinod was incredibly happy in life; he acknowledged his dyslexia ensured he could not live up to his mother's stringent demands for academic qualifications, and whilst he could never claim the same level of glamour as his father (who was a quantity surveyor) professionally, he realised that his mother would always resent his earning a very comfortable living as a dealer of prestigious second-hand cars.

As far as his mother was concerned, Vinod was only ever going to be a second-hand car dealer.

And she could never forgive her son for marrying an Englishwoman. Anjali Prasad wanted her son to marry the daughter of a rich Hindu friend. A marriage had even been arranged for them, as far as she could arrange a marriage in Isleworth.

That Vinod and Pippa had been happily married for forty years and had three privately educated children (one was now a quantity surveyor) and were now grandparents themselves, were an irrelevance for her. Vinod had married against the wishes of his family, specifically his mother, and she had never forgiven him for that.

She had most recently resented the fact her son moved her from her hospital bed in Hounslow to be nearer to him in Gretford.

She had recently told Vinod all that before losing her power of speech.

Vinod sat beside his mother's deathbed as she vented her last poisonous spiel to him. Fifty years of unfair disappointment cascaded from her as her son sat passively beside her, holding her hand.

For Vinod, there was nothing shocking nor surprising in what his mother had said. She had been saying it for years. He used to respond, giving her the argument that she so desperately craved.

He realised that denying his mother an opportunity to argue angered her more than had he argued.

That was a week ago.

Now, blissfully for Vinod, Anjali Prasad was incapable of speech, as the infection in her lungs drowned out her vocal cords.

Vinod's daily visit followed the same pattern. He would arrive at three o'clock in the afternoon, kiss his mother on the forehead, sit down next to her, explain the latest news from her grandchildren and great-grandchildren, and provide the latest news from his business (which he only did because it was sure to annoy her). At exactly half-past three, he would get up, kiss his mother's forehead again and leave.

On that Wednesday, however, he had brought his visit forward to the morning. The reason for the change in time was because of his reading his mother's will the night before. Whereas the contents of a will would not have been a mystery to most sons, Anjali Prasad had never allowed Vinod the pleasure of seeing it.

Afraid that Vinod would share the contents with his wife, Anjali had refused to have a non-Hindu know her business. Vinod had found the will amongst his mother's possessions in her room the day before. Not that he was deliberately searching for it. Noticing that his mother was shivering in her sleep, Vinod had taken a duvet from his mother's wardrobe and the will had dropped out of the closet.

Trust his mother to have secreted it away from him, he thought.

Vinod had sat reading the will that night after dinner, appalled. It was not that Anjali Prasad had left all her estate divided equally amongst her three grandchildren (Vinod had expected as much, and besides, he did not need the money). What appalled him were the funeral arrangements.

'Turns out she wants a traditional Hindu funeral,' Vinod said.

'Oh, that's nice,' Pippa had said, not looking up from her book. Ignoring the fact his wife was not really listening, Vinod continued.

'That means that she believes in reincarnation.'

'Really?' Pippa said, still not listening. Her interest in her mother-in-law had died years before.

'Yes, she believes that her soul will be reborn once she dies.' Vinod fell silent, appalled by the nightmare that his mother could be reborn into another individual to haunt him for years to come.

Hopefully his children would refrain from providing him with another grandchild for a few years yet.

'And she doesn't want any unnecessary touching by any funeral directors, as it is impure. Doesn't surprise me. She hated being touched so much in life, I'm amazed that she ever allowed my father to touch her. Given that Esha's birthday was two weeks after mine, I think she only allowed him to touch her twice during his life.' Vinod continued reading. 'Oh God,' he said.

'What now?' Pippa snapped, irritated that her husband was interrupting her reading.

'She wants the cremation to follow Hindu practice.'

'Which means?' Pippa asked.

'Which means she wants me and her other male relatives to push her coffin into the furnace,' Vinod said, dreading that particular nightmare. Another more practical issue came to his mind. 'How am I going to organise a Hindu funeral?' he asked.

'Weren't you raised a Hindu?' Pippa asked, knowing that her husband now considered himself to be a practising atheist.

'Doesn't mean I know how to organise a sodding Hindu funeral.'

'What about your father's funeral?' Pippa asked. Prasad senior had conveniently died whilst visiting relatives in India.

'Traditionally, a Hindu funeral has to take place within twenty-four hours of death. By the time I got out there, all that was left for me was to deal with my wailing mother,' Vinod answered. The image of the amateur dramatics his grieving mother put on for the rest of her family on the day his father's still-warm ashes were cast into the Ganges was one which would never leave him.

At one point, Vinod took a step towards his mother, who was by this time kneeling in the river, in order to save her in case she would throw herself into the Ganges after his father's mortal remains.

'Where does a Hindu funeral even take place?' Vinod asked.

'At the local crematorium?' his wife asked.

'Darling, this is Gretford. I think it's fair to say that not only am I the only Hindu in the town, I think we can say with some certainty that Gretford has never hosted a Hindu funeral before.'

'Then why don't you contact some Hindu funeral directors?'

'In Gretford? I'm sure there's plenty of them.'

'There's plenty of non-Hindu undertakers, so why don't you ask them?' she asked, going back to her book.

And so the following day, Vinod Prasad went to organise a funeral.

Vinod left his mother's nursing home at eleven thirty that Wednesday and drove into Gretford town centre. Realising the complexity of the issue that he now faced, Vinod visited Gretford's premier funeral directors, B Todd & Sons.

Located towards the industrial centre of Gretford, B Todd & Sons occupied large premises in the outskirts of a quiet residential area, somewhat ominously located next door to Gretford's branch of the Samaritans.

Or fortuitously, depending upon your viewpoint. Vinod wondered if there was a secret underground corridor connecting the two buildings.

Vinod parked his Mercedes outside the undertakers and walked through the discreet door, with blinds hanging down the front windows to offer privacy to bereaved relatives.

Vinod entered a waiting room which also served as an office. A large desk with a computer faced the door. Two chairs faced the desk and a coffee table with two sofas filled one corner of the room.

A door was located behind the desk, which had been left opened to reveal the innards of the building. A large man in his thirties sat behind the desk, talking on the office phone. He had jet black hair with the first dusting of grey. He wore black suit trousers, a crisp short-sleeved white shirt and a black tie. His black suit jacket hung from a coat hook behind.

The man interrupted his call to greet Vinod. 'Will you please take a seat, I shall only be another minute,' he said, offering Vinod a sympathetic smile.

Vinod sat on one of the chairs and studied the framed certificates and awards adorning the cream vinyl walls, the accepted interior colour for funeral directors across the country. Vinod noticed that B Todd & Sons had won the prestigious National Association of Funeral Directors' first prize award for the south-east division for the past three years.

As the man finished his call, Vinod sat wondering how a funeral director could possibly win such an award, or even how such awards were even judged.

Did a judge secretly pretend to be a cadaver for a day and therefore experience the embalming process? Or did he (Vinod assumed the judges were all male) sit in on the entire process? In which case, how could one funeral director be any better than another? It's not as though they're doctors and have different degrees of caring for their clients, who would be blissfully unaware of the process that they subjected their mortal remains to.

Perhaps the bereaved relatives were asked to give their opinion on the funeral directors? In which case, how would they know if B Todd & Sons did a good job, as they would only have witnessed a small fraction of the work done?

An entire range of distinct possibilities flickered through Vinod's mind as the man opposite finished his conversation and turned to face him.

'Good morning, I am very sorry for being on the phone,' he said calmly, much like a psychiatrist talking to a patient.

'Oh, that's quite alright,' Vinod answered, immediately aware that he was not perhaps sounding as upset as most of the man's clients would be. Was he even the client? Vinod thought. Surely that would be the deceased, as they were the ones receiving the service. 'I'm here to organise a funeral,' he added, immediately regretting it. Why else would he be there?

'Of course, sir,' the man said, opening a blue notebook. 'And may I have the name of the deceased?'

'Anjali Prasad,' Vinod answered.

'And what relation was she to you?'

'My mother,' Vinod answered, resisting the urge to add 'and not much of one.'

'And when was mum born?'

'The 22nd May 1931,' Vinod answered, watching as the man wrote it down.

'Lovely, a great age. And when did mum die?' he asked.

'She hasn't yet.' Vinod answered.

'I'm sorry?' the man opposite asked, aware that the speed with which he asked it betrayed his own sense of growing unease.

'She's not dead yet, but she will be soon.'

For once, the man opposite was quite literally speechless. The son of the founder referred to in the business's name, Todd, could not but help look to the phone on the desk.

Aware that the man opposite him was, not unreasonably, eyeing up the phone and also aware that Vinod had made himself sound like a clairvoyant at best and a deranged maniac at worse, he answered just as rapidly.

'She's currently receiving palliative care for lung cancer. To be honest, she has only days left to live.'

'I see,' Todd said, putting down his pen. 'I am very sorry for the appalling situation in which you find yourself in, but as I hope you appreciate, it's not possible to arrange a funeral until a relative has already left us. However, we can offer you various funeral planning packages. Though, if your mum has only a few days left to live, it might be better to wait until she has passed.'

'Passed where?' Vinod asked.

'Passed away,' Todd answered.

'Passed away to what?'

'Died, Mr Prasad,' Todd answered, unaware if Vinod was being deliberately obtuse or if he was genuinely unaware of the modern and woke way of saying someone had died.

'Appreciated, but I was hoping I could get some advice from you.' Vinod briefly described his problem to the earnest younger man.

'I see,' the funeral director said. 'The issue is, is that you require a Hindu funeral director to provide you with the service that you require.'

'Are there any in Gretford?' Vinod asked.

'I am afraid not. The nearest one is Isleworth.'

Faced with the prospect of returning to an area he had thought he had finally said goodbye to after forty-plus years of trying, Vinod persisted with his enquiry.

'Can't you do it?' he asked.

'We certainly could organise a funeral,' Todd said, now convinced that the man opposite him was no longer a soon-to-be murderer but rather a judge from the National Association of Funeral Directors' south-east division. Aiming for a record fourth successive best undertaker award, Todd was on the lookout for a judge who would be bound to have thought of an imaginative professional ethic point for him.

'But the issue,' he added, 'is that we cannot provide the level of service which you would require as a practising Hindu. For a start, there is not a local crematorium which provides the facilities required, and secondly as non-Hindus ourselves, morally we could not do the job. As non-practitioners of the Hindu faith, we would, in the eyes of Hinduism, be tainting the soul of the deceased.'

Not convinced that his mother had much of a soul to tarnish, Vinod tried one last tactic.

'What's wrong with Gretford Crematorium?' he asked.

'Unfortunately,' Todd answered, 'the building was built in the 1950s, when Christianity was still the predominant faith for funeral services. As such, it is now somewhat dated and is unsuitable for anything but a Christian service.'

'But a non-Christian service could be held there?'

'Certainly, the manager at the crematorium goes to some considerable lengths to ensure that the Christian influence could be hidden if that is the wish of the client. Furthermore, we have not yet discussed the additional problem of availability. Unfortunately, Gretford Crematorium is booked up to three weeks in advance. I understand that a Hindu funeral must be undertaken much sooner than that.'

'Oh, I wouldn't worry too much about that,' Vinod said. 'We're in Gretford, not India.'

'And of course, your mother would have to return to the family home the day before the service,' Todd said.

'Not bloody likely,' Vinod said. For Pippa, it was bad enough his mother stalking their home whilst alive, let alone haunting it as a corpse. Seeing the latest questionable look Todd was giving him, Vinod changed tack yet again. 'So the nearest venue with all the necessary support is in Isleworth?' Vinod asked.

'I believe so, sir, yes. Have you ever been to a Hindu funeral service, sir? I went to one once. It was quite a sight; dozens of coaches transported the mourners to the service, all dressed in white, as opposed to the more common black.'

'You've already said that Gretford Crematorium can be kitted out for non-Christian services, so it's not beyond the realms of possibility that it could be kitted out for my mother's?'

Todd talked slowly, thinking every word through, so he could not be held to have been unethical. 'I would have to check with the crematorium, but I don't see why not.'

'And the embalming process. Surely you naturally want to have as little to do with a dead body, anyway?'

'You'd be surprised, sir,' Todd answered, then remembered himself. 'What I mean to say, sir,' he said hurriedly, 'is that you would be surprised about the level of work that the average deceased requires.'

'But you could keep touching to a minimum?'

'Certainly, sir,' Todd answered.

'And the pushing of the coffin into the fire? Could that be organised?'

'I would have to check with the crematorium, sir?'

'Perfect, so you can do it. Any idea about costs?'

'Perhaps that is a discussion that we should have once your mum has passed?'

'Or died?' Vinod responded.

'Indeed, sir,' Todd said. 'But don't you want the larger service that one would expect of a Hindu funeral?' he asked, hoping he had not betrayed his eagerness not to have anything further to do with the man opposite him.

'Oh, I wouldn't worry about that,' Vinod answered. 'There's few relations left, and none of them are practising Hindus. In fact, the younger generation were all educated at Christian schools.' Vinod rose from the chair, smiling. 'Thank you very much for your time today. It has made me incredibly happy to know that you will be able to organise everything for me. I shall be in again when mum dies, which should only be in a couple of weeks.' He extended his hand for Todd to shake, which Todd did reluctantly and with the firmness of grip that could be expected from one of the cadavers in the company's cooler.

'I didn't catch your name?' Vinod asked.

'John,' Todd answered.

'Thank you, John. I shall see you again shortly,' he said as he left.

John Todd had his lunch firmly in the belief that he would be hauled up in front of the National Association's Professional Ethics Committee. The fourth successive prize now became a fading dream.

Woake was in the robing room of Gretford Crown Court. The verdict had just been returned in Woake's latest trial. The defendant was found guilty of handling stolen goods and money laundering, a success for Woake who had been prosecuting. The sentence was adjourned for three weeks, pending a report from the probation service.

It meant that tomorrow would be an easier day. Whilst he might not be earning, he needed to check the figures in the Westbrook case, which he would do in the Inner Temple library.

At least it meant he could attend Chambers' afternoon tea and therefore keep Myers happy.

His phone buzzed as he was de-robing. Checking the number, he saw it was Charlotte Bateup, the district's Director of Finance, calling.

He answered.

'Hi Seb, we need to talk,' she said.

'I can talk now if that's ok?' he asked.

'Not really Seb, we need to speak face to face.'

'OK Charlotte. I can't get in this afternoon, but how about tomorrow at six?' Woake asked.

'That will have to do,' Bateup answered.

'Everything OK?' Woake asked.

'Sort of,' Bateup answered. Woake detected a slight hesitation in her voice. 'It's about the crem. I'll explain tomorrow,' she said hurriedly before ringing off.

Twenty Six

Woake was working on the top floor of the Inner Temple library. Laid out across two floors, the large building reminded Woake of his school days.

Large bookcases adorned the walls, reaching to the ceiling, requiring ladders for any who wished to reach the top row of books. A large rectangular room, tables were laid out in the middles. Alcoves led from the centre, adorned with bookcases ranging from every legal practice, political record and history books, many decades if not centuries old. Carpet and bookcases were all immaculately clean, the lights from above glistening off the polished wood.

Suited barristers, pupils and law students sat at the tables, case files, research exercises and assignments all spread out in front of them. Every few minutes, one of them would silently walk to a bookcase and just as silently remove a book before returning just as quietly to their chair.

Woake was wearing a pair of sand-coloured Gant chinos, a pair of moccasins and a blue-and-white-striped Gant shirt, his shirt specially chosen so that it had neither collar buttons nor a chest pocket. He had hung a dark blue sports jacket on the back of his chair. He had been in the library since ten that morning. The time was now two thirty in the afternoon. As it was a weekday, Woake knew Chambers would serve afternoon tea for all members not attending court at three thirty that afternoon.

Woake could have worked in Chambers; indeed, as Myers explained to him earlier, such conduct was expected of members when not in court.

However, Woake shared a room in Chambers with five other members. In their room were three desks, each with two chairs facing opposite each other. All three desks were littered with counsels notebooks, abandoned case papers and legal textbooks, as harassed barristers rushed home after a long day in court and an even longer night ahead studying their papers in their sitting rooms for the following morning.

Bulging filing cabinets, a fireplace stuffed full of old case files and bookcases holding legal textbooks of dubious vintage added to the sense of claustrophobia. That, and the fact Woake had long since donated his half of the desk to a fellow member, had led him to find solace in the library.

As a predominately criminal Set, most members spent their days in court, working only in Chambers if a case finished early or when they took a day off to study a particularly demanding trial.

The only member of Chambers to have the privilege of his own room was Richard Myers, as Head of Chambers. And even that was equally shambolic.

For Woake, the most important area of Chambers was his pigeonhole, located in the clerks' room and where his post and, more importantly, where his new cases lay in wait.

On the desk in front of him was a calculator, his laptop, the Westbrook case file, a counsels notebook and a single sheet of paper.

Woake had spent that morning studying the single sheet of paper, which were typed notes, supplied by the DWP, detailing the exact monetary value of all her claims between June 2012 and November 2015.

Using his Mont Blanc fountain pen, Woake drew a line down the middle of a page in his counsels notebook.

In the left column, he wrote all the claims which she legitimately claimed, such as jobseeker's and disability allowance. It was never in dispute between the parties that Westbrook was entitled to receive these claims, nor was the home address of her children important in determining the legitimacy or otherwise of these claims.

In the right-hand column, he wrote down all the claims which the DWP claimed she attained fraudulently, namely the single parent allowance and housing benefit.

Once completed, Woake added up the total of all the, alleged, fraudulently claimed benefits.

Woake wrote the total at the bottom of the right-hand column. The amount was £44,854, significantly less than the £90,000 Marla Rajeesce claimed it to be.

Turning a page in his notebook, Woake repeated the process

a further three times. He reached the same amount on all three attempts.

A little alarmed at the inadequacies of his instructions, Woake sat in thought, staring at the figures in the notebook.

A solution eventually presented itself.

Using his calculator, Woake added the benefit claims to which she was entitled to make, and like before, Woake wrote the amount underneath.

The amount was a little over £45,000, the difference between his and Rajeesce's amount.

Woake checked his figures one last time before sending a message to Myers.

Def solicitor correct. Amount is wrong. Should be 44k, not 90. Going to be in Chambers later, will explain Rajeesce's mistake.

Woake was packing up for lunch when Myers responded.

Looking forward to seeing the prodigal son again.

Woake took lunch in the Temple, eating in the lofty dining hall, complete with stained-glass windows and adorned with heraldic badges from all past Masters, the symbolic head of the Inn.

Every barrister must join an Inn of Court, professional associations providing supervisory, disciplinary, training and professional accommodation to all members. Woake had joined the Inner Temple for no greater reason than he had heard the wine served was the best out of the four.

The hall was half-full and Woake sat alongside two fellow barristers and a QC, all of whom were suited. Conversation at first was somewhat stilted. The other three, having made the mistake that Woake was a mature law student, were reluctant to speak lest Woake would beg for professional advancement, the pastime for most legal students.

It was only when Woake explained the shortcomings of his latest instructions did the other three finally relax.

Woake ate roast loin of pork, complete with crackling. The mediocrity of the meal was reminiscent of school dinners, and the total lack of fulfilment in the meal, so typical of mass catering, meant that a second meal later that day would certainly be required.

Fortunately, Woake was having dinner with Serena Kildare later that evening.

After lunch, Woake returned to the library and, using his

laptop, wrote a timeline of all the facts in the case. Woake wrote the date of Westbrook's first claim, the dates of payments made by the DWP, the date the investigation was first launched, details of Rajeesce's investigation and Westbrook's arrest. He also typed up the arithmetic of the fraudulent amount.

Such a document would not only aid Myers in court but it provided an easy-to-read summary of all the key points, a vital tool for Myers when formulating his case theory; the line of attack he would use against the defence and how he would also hide the defects in the prosecution's case.

Woake looked at his Omega watch. The time was now three thirty. He would finish the document after court the following day. Collecting his files and laptop, Woake left the library and left them in the boot of his car, which he had parked in the Inner Temple car park.

Locking his car, Woake made his way to Chambers and a cup of tepid tea.

Woake climbed the steps leading into Chambers, located in Griffin Court; a little-known part of the Inner Temple impossible to find by tourists and most lawyers, but accessible through two archways, one leading off Middle Temple Lane and the other from the better-known Hare Court.

As Griffin Court was used primarily by the administrators of the Inner Temple and for residential suites for Inn members visiting London, Chambers was the only barristers' Set in the small quadrangle.

The entrance into Chambers was through a Georgian façade, the large navy-blue door left permanently open during working hours. The immaculate ground floor, complete with sweeping staircase up to the barrister studies on the first and second floors, was in stark contrast to the chaos upstairs.

The clerks' room was to the immediate right, doubling as a reception area. Behind the clerks' room, and opposite the staircase to the left, was Chambers' meeting room, a large rectangular room used infrequently by members for conferences and interviews.

Woake's own pupillage interview, and subsequent tenancy interview, took place there.

Its primary use was the location for Chambers' daily afternoon teas.

Woake walked through the Georgian façade and stopped in the doorway of the clerks' room. His clerk, Louise and her assistant, Toby, were working at their computers.

Louise looked up as she saw Woake looking down on her.

'Afternoon, stranger,' she said.

'Good afternoon, Louise. How are you?'

'Fine, thanks. You've got some new cases in your pigeonhole,' she said, watching as Woake walked towards the pigeonhole cabinet.

'Anything juicy?' he asked, flicking through the large bundles.

'A burglary trial and an attempted murder,' Louise answered. 'They're in there,' she said, flicking her head towards the meeting room.

'Thanks, I'll pick these up on my way out,' Woake said, placing them back in the pigeonhole and walking towards the meeting room. 'Time to have stewed tea.'

He could hear a soft hum of voices as he approached the room. As he entered, he saw two groups. The first, smaller group, comprised Chambers' pupil and her pupil-master who were speaking to two other members.

Woake nodded his head to them in acknowledgement as he walked towards the central table.

A cafetière and teapot were laid out next to the milk and cream jugs. Toby had neatly placed twenty cups and saucers, along with a selection of biscuits and bottles of sparkling and still water.

Woake winced as he poured a cup of stewed, tepid tea and listened to the conversations from the two groups. Both were discussing the two most important political issues of the day; the EU referendum and the forthcoming US election.

Deciding that Chambers' pupil had done nothing to deserve hearing his opinion on either subject (as a former officer and now lawyer, Woake was a committed Leaver), Woake placed two Bourbon biscuits on the saucer as he walked towards the larger group, consisting of six members congregating around Richard Myers.

'Ah Woake, how goes my Junior?' Myers asked as he saw Woake approach. 'Decided to dress up for us?'

'Thanks Richard, good afternoon all.' The other members, all suited, acknowledged Woake. 'Just been working in the library for our DWP case. I'm afraid that our opponent is correct.'

'So you say, what's the bad news?'

'It would appear that the fraudulent amount should be half of what we claim. It would appear that our OIC included the entire amount of benefits claimed, some of which she was entitled to.'

'Stupid bloody woman,' Myers muttered.

'Doesn't surprise you, does it, Sebastian?' Angela Goodwin, a forty-something member, asked. 'I was up all night a couple of weeks ago dealing with a case in which the defendant had a criminal record as long as your arm, and at no point did it occur to the CPS to apply for bad character evidence.'

'What happened?' Myers asked.

'I spent the first morning of the trial trying unsuccessfully to convince the judge to make the bad character evidence admissible. He said that had it been made at the correct time, i.e. at the start of the process, then it would have been granted. As it was, it was too late.'

'That's bloody typical,' Myers said 'of the Bar post-Blair.'

'In what way, Richard?' David Jolley asked. Jolley was the most junior of Chambers, except for the pupil. In his mid-twenties, Jolley's experience of the Bar was still confined primarily to the Magistrates Court.

'In that,' Myers answered, 'the CPS only ever used to manage the administrative side of criminal cases, which would be instructed out to barristers to appear in court right at the beginning of the process. Indeed, the decision on whether to charge rested primarily with the police. If there were any important decisions to make, such as to make a bad character application or not, they rested with us. Unfortunately, such decisions were taken away from the police and the Bar, so the process is now overseen by people who lack the intellect, experience or ability to realise that such decisions need to be made.'

'But why did this happen?' the naïve Jolley asked.

'Two reasons. Firstly, the police made a few high-profile mistakes, namely the Birmingham Six and the Guildford Four, in that they allegedly fitted up ten otherwise innocent individuals. And secondly, the left-wing liberal political establishment has a natural suspicion of a profession which it cannot control. Therefore, the expansion in recent decades of the CPS is nothing more than a means in which to control us.'

'And you would change this?' James Melville, Myers's Deputy Head of Chambers, asked.

'Absolutely, which brings us back to the conversation we were having before Woake joined us. Say what you want about Trump, but at least he wants to shake a few things up.'

'Screw a few things up rather,' Angela Goodwin said. 'You can't honestly say that you're supporting Trump?'

'Why can I not?' Myers responded. Is it because of the perception that just because I am black, I must therefore follow the consensus of perceived correct thought and support Hillary Clinton?'

'Well, not really, Richard,' Goodwin spluttered 'it's more of a case of the fact that you're an intelligent, well-rounded individual.'

'Certainly well-rounded,' Woake said, looking at Myers's paunch.

'Do you have any idea how utterly patronising that is?' Myers said. 'The entire assumption that I, as a member of the black and minority ethnic community, must adhere to the doctrine as spouted by most media outlets is in itself a demonstration of how utterly hypocritical the so-called liberal faction of this country is. Just because I do not conform, I am therefore wrong.'

'But are they really saying that?' Melville asked.

'I would argue that they are. The fact Bill Clinton was one of the greatest shaggers in US history is a fact conveniently overlooked, whilst Trump is made out to be a sexual predator. Which he may or may not be.'

'But surely you must find some of Trump's language inflammatory?' Goodwin asked, hoping to regain the initiative.

'It's no more inflammatory than these liberal students wanting to rewrite history because the past no longer conforms to their own twenty-first century sentimentality. Of course, there were slaves and businessmen who made fortunes out of the vile trade, but do these students and liberal activists have any notion of how slavery in Africa actually worked?

'The slaves bound for the Americas and the West Indies were sold to the white traders by their fellow black Africans, either after some local war or taken during some raid. The notion that a group of whites traipsed through Africa, finding innocents, is actually a total myth.'

'So what are you saying?' Melville asked.

'What I am saying is that we have a predisposition in this country that says people must think and act in such a perceived correct way, otherwise they are branded bigots and racists.'

'And you're saying that as a black man?' Goodwin commented.

'No, I'm saying that as a coconut.'

'As a what?' Woake asked.

'As a coconut. I'm black on the outside and white on the inside. I even heard someone, who I am sure must have been black, saying that the white population of this country, which makes up about eighty-five per cent of the population, should no longer help Africa. Obviously, he feels that the white British have done enough in Africa, such as helping to build schools, hospitals, infrastructure and governance, that the millions raised every year in Comic Relief are no longer required.

'But that in itself, I would argue, is a form of prejudice and racism. This black individual assumed that everybody who is white in this country is a racist and guilty of the crimes of a few individuals centuries ago. Of course, you're all victims of positive discrimination,' Myers said to blank faces.

'Those ethnic and diversity monitoring forms we all have to keep filling in,' Myers continued 'are collated into one large spreadsheet. This spreadsheet contains information about your race, sexual orientation, disability (if any), religion, gender and education. This spreadsheet is then used as the principal tool by the CPS caseworkers when handing out cases; caseworkers who must hand out a certain number of cases each week to members of each minority group. It has very little to do with your success. I would therefore recommend that you all start sweet-talking your contacts at the CPS ASAP.'

'Tell you one thing about Trump,' Woake said. 'At least he can project strong leadership.'

'You would say that,' Goodwin said. 'You're a Conservative.'

'Now now, Angela,' Woake responded. 'Have you not listened to a word that Richard has said? Why would I, as a Conservative, naturally support Trump? Perhaps I may think of him as you do, a racist, misogynist shit?'

'I'll tell you one thing I do respect Trump for,' Myers said, noticing that Ian Matthew and his pupil had joined their group. 'Apparently he has started to tell his campaign team to refer to him as "The Donald". I may make it Chambers policy for everyone to start to refer to me as "The Richard".'

'That shouldn't be too difficult, Richard,' Woake replied. 'Bearing in mind that we already call you "The Dick" behind your back, calling you "The Richard" won't be too difficult for us.'

Angela Goodwin smirked, pupil looked nervously at her pupil-master unsure whether to laugh at a perceived insult at her Head of Chambers. Ian Matthew indicated she should remain passive. The other members looked on uncomfortably, embarrassed.

Myers guffawed with laughter. 'Woake, you bastard,' he said. 'Right, that's enough insulting for one day. I'm going back to work. Woake, can you call me this evening to discuss our case in more detail?'

'Afraid not Richard, I'm busy tonight,' Woake answered.

'Not another bloody Council meeting?'

'Thankfully not, I'm out for dinner.'

'Oh yes. Who with?' Myers asked mischievously.

'None of your bloody business.'

'Poor girl,' Goodwin commented. 'Is she just deranged or is she an idiot?'

'Please, Angela. Don't be jealous. If you must know, she's a doctor and very attractive. Right, that's enough inquisitiveness for one day. Richard, I'll call you tomorrow.'

Woake checked his voicemail as he walked back to his car.

He had only one message, from one of his ward colleagues, Simon Booth, the sincere little Welshman.

Woake phoned Booth as he drove through Gretford. Booth answered.

'Hi Sebastian,' the Welshman said. 'How are you? We haven't heard from you in ages.'

'Sorry, been hectic at work,' Woake answered.

'How is saving the world from villains?' Booth asked. Woake smiled. Despite being Welsh and a Lib Dem, Woake actually quite liked Booth.

'Very busy, which is good. Obviously, as I'm self-employed, I only earn when I work. Unfortunately, I've had to spend most of today working in Chambers on a big case I have coming up. Thankfully,

I'm at the Old Bailey tomorrow.'

'Appearing in Court 1, are you?'

'I wish, despite its reputation, the Old Bailey is a court like any other. Which means it deals with the same dross as all the others. It's because of its closeness to the Chambers in Holborn that has ensured it became as important as it has.'

'And how is life on the Cabinet?' Booth asked, so blatantly attempting to fish for information he already knew wouldn't be forthcoming.

'The usual fun and games,' Woake answered. Despite liking Booth and his own animosity towards playing political games, Woake was still wary that he was talking to a member of the Opposition. And Woake realised that he owed some loyalty to the Cabinet.

'Oh, I appreciate you cannot tell,' Booth responded. 'I have a bit of a problem with a resident which I hope you can help me with.'

'Of course, what's the matter?' Woake asked.

'Have you seen the email from Mrs Robertson from yesterday?' Booth asked. Woake explained that as he had been working solidly on a trial, he had not yet checked his Council emails that week.

'Mrs Robertson,' Booth explained, 'is one of our residents on Scillian Road. She has emailed to enquire why she and her neighbours had not received a planning notification from the Council regarding the development of the crem. And as you are taking such a lead role of the project, I thought I would ask you to look into it.'

'You mean, can you please do some work for the ward rather than always leaving it to us old blokes?' Woake asked.

Booth laughed. 'I wouldn't quite say it like that, but yes.'

'How far away from the crem does she live?' Woake asked. Since authorising the spend on the crematorium, the Council had instructed architects to draft plans and prepare a planning application. As the authority to decide on the merits of the application, nobody at the Council expected permission to be refused.

Woake knew that the planning application had just been submitted, and as part of the process, letters of notification would be sent out to all the neighbouring houses and businesses.

'From looking at the map, I think about a kilometre,' Booth answered.

'In which case, that's probably your answer. She probably lives sufficiently far away from the development that she will not receive notification.'

'But could you look into it?'

'Will do, I've just arrived at Fordhouse. Could you text over her address now please and I'll speak to Planning.' Woake rang off a couple of seconds later as he parked in the Council car park. His phone pinged as a text message arrived.

Booth had sent the address as promised. Woake opened Google Maps and checked the address. He smiled when he realised he was correct. Mrs Robertson lived far enough away that she was outside of the area of interest for the proposed development.

She would therefore never be notified.

The majority of ward work involved busybodies. Those who held no concept of privacy, the retired or unemployed with too much time and, sometimes, the mentally deranged.

What would have angered Mrs Robertson would not have been that she had not received a letter from the Planning department, but rather someone else (in her mind) would have been privy to information that she had been denied access to.

The application was now in the public domain. *Let her find it*, Woake thought.

Woake walked through to the leadership suite, greeting all the directors. It was before five o'clock, so all the directors were still at work. Hughes (Planning), West (Environment), de Lusignon (Sustainable Projects) and Bateup (Finance) were present.

The three PAs were at their stations. Woake greeted them.

'Hi girls,' he said 'busy in here, isn't it? Haven't seen it like this in a long time.'

Louise looked at him questioningly. 'Not really,' she said 'usual day here.' Woake nodded towards the leaders' office. 'Neither are in,' she answered.

'Hiya Sebastian,' the ever-grinning Managing Director welcomed Woake, 'long day today?'

'Yep, been working in Chambers today. So an early bath for me.' *Better not mention dinner with Kildare*, Woake thought.

'Ah, life must be so hard for you,' Bane said.

'Never been better.' Woake approached Bane and lowered his voice. 'Giles, I think I have a problem in my ward. Do you mind if I have a word with you later?'

Bane turned serious. 'Of course, come into my office.'

'Can't. I have a meeting with Charlotte. Could we talk later?' Woake asked.

'Sure, come in once you've finished. I'm here until six,' Bane said.

'Working late, are we?'

'Hello Seb, come in,' Bateup said as she looked up from her desk. Despite her office door being open and her being visible from the doorway, Woake still knocked before entering. He was the only member of the Cabinet to do so.

'Hi Charlotte, you wanted a word?'

'Yes, I did. Could you please close the door?' Woake did as directed. 'Do you mind if we sit down at the table?' she asked as she pulled out a chair for Woake. She sat next to him and whispered, 'We have a problem with the crem. Do you remember we were told during the tour that the cremators could not be operated at full capacity?'

'Yes, something to do with it being environmentally unfriendly to burn more than six coffins a day.'

'Quite, but that's not really the reason why so few coffins are processed daily.' Bateup took a deep breath. 'The issue is that the two cremators are actually relatively new, only being installed about ten years ago. Unfortunately, they were improperly installed.'

'In what way?'

'In that the two cremators do not have a sufficiently adequate cooling system.'

'Meaning?'

'Meaning that if we ran them at full capacity then the cremators could blow up.'

'Excuse me?'

'It's quite complicated, but cremators need a cooling system. Otherwise they get too hot, which causes high pressure. If the pressure gets too high, the cremators will explode.'

Woake fought hard to suppress a smile. 'And has this happened yet?'

'It nearly happened last week.'

'You're kidding?'

'Wish I was,' Bateup answered. 'The technician was using the cremators when the alarm went off. He was able to shut the cremators down before they exploded. Apparently the only thing that happened was that ash exploded out of the chimney. Thankfully, the only witness was a gardener who reported it immediately.'

'So have the company who supplied and maintain it sort it out. I'm assuming that it comes with a warranty?'

'The company which supplied and fitted it has gone out of business.'

'Not surprised,' Woake said. 'Can't imagine that there's much of a demand for cremators. Where does that leave us?'

'We have had another company inspect them,' Bateup answered. 'The cremators have been condemned.'

'And the solution?' Woake asked.

'I need you to sign this bit of paper authorising us to spend £250,000 on two new cremators. The good news is that we can recycle them into the new crem. So all we're doing is spending the money sooner rather than later.' She handed Woake an A4 piece of paper for him to read. It was the authorisation Bateup referred to. He signed it.

'Sebastian,' Bateup said, 'this is a very serious problem. If it became known that the crem could blow up, then it would be a PR and financial disaster. Given the amount of pressure that these things create, the explosion could be quite severe.

'Not to mention, if the local funeral directors found out, they'll take their business elsewhere. Which would be a commercial disaster for the Council. So please do not tell anyone!'

'Of course. Who else knows?' Woake asked.

'Apart from you and I? The directors, and Will and Craig. No one else.'

'Understood. I promise I will not mention this to anyone else.'

It was gone five o'clock when Woake left Bateup, who followed him out as she left the office for the night. The PAs had already gone home. Bane's office door was still open. Woake knocked as he entered. Bane was working on his computer. He looked up.

'Hi Sebastian, come on in.'

Woake sat opposite Bane. 'Giles, I have a problem.'

'Of course Sebastian, what's the problem?'

'It's about the crem,' Woake answered.

'Of course,' Bane answered, looking concerned. He took out a pen and a notebook and began taking notes. 'What's happened?'

'I have just received a phone call from one of my ward colleagues, Simon Booth. Apparently one of the residents, a Mrs Robertson, was visiting her late husband's memorial at the crem last week when she heard a loud explosion and was horrified to see a cloud of white ash explode out of the chimney.'

Bane's face had gone from mild concern to panic in a space of only a few seconds. Woake continued.

'Apparently she mentioned this to a couple of her neighbours, who have all seen something similar in the past few weeks. She would like an explanation.' Bane stopped writing as Woake finished.

He looked up at Woake. The blood had drained from his face.

'Only joking,' Woake said. 'Apparently this Mrs Robertson hasn't received a letter of notification from the Planning department, which she says she's entitled to as a neighbour. I have her address for you. Perhaps you could be kind enough to have Sharon Hughes look into this in the morning?'

Bane stared intently at Woake for a few seconds. 'You bastard,' he said.

Vicky Walsh walked out of her monthly meeting with Peter West, her latest report into the work of the JETs. West had been impressed by the statistics that Walsh had provided with evident pride.

The contribution which Gabriel had made in combating petty offences was particularly impressive.

'Keep up the excellent work,' West had said as Walsh left.

Walsh walked through the leadership suite, past the empty PAs desks and past Bane's office. She walked deliberately slowly, as befitted the leader of the JETs, determined that no one would hear her approach.

Walsh could hear voices from Bane's office. One was obviously Bane. The other? It took her a while to place the voice, but she soon recognised the well-spoken arrogance of a man she resented for his non-liberal views. She stopped short, listening intently.

Both men were unaware of her presence and as there was no one else in the leadership suite, she stood listening.

She could hear Woake talking. 'Apparently one of the residents, a Mrs Robertson, was visiting her late husband's memorial at the crem last week when she heard a loud explosion and was horrified to see a cloud of white ash explode out of the chimney.'

So Gretford Crematorium had a health and safety problem? Walsh left the leadership suite immediately, not caring to remain to hear the rest of the conversation.

With the enthusiasm only born out of total ignorance to the facts, Walsh returned to her desk to plot her investigation. Failing to realise, or not caring to investigate, the ownership of the building, she turned to the one man she could trust to conduct the investigation with the zeal for which it deserved.

Walsh took out her mobile phone and scrolled down until she had found the name she wanted.

Twenty Seven

Two days later, Councillor Charles Williams parked his Porsche 911 in the Fordhouse car park, in a space reserved solely for members of the Cabinet. The Porsche was adorned with a personalised number plate, its intention exactly the same as personalised number plates the world over; to hide the age of the car.

An ex-demo, Williams had mistakenly bought the car when poor timing dictated that the six-month registration would ensure that the number plate would no longer be brand new. Disgrace would certainly follow embarrassment when his wealthy friends would notice the age of the plate; especially as he had been boasting to them that he had bought a brand-new sports car.

Williams had therefore purchased a personalised number plate to protect his modesty.

If Woake's speedy promotion to the Cabinet had caused a few raised eyebrows, then Williams's was meteoric. A property solicitor of over thirty years' experience in Gretford, no other councillor could claim his level of expertise in the commercial and residential markets. Especially at a time when Gretford's planning policy was under so much pressure.

Unofficially, Williams's promotion owed more to his donations to the local Conservative Party and the hospitality he had latterly provided the leadership. Williams left school at sixteen. With minimal qualifications, Williams went to work as a clerk at the local firm of solicitors.

His tenacity, hard work and natural ability in his chosen profession provided him with the strong foundations for a successful, if unspectacular, career. However, these virtues were combined with another talent. His utterly sycophantic nature, which many found charming and only a few found alarming, had allowed him to become firm friends with many within the local property market.

Deciding to strike it out alone just as he became fully qualified, Williams's new contacts provided him with invaluable insights into the latest news. It was now that his natural ability at deal-making came to the fore.

Williams started small. With a commercial mortgage, he was able to secure an excellent deal on an industrial site which was due to come on the market. Using the interest earned on his investment, he could secure additional property.

As Williams was to discover, knowledge really is power.

As his success grew, so too did his circle of friends expand to match. His new friends were wealthier than those when he first started his career, but the type of friends subtly changed too.

A natural Conservative, Williams discovered in his late forties that the local Conservative Party provided a unique opportunity to network.

He therefore became one of the Conservative Association's largest donors, and in return his friendships with councillors ensured that he always knew the locations of likely Council targets for acquisition or selling.

Keen to always ensure that there could never be any hint of bribery, Williams started to entertain senior councillors at his country home in Hampshire. Over a weekend of free-flowing food and drink, Williams would subtly prise out of them where Gretford District Council was seeking to buy or sell.

If it was selling, Williams would ensure that a company in which he was quietly involved would purchase the site at a lower rate. If it was an area or a particular type of site which the Council was interested in, Williams would ensure that another company would be the one selling.

By now, Williams was in his late sixties and was looking to retire, and when the opportunity presented itself to replace Gerald Gallagher as a councillor, Williams knew that this would provide him the status in order to impress his many friends.

Not sufficiently happy at being a backbencher, Williams ensured that the value of his assistance to the Conservative Party would be explained to Foster by no less than the local MP, who strongly stressed the virtues of Williams as a Cabinet member.

To ensure that Foster and Overton understood, he entertained them during his election campaign. First it was dinners out, then it became free helicopter rides (Williams was proud to say he was a pilot) and finally a weekend in the country.

Embarrassed, and not a little concerned by his connection, which had built up over the last few months with Williams, Foster had little choice but to agree.

Now Williams could look forward to a very fruitful retirement.

Williams was at Gretford District Council because it was the night of ManCab. Despite driving his Porsche, Williams wore clothing more in keeping with a country gentleman; tweed jacket and bronze-coloured corduroy trousers.

Williams had already studied the meeting's agenda, ever on the lookout for that nugget of unforeseen information. He was looking forward to the meeting. Here finally would be where policy would be discussed and decided, often weeks before it became public knowledge.

What an advantage he would have over his rivals in the local market.

Williams took his seat at the board table, smiling at the leaders at the top of the table. An empty space was to his left, to his right sat Reg Swaden; an amiable man Williams had already correctly identified as a potential source of unwitting knowledge.

Further down the table, and nearest the leaders, sat a young tall athletic man, with a look of mild mischievous amusement combined with what Williams believed was an air of boredom. How could anyone be bored here? Williams thought, with the unique insight and the joy of the game of politics.

At the stroke of seven, Foster started the meeting. 'Good evening everyone, I see we're all here but one. Has anyone heard from her?' Foster asked.

'She's just left the hospital, she's stuck in the usual Gretford rush hour,' the young man said curtly. Was there a hint of defence displayed for "her"?

'Thank you, Sebastian,' Foster said. So that was Sebastian Woake, Williams thought. The money man who had already earned himself a questionable reputation. Foster continued.

'I would like to start tonight's meeting by welcoming our latest member, Charles Williams.' Williams sat in smug silence, attempting to look modest as all eyes turned in his direction; the directors reflecting on the latest political promotion and wondering how many more they will see during their careers, the councillors wondering if Williams was a future rival for the top job.

Foster continued. 'The first item on tonight's agenda is the grants to the local Parish Council. Seb, over to you.'

Woake leant forward.

'Thank you, dear Leader,' Woake said. *Was that just a hint of sarcasm?* 'This is a relatively quick agenda item and involves the grants which all fifteen Parish Councils in our district have applied for. As I'm sure many of you are aware, by law we have to provide funds for several projects which all the Parish Councils can apply for.

'In the last number of years, this has been a bit of a formality. But the discretion to grant the applications lies with us. This year, the grand total of grants the parishes have applied for is £500,000.' Woake was interrupted by the door opening, as a blonde-haired councillor Williams knew to be Serena Kildare entered the room.

'Sorry I'm late,' she said.

'Don't worry Serena,' Woake said. 'You're only missing me declaring war on the parishes.' Woake continued with his speech, but Williams was no longer listening; he had read the applications last night and had decided that they were of little interest to him.

What was much more important to him now was Kildare. Williams had seen Kildare smile at Woake. Was that a private joke between the two of them? And, just as importantly, was Woake's comment intended to ensure that Foster could not publicly chastise Kildare for being late?

Williams helped Kildare as she took off her jacket and hung it on the back of her chair for her, which he pulled out from under the table for her. It gratified him to see her smile at his manners.

Woake was nearing the end of his speech. 'I am quite disappointed that the reason Holt have given for a play area which totals £24,000 amounts to no more than a fifteen-word sentence. Furthermore, it is worth noting that Binham Parish Council currently has £1.5 million sitting in its bank account, which it hasn't spent on anything for the past three years. I don't think it's unreasonable for it to pay for its own five applications, which between them amount to just under £250,000.

'In conclusion, dear Leader, it's my belief that the larger wealthier parishes should pay for their projects and the smaller poorer ones should put a bit more work in. Especially Burford, which wants us to spend £5,000 on three park benches, which are bloody expensive benches.' Woake finished.

'I have some sympathy for what Sebastian says,' Swaden said. 'As a councillor who represents three parishes, I know full well how they try to act poor when it suits them, but are somewhat fiscally stronger than they appear. I just wish that my learned friend could choose a better example than Burford, which you know, is one of mine.

'I would stress to Seb, however, that not all Parish Councils are raking it in. A couple of them are quite poor, like Biscombe, which has a hand-to-mouth existence as it represents only about fifty people and their dogs. Having said that, I can see why the money man is having some problems with this.'

Charlotte Bateup faced off with her lead councillor, who sat opposite her. 'As Seb said, we are under an obligation to grant these applications, and despite the somewhat limited length of some applications, they know full well that it's a formality the money will be granted to them. Indeed, practice in recent years has been to submit a minimum length application, to save time for everyone.'

'Thanks Charlotte,' Woake said. 'I am not disputing the merits of otherwise "restocking the Clay village hall with new tables and chairs" at a cost of £10,000, although it begs the question of where on earth they're buying this kit from. All I am saying is that every Parish Council already receives an annual grant from this Council, relative to the size of its population. Frankly, if they want even more money, then I would appreciate it if they supplied proper quotations and invoices. Let them work for their money. I therefore recommend that we do not agree to this.'

'What do you want?' Foster asked, desperate to move the meeting onto more interesting matters.

'The Parish Councils currently receive approximately £5 million from this Council every year. I would like a review of this, as I am sure that we can save money here,' Woake answered.

'Charlotte, can you arrange this?' Foster asked. Bateup reluctantly nodded. 'Excellent, then the grants for Parish Councils will be postponed until our next meeting, pending a review into their funding.' He turned to Kildare. 'Serena, now that you are here, the next item is yours. Inspire to Aspire.'

Williams looked alert as all the eyes in the room turned to Kildare, sitting next to him.

Williams listened to Kildare introduce her item, explaining how Inspire to Aspire was set to help the lives of the most vulnerable young people in the district. Williams admired everything about her, from her attractiveness, to her passion, to how she responded to his show of gentlemanlike behaviour earlier.

Kildare ended her speech thanking Woake for agreeing to providing the funds, secured only in the last couple of weeks.

'Thank you, Serena,' Foster responded. 'Are we all agreed to authorise Inspire to Aspire?' Before ManCab could agree to it, Cathy Fulcher-Wells interrupted.

'I would just like to ask Will, why it is that Serena's project received money, but yet my own requests have been turned down?'

Did Williams detect a trace of a blush cross Kildare's face?

'Sebastian, would you like to answer that?' Foster asked. Williams studied Woake as he answered, not moving from his relaxed posture.

'It's quite simple, Cathy,' Woake answered. 'Because Inspire to Aspire will cost £250,000 and will benefit up to two hundred vulnerable youths in its first year, rising to four hundred the year after. Whereas your last request over Edgeborough Farm was to cost £250,000 and would only benefit fifty of the wealthiest Gretford residents.'

'And Gretford Museum?' Fulcher-Wells asked.

'We haven't decided yet, but you're asking for £3 million for the redevelopment of a building which last year only attracted ten thousand people. Most of them were school groups and people wanting to escape from the rain.'

'And the Gretford Symphony Orchestra and the Gretford Shakespeare Company? Their grants are coming up for renewal and I will come...'

'I hope not.'

'To you for approval,' Fulcher-Wells answered.

'No comment at the moment, but I would say that it's a joke for amateur groups such as those to receive public funds at a time when we're facing bankruptcy. There are things we have to spend money on, things we need to spend money on, and things we would like to spend money on. Those are the latter.'

Williams had been studying his colleagues during this exchange. Whereas Woake had remained completely passive and relaxed in his demeanour, Fulcher-Wells had grown ever more animated and excited. Williams noticed a thin smile break out on Kildare's face.

Were Woake's answers all but a wind-up?

'One point if I may, Mr Chairman,' Mark Skelding said. 'I don't want to be too clever,' he said, taking the poise of someone who was about to do just that; head bowed to one side, dominant hand raised, 'but I would just like to point out to everyone that it is worth remembering when deciding about grants, that many of these groups which have just been mentioned all vote Conservative, as do many of their supporters. Which is more than can be said for Inspire to Aspire, no matter how noble a cause. We need to fund politically.'

Williams saw that it was now that Woake became more animated. 'Can I just say that if we decide to fund groups solely based upon their political allegiance it is an absolute disgrace, and it's little wonder that the public, and indeed the officers in this Council, hold us in such contempt.'

Foster interrupted Woake, more to save him from embarrassing himself through his political naivety rather than preventing a public confrontation in the Cabinet. 'Thank you, Mark, for your comment. I have to say Sebastian, that if you pick a fight against the Gretford Symphony Orchestra or Gretford Shakespeare Company, then that is a fight you are going to lose. Is this item agreed?' he asked the meeting.

In one voice, the meeting shouted 'agreed'.

Save for Williams, who muttered his agreement. Having never done this before, he did not want to embarrass himself by saying the wrong thing at the wrong time.

'Item 3,' Foster continued. 'Binzhou, and the itinerary for our hosting of the two-day delegation.'

Foster then addressed the meeting himself. He presented the ideas of the Conservative Group and asked for additional feedback. After half an hour of suggestions from councillors and officers alike, an initial itinerary had been drafted. The document would be sent around to all the ManCab members for their approval.

'I especially like the suggestion about visiting the crematorium, which will show the delegation how well we can organise a major infrastructure project. That's bound to impress them,' Bane said. The visit to the crematorium had been agreed for the second day of the visit.

'And I like the idea of them visiting Full Council. It would be great for them to see British democracy in action,' said the effete de Lusignon.

Williams leant forward and raised his hand. 'Sorry, excuse me, Will. I have a suggestion,' he said, feigning embarrassment. It was the first time he had spoken during the meeting.

'Just talk away, Charles,' Foster said 'everyone else does.'

'While, as I am sure some of you know, I own a helicopter and I was wondering if the committee would like me to put on a couple of flights? You know, take them on a tour of Gretford, show them our plans for the town from another perspective,' Williams said modestly, basking in what he perceived to be glances of admiration from the directors opposite. 'Although, I appreciate the Mayor is planning his own tour,' he added, purely for effect.

'Charles, great idea,' Foster exclaimed enthusiastically, hoping that he would be included in at least one flight, as befitted his status as Leader.

'Yes, Charles. Do that,' Overton agreed with Foster, predictably. Williams could see the other councillors nodding their enthusiasm. 'You could fly them over EARP and show them what their money will bring in.'

'Yes, brilliant idea,' Woake quietly said.

'Sorry, Sebastian,' Foster said, 'did you want to add something?'

'Not really, dear Leader. If the Cabinet thinks it's a great idea then brilliant. But why the Chinese would be excited by a helicopter flight over Gretford beats me. What are they going to see? Congested traffic at all hours of the day? A leisure centre roof finally caving in? Or even better, the site of a clapped-out waterworks? Frankly, it appears to be utterly pretentious.'

The councillors, to Williams's relief, all looked at Woake in total alarm. Save for Kildare, who stared straight ahead of her, determined not to look at Woake, less she should smile.

To Williams's horror, the directors (including Bane) were all smirking. It was not so much that Woake had criticised him which angered Williams, but rather the reaction it caused from the directors. He had wanted, not just expected, looks of admiration from the officers. Not to be a subject of fun.

'I don't have to do that,' Williams said, playing the hurt victim.

'Is there anything else you would like to add, Sebastian?' Foster asked.

'No thanks,' Woake answered, seemingly oblivious to the effects his words had had.

'In which case, I would like to thank Charles for his kind offer.' Foster turned to Overton. 'Craig, can you ensure that the helicopter ride is organised for the Chinese delegation? And also make sure that the minutes from tonight's ManCab are circulated to the Conservative Group as per the Group's procedure rules?'

'And as you can see from the planned itinerary for the visit of the Binzhou delegation, a helicopter tour of a green and pleasant district is planned on the same day as the Full Council will vote whether this sham of a Local Plan should go out for public delegation,' Councillor Patricia Lafontaine said, as she addressed the Gretford Guardians Liaison Committee.

Like every committee, the Gretford Guardians Liaison Committee contained far too many members, all determined to voice their opinion whilst enjoying the sound of their own voices and hating the sound of anybody else's.

The GGLC was formed by the Gretford Guardians' own Management Committee (twelve members) and representatives (two from each) from the affiliated campaign groups from across the district's rural wards, all determined to stop any form of development in their own villages. Members from the Cobe Action Group sat next to the Save Chalk Pit Farm campaign, which in turn rubbed shoulders with the Prevent Garlich's Arch.

In total, twenty-four Gretfordians ranging from fifty to eighty years old, and all grey in clothes and hair, sat listening to Patricia Lafontaine as she quoted straight from the minutes of the latest ManCab, held only forty-eight hours previously.

Unlike most promises made by politicians when voting, there was one promise which Foster had no option but to keep, primarily because it was made separately to every backbench councillor. Except to Woake.

It had been a constant complaint (somewhat justifiable) that after

Gallagher had taken over as Leader from Newton, that decisions taken by Cabinet had been made with no consultation with the backbenchers, also somewhat justifiable.

A lack of transparency in the decision-making process had been a constant theme from all councillors in every Group throughout the previous administration.

To rectify this, Foster had promised the Conservative Group that he would publish the minutes of every ManCab within twenty-four hours. It was hoped that this would allow any backbenchers to voice their (valid) opinions before the reports were written and the decisions taken were formalised.

However, there was a reason why Gallagher had cultivated the sense of opaqueness in the Group. He knew full well that the Conservative Group had more leaks than a water main supplied by Thames Water.

Overton, to his credit fulfilling an election pledge, had published the latest ManCab minutes to all the Group members. Within minutes of reading about the Binzhou delegation, Lady Turton had logged into an email account that only she and Patricia Lafontaine could access.

Turton had little concern about her relationship with Lafontaine. Yes, they belonged to separate parties, but at seventy-two, Turton knew that this was going to be her last term as councillor. From her perspective, she felt she owed the Group nothing. Not only had she never been promoted beyond chairmanship of a couple of minor committees, it now transpired that the Group was planning on building over Gretford's rolling countryside.

For Turton, a conservative as well as a Conservative, the Local Plan represented the biggest crisis in her municipal life.

That she lived in a quiet village which would undoubtedly be massively impacted on by the proposed Cobe development was only a very minor consideration.

Patricia Lafontaine continued to address the Liaison Committee. 'That the dominant Conservative Group is planning hosting a delegation from communist China on the day of such potential momentous change to the future of our beautiful town is, I would say, an insult to the people we represent. I therefore propose the following.'

For the next half hour, the other members of the committee sat in silence as she unfurled her plans. 'Are we all agreed?' she asked at the end of her address.

'Agreed!' all twenty-four members of the committee shouted back.

Twenty Eight

1st August 2016

Twenty-four hours after the Gretford Guardians Liaison Committee, it was Martin St John's turn to address the Management Committee of his own pressure group.

Like Patricia Lafontaine, St John had also been provided with a copy of the latest ManCab minutes. But Lady Turton was not his leak, rather his own councillor, Jeremy Pakeman. Whereas Turton could (arguably) justify her leak on the basis she was protecting her residents rather than furthering her own political career, Pakeman's own reasoning was much less noble.

Alarmed by the rise of GAG and the implications it would have on his own chances at the ballot box, Pakeman had suggested that they meet for a drink in a pub located safely outside the boundaries of Gretford District Council, where an agreement was reached.

In return for the latest news from the district (including reports), St John would ensure that no GAG candidates would stand against Pakeman at the next election, and would also actively campaign on his behalf.

'As you can see,' St John addressed GAG, 'GDC has insulted every urban resident by the insane decision to showpiece the development of the crematorium to a delegation from a communist state. That the Council has decided to showcase urban sprawl to a smog-ridden city of over a million dwellers emphasises the appalling direction in which this Council intends to take our town. I therefore propose the following.'

St John spoke for twenty minutes, detailing his own planned response to the delegation from Binzhou.

'Are we agreed?' he asked the committee once he had finished explaining his plans.

'Agreed!' the committee responded.

It was a harassed Giles Bane who hurried across the car park at Fordhouse. Not that anyone, officer or councillor alike, would have noticed. Not for a second did Bane drop his cordial demeanour. For Bane, the Andrex puppy dog routine beloved by Kildare, mistrusted by Foster and occasionally mocked by Woake was a mask, a shield for protecting himself and his district officers (all twenty thousand of them) from the intrigues of the elected members.

It was normally one highlight of Bane's day to walk through the main entrance of Old Fordhouse and walk the fifty metres to the entrance of New Fordhouse. For the offices of Gretford District Council were essentially two separate buildings.

Old Fordhouse was the original Council building, but as the size of local Government expanded rapidly during the 1980s, until each local authority began to rival Whitehall in size, the somewhat limited space of the central office became apparent.

It was, perhaps, a shame that the architect of the original 1920s building lacked the foresight to predict that GDC would become the second biggest employer in the area.

The first being the NHS.

The result was that New Fordhouse was built in the early 1990s, to house the growing empire. In revenge for the tendering process, which was ludicrously convoluted even then, the architect had designed a two-storey bridge connecting the two buildings. Unfortunately for the Council officers, this bridge was positioned in the least accessible part of the two buildings.

In a further act of revenge, the architect had placed the meeting rooms and the Council Chamber as far away from the bridge as he could place it.

The result was that it was actually quicker for Council staff to walk out of one building and across the car park to the other.

Not that Bane ever cared for this annoyance. As Managing Director, he could often conduct this walk half a dozen times a day, and each walk reminded everyone (from the Leader of the Council to the caretakers) that he was the Managing Director.

This late afternoon, however, Bane's attention was firmly on other matters.

Towards the end of the month, the Binzhou delegation would be visiting Gretford. During the past month, Bane had had to implement the often-conflicting wishes of the Conservative Cabinet.

The Foreign Office had been in constant communication, hoping to ensure that no miscommunication between English or Chinese could lead to any unfortunate diplomatic incidents.

Bane had to contend with the pretentious pomposity of Foster, the arrogant careerism of Overton, the ego of Skelding, the unrealistic fantasy of Fulcher-Wells and the scheming of Williams. Combined with the determination of the Mayor to present himself as the leading citizen of the district whose right it was to monopolise the entire visit.

Tours in the mayoral car competed with a flight in a helicopter. Tours of the museum and children's theatrical productions rivalled a pub lunch in the countryside. Rumours of unrest and demonstration went unheeded by the Cabinet, and the Planning Policy department grew evermore uncertain whether the Local Plan would ever be voted for consultation.

The Cabinet was determined not only to showcase Gretford, but to also gain whatever it could from the Chinese in a desperate attempt to safeguard its future projects.

For some, it was pure ego. For others it was to secure funding for a project they cared little about save for the advantages it could bring them.

Bane followed the other directors as they walked across the car park. He barely acknowledged Woake as he joined Bane's side as they made their way into the main meeting room. And he certainly did not notice that Woake was carrying an old sports bag over one shoulder.

Bane and Woake were the last into the packed committee room. Bane took his position at the head of the board table. Woake took the last position to the left, a chair in the far corner of the board table, guaranteed to ensure the minimum amount of notice by anyone at the head of the table.

A situation Woake was more than happy with.

The plea and case management hearing of the Westbrook case was to be heard the following day, and Woake had a full night's work ahead of him re-reading through the case papers.

His location at the bottom of the table provided him with the opportunity to get a head start on the work, and he doubted anyone else present would notice. Not that he would have cared anyway.

Bane started the meeting, grinning as he welcomed everyone to the first meeting of the newly formed Major Projects team.

It had been yet another discussion between him and Foster as to who was going to chair the meeting.

'Giles,' Foster had argued 'as Leader of the Council, it is my role to set policy for the district. The Major Projects team is essentially a policy-deciding body, it is therefore only appropriate that I chair it. I must be seen to be fulfilling my role.'

'You can be seen to be fulfilling whatever you want,' Bane had responded. 'The formation of the Major Projects team was an officer initiative, and will be formed primarily by officers as we will bring together the most senior members of the various teams responsible for implementing the decisions taken by senior officers and councillors.'

'Exactly, senior councillors,' Foster had retorted 'it's our role to make the decisions, and it's our careers on the line if the electorate dislike the decisions we take.'

'It's precisely because you all could be voted out that is so important that this is officer-led. We have to provide continuity,' Bane had added, hoping that was indeed just the case. In the end, it was the realisation that the officers would outnumber the councillors four to one, and that Bane could arrange the meeting at a time he knew would be impossible for councillors to attend, that had ensured Foster had capitulated.

Not for the first time.

Bane started the meeting. 'Good afternoon and welcome all to the first meeting of the recently formed Major Protects team. This is an officer-led committee hoping to provide oversight on the advancement of the major developments which this Council wishes to take forward in the short and medium-terms.

'I would like to thank the councillors present for agreeing to join the committee and they will help to provide drop-down policy and direction from their respective departments. As I am sure you are aware, this Council is confident about securing the required level of finance in the very near future. Is that not right, Charlotte?' Bane asked Charlotte Bateup, Director for Finance.

'Indeed it is, although it is worth stressing that we could do this anyway through other means of finance, such as through the Public Works Loan Board and other investors. Although we are not willing to do just that, are we Seb?' she asked Woake.

'Indeed, we're not, Charlotte,' Woake answered, not bothering to look up. To all appearances, Bateup could have said anything to Woake and he would have agreed. Appearances would have been deceptive; Woake had mastered the basic barrister's skill of listening intently to his surroundings whilst reading his case papers.

Bane continued. 'The major developments which we will concern ourselves with are the proposed regeneration of the Enton area of Gretford, including the rebuilding of the current ageing water treatment works. The redevelopment of the bus station. And the possible building of ten thousand homes for student accommodation on the university campus.' This last item was known only to the directors, and Bane enjoyed the looks of surprise on the faces of all the councillors present.

'The crematorium is obviously much more advanced than the others, but we will be providing oversight as that particular development advances. Without further ado, may I welcome Mike Warsop. Mike is a chartered engineer with over thirty years' experience in project management. He has recently been appointed our new committee manager and I think now is a good time for him to address us all.'

'Thank you, Giles,' Warsop said. A short man with a small pointy face, the thick glasses he wore finished his mole-like appearance. By way of devotion to the adage "male, pale and stale" Warsop wore a brown tweed jacket to complement his sandy chinos. His hair matched his skin colour, both fading to a near translucent colour due to the number of years he had spent indoors.

Warsop stood in front of a projector screen, using a PowerPoint as an aid for his address. To Woake's amusement, Warsop was unfortunately cursed with perhaps the most dreary, monotonous voice he had ever encountered, at least outside of the Council Chamber.

For the next half an hour, Warsop droned on about each

individual project; what the Council hoped to achieve, what the return on the investment meant for Gretford, the advantages and the challenges faced with each development.

The audience sat patiently through slide after slide, the officers accepting that the meeting provided them with the opportunity to have unlimited tea, coffee and biscuits.

As well as the opportunity not to do any actual work.

Bane sat throughout the entire presentation with his trademark smile. He observed the rest of the committee. Many departmental deputies had accompanied their directors, although some middle-ranking officers were also present. These were all officers with a specialism, whether accountants, lawyers or in-house surveyors whose expertise were greatly needed.

Bane was particularly amused to see all the Cabinet members present sitting together; Foster, Overton and Williams sat as one group, as redundant as they were outnumbered. Save for Woake, who seemed oblivious to the fact he alone sat with the officers.

Warsop was continuing to talk about the Enton development, or EARP, as the Council's devotion to jargon and acronyms had christened it.

'As you can see,' Warsop said, 'this video shows the footage taken from a drone which shows the enormity of the proposed water treatment works.' The audience looked on, many happy to watch it; for some, it ensured yet more minutes when they were not required to do any work. For others, they were merely relieved that they were senior enough that their presence was required.

The video showed a huge green field on the edge of an industrial estate. 'You can just about make out the current water treatment works, which will be knocked down and turned into housing.'

'Truly fascinating,' Woake said, not too quietly. Warsop ignored it, believing in Woake's sincerity.

'The video will now show the angle from the return leg of the journey.'

'Excellent, what a sight,' Woake said as the video played exactly the same footage, only this time in reverse.

'Charles, we should have got you to take this footage from your helicopter,' Overton said, hoping to impress the committee.

'Always willing to help, Craig,' Williams said modestly, privately enjoying the faces of those present turn to him, clearly impressed with his professional success. For all there present, even Bane as Managing Director, the financial success Williams was blessed with could be nothing more than a fantasy.

Warsop looked like he was about to say something to Williams, but was interrupted.

'Charles, do you own a helicopter?' Woake asked. Williams's enjoyment was turned sour as all the officers either laughed or smiled, depending upon their seniority. Blushing red with embarrassment, Williams looked down towards the desk in front of him, his humiliation complete.

All except for Bane, who quickly turned stern, as befitted the Managing Director when a Cabinet member was being laughed at.

Bane, however, found himself blushing as Woake winked and blew a kiss at him.

Warsop turned back to the video, the moment clearly gone.

The meeting droned on for another hour, as all the directors and the leadership insisted on addressing the committee. As with most Council committees, a lot was said; most of it irrelevant, a lot of it repetition, where the need to justify an existence or to reinforce power became the primary concern of many of those present.

The purpose of the meeting quickly became immaterial.

The meeting finished at six o'clock, many of the participants grateful that it meant the end of their working day.

Woake's phone rang as he was leaving the committee room. It was Myers. He answered.

'Woake, I understand that we're in court together tomorrow.'

'Just like old times,' Woake answered. He had spent six months with Myers for his first non-practising six months of his twelve-month pupillage.

'Quite, for that reason you can drive me to court.'

'Happy to. Why don't you get to mine for seven thirty? That should mean we get to Winchester by eight thirty.'

'Why the fuck won't you pick me up from my home, most Juniors would?' Myers asked.

'Because you live twenty miles away from me, in the opposite direction.'

'So I've got to drive instead?'

'Afraid so. I've got the case papers and will update you on the latest news. See you in the morning.' He rang off as he saw Charles Williams approach him.

'Hi Sebastian, I just wondered if I could have a word?' Williams asked.

'Go for it,' Woake said as he walked to his car. By chance, Williams had parked nearby.

'I am just concerned if I mention the helicopter a bit too much?' Williams asked.

'Not at all Charles, I've only been in two meetings so far with you and you mentioned it on both occasions.'

'But are people talking?' Williams asked.

'About what?' Woake answered, hoping his feigned ignorance of Williams's intention would suitably annoy him.

'About the helicopter?' Williams was all smiles as he spoke.

'I'm not sure, shouldn't imagine that anybody really cares,' Woake said, knowing that particular answer would certainly annoy him.

'I'm just a bit concerned that I'm coming over to be something that I'm not,' Williams said.

'I honestly wouldn't worry Charles about how people view you,' Woake said, opening his car door.

'That's a relief. But you should know that I am absolutely fine with banter. But be warned,' Williams said, appearing to be extremely friendly. 'I do retaliate in kind,' he said, laughing.

'I know exactly what you mean Charles,' Woake said, knowing as he drove off that he had just made an enemy.

Williams would have been extremely upset to have known that Woake could not have cared less.

Vinod Prasad's deep sleep was broken by the ringing of the bedside telephone. Vinod checked the time before answering. It was five o'clock in the morning, the summer dawn breaking through the curtains.

His wife Pippa stirred in her sleep as he answered the phone.

'Hello,' he said sleepily, trying to drive the sleep from his voice and failing, like everyone else in the same situation.

'Mr Prasad?' an irritatingly alert woman asked, typical of

someone who worked nights.

'Yes,' Vinod answered, taking an alarmingly long time to think of the answer.

'Good morning, I'm Jane Turner. I'm calling from the Ford View Nursing Home. I am afraid that I have some bad news. I am afraid that your mother has just passed away.'

'Oh,' Vinod answered, not sure how to answer that at any time of the day, let alone in the early hours of the morning.

'At least I think she has,' Jane Turner added.

'What do you mean, you think she has?' Vinod struggled to ask coherently.

'Well, I'm pretty sure she has. She isn't breathing. I was just conducting my rounds and noticed that Mrs Prasad wasn't moving. I've checked for a pulse and cannot find one. A doctor has been called to confirm death, but I'm sure that's not necessary.'

'Is there anything I can do?' Vinod asked.

'Not really, she's already passed on, so there isn't much point being here until the morning.'

'You sound a bit more confident now.'

'Well, she certainly hasn't been breathing since we've been talking,' Turner added. She did not want to mention that she was calling him from his mother's room.

'OK, thanks for letting me know. I'll be over in the morning,' Vinod said.

'Of course, Mr Prasad. And I am very sorry for your loss,' Turner added as Vinod hung up the phone.

'Who was that, darling?' Pippa asked in her sleep.

'The home,' Vinod answered. 'Mum's dead.'

'Oh, I'm very sorry to hear that,' Pippa said as she rolled over, back to sleep.

Vinod lay awake on his back as his wife breathed softly in her sleep beside him. It was not the thought of his mother's death which kept him awake. But rather the questions which many had asked in the same situation.

What was the point in phoning him at five o'clock in the morning in order to tell him the news? What could he do about it?

Why not tell him at a more reasonable hour, like seven o'clock?

Twenty Nine

The sun shone brightly on Myers and Woake as they made their way towards Winchester Crown Court. The time was half-past eight, an hour and a half before their court time of ten o'clock, as Myers had wanted to arrive early in order to sort out the number of problems which the Department of Work and Pensions had left for them to solve.

It had always annoyed Woake when he heard laymen complain about courts sitting at the relatively late time of ten o'clock. Why not bring the sitting time forward an hour in order to provide more time for the hearing to be heard, was the usual complaint Woake was used to hearing.

The answer, as Woake was always keen to point out, was that the late start provided both sides time to attempt to reach a compromise. As he had once told Melanie Shone, most defendants were guilty. It was just a question of what.

The late start provided the opportunity for the two sides to determine the answer to that question, thereby often negating the need for a trial.

Woake followed Myers into the court building. Being the summer, and what Myers called the "silly season" because of the number of absences caused by summer holidays, the Crown Court was blissfully quiet.

'That's our girl over there,' Woake said as he took off his Ray-Ban's. 'Large girl, short blonde hair, sitting at your four o'clock. The man next to her is Paul Adams, her solicitor.'

'Will you inform them we're here and meet me in the robing room?' Myers asked, before adding, 'and if you see our case officer, try not to upset her.' Myers left Woake, pulling his holdall behind him.

Woake carried his sports bag over his shoulder as he walked to Westbrook and Adams.

Adams stood as Woake approached him, his ill-fitting brown suit a sad comparison to Woake's own tailored Gieves & Hawkes, a mark of the difference in status between the two lawyers.

'Hi Sebastian, good to see you again,' Adams said.

'Appreciate you probably don't mean that, but thanks for the courtesy. My senior is also here,' Woake answered, turning to Westbrook. 'Good morning Ms Westbrook, I'm Sebastian Woake. I'm involved with the prosecution, I'm afraid. We met back in Aldershot.'

Westbrook smiled weakly at him, the nerves of the occasion rightly getting the better of her.

In Woake's experience, it was only when the enormity of the occasion hit the defendant that they realised the severity of the predicament in which they now found themselves.

Woake turned back to Adams.

'Thank you for the note you sent through a few weeks ago. As promised, I've looked and agree that the amount in question is perhaps erroneous. Unfortunately, my calculations are not quite the same as yours. Perhaps we could let our respective seniors discuss it and then see if we can reach some form of agreement?'

'That seems fair. Your opponents arrived a few minutes before you did.'

'In which case I had better check that my senior has not got lost on his way to the robing room. I'll see you're called when we have our conference.'

Woake left the defendant and her solicitor and made his way up the stairs to the robing room.

As he approached the room, he noticed Marla Rajeesce sitting outside a courtroom door. She failed to recognise Woake, even though she was looking straight towards him.

Woake ignored her as he walked into the robing room.

Myers was already talking to his opponent, a small thin man with a long face and swiped grey hair who, Woake noted, bore a striking resemblance to Kenneth Williams.

The two QCs were distinguishable from the other barristers in the robing room by their pinstripe trousers and long-sleeved black waistcoats which, along with the silk gown, formed their court dress.

Woake began putting on his bands as he walked towards Myers, who introduced him to his opponent.

'Gavin, this is Woake, my Junior. Seb, meet Gavin Teague.'

'Good morning,' Woake said, to be met with a slight bow of the head from Teague.

'Give us a sec, will you, Seb?' Myers asked. Woake retreated to his sports bag, and fished out his gown and trial bundle, a lever arch file he had prepared the night before which contained every document, statement and piece of evidence needed for a trial. It would be his bible for the duration of the trial. Small blue Post-it notes were placed on the first page of each document, allowing for quick reference.

If the matter was to proceed to trial, then Woake would bring in the remaining half dozen files, in case he had inadvertently forgotten an important document.

Myers broke away from Teague and motioned for Woake to follow him out of the robing room, carrying his gown under his arm as he did so.

Woake followed, carrying the trial bundle, a notebook each for himself and Myers, and his own gown.

'What's the story?' Woake asked.

'Teague's confident he can get her to plead,' Myers answered, delighted at the prospect of half fees for a cracked trial for doing not even a tenth of the work. 'As long as we can firm up the fraudulent amount. How confident are you of your calculations?'

'In all honesty? Not very,' Woake answered, who had spent a day after the Aldershot hearing attempting to understand the convoluted formula used by the DWP to calculate benefits. After his tenth attempt had yielded a tenth different result, Woake had decided that such calculations were more of an art form than a science, and the amount a recipient could claim was down entirely to the intellect of the caseworker.

Myers led Woake out of the robing room and made straight for Marla Rajeesce, whose sole activity had graduated from staring at the wall opposite her to writing in what Woake assumed was her diary.

'Good morning, Marla,' Myers said, holding out his hand 'good to see you again,' he added, with a slight implication which Woake took to mean that it was anything but.

Rajeesce looked up blankly at Myers, who said to her 'we met at your office back in February.'

Rajeesce still failed to respond, forcing Myers to try one last time. 'I'm prosecuting Tiffany Westbrook, the case we're here for today. This is my Junior, Seb Woake, who you were due to meet at Aldershot.'

'Oh yes, now I recognise you. What did you say your name was?' The formality of the introductions dealt with, Myers motioned her into an empty conference room.

Myers and Woake both stood by the door into the conference room and watched as Rajeesce, not without effort, pulled her large purple holdall behind her and entered the room.

Myers sat down at the far end of the single table, Rajeesce sat opposite him, laying her holdall flat on the floor by her side.

Woake sat between them, opening his notebook in anticipation for taking notes. He need not have worried.

'It looks like our girl will plead,' Myers told Rajeesce.

'Plead what?' she asked, her mole-like face staring intently towards Myers.

'Plead to the indictment,' Myers answered.

'Can she do that today?'

'Of course she can.'

'And if she pleads, what does that mean?' Rajeesce asked.

'It means that we won't be going to trial,' Myers answered abruptly.

'The only slight issue being the fraudulent amount which she is alleged to have claimed,' Woake said.

'What's wrong with it?' Rajeesce asked. As the investigating officer, even she knew that calculating this amount was her ultimate responsibility.

'In the way that it is incorrect,' Myers answered on behalf of Woake.

'How?' Rajeesce persisted.

'The amount she was originally charged with was £90,000,' Woake answered. 'However, this amount encompasses her jobseeker's allowance and disability allowance, though what her disability is will remain a mystery to me.

'However, these are benefits which she was entitled to claim and are not in dispute between the two sides. What is the fraudulent amount is the housing allowance, which only represents a proportion of the £90,000.'

'So how much are we saying?' Rajeesce asked.

'About £45,000 instead,' Woake answered.

'How did you calculate that?' Rajeesce asked.

'By using the formula which you guys use, considering such things as family and dependants, other benefits claimed and market rent.'

'How did you calculate it?' Myers asked her.

'We don't tend to. If there's an allegation that any money has been fraudulently attained, then we just claim the whole of the benefits provided. In cases like these, it's usually impossible to accurately work out how much is stolen and how much isn't. So what are you proposing?'

'What I am proposing,' Myers said 'is for us to accept that she is not guilty of taking the full amount by fraud, and to meet with the defence to see if we can find an agreement which doesn't force us to go to trial. Would the DWP be mindful to accept a plea on that basis?'

'I'd have to check with the legal team, but I imagine they would be happy with any result.'

'In which case, Sebastian and I will meet with our opponents now.' He got up to leave.

'One more thing,' Woake put in. 'Have you got the indictment? That was the one document missing when I was putting the trial bundle together.'

'What's the indictment?' she asked.

'It's the piece of paper which names the alleged crime which has been committed and the details of the said crime,' Woake answered.

'Oh, you mean the charge sheet,' Rajeesce said.

'No, I mean the indictment,' Woake said. 'You'll be able to tell what it is. It is usually a document with the word "indictment" written on it.'

'I'll have to have a look in my files,' she said. Rajeesce then bent forward, towards the purple holdall, and to the disbelief of both Myers and Woake, opened it to reveal a suitcase worth of paper, thrown in with apparent disregard for any semblance of order.

'How long have you been doing this?' Myers asked.

'What? As a caseworker?' Myers nodded. 'This is my twentieth year.'

Woake followed Myers out of the conference room and made straight towards Teague, who was standing beside a tall, fat man in his early fifties, dressed, like Woake, in the robes of a Junior barrister.

'My Junior, Tony Martin,' Teague said. Martin greeted Myers and Woake. 'This is my client, Ms Westbrook and her solicitor, Paul Adams. Any news?' Teague asked.

'Probably better if we talk in private,' Myers replied, not wanting Westbrook involved in any discussion, in case she added an unwelcome degree of emotion.

'I'll go in for you,' Adams said to her kindly, smiling at her. 'Please don't worry, everything will be fine.'

Woake held the door open as the other four lawyers entered another conference room. Woake was about to close the door behind him when Rajeesce left her conference room, pulling her holdall in one hand and carrying a piece of paper in the other.

'I have the indictment for you,' she said.

'Thank you,' Woake said, as he took it from her.

'What's going on now?' she asked.

'We're just about to have a meeting with the other side,' Woake answered.

'Am I needed?'

'Not at the moment, I'm afraid,' he said as he closed the door behind him.

John Todd sat in the front office of his undertakers, drafting an invoice for services rendered to a customer the day before.

Todd sat up with a start as the front door opened. He was further shocked when he recognised his visitor as Vinod Prasad.

'Oh, hello,' he mumbled as Vinod sat down opposite him, looking alarmingly cheerful. For Todd, it was imperative to maintain an aura of dignified respect between funeral director and the relative of the client. An aura that Vinod had not only broken by sitting down uninvited, but had been enhanced by the smile that Vinod wore.

'Good morning, Mr Todd. I hope you remember me?' Vinod asked.

'Indeed, I do,' Todd answered, tempted to add that he was unlikely to ever forget Vinod.

'My mother died last night,' Vinod said, not realising that his directness would only further unnerve the funeral director.

'I am very sorry to hear that,' Todd answered, recovering his professionalism.

'And now we need to organise her funeral.'

'Indeed, we do.'

'Can you please organise it as we discussed a few weeks ago?' Vinod asked.

'Are the details the same as when we last spoke?' Todd asked, scrambling to find the file for Mrs Prasad, wishing that he had prayed harder that he would never have to look at the file again.

'Indeed, they are,' Vinod said, beginning to imitate Todd. Both had realised that they wanted this conversation to end.

'And your mother still requested a Hindu ceremony?'

'Unfortunately she seemed quite determined on that matter.'

'Are you sure that you do not want to use a firm,' Todd fell silent as he considered the appropriate phraseology 'with more experience in these matters?'

'Oh no,' Vinod said with alarm. 'That will not be necessary. Anyway, there aren't any Hindu undertakers in Gretford.'

Nor indeed were there any suitable facilities, Todd nearly added. 'I am sure that something can be arranged,' Todd said, resigned to his fate.

'Excellent,' said a happy Vinod. 'Can I leave all arrangements with you? Mother was residing at the Ford View Nursing Home and I'll let you talk with them. I'll be in contact with you in a couple of days to check the arrangements regarding the Hindu priest,' Vinod said as he rose from the chair.

'I understand that a Hindu priest is called a pandit, Mr Prasad.'

'Of course.'

'One more thing, Mr Prasad,' Todd said, raising a hand to halt him. 'We need to arrange a date. Is there any date you have in mind?'

'Don't think so,' Vinod answered, quickly sitting down again, embarrassed for forgetting such an important detail. 'There'll only be a few of us, so we can proceed with any date.'

'In which case I will contact Gretford Crematorium now,' Todd said as he picked up the phone and dialled a number. It was shortly answered and Todd introduced himself. 'Will Thursday 25th August be suitable?' he asked Vinod as he held the line.

'Perfect,' Vinod said.

Woake took his seat next to Myers, sitting opposite Teague, who sat next to Martin, who sat opposite Myers. Adams sat at the head, in between both sides.

'So, are we in agreement that the figure needs to be looked at?' Teague asked, staring straight at Myers.

'That very much depends,' Myers responded, staring straight back 'upon your client. How likely is it that if we were to lower the amount, that she would plead?'

'That depends upon the figure we reach,' Teague responded, maintaining eye contact. 'How likely is it that your client will accept a lowered amount, which, in all likelihood, will lead to a reduced sentence?'

'That all depends upon the figure we reach,' Myers said. He turned to Woake. 'My Junior has been looking into this matter.'

'Mine has done likewise,' Teague said.

'Woake, what is the exact figure that we believe should be the correct amount?' Myers asked.

'Having used the formula and the benefits application disclosed by the DWP,' Woake answered, pretending to look at his notes 'I make it £44,854.'

'So let's say £44,000,' Myers said.

'Tony, the same question, please,' Teague said.

'I make it £41,682,' Martin responded, in a surprisingly high-pitched voice for such a large man.

'So let's say £42,000,' Teague said.

'A bit of luck you two have different amounts,' Adams piped in. 'I've also used that nonsensical formula the DWP disclosed and came up with £36,000.'

'On the basis that we are only talking about a £2,000 difference, I would be happy to accept your figure,' Myers said, hoping that by appearing to be reasonable, he would secure the conviction.

'What are the chances that your client will accept the lower amount?' Teague asked.

'Impossible to say. On the one hand, there's a general reluctance on the part of the DWP to prosecute such cases. However, as they've gone this far, I believe it is a reasonable assumption that they would accept any figure which secures a conviction without having to go to trial. I will, of course, have to take instructions.'

'Of course.'

'What are the chances that your client will now plead?' Myers asked.

'I cannot say for certain,' Teague answered. 'But considering the overriding evidence against her, not to mention that I am sure the enormity of her predicament has finally reached home, I believe that she would do what she can to avoid a custodial sentence, or in the very least, limit any such sentence.'

'And pleading to a lower amount at the first opportunity will certainly do that,' Myers said, trying not to sound too doubtful.

'I have my hopes, as any defence would. It is, however, her decision alone and I will, of course, need to take instructions.'

'Of course.'

'How are your witnesses today?' Teague asked.

'That will be my next job,' Myers said. 'Will you be relying on any?'

'There was talk of her ex-husband giving evidence in support of her,' Teague answered.

'If only my ex-wife would be so accommodating,' Myers said. 'Might I suggest that we both take instructions from our respective clients and meet back in half an hour?'

'That sounds good,' Teague answered.

Teague, Martin and Adams rose and left.

'Right, well, I'm glad we got that bollocks out of the way,' Myers said after a few minutes. 'What an absolute disgrace the DWP is. Tell you what, could you bring Rajeesce in and we'll see if we can nail this rubbish.'

Woake ushered Rajeesce in, who struggled to enter with her holdall. 'May I help you with that?' Woake asked.

'No thanks, I have it,' Rajeesce answered, smiling.

'Thanks Marla,' Myers started. 'We've just met with the defence, and it looks like our girl will plead if we accept the lower amount of £42,000.'

'But I thought you said it was going to be £45,000?' Rajeesce said.

'Indeed,' Woake answered 'but as I am sure you will agree, calculating such claims is far from an exact science. Hence, no doubt, why you chaps only prosecute for the full amount.'

'And will she definitely change her plea?' Rajeesce asked.

'Can all but guarantee it,' Myers answered.

'What do you want from me?' Rajeesce asked.

'You need to contact your legal team ASAP and ask for their authorisation. Explain to them the facts and say that we can have conviction secured by lunchtime,' Myers answered.

'OK, will do,' Rajeesce asked, fishing out her mobile phone from her handbag. 'Do you have the number for the legal team?' she asked.

'No, I am afraid that I don't. No doubt it is in your papers. Sebastian, can you please check on the status of our witnesses in case we go to trial? I'll meet you back here once you've done.'

Woake rose and left, leaving Myers alone with Rajeesce, who had her head in her holdall, desperately trying to find a piece of paper with the phone number of the DWP's legal department.

'So you think that the difference in the amount and a guilty plea will be the difference between me going inside?' Westbrook asked.

'Well, to be honest, we don't know that,' Adams answered before Teague could. Despite the difference in seniority, Adams knew that he would be slightly more honest than the QC who seemed to be solely interested in the merits of a cracked trial.

'In all honesty, it's still a large amount that you claimed and have spent, so you will be extremely lucky to avoid custody.'

'But what we can do,' Teague said, hoping to regain the initiative, 'is use a guilty plea as an excuse to ask the judge for a probation report. During your meeting with probation, you can plead poverty, desperation, stupidity, all of which we can use in an attempt to either limit the sentence or even to ask the judge to suspend it.'

'But there's no guarantee?' Westbrook asked desperately, tears forming in the corners of her eyes.

'Unfortunately, there's never a guarantee,' Teague said. 'All I can say is that you have a greater chance of getting what you want, which is avoiding jail, if you accept the deal in front of you.'

'All present and correct,' Woake said as he re-entered the conference room thirty minutes later. Rajeesce was missing, but her closed holdall was still in the room. 'Any luck with the DWP?' he asked.

'She's only just made contact with them,' Myers answered. 'And only then that was because I contacted Chambers and asked them to get us the number. She's on the phone to them now. Any issues with our witnesses?'

'Apart from Rajeesce, there's only two others giving evidence. The representative from the DWP is here, and he's prepped about being able to explain how the applications are dealt with, and the landlord.'

'What mood was he in?' Myers asked.

'Moaning about being here, claiming he's damaging his business if word gets out where he is today. He even asked if we could organise it so that he gives evidence anonymously.'

'What did you say?'

'That on the basis he isn't the victim of domestic abuse, sexual assault or child abuse, the answer is no.'

'Bet he wasn't too pleased with that,' Myers said as Rajeesce entered the room, a smile of triumph etched across her face.

'They say that if you can guarantee a conviction, then they're happy to accept the lower amount,' she said.

'Excellent,' Myers answered 'all we need now is for the defence to play ball then we'll be out of here by lunchtime.'

'Marla,' Woake said, smiling. 'Might I please ask you for a huge favour? Could you please organise for the indictment to be amended?' he asked, handing her his annotated copy. 'All you need to do is change the amount,' Woake added.

'And how do I do that?' Rajeesce asked, taking the piece of paper.

'Well, it's quite simple,' Woake answered. 'You go to the police room and ask to borrow one of their computers.'

'But I'm not the police.'

'No you're not. But you are a DWP caseworker, who has the same power of arrest and stop and search. Plus, you're the OIC in a serious fraud trial, therefore you're entitled to the same right of access as a police officer.'

'OIC?' Rajeesce asked.

'Officer in the case,' Woake said. 'Any problems, then phone me and I shall deal with it for you, but there shouldn't be.'

'But how will I know the correct login information?'

'Ask,' Woake answered. 'And we need five copies, please; one for you, one for us, one for the other side, one for the judge and one for the court,' he added, confident that Rajeesce would only think to print one off.

Myers and Woake watched as she left the room, leaving the holdall behind.

'Bloody frightening to think she has the power to arrest you,' Myers said, looking at the holdall which was laying right across where the defence team would still be sitting. 'Better move that bloody thing,' Myers added.

Woake stood and strode towards the holdall. Reaching out with one hand, he grabbed the top handle and with one sudden action pulled the holdall upwards.

'Jesus,' Woake muttered under his breath, although his struggling with the weight of its contents was quickly replaced by amazement at the sudden loss of weight. 'Oh shit,' Woake said as he stared down, having inadvertently strewn the entire contents across the floor.

'It would appear that our OIC failed to zip the holdall up,' Myers said. 'Better clear that before our opponents come back.'

Woake placed the holdall horizontally back on the ground and quickly grabbed the papers, throwing them back into the case with no regard to order or organisation.

'I do hope that you are filing those papers in proper order, Woake,' Myers said, who remained firmly in his chair.

'Fuck off, Richard,' Woake responded. 'It's not my fault we're dealing with an idiot,' Woake said, as he struggled with the zip. 'Daresay that the papers are in a better order than they were previously, and she'll probably have more of an idea where to find something now than she did before,' he said as he placed the holdall up against a corner of the room.

Woake had just returned to his seat when the defence team came in.

'Richard, do we have any news?' Teague asked as he, Martin and Adams took their seats.

'Yes, we do,' Myers answered. 'How's your girl?' he asked, wanting to know as much about the other side before committing.

'Depends upon you,' Teague answered, equally experienced in pre-trial negotiations.

As prosecutor, Myers had little option but to now disclose.

'My client will agree to the lower amount, on the undertaking that your client will change her plea. If not, the original indictment stands.'

'Thank you, Richard, for your efforts. They are very much appreciated,' Teague said, maintaining the professional courtesy expected of senior members of the Bar. 'My client is of a mind to plead to the indictment, as she is most eager to avoid jail.'

'Not much I can do about that,' Myers said.

'Agreed,' Teague responded. 'Although please be aware that I will push for a probation report before sentencing.'

'Who will, of course, be the first to highlight single-mother status, poverty-induced greed and lack of employment amongst a host of other reasons as to why a custodial sentence should be avoided,' Myers said, knowing full well that the probation services were best placed to plead leniency to the sentencing judge far better than any QC.

'I will not go too far to ask if you would not object to a probation report,' Teague said, fully in the knowledge that Myers was honour bound to push for as tough a sentence as he could.

'Of course not,' Myers said.

'But I would urge you to remain receptive to any possible mitigation made on my client's behalf.'

'Of course,' Myers said. 'In which case there is little for me to add but to say that I will now inform the court that we are ready to proceed. Hopefully, they can deal with this sooner rather than later. Thank you, Gavin, very much for your efforts. They are very much appreciated.'

'Always good to see justice being seen to be done,' Teague said.

It was midday and John Todd still sat at his desk, pondering the forthcoming funeral.

As Gretford's leading funeral director, Todd prided himself on his ability to organise a Christian funeral; an atheist funeral provided his only challenge. Or humanist, as the current phraseology would have it.

Todd always privately smiled when a client requested a humanist funeral. Surely every funeral his firm organised was humanist, considering the client focus? For Todd, the current fashion of humanism was the antithesis of taste. The spectacle of the deceased being pushed in a wicker basket on a trolley to the murmurings of Andrea Bocelli's Time to Say Goodbye as if a large picnic was to be supplied to the five thousand was a sight which always brought a shiver down his spine.

As he once told a bereaved relative, the trolley was essential. Unfortunately, the wicker baskets lacked the structural integrity which defined an oak coffin, ensuring that they were impossible to carry when fully laden.

Todd had once filled such a coffin with a set of ninety kilo weights in order to impersonate a body. The result had not been encouraging. As the pall-bearers had lifted the handles, the ninety kilos had proved too much for the structural integrity of the coffin. The handles had made it onto the pall-bearers' shoulders. Unfortunately, the coffin had not, which remained in one piece on the trolley.

The image of a corpse spilling down the nave of Gretford Crematorium had ensured a sleepless night for Todd.

Now, the challenge was different.

As he had tried to tell Vinod Prasad, Gretford was just not a town designed for a Hindu funeral.

It was not so much the days leading up to the funeral which concerned Todd; contrary to popular belief, undertakers gained little pleasure in physical contact with a cadaver. Therefore, maintaining minimal contact with the Prasad corpse was the straightforward part.

Rather, it was the service itself which filled him with dread.

There was only one thing available for him to do. He phoned Angelina Burbridge, the manager at Gretford Crematorium.

'Hi Angelina,' he said when she answered the phone 'it's John Todd. I have a funeral booked with you on 25th August and there's just a couple of things which I need to discuss with you.'

'And they are?' Burbridge asked.

'The family has requested that it be a Hindu funeral.'

'What?'

'As I say, it's a Hindu funeral.'

'I hope you told them that is quite impossible.'

'Far from it, you always say that your crem is a location for all the faiths.'

'No, I always say that my crematorium is for people of faith.'

'Quite, but the funeral has already been paid for,' Todd said, knowing that the income would be a deciding factor for her.

'How on earth do I organise a Hindu funeral? The maximum capacity of the chapel itself is only a hundred people,' Burbridge had said, images of countless coach loads of relatives disembarking in the car park flashing through her mind.

'Oh, I wouldn't worry too much about that,' Todd answered. 'The family is quite anglicised. I shouldn't imagine that it will be too much of a challenge for you. Just hire an appropriate preacher, hide the crucifixes, cover the chapel and Room of Remembrance with plenty of white flowers and ensure that the family can push the coffin into the cremator on its last journey, and I am sure that you will have it cracked,' Todd said.

When he hung up the phone five minutes later, he felt decidedly better.

The same could not be said for Angelina Burbridge.

The case was called on at half-past ten.

Drawing inspiration from the Colosseum in Rome, the courtrooms at Winchester Crown Court had been designed to be large hollow auditoria. At the bottom of each shell was the dock, in front of which were three rows for the legal teams. To either side of these rows, and set higher, were the stalls for the jury and members of the media.

Higher still is the judge's bench, providing an excellent view of the courtroom below. Located even higher, and accessible only by a separate staircase, was the public gallery, set on three sides of the courtroom and thereby paying homage to the adage that justice must be seen to be done.

A thick glass screen partitions off the courtroom from the public gallery. Officially installed to provide protection to those in the courtroom, it provided one added bonus. The glass was soundproof. Rather than be disturbed by any unpleasant behaviour, the matters in each courtroom could progress oblivious to any riotous behaviour in the galleries.

Unfortunately, it also meant that the public were unable to hear proceedings.

As one QC once said, 'Whilst it is important that justice is seen to be done at Winchester, it doesn't necessarily mean that it needs to be heard.'

Woake held the door open for Myers as they walked through the first set of double doors into the courtroom. Rajeesce followed Myers, struggling with the holdall. 'Thanks,' she said as she walked through the open door. 'I'll follow you, easier that way.'

Myers was already through the second set of doors and was in the courtroom proper when Rajeesce asked, 'I am in here?' pointing to the staircase.

'Yes,' Myers said, not bothering to turn around. Woake also made the same mistake.

Myers placed his papers in the front row, next to Teague but furthest away from the jury. Woake took his position in the second row, directly behind Myers and next to Tony Martin. Adams was relegated to the third row.

The courtroom was not yet sitting, so the two QCs were engaging the clerk of the court in small talk. Woake attempted the same with Martin, who sullenly sat in silence.

'Your client must be feeling confident,' Woake said. 'She's brought an overnight bag with her.' Martin ignored him. Adams had turned around to offer Westbrook a reassuring smile as the defendant entered the dock.

A large whack from behind the dock suddenly disturbed the quiet hum of the pre-hearing small talk. All five lawyers turned around and stared at the wall behind Westbrook.

The first whack was followed a second later by another, and then a third, then a fourth, as the lawyers followed the sound with their eyes as it rose diagonally across the rear wall.

'What the fuck?' Myers asked.

'Where the Hell is Rajeesce?' Woake asked, looking alarmingly around the courtroom to see where she was sitting.

'I thought she had followed us in,' Myers said, following the sound of the whacks as they continued to raise to the public gallery.

'You know, Richard,' Teague said, 'I do believe that that is your case officer.'

'Woake,' Myers said, 'can you run up there and tell that fucking halfwit that I need her down here, now?'

Woake rushed out of the courtroom and turned right, straight up the public gallery, taking two steps at a time. Woake burst through the door leading into the gallery, to see Rajeesce sitting cross-legged with a notebook in her hand. Her holdall lay open on the floor next to her.

Thankfully, she seemed oblivious to Woake's attempt at filing her papers.

'What are you doing in here?' he asked her.

'I asked Richard where I had to go, and he said in here,' Rajeesce answered.

'He thought you meant the courtroom,' Woake said, watching as the occupants in the courtroom rose as one. 'There's no time to discuss this, we need you down there now.'

'So not up here?' Rajeesce asked as the judge entered and bowed to the barristers in front of her, who dutifully bowed back.

'Yes, we're both needed now.'

'OK, let me get my papers,' she said as she rose slowly from the chair. Zipping up the holdall, she pulled it behind her as she walked through the door held open by Woake.

'May I help you with that?' he asked, not so much out of chivalry but more to prevent a repeat of her ascent into the gallery.

'No thanks,' she smiled in response, 'I have a system now.'

To Woake's horror, she took each of the twenty steps individually, lowering the holdall on each step, causing a loud thud, which was repeated all the way down.

Unbeknown to Woake, Judge Toms had added her wonderment at the looks the lawyers gave to Rajeesce's descent.

Oblivious to any sense of embarrassment, Rajeesce entered the courtroom and promptly took the first seat she could see, which was directly outside the dock. Bowing as he entered the court, Woake pointed to the third row. 'There!' he whispered angrily.

Westbrook was standing in the dock as the indictment was read out to her. 'How do you plead? Guilty or not guilty?' the clerk asked.

'Guilty,' she said back.

Woake made a note of the time, in case he had reason to refer back to the transcript in the unlikely event that there would be an appeal.

Myers handed him a note as the indictment was read out. *What the fuck was that noise?* he had written.

Woake scribbled his answer back. *The holdall*, he answered.

Didn't you offer to carry it for the stupid cow? Myers responded.

Said she had a system, Woake noted as Her Honour Judge Toms addressed the court.

'In light of the guilty plea, I am minded to move to sentencing,' she said. Myers rose to respond, but he was beaten by Teague. Halfway to standing, Myers sat back down, removed his glasses and sat sideways so he could observe his opponent.

'Your Honour,' Teague said, 'I beg the court's forgiveness, and that of my learned friend, but might I please address you before my learned friend?' He stopped as Toms looked at Myers, who responded, 'I have no objection, Your Honour,' he said, sitting back down as quickly as he rose. Toms indicated for Teague to continue.

'I am grateful, Your Honour, and to my learned friend. The reason I sought leave to address you before the prosecution, as is its right, is so that I could apply for a delay to sentencing so that a report by the probation service can be conducted.'

'I am mindful to proceed to sentencing now, Mr Teague,' Toms persisted.

'I note your intention, Your Honour, and might I say in normal circumstances I would agree. However, I respectfully submit that these are not. Whilst the defendant has admitted to her wrongdoing and is prepared for the consequences, there is the issue of her children.

'I think we all now accept that they are not living with her, but there is the outstanding matter as to what will happen to them should their mother be handed a custodial sentence today. Namely, where will they live? Who with? Will they go into foster care or live with their father? A probation report will answer these matters.

'The defendant has entered a guilty plea at the first available opportunity, to which she is entitled to maximum credit.'

Toms turned to Myers. 'Mr Myers, do you have anything to add?'

Myers rose, replacing Teague, who sat down. 'There is not much to say, Your Honour. Like you, I would be happy to proceed straight to sentencing. But I have some sympathy for what my learned friend has just said. It is important that we remember that there are two young children to consider, and perhaps the court should reflect that.' Myers sat down.

'Mr Teague, how old are the children?' Toms asked.

Teague rose to respond. 'I am afraid that I do not have the answers to hand. May I turn my back?' Toms nodded, allowing Teague to turn around and confer with Martin and Adams. A quiet conversation ensued before Teague turned back to the judge. 'They are nine and five, Your Honour.'

'And they live with their mother?' Toms asked.

'No, Your Honour, I understand they lie with their father.' Teague answered.

'Thank you, Mr Teague,' Toms said, smiling for the first time during the hearing. 'I appreciate that was a rather obvious answer, but I still wanted it confirmed.'

'No need to apologise, Your Honour,' Teague said, smiling back.

'In which case, I adjourn this matter for the first available date after three weeks, which is?' Toms said, looking down at the clerk of the court.

'Thursday 25th August, Your Honour.'

'Until Thursday 25th August. In which case I wish you gentlemen good morning and I warn you Mr Teague that your client should be prepared for a custodial sentence.'

'I think she is prepared for one now,' Woake said, quietly enough that only Myers could hear.

The judge stood.

'All rise!' the court usher shouted. Judge and barristers solemnly bowed to each other before Toms left the courtroom. The G4S security guard standing beside Westbrook in the dock unlocked the door, allowing the defendant, who had remained completely silent throughout the proceedings as her future was being decided for her, to leave.

Myers and Woake remained standing by the door leading out of the courtroom, allowing the defence team to pass through before them. Rajeesce followed them out.

'So that's the case dealt with,' she said after they had left the courtroom.

'Apart from the sentencing,' Myers responded.

'Which will be when?' she asked. Myers told her.

'So what just happened?' Rajeesce asked, oblivious to the incredulous looks that Myers and Woake were giving.

'Sebastian,' Myers said, 'would you please check on the witnesses and discharge them whilst I explain what has happened to Marla. I'll meet you back in the robing room.'

***

Ten minutes later, Woake was back in the robing room. There was no sign of Myers, but Teague and Martin had already disrobed and were about to leave. They both pulled holdalls.

Teague noticed Woake disrobing. He also noticed that Woake had not put a soft collar back onto his tunic shirt and was therefore tieless.

'We're just off now,' Teague said to him. 'But I just wanted to pass on my thanks to Richard for allowing the matter to go to a probation report.'

'No problem at all,' Woake replied. 'I shall pass on your thanks.'

'Thank you,' Teague responded, falling silent for a second, as if he was deciding whether to trust Woake with what he had to say next. He leant forward. 'I do hate these bloody benefit cheats.'

'You did what you had to do for her, and for her children,' Woake answered.

'Wish I didn't have to. Would have liked to have seen the bitch roasted,' Teague leant backwards, and smiled. 'Looking forward to seeing you on the 25th,' he said as he and Martin left.

As a solicitor, Adams was not allowed into the sanctum of the robing room.

Woake was sitting cross-legged in an armchair, reading his council emails on his iPad when Myers walked back in.

'Enjoying ourselves, are we?' Myers asked.

'Just catching up on pro bono. How was Marla?'

Myers cut Woake a sharp look. 'Tell you what dear boy, in light of the fact we have just secured for ourselves a cracked trial, why don't we celebrate with a pub lunch somewhere in the Hampshire countryside?'

'And Marla?' Woake asked with a grin.

'Don't speak to me about that bloody woman. Just spent half an hour of my life explaining to that idiot what had just happened. You know what women like that are, don't you? They're life support machines for a fucking clitoris.'

'Have bad news, Richard,' Woake said, ignoring Myers.

'In what way?'

'I'm unable to do the 25th August,' Woake answered. Seeing the questioning look Myers was giving him, Woake decided it was political to carry on before Myers interrupted him. 'I've already booked the day off as I have a personal appointment that day which has been in my diary for a while.'

'Playing bloody politics again, you mean,' Myers said.

'No comment, Richard.'

'In that case, I'll have to find another Junior to appear with me. Although this will mean a reduction of the fee you can expect. In the meantime, can you dig out of the library some case history of sentencing which other benefit cheats have received?'

'Of course,' Woake answered.

Angelina Burbridge sat at her own desk, with the same feelings John Todd had felt a couple of hours earlier. It was nearing the evening, but Burbridge was nowhere near finishing her work for that day.

She had spent the intervening hours working on the Prasad funeral.

A viewing room had been organised, so that Anjali Prasad's family could pay their respects to her open casket. For that, Burbridge had organised for the Room of Remembrance to be emptied, with express guidance that the contents were to be replaced as soon as the viewing had been over.

Hopefully, no one would decide to remember a dead relative during the service. In Burbridge's experience, very few mourners ever returned to the crematorium following a service. She did not feel like telling the councillors during the tour that the flowers which had filled the room had been put there during the day solely to make the Room of Remembrance look more popular than it otherwise had been.

Preparing the chapel had been easy; white flowers were to be placed strategically around the Christian tokens, whilst a pujari had been hired to lead the chanting of the mantras and lead the service.

The most challenging aspect of the organisation was the cremation itself. As Vinod had rightly stated to his wife, Hindu practice dictated that the relatives lead the cremation itself and can only leave once it had been completed.

For this, Burbridge required the assistance of Robbie Cole, the vertically challenged technician in charge of the cremator.

Unable to face the prospect of discussing the details of the Prasad funeral with Cole (the moving coffins were still an image too fresh in her memory), she instead wrote him an email.

As is typical of a person in management conversing with an individual of more practical expertise, Angelina Burbridge confused Cole's lowlier status with a lack of intellect. She therefore detailed in exceptionally simple language the requirements she needed.

Unfortunately, as is typical of a person in management, Burbridge had overestimated the efficiency of email.

In the spirit of inclusivity, Gretford District Council had previously granted every employee an email account, regardless of whether they needed it, wanted it or even required it. To that end, employees such as cleaners, gardeners and caretakers had been given their own unique Gretford email address, accessible at their workstations.

However, for many of them, a computer was not a required tool for their workstations; so not only were they unable to check their emails, but many were oblivious that they were even granted an email account in the first place.

This included Robbie Cole.

As she sent her email and left for home with the contentment that can only come by passing responsibility further down the chain of command, Angelina Burbridge was blissfully unaware that Robbie Cole would never read her email.

That evening, *The Gretford Gazette* broke the news of the formation of the Major Projects team. The article provided full details of the formation of the committee, including details of the planned projects and the membership of the team.

The article speculated on the source of the finance.

In keeping with the fine tradition of the district leaking like a sieve, knowledge of the team's formation had been made known to *The Gazette* by a leak.

Three to be precise.

As angry messages were flying on the Cabinet's WhatsApp group, nobody questioned why Foster, Overton and Williams were all the most passionate in their annoyance.

Unbeknown to the other two, each one had been the source. Their motive, however, was the same; to further their own standing in their respective political careers.

Thirty

Wednesday 24ᵗʰ August 2016

The sun rose brightly, promising the people of Gretford a warm summer's day. At ten o'clock that morning, the Gretford welcoming committee congregated at the bottom of the cobbled high street.

William Foster, Craig Overton and Charles Williams represented the Cabinet, Williams having already established himself as a key ally to the leadership. They stood on one side of Mayor Joplin, resplendent in his full scarlet robes and bicorne hat.

Not that Mayor Joplin felt overly resplendent. Gretford's low slung shops provided little shade from the warm summer sun.

The Binzhou delegation was due to arrive at half-past ten, having spent the previous night at Sam Tong's university residence. Tong was to accompany the Binzhou delegation as its official translator during the course of its visit.

Sam Tong's presence would also provide the Binzhou delegation with one further benefit. Being a Binzhou citizen, Tong knew his loyalties lay with the town of his birth as opposed to the town of his adoption. However, his position as vice-chancellor of the local university provided him a unique knowledge into the otherwise confidential workings of Gretford District Council; a knowledge he saw as his duty to pass onto Binzhou.

The confidential messages from the University of South-East England to the Council had been encouraging; the Chinese had shown their willingness to invest heavily in the university's proposed development of its science park and the university student housing project.

The Council was therefore confident that they too would receive financial assistance.

Not that Mayor Joplin felt overly confident.

When his chauffeur had parked his car outside the guildhall at nine thirty, Mayor Joplin had all the confidence of a councillor who was the only one to have been driven by his chauffeur to a welcoming committee for a foreign delegation (and a Far-East Asian one at that).

It was for that reason he had shunned his PA's advice not to wear his ceremonial robes, but just the gold chains of office instead. As most westerners do who lack any knowledge or experience of Chinese culture, Mayor Joplin was firmly of the opinion that Chinese history started only in the communist takeover of 1949.

Believing that the Binzhou delegation would be awed by pomp and tradition, Mayor Joplin had elected for full robes. Besides, he remembered seeing on some television advert that the colour red was a sign of luck in China.

It was with great pride that Mayor Joplin admired himself in front of the mirror in the guildhall parlour, believing that his scarlet uniform would bring luck to his residents that day.

Now, at ten minutes past ten that morning, Mayor Joplin was not so sure that he had not erred in his choice.

It was with some trepidation that Mayor Joplin first felt a trickle of perspiration flow down his spine, which by ten thirty had become a flood. As the sweat flowed into his eyes, steaming his glasses, Mayor Joplin felt with growing anxiety his cheeks beginning to flush.

If his robes were worn as a symbol of good luck, then by the time the delegation arrived, he was positively a symbol of fortuitousness incarnate.

Of course, Mayor Joplin's growing sense of unease was further exacerbated by the sight of the three other councillors standing quite coolly to one side, and Giles Bane and the other directors standing just as serenely on the other.

The high street had been closed off specially for the arrival of the Binzhou representatives. With uncharacteristic efficiency, two taxis had picked the delegation up at the appointed time of ten fifteen.

As Peter Lo's residence was located on the western side of the town, the delegation (and their Gretford counterparts) was blissfully unaware of the build-up of traffic on the northbound A32, the main dual carriageway located to the north of the district.

Craig Overton stood smiling as the two taxis arrived. Whils
would only admit his nervousness to his boyfriend later that even.
Overton dreamt of his future political career; being welcomed by
and welcoming foreign dignitaries from around the world.

For a brief moment, Overton allowed himself to exaggerate
the importance of the Binzhou visit, believing himself to be a
senior Government minister, rather than a deputy leader of a local
authority unheard of by anyone from outside of Sussex.

The minibus stopped in front of the Gretford delegation, and
Sam Tong stepped out cheerfully.

Behind him emerged the eight delegates from Binzhou.

Overton was struck by the similarities of all eight of them. Hailing
from a country not known for encouraging individualism, all eight
Binzhou men were dressed in exactly the same suit cut and colour,
but shared the same skin complexion and hair style. The group
was split evenly between old and young, the young obliviously the
deputies for the older half.

All eight delegates were male; the eldest could have been anywhere
between forty and sixty years old, the youngest between thirty and
forty.

Mayor Joplin walked towards the Binzhou delegation as soon as they
had alighted from the taxis, not waiting for Sam Tong to introduce
him. He stuck out his hand to the one who he considered to be the
leader of the group, who stood in the centre of the nine Chinamen.

'Good morning gentlemen, and welcome to Gretford. I am
Mayor Joplin and it is my great pleasure to extend to all of you the
warmest possible welcome.'

It was with some surprise for his intended victim that Mayor
Joplin grabbed the delegate by the hand and warmly shook it.

Not used to returning a handshake, the Chinaman's hand hung
limply like a landed fish in the Mayor's hand. It was also obvious by
the way he stood awe-struck, that the Chinaman had no knowledge
of what either an ill man or a deranged lunatic dressed as a lobster
was saying to him.

Thankfully, he was saved by a quick translation from Sam Tong.

The man spoke back.

'Jianjun Li would like to thank the Mayor for his warm welcome and would like to extend his warmest welcome back,' Tong said diplomatically.

"What the fuck is this lunatic saying?" would have been a more realistic translation of what Jianjun Li had said.

'He's welcoming you to Gretford,' Tong told Li, reverting back into Mandarin.

'Who is he, except someone who looks like he's about to have a fucking heart attack?' Li asked as he returned Mayor Joplin's handshake. 'Very nice to be here,' he added in broken English.

'He's the Mayor of Gretford,' Tong said in Mandarin, causing Li to smile even more warmly at the Mayor. Li was more used to the American executive style of Mayor.

Realising that, Tong explained the importance of an English Mayor. 'All he is, is the leading citizen in the town. He doesn't actually have any actual power. He's purely ceremonial.'

'So what does he do?' Li asked in Mandarin, breaking back into English as he spoke to the Mayor. 'Lovely day today, yes?'

'Chairs meetings and meets the public. Oh, he also meets guests like you,' Tong answered in Mandarin.

'So he doesn't have any real power?' Li asked. 'I'm very much looking forward to seeing your lovely town,' he told the Mayor.

'None at all, though he likes to think he does,' Tong answered.

'Then who does?' Li asked in Mandarin. 'Do you often wear those clothes?' he asked in broken English.

'The man to his right, who's called Giles Bane, he's the Managing Director. The short fat man to the Mayor's left is the Leader of the Council. He holds chief political office.'

Mayor Joplin had stood still as Tong and Li had conversed in Mandarin, all the while growing as uneasy as any man would who sensed that he was the subject of intense debate in language of which "limited grasp" would have been an exaggeration of his understanding.

This was confirmed when, to his horror, Li walked away from him as he explained the importance of the mayoral robes and instead spoke to Bane.

'I understand that you are the one with power here?' Li asked, oblivious to the stirrings from the rest of the district delegates, mostly from the councillors. 'Perhaps Sam could introduce us?'

Sam stood forward, accompanied by the other seven Binzhou

delegates, as both sides were introduced to each other.

'It really is my pleasure to welcome you all to our special, beautiful district,' Foster said to the Chinese, through the interpreting of Sam Tong. Foster was as annoyed as the Mayor by Li's focus on Bane, and therefore keen to gain the initiative for the Cabinet over the directors.

'We have a full agenda for you over the course of the next two days. To start with, one half of you will attend an address in the guildhall followed by lunch, whilst the other half will join a tour of the district with the Mayor.'

'Who's going on the tour?' Li asked one of his younger colleagues from Binzhou. As the Mayor had quickly surmised, as deputy secretary of the Binzhou Communist Party, Jianjun Li was the most senior delegate present.

'You sir,' Zhang Yong responded, 'as well as me, Ying Han and Wang Wei.' Ying Han was the Deputy Chief Executive of the Binzhou prefecture and the delegation's treasury spokesman, whilst Wang Wei was the city's Deputy Director for Information, Technology and Enterprise.

'So the three most senior of us have to go with the lobster whilst three of the most junior have to go with their policymakers?'

'So it would seem, sir,' Yong responded, his ever-diligent deputy. Li turned back to face Foster and the other Gretford leaders and addressed them through Tong.

'There is some mistake. Me, Ying Han, Li Qiang and Wang Wei will go with you, and Zhang Yong, Li Jie, Donghui Niu and Junjie Meilin will go with his highness.' Mayor Joplin turned red at this address, though was unsure whether this was because of the heat, his embarrassment at being addressed in such terms or his anger at this slight.

'I am afraid it's quite impor...,' Foster started to answer, only to be interrupted by Jianjun Li.

'Shall we get going?' he asked, already walking away from the meeting, directed towards the guildhall by Sam Tong. Han, Wei and Qiang following loyally behind. The Gretford delegates had no option but to follow in their wake.

The more junior Binzhou delegates remained with the Mayor.

The Mayor stood on his own, facing four Chinamen in front of him.

'Shall we get going then?' he asked, to no response. It was with a growing sense of despair that he stood silently facing the four men.

A photographer and a reporter had been invited from *The Gretford Gazette* to report on the historic meeting between the Gretford and Binzhou authorities.

'This represents a new age for the people of Gretford,' Foster had told the reporter as the two political leaders were photographed shaking hands in a symbol of future cooperation. For Foster, it marked the pinnacle of his political career, an opportunity for him to play statesman.

'At a time when the UK retreats away from our European neighbours, it becomes ever more important that leaders, whether they be at a national or local level, reach out the hand of friendship to any potential friend and ally, in order to strive for mutual benefits for our people, to take advantage of our respective strengths and to propel our towns across the world,' Foster had concluded.

'And you sir?' the reporter had asked Li, 'what do you hope to gain from it?'

'For Binzhou, this new friendship represents many exciting opportunities of significant benefit to both the people of Binzhou and Gretford,' Jianjun Li answered through Sam Tong. "To make money" would have been a rather more accurate translation of Li's response.

The reporter and the photographer had been ushered away shortly afterwards, and the two delegations sat at a horseshoe-shaped board table in the centre of the guildhall, facing each other with Sam Tong sitting in the middle, ready to act as translator if the need arose.

A microphone was positioned in front of each delegate.

Giles Bane sat in the centre of the Gretford delegation, a position he had ensured for himself.

'Kate,' he had told the Mayor's PA, who had been tasked with organising the meeting, 'will you do me a favour? When it comes to our guildhall meeting with the Chinese, would you stick me in the middle, opposite Jianjun Li? And stick Will to my right and Craig next to him.'

In a move that would not have surprised Bane, Foster had also asked Kate exactly the same thing. As the political leader, Foster felt it to be his place to sit opposite Li.

Reflective of either his own lack of standing amongst district officers, or perhaps because Kate was married to a banker (as her brand-new Range Rover and endless supply of pashminas would testify) and was in one of the most enviable positions of all Council staff, she could vent her lack of respect for the leadership. Foster now sat sulkily next to Bane.

Giles Bane leant forward to address the meeting. 'I think we have exhausted all our welcomes, and as we have a full agenda for the next two days and only limited time in which to talk, why don't we press ahead?' he said, as Tong translated.

'There are many areas in which we can discuss future friendship and cooperation between our two towns, from different insights into technologies, to investment in each other's projects, to provision of hubs for Binzhou and Gretford businesses, to potential commercial links.

'You are very fortunate to be here at a very exciting time for Gretford. After years of very limited investment, Gretford is now planning to start some major new projects. With that outcome in mind, the Council has recently formed its own Major Projects team to provide oversight to these developments.

'Without more ado, may I please introduce our recently appointed Major Projects manager, Mike Warsop, to discuss the projects in greater detail.'

The Chinese turned towards Tong, as the man who was responsible for translating Warsop's presentation.

Warsop spoke for the next half an hour, repeating much of his presentation from the first Major Projects team meeting. For the Gretford team, they appeared to be listening intently. As far as outward appearance would show, this was the first time they had been told about EARP.

For the Chinese, Li had other ideas. Within minutes of listening to Sam Tong's dire interpretation of Warsop's dull presentation, a spurt of Mandarin from Li, which also stopped Tong's translations, interrupted the presentation. Li turned back to Bane, all smiles on his face. 'Sorry,' he said 'our English is good enough in order to understand you.' As their own limited grasp of the English language had saved them from the mind-numbingly dull tones of

Mike Warsop, the Chinese sat, pretending to be entranced by the architectural plans, the overhead photographs and the diagrams of projected growth across the district in the next twenty years, which were being shown on the large screen behind Warsop.

The Chinamen watched the presentation. Except for Ying Han, the Binzhou treasury spokesman, who sat oblivious to the screen. Instead he concentrated on the print out which had been supplied to all delegates.

'Sam, can you translate?' Ying Han asked, cutting straight across Warsop, who sat silently furious at the disrespect which had been shown to him. Tong sat, ready to translate. 'I am looking at the figures for each of these projects. How much will the grand total be?'

'The Enton Area Regeneration Project will cost approximately £150 million. The water treatment works about £20 million, with a £10 million contribution from Thames Water and about another £15 million for the bus station,' Warsop answered.

'Our latest oil refinery alone cost that much,' Han responded in Mandarin.

'A very impressive amount,' Tong translated into English.

'Where will you get that investment from?' Han asked.

Charlotte Bateup responded. 'There are many avenues of investment available to us. We can borrow money from what is called the Public Works Loan Board at a cheap level of interest.'

'Who owns that?' Han asked.

'The Government,' Bateup answered.

'So your Government gives you the money to do something, and it then makes money out of you, all the time it funds its own investment scheme through tax as well as its loans from other countries, mainly China?' Han asked.

'A very sensible policy,' Tong said instead.

'We can sell assets to raise the capital, or we can approach third-party investors.'

'Such as us?' Li said in Mandarin. Tong decided it was policy not to translate this.

'So you cannot afford to pay for these projects yourself?' Han asked.

'It represents a struggle, but as I say, there are many avenues for us to investigate and many opportunities as we gain the level of investment required.'

'No,' Tong translated.

'How are you going to invest in our projects if you cannot invest in your own? What do you have to offer us in return?' Han asked.

The Gretford delegates looked amongst each, wide-eyed and open-mouthed. Safety came from the unlikely source that was Mike Warsop.

'Perhaps we should look at the finances in greater depth.'

For the next hour, Warsop and Bateup led the Binzhou politicians through a masterclass of delay, bluster and ossification. Graphs, tables and pie charts were all used in order to sell the attraction of investing in such a forward-looking district.

At the strike of one o'clock, a mentally drained and physically hungry Managing Director noticed with relief that it was now lunchtime.

'I think that this is a good time for us to stop for lunch. As I hope you can see, we can provide an excellent opportunity for any investor looking for a very attractive proposition.

'After lunch, we will take you on a helicopter tour of our very special district. Now, if you would like to follow me into the Mayor's parlour, I believe that our lunch is now ready.'

Foster piled high a plate full of dry sandwiches and limp canapes and with a large glass of tepid Chardonnay in his other hand, walked towards Jianjun Li, who was busy explaining the latest developments in oil technology to a mystified Peter West, whose only responses to oil refinery comprised 'Really' and 'You don't say'.

Jianjun Li saw Foster walk towards him.

'How are you finding your time in England?' he asked, placing the wine to one side as he began to clumsily eat his lunch. In contrast, Li was not eating and was only drinking sparkling water.

'You're very fortunate to live in such a beautiful area,' Li answered through Sam Tong as Foster ate yet another canape 'but are you not concerned about your ability to see the projects through to their conclusions?'

'I appreciate that finances are a potential issue, but you have to remember that these are very challenging times for the UK, not to say quite unprecedented.'

'I wasn't referring to your ability to pay for the projects. Though at the moment, it appears that Gretford can offer Binzhou a lot less than what Binzhou can offer Gretford.'

'I wouldn't say that,' Foster said 'we could provide a unique opportunity to provide access to UK markets for many of your companies,' Foster said, remembering the briefings.

'Many of which are oil and energy companies. How is your own oil industry?'

With a face drooping to mimic the limp sandwich in his hand, Foster had to admit that it was non-existent.

'But of course, by what I mean by your ability to see the projects through is more to do with your political situation.'

'I can assure you that Gretford is a very strong and stable local authority. My own Group is totally dominant in Gretford.'

'For the time being, yes, but who is to say that it will be after the next election? Which is when?'

'In two years.'

'So in two years, your Group could have lost power, and where will the projects be then?'

'Rest assured that I am determined not to lose the next election.'

'So says every politician. But what happens if another political party takes over and cancels these projects?'

'Don't you have elections?'

'Yes, but we have the advantage that we select who stands and select the results. The public is very understanding in accepting that their political leaders always have their best intentions at heart.'

'You don't say,' Foster said, somewhat envious of the Chinese political system.

'Unfortunately, we are going to have to see some long-term security in these proposed projects before we consider investing.'

When the lunch finished, a taxi arrived to take the Binzhou delegation and Councillor Charles Williams to Fairbourne Airfield, located in the neighbouring town of Hinton.

As the delegation left, William Foster sent a message to the rest of the Cabinet on the Cabinet's WhatsApp group.

Very successful lunch with our new friends from Binzhou. Early indications for greater cooperation are very encouraging and we must all work hard over the next 24 hours to secure a basis for future agreement. Good luck Charles with the flight!

One man who at least was not quite so publicly confident was Mayor Joplin.

After the indignity of being forced into a minibus with what was obviously the more junior members of the Binzhou party, the Mayor had been alarmed to realise that only one member of the party had any grasp of English.

Or at least pretended to.

The other three spent the rest of the tour studying their mobile phones, seemingly oblivious to events around them.

As the taxi left Gretford High Street and turned onto the gridlocked gyratory system, the Mayor attempted to engage the one English-speaking delegate in conversation.

It had not been a success.

'I'm going to show you the location of EARP. A site in the urban suburbs of Gretford which will provide housing, restaurants, cafes, schools and doctors' surgeries.'

'How many houses?' Li Jie asked.

'I understand about a thousand,' the Mayor had responded, not at all sure if he had given the correct answer, but at least one thousand sounded impressive.

'Our latest housing project in Binzhou provided ten thousand homes,' Li Jie had responded.

The A32 dual carriageway provided the opportunity for the Mayor to talk about one of his passions, the expansion of the carriageway into three lanes in order to aid congestion.

'This road provides the main traffic artery through the district, as you can see it is very busy, even at eleven in the morning.'

'How many lanes does the road have?' Jie asked, interrupting the Mayor.

'Two, although there are many of us.'

'Our largest road has four,' Jie said, interrupting the Mayor, who would never have the opportunity to explain his theory for traffic easing, let alone ask the Chinese for the financial assistance, which represented the biggest hurdle for the Mayor's plans.

'Is the traffic usually this busy?' Jie asked. The taxi had travelled half a mile in an hour.

'It's an absolute bloody disgrace, mate,' said the taxi driver, not one to pass up on the opportunity to vent his frustration to a councillor. 'It doesn't help that there's an accident on the A32, but all we hear is bollocks from the Council like sustainable corridors and model shift. Look at that lane over there. It's a bloody bus lane, but where are the buses? Stuck in all the other bloody lanes, attempting to make their turns either on or off the roads.

'I've told them many times, but they're not bloody interested. Remove the bus lane and free the lane up. This will provide the additional space which is needed for all the traffic. But they're not bloody interested. Apparently, it's to do with pollution and climate change, attempting to get more of us onto buses. But what the idiots don't realise is that stationary traffic causes yet more pollution.'

'Do all your drivers interrupt their betters?' Jie asked.

'Who are you saying is my better, matey? Because I'm driving a cab and you're in a sodding suit?'

'In China, none of our drivers would ever dare interrupt.'

'We're not in sodding China, matey.'

To the Mayor's relief, the taxi eventually found its way to the site of the Enton Area Regeneration Project.

'What is it?' Jie asked, not hiding the disappointment in his voice.

'You're looking at it,' Mayor Joplin answered 'it's going to be built on this industrial unit. To maintain an income, the Council has just bought a disused industrial estate half a mile away, to which we'll move all the businesses across.'

'How big is the estate you have just bought?' Jie asked.

'About 100 acres. I understand that it's the biggest estate we have ever bought.'

'Our smallest estate is 100 acres in size.'

Considering the disappointment of Gretford's urban offering, the Mayor hoped that the tour of the majesty of the surrounding countryside which formed the start of the South Downs would awe his Chinese audience.

As the minibus wound its way through country lanes, the Mayor explained the challenges facing Gretford's housing need.

'The issue we have is that we need houses, but yet we don't have anywhere to put them.'

'Why not over there?' Jie asked, pointing to open farmland.

'Can't build there,' the taxi driver said. 'It's protected.'

'Why is it protected?'

The driver answered before the Mayor could. 'Protected to make sure that nobody can build on it. It's all about maintaining the countryside.'

'But if you need the homes, why not build?' Jie persisted.

'Not as simple as that, that there is someone's property, their land. Can't buy unless they want to sell, and you can't take it either. That's communism.'

'That's what we do,' Jie answered. 'If we need the houses, we build them.'

'Won't happen here mate, we've got laws.'

'Can't get in the way of progress.'

'You bloody can here, mate. Some of us like to look at the countryside.'

'I think we should get back to Gretford,' Mayor Joplin told the driver.

'I agree, can't wait to get rid of these bastards.'

'Where are we going?' Jie asked.

'We're going to drop you off at Gretford Museum, which celebrates our town's centuries old history. My colleague, Councillor Fulcher-Wells, is going to talk you through the £3 million redevelopment of the museum.'

'How big is the museum?' Jie asked.

'It's currently in a small building in the castle grounds.'

'Binzhou's is in a purpose-built facility in order to celebrate our own glorious history,' Jie said, displaying the communist ability to disregard facts.

Especially as Binzhou had only been established in the 1980s.

The sky over Gretford remained clear as the sun beat down upon the town, basking the town in glorious sunshine, an urban oasis in the Sussex countryside.

Few Gretford residents dared leave their offices, preferring to seek shelter from their air conditioning. And those few who were outside would have been too awe-struck by the magnificence of the sky to notice the high-flying helicopter, and would have cared even less for those who flew in it.

Shortly after lunch, the more senior half of the Binzhou delegation, accompanied by Sam Tong, were escorted into a taxi, accompanied by Charles Williams.

Williams sat in the front of the taxi, turning around to face the Chinese, barely able to hide his excitement. At last, here was a councillor with the ability to properly impress the Chinese.

'As we take off, you'll get an excellent view of the latest building developments at Woking,' Williams informed the group. 'Now you won't be impressed with Woking. Frankly, nobody is. The most famous thing about it is that it is the original setting for War of the Worlds. You know, that film with Tom Cruise?'

It surprised Williams to see the Chinese nod back; little did Williams know that a film featuring the total destruction of the US was a box-office sensation in China.

'Not that the aliens would be particularly interested in Woking nowadays, they'd take one look at it as soon as they arrived, realise it's not worth the effort and then leave.'

The minibus made it to the small private airfield and at Williams's directions, drove straight towards a wooden barn seconded as a hanger. Its large wooden doors were opened and a blue medium-sized but ageing executive helicopter had been rolled out of the barn.

A beaming Williams walked straight towards it. 'I had the girl taken out this morning for us. It's a bit of luck actually you being here from my point of view. We're going to be flying into another airfield towards the south of Gretford for its bimonthly service. Oh, no need to look too concerned, I've organised for another taxi to collect us and bring us back.'

For the first time in many years, Williams had misread facial expressions. The look of apprehension on the faces of his passengers were not born from wonder at how they would return from their destination, but in the wonder of whether they would even reach their destination in the dated machine.

The party climbed into the helicopter, Williams taking the controls with three of the Chinese sitting in the second row. Li took his place next to Williams. Williams completed the pre-flight checks and the engine spat into life.

Passengers and pilot put on their headsets and there was a sudden lurching as Williams applied the throttle and the helicopter rose into the sky.

Unbeknown to Williams, this was not the first time that any of the Binzhou representatives had been in a helicopter, being the mode of transport of choice for Binzhou councillors wishing to avoid their city's busy congestion.

As the ground grew smaller beneath them, Williams eased the stick forward and applied the rudder to the right, providing the occupants of the helicopter with a view of Woking to the left and, nestled gently in its valley, Gretford.

The contrast between the two towns could not be starker. One resulted from gradual development, continuous throughout the centuries, with its low-rise buildings and cobbled high street and suburbs ordered neatly around the market town centre.

The other resulted from overenthusiastic development since the 1940s, whose modernity had ensured little remained of the original village settlement, but yet whose characterless 1960s development had ensured continual build ever since. Its sprawling suburbia offered little in the way of character and provided even less in the way of community for its residents.

Williams and his passengers were afforded the perfect view of the latest victim for an insatiable demand for American imports; the skyscraper.

The Chinese smiled in appreciation as below them a complex of four skyscrapers, each measuring thirty storeys, rose from the centre of Woking. The two towns stood facing each other, like David and Goliath; symbols of an unfair battle waged between conservatism and reckless modernity fought throughout the twentieth century.

Jianjun Li turned to Williams, who piloted the helicopter away from Woking and towards Gretford.

'Lots of construction in that town,' Li commented.

'The local council has invested heavily in inner-town development, including those high-rise buildings that you can see. But they are also building a new shopping centre, or mall as you probably call it. As well as restaurant plazas and apartment blocks more akin to central London,' Williams answered as fully as he could, never being one not to demonstrate his expert knowledge on all things relating to property.

'Why don't you do the same in Gretford?' Li asked.

'Can't do that.'

'Why not?' Li persisted.

'Not how we do things in Gretford, dear boy. The residents won't like it for a start. Not to mention the money situation.'

'Why are the residents important? You mentioned earlier that you have a housing shortage. If you build them houses, why should they care where they're built?'

'Can't ignore the residents,' Williams answered 'elections are vital. If we build something our residents don't like, they'll chuck us out.'

Li spoke into his headset, addressing his colleagues in their native Mandarin. To his alarm, Williams heard Li mention several times not only Woking but also his own name, as a conversation quickly developed between the Chinese. Williams could only surmise that the Chinese found Woking a much more attractive investment.

'Below us is the Prism, Gretford's main leisure complex. In addition to its own Olympic-sized swimming pool, its ice rink is home to the Icicles, Gretford's very own major league ice hockey team.'

'Why is it surrounded by scaffolding?' Li asked.

'Repairs to the roof,' Williams answered, his unease over the conversation in Mandarin having ensured he answered the question perhaps too quickly as he otherwise should have.

'What's wrong with the roof?'

'It unfortunately leaks,' Williams answered.

'Is it not weatherproof?' Li asked.

'Unfortunately not. The design was very far-sighted back in the 1980s,' Williams responded, believing that his best tactic now lay in confusing Li by answering as fully as possible.

'The Prism is essentially one large greenhouse,' Williams continued 'with a roof made entirely of glass, supported in position by steel struts. Unfortunately, the designers failed to consider two factors. Firstly, that such a large structure will move with the weather and the steel struts are totally inflexible, which causes the roof to crack in high winds or in periods of high humidity or cold weather.

'Secondly, the glass roof causes the building to have its own microclimate. About a million and a half people visit the building per year. The heat from that many people obviously rises to the top of the roof, which, because it's made of glass, turns into water. If enough water forms on the underside of the roof, it falls back to the ground, essentially as rain. Quite clever actually.'

'How do you stop that from happening?'

'Quite ingenious, actually. Apparently, we have tied large tarpaulins underneath the roof in order to collect the water, and every so often the water is emptied. The reason I have brought you here is to show you the planned location of its intended replacement. Our intention is to build a new leisure centre and then knock this one down.'

'How long before the replacement is built?'

'We're moving quite quickly on this one. We're hoping to be in a position to start building in about ten years.' Williams saw the look Jianjun Li was giving him. 'Obviously, we need to consult with residents, get architectural plans, apply for planning permission and appoint contractors,' Williams added. He felt it prudent not to add "and secure finances".

'What he means is, he wants us to finance another giant greenhouse,' Li said to his fellow compatriots in Mandarin. 'Judging from the state of this dump, looks like this thing will fall down in ten years anyway.'

The helicopter tour continued, with a flight over the planned EARP (mixed interest in this from the Chinese), to the rolling countryside of the South Downs (minimum interest in this) and the proposed sites of the major housing projects (lots of interest in this).

Towards the end of the afternoon, and with the helicopter low on fuel, Williams concluded the tour with a flyover Gretford high street.

'And this is where you first saw Gretford,' Williams said, 'the high street with the famous cobbled setts.'

'What are all those people doing down there?' Li asked.

'Oh, I think they're something to do with tonight's meeting,' Williams answered, not wanting to voice his suspicion that they looked like the rumoured demonstrators gathering outside the guildhall.

'Looks like they're carrying banners,' Li added.

'Uhm, could be something for tonight's Full Council. I understand that you're going to that,' Williams said, wanting to divert the conversation away from the crowd on the high street, which disappeared as he guided the helicopter towards the second airfield.

'You know you should be honoured to see tonight's Full Council. As I'm sure you're aware, we'll be voting on whether to put our plans for future development to the people for consultation.'

'Are you happy about the demonstrators?' Li asked.

'Not much you can do about that, dear boy, living in a free country and all that. Don't you ever have demonstrators in Binzhou?'

'Never, the people are always grateful that we, as their elected representatives, always make the correct decisions which are in their best interests.'

Williams did not respond to this, privately envious of an electoral system which could guarantee him victory every four years.

Later, after the Chinese had been collected, Williams messaged his Cabinet colleagues.

Very successful trip. The Binzhou lot seem to be very impressed with our future plans and appear to be interested in discussing this further. BTW, looks like a lively crowd on the high street.

Thirty One

Councillor Patricia Lafontaine took her position outside Gretford Guildhall at exactly five o'clock that evening. Three other Gretford Guardians were with her; her two fellow councillors and her husband, who had been subpoenaed (somewhat reluctantly and certainly silently) into helping with the protest.

The four unveiled a large ten-by-four-metre banner, which required all four of them to carry. Within minutes, other protesters had joined the four Guardians.

It started as a trickle of protesters, the most dedicated of campaigners to protect intrusion into the Gretford countryside. By a quarter to six, over a thousand Gretford residents from the villages congregated to vent their frustration.

Representatives from the Campaign to Protect Rural England mingled with those from Save Chalk Pit Farm, who rubbed shoulders with the Cobe Action Group, who in turn were supported by a joint group representing all the district's Parish Councils.

Hundreds of banners fluttered in the early evening sun as the protest effectively closed the high street to pedestrians and cars. Shoppers, unable to pass the mass of people, were forced into side alleyways and lanes. Shops, cafes and pubs became refuges for residents, waiting for the storm to pass.

Cars, unable to drive up the high street, ground to a halt, causing gridlocked traffic on the already busy gyratory.

At precisely ten minutes to six, Lafontaine held a microphone to her mouth and addressed the demonstration.

'This Local Plan represents the biggest change for Gretford! Are we going to stand by and let our beautiful countryside be trashed by this Tory Council?' she asked the crowd.

'No!' came the unanimous response.

'Are we going to let this Tory Council know we will fight them?'

'Yes!'

'As a typical mark of this Council's arrogance, this Tory administration has invited a group of communist investors all the way from China with the sole intention of stumping up the cash to bulldoze over your villages! Will you let them?'

'No!'

'Are we going to send the Council and the communists a message?'

'Yes!'

Lafontaine turned her back on the crowd, holding the banner in her left hand and the microphone in her right. Taking a deep breath, she took her first step as she led the demonstration down the high street towards the Council Chamber.

Like Moses leading his people from Egypt, Lafontaine swept down Gretford high street, the waves of shoppers parting in her wake.

Lafontaine did not need to look behind to check that her supporters followed her.

'Save Gretford!' she shouted.

'Save our villages!' her followers shouted back.

'Protect our wildlife!' 'Protect our countryside!' 'Sod the Chinese!' rang out across the high street as the largest collection of retirees, tweed, chinos, Musto and Barbour in Gretford history made its way towards Fordhouse.

Sebastian Woake had just parked his car in the Council car park and was sorting that evening's papers in the boot of his Discovery when he first noticed the sound of a loudhailer and the growing hum of a large crowd making its way towards him.

'Save Gretford!' the crowd shouted

'We are not prepared to let this Council trash our countryside,' shouted a voice he recognised on the loudhailer.

'They will not trash our town!' the crowd shouted back.

Woake looked up from his boot; he had reversed into the space so he could quickly drive out again, a habit he had acquired from his days in the army. He looked on passively as a huge green banner was carried through the narrow car park entrance.

Behind the banner, hundreds of people attempted to file their way through the entrance and into the Council offices.

Alarmed by the sight of the approaching campaigners, the four on-duty caretakers had called out for Giles Bane, who now stood on the top of the staircase.

Fully in the knowledge that he would have as much success as Canute with an incoming tide, Bane held out his hands to the demonstrators in a sign of peace.

To Bane's relief, Lafontaine stopped the demonstrations a couple of steps away from him.

'We have the right to pass,' she said through her microphone, not through malice but through recent habit. Unfortunately, this was not much solace to Bane or the four men standing behind him, who all fell backwards as if by an unseen hand.

'Sorry,' she mumbled.

'You can pass, they can't,' Bane shouted back, owing to temporary deafness.

'Bully!' the crowd shouted. 'Patricia, lead the way!'

'This is a public meeting and members of the public are entitled to attend. And you don't have to shout!' she replied, shouting to Bane so all her supporters could hear her.

'I'm shouting because you used that bloody thing and I can't hear anything!' Bane shouted back.

'We're entering the Council building. As Gretford district councillors, it is our duty to attend as stated by law. Also stated by law are the rights of those standing behind me to attend too!'

'We only have space for three hundred people today, and we have to allow provision for other people of different opinions to you!' Bane shouted back.

'Shame on you!' voices shouted from the demonstration.

'In which case, two hundred people will follow me in!'

'Quite right, Patricia!' her supporters shouted back. 'Tell it to the bastards!'

'No they bloody won't, Patricia,' Bane shouted. 'We're already at half capacity, you can have a hundred supporters, and don't forget that it's this Council's right to refuse entry to such a large number on health and safety grounds,' he added, though he was not confident that he had the natural ability to order the demonstration aside.

Ben Jones, a local journalist from *The Gretford Gazette*, looked on from the reception area. Jones's role for that evening was to provide a live commentary feed on the gazette's website before publishing a full article in the morning.

Mass Demonstration Comes to Council, along with a photograph and a quick report, was Jones's first post.

GDC's Managing Director Seen Swearing and Shouting at Leader of the Gretford Guardians was the second.

Woake collected his papers and walked towards the Council offices. The nine-hundred Gretford Guardians demonstrators who had been denied entry congregated in the car park, banners and chants aplenty, hoping to intimidate as many Councillors and other members of the public as possible.

Woake walked through the demonstrators, ignoring the insults and the shouts that were thrown in his direction.

'Tory bastard! Shame on you!' a well-spoken middle-class woman shouted at him.

As he walked up the steps towards the foyer, a professional looking man in his forties held out a piece of paper to Woake. 'To remind you of your election promise,' the man said. Woake stopped and looked at the document. It was an election flyer.

The headline read *Greenbelt to Stay, Promise The Conservatives*, above a picture of Woake standing in a field.

'I'm sure that you won't believe me,' Woake said to the man 'but this is the first time I have ever read this document!'

Woake handed back the document and walked through into Fordhouse.

Woake entered the Council Chamber, to be greeted by Reg Swaden. 'Reminds me of being back in Northern Ireland with old rent-a-mob downstairs.'

'It does promise to be a rather lively evening,' Woake answered. Swaden noticed Woake looking at the regimental tie Swaden was wearing.

'I was firstly a gunner and then ended up in intelligence, if you can believe that. I understand you were a para?' Swaden asked.

'Spent three and a half years in second battalion.'

'Good for you, won't insult you by making any jokes about this reminding you of Afghanistan. Tell you one thing, that bloody bitch has riled that crowd up properly, expect a lively evening,' he said as he walked out of the Council Chamber and towards the gents.

Woake held the door open for councillors Turton and Alexandra Rushworth; Rushworth being one of only two Labour Party councillors in Gretford.

'Good evening, girls,' Woake addressed them. Turton smiled at him.

'Girls? How dare you be so patronising?' Rushworth said with forced pique.

'Now, now, Alexandra, if the PAs upstairs don't mind me referring to them as girls, then there's no reason why you, as the representative of the working person, should object too,' Woake said as he left them in the doorway.

It was a quarter to seven and the Council Chamber was already nearly full. The last remaining councillors were making their way to their seats. Councillor Kildare was, customarily, the last to arrive.

There were obvious deep divisions within the public gallery. One half of the public gallery comprised the Gretford Guardians supporters who had been allowed in, with more spilling into the extra room provided.

Another small group consisted of nervous looking men and women, who were all of working age and wearing suitable office attire. Woake correctly surmised them to be representatives of various property developers, surveyors and other interested commercial parties.

The third group comprised the supporters of Gretford Advisory Group. Banners opposing town development competed with banners opposing urban sprawl into the countryside.

The four rather nervous, not to mention still temporarily deaf, caretakers stood to attention on one side of the public gallery.

The Binzhou delegation, along with Sam Tong, sat on the edge of the Council Chamber.

Woake winked at Kildare as she sat down, who smiled back. Fulcher-Wells and Skelding sat on either side of him.

'Not wearing a tie tonight, Sebastian?' Fulcher-Wells asked disapprovingly.

'Afraid not, Cathy,' Woake answered, who sat in an open-necked tunic shirt under his suit. 'I was hoping to be able to have time to shower and change, but unfortunately the usual Gretford traffic had other ideas.'

Fulcher-Wells turned to Kildare. 'I think it's essential that male councillors look properly dressed at Full Councils, especially one as important as this. Wouldn't you agree, Serena?'

The arrival of the Mayor saved Fulcher-Wells before either Kildare or Woake could respond.

The hum of the packed Chamber fell into silence as the Mayor took his seat on the dais. Bane and the leadership sat beside him.

'Welcome ladies and gentlemen to this extraordinary meeting of Gretford District Council,' Mayor Joplin opened Full Council. 'I would also like to extend a welcome to our friends from Binzhou.'

'Bollocks to them and to the Local Plan!' a member of the public shouted from the public gallery, to warm applause.

'This meeting,' Mayor Joplin said, raising his voice 'has been called in order to discuss and vote on the next stage of the Gretford Local Plan.'

'Bollocks to development,' the same voice shouted back, to an even greater applause.

'I would remind the public that their presence here is a privilege and not a right. They will behave or I will ask them to leave.'

'Save our countryside!'

'Save our town!'

'There are three public speakers tonight. May I please call Martin St John from the Gretford Advisory Group to be the first speaker.'

St John walked towards the space on the benches reserved for public speakers, accompanied by cheers and boos, depending upon viewpoint.

'Thank you, Mr Mayor. It is my privilege to be chairman of the Gretford Advisory Group. It is the aim of our Group to not only challenge the Local Plan but to advise the Council as to the best way forward as to the future of our town. As I say, our aims are to challenge and to advise.'

'Start challenging by abandoning this bullshit!' a protester called.

'It is in the opinion of Gretford Advisory Group that this

Local Plan is in the worst possible interests of the town. The unprecedented level of development combined with the level of changes in infrastructure represent the biggest change in the fabric of Gretford in generations.

'The town cannot cope with the level of housing being imposed on it by the Council. It cannot cope with the level of traffic, building works and the extra thousands of people who will be living in the town.

'Gretford is an old historic town, and this Local Plan will ride roughshod over it. It would make more sense to build in the countryside, in the villages where we can start afresh, where we can build the necessary roads and traffic network, where there can be new towns and villages.

'No one at GAG denies we are in the grips of a housing crisis, that we need houses, especially affordable for frontline service providers on low incomes. We do not deny that the town could not benefit from investment. For that reason, GAG's official response to this Local Plan is currently being drafted and will set out proposals for what we consider to be sustainable development.

'Our Master Plan will be ready for publication within weeks and will be published regardless of the progress of the Local Plan.

'We urge the Council to do the decent thing and postpone consultation of the Local Plan until they have had the chance to read our own proposals.' St John stood up and made his way back to the public gallery, to a mixture of cheers and boos.

'May I please call James MacNulty,' Mayor Joplin said, relieved that his role so far was relegated to merely an observer.

A large rotund man, with red chinos and, in defiance to the hot evening, a tweed jacket, MacNulty made his way to the front of the Council Chamber.

'For the interests of openness and transparency, I should divulge that I am a quantity surveyor with over thirty years' experience,' MacNulty said, obviously believing that his professional experience gave him a unique perspective that anyone else would be foolish to disagree with. 'I should also divulge that I am chairman of the Cobe Action Group, which is an affiliated member of the Campaign to Protect Rural England and a member of the Gretford Guardians. I am speaking to you tonight in relation to this disastrous Local Plan, which this incompetent Council is disgracefully intent on forcing through the poor residents of this district's countryside,' MacNulty said, belonging to the school of thought that the best way to persuade your audience is by insulting it.

MacNulty continued.

'This Local Plan will destroy the countryside and our beloved villages. The green belt policies, long established over decades, will be spectacularly destroyed within months of the adoption of this abomination of a plan.'

'Here here!' cried a member of the audience.

'Tell the sheep what it's worth,' shouted another, causing a chorus of "baaing" sounds from the gallery.

'Save the town!' cried a lone voice, to murmurings of support from her side of the public gallery.

'In order to cope with the three thousand extra homes from the three largest developments, we will require more roads, more buses, more trains, more electrical and sewerage infrastructure, not to mention greater pollution.'

'There'll be more pollution in the town!' an urban resident shouted.

'All causing the destruction of our green and pleasant land. There is only one place in the whole of the district which can cope with the level of housing required and that's the town centre.'

'The town is full!' shouted a member of GAG. 'Build on your own garden!'

'Only the town has the capacity to cope with the influx of residents projected by this disgrace of a plan. Only the town has the space. Why not follow the example of Woking and build upwards?'

'You have thirty seconds left, Mr MacNulty,' Mayor Joplin said.

'Build large-scale towers, but keep the villages safe. The Gretford Guardians have the funds, we have the numbers and we will never stop fighting this pathetic Council.'

'You're out of time, Mr MacNulty,' Mayor Joplin said.

'We will fight you in the courts and on every...'

'Mr MacNulty,' Mayor Joplin said.

'Planning application,' MacNulty continued, oblivious to the Mayor's interruption.

'That is your five minutes. You have to stop,' Mayor Joplin persisted.

'We urge you to abandon this Plan and to meet with us.'

'Mr MacNulty, I must ask that you stop,' the Mayor added, pathetically.

'In order to seek a way forward for the benefit.'

'Oh, turn the bloody idiot's mike off,' Bane told the Council secretary, in a volume he considered to be a whisper. Unfortunately for the still deaf Bane, what he thought was a whisper was in fact loud enough to be heard by the entire Chamber. Within seconds, the Gretford Guardians' half of the room was in uproar.

'Stifling free speech!'

'Contempt for the people!'

'Insults! Shame on you!'

'Now we really know what this Council thinks of us!'

'Point of order Mr Mayor!' Councillor Lafontaine shouted.

Outcry as GDC Managing Director labels Gretford Guardian activist a "bloody idiot" was posted on *The Gretford Gazette*'s live feed.

'I now call Mrs Philpotts from P&A Architects and Surveyors,' Mayor Joplin said, looking more like a man with a growing sense of panic that he was losing whatever grip he had on proceedings.

Joanna Philpotts made her way nervously to the chair finally vacated by MacNulty.

'I am a representative of the Gretford Association of Architects and Town Planners. To say that the UK is facing a housing shortage would be an understatement. Gretford is typical of most Councils throughout England that has to wake up to the reality that we cannot continue with such unsustainable housing developments.'

'Bollocks!' shouted a protester.

'Build in Surrey! No to developers!'

The rest of Philpotts' five minutes would be lost forever. Where St John and MacNulty had failed, Philpotts had achieved with surprising speed; she had united the opposing forces of town and country against a common enemy. The clamour of protest from the public gallery grew in tempo until it drowned out whatever it was that she was attempting to say.

Even Woake, sitting in the same row as Philpotts, struggled to hear her. 'Come on Joplin, get a grip!' Woake said, deciding, as everyone else had, to ignore any sense of formality.

He was supported by Swaden. 'Enough Mr Mayor, chuck them out!'

'Order! Order!' Mayor Joplin shouted. 'Any further interruption would be dealt with by the perpetrator being asked to leave.'

The sound from the public gallery eventually exhausted itself and the Mayor turned to Council Leader, William Foster.

'Councillor Foster, as Leader of the Council, would you like to propose the motion?'

'Thank you, Mr Mayor. This is an exciting time for Gretford. This Plan in front of us represents a culmination of many months of hard work from not only Council staff, but Councillors as well.'

'And it's still fucking shit!' shouted a protester.

'I would remind the public here tonight of my previous warning,' Mayor Joplin said.

'Just chuck them out,' Woake said. Fulcher-Wells sniffed. Swaden winked.

'We are in the unfortunate position that planning policy is being dictated to us by central Government, including a housing target we need to meet. The sad reality facing us is this; adopt a Local Plan and keep control over our planning policy and decision-making, or lose it.'

'Or build over it!' shouted a protester.

'But it is important that we all remember this. This evening is not about adopting the Local Plan, it is about publishing it for public consultation. Every Gretford resident will have the opportunity to comment and the comments will be duly noted.'

'Then ignored!'

'And duly acted on in order to formulate a second draft. I would like to reassure all members of the public here this evening that I met with senior politicians, including members of the Cabinet,' Foster said, enjoying how this made him feel more important 'and I can assure you all that I emphasised in the strongest possible terms our anger at the position we have been placed in. And the Cabinet minister agreed.

'Mr Mayor, this motion relates to publication only and not formal adoption, which is some time away. I urge all my Council colleagues to support this and I commend it to this Council.'

Council leader met cabinet minister to agree Local Plan, Ben Jones immediately wrote. 'Thank you,' Mayor Joplin said. 'I now call Councillor Overton to second this motion.'

'I so second, Mr Mayor, and I reserve my right.'

'I have received no notification that any councillor wishes to make a speech tonight. Are there any?' the Mayor asked, more in hope than expectation. Within seconds, forty hands rose sharply in the air. With a sickening feeling in the pit of his stomach, Mayor Joplin looked at the list of speakers, hoping that the first name on the list would be a friend. He was to be disappointed.

With an impending sense of doom, the Mayor turned to Patricia Lafontaine.

'Thank you, Mr Mayor,' Lafontaine started her prepared speech. 'I would like to thank Mr MacNulty for his excellent speech, which has already highlighted many key ishues which I would like to raise.' Cries of support from one half of the public gallery interrupted her speech. 'However, I would like to raise in the strongest possible terms the appalling way in which Mr MacNulty was treated by the Managing Director, which really does highlight the utter contempt in which this Council holds the residents it alleges to serve,' she said, her voice raising to a shout as her support from the public gallery grew.

Lafontaine continued for a full five minutes, accusing the district of lying to its residents, of insulting them, of trampling over their rights in the pursuit of profit and of being beholden and benefitting from the money provided by offshore property developers.

By the end of her five minutes, both halves of the public gallery were cheering her. She concluded with her most damning statement of her Council colleagues.

'This Council should tonight do the decent thing and abandon this appalling document. However, I have no doubt that the sheep which sit on thirty-five of these forty-eight benches will do what they always do, meeting after meeting. And that is to blindly follow the wishes of their leaders without question or hesitation, like the pathetic sheep they are.'

Lafontaine leant forward to turn off her microphone, to public cheering. Certain members of the public even started to "baa".

'Thank you, Councillor Lafontaine,' the Mayor said, attempting to make himself heard over the sound of farmyard noises. 'I now call Councillor Newton.'

'Thank you, Mr Mayor, and might I say what an absolute disgrace the behaviour is of some of us here tonight,' Councillor Newton said. His statement, intended as a reprimand, only acted to incite the public hatred even further. Newton spoke for his full five minutes, little knowing that his speech would have bored anybody who cared to listen.

Unfortunately for Newton, nobody did care to listen. Or rather were unable to listen as the public heckles drowned out his speech.

Had anybody been able to hear Simon Newton, they would have heard a passionate plea in support of the motion.

Kildare, Skelding, Swaden, Woake, the leadership and Bane all urged the Mayor to intervene, who sat on his high chair unmoving, with little idea how he could regain control over the meeting.

Not, as the Chinese observed, did he have any control to start with.

'Can I please remind everyone to behave themselves tonight, otherwise I would have to ask you to leave,' the Mayor said pathetically at the end of Newton's speech.

'You've already said that, act on it,' Woake said, to support from his Cabinet colleagues. Only Fulcher-Wells and Williams remained silent.

Cabinet councillor urges Mayor to remove public, Jones posted.

The meeting progressed.

For the next two and a half hours, Woake sat in silence as speech after speech was made, either in support of the motion or against. The public gallery sat in silence for a councillor whom it suspected was against consultation and heckled all those who supported it.

The Liberal Democrats reluctantly supported the motion, and most Tories were also in favour. All those who supported it were subjected to "baaing" chants from the public. Those against were treated to rapturous applause.

For the first time in his brief political career, Woake wondered why anybody would subject themselves to this level of harassment and abuse whilst attempting, rightly or wrongly, to carry out public service.

Only Lady Turton and her ward colleague were dissenting Tories.

'I found it hard, not to say bewildering,' she said with her sly smile, which so irritated Gerald Gallagher and any other whom she disagreed with 'that this Conservative-led Council takes so much pleasure in disregarding and alienating its core support. This Local Plan will mark the destruction of communities and the destruction of our cherished countryside.' The rest of her speech was lost amongst the cheers from the Gretford Guardians supporters in the public gallery.

Jeremy Pakeman was another half-dissenting voice. 'I am struggling with this motion,' he said to silence. He held his hands together with his two forefingers pointing upwards towards his chin as he spoke. It was not for nothing that he was known as a thinking councillor.

'We are asked tonight to open this Local Plan for consultation, not for adoption. Therefore, I think we should all take the emotion out of this. If we were discussing adoption, then there would be no way I could support it. This Local Plan will destroy an already delicate and fragile town centre, which is already straining under the pressures which it is unfairly being treated to. I know I am not alone in this concern.'

Cheering and applause greeted Pakeman's comment from the GAG side of the public gallery. 'We must therefore look to the countryside to shoulder most of this burden. A countryside which is ideally placed to welcome three new garden villages.'

'Sod off!' someone from the Gretford Guardians side cried out. 'Build in the bloody town!' another shouted.

'Fuck off back to the sticks, you toffee-nosed bastards!' was supported with loud cheering from the Gretford Advisory Group.

'What the Hell is the idiot doing?' Kildare asked. Woake winked at her.

'But we are not doing that,' Pakeman continued, oblivious to the growing turmoil he was causing. 'We are discussing consultation only, and I believe that every Gretford resident should have the right to voice their opinion on what is the most important document that this Council has had to discuss for a generation. It is therefore with reluctance that I will support this motion, but I do not support the Plan as it stands,' he concluded, ever aware of the next election.

Reg Swaden was called as the next speaker. 'Thank you, Mr Mayor. I shall be very brief. Many people here tonight, including some Councillors, either lack the wit or the ability to understand what we are discussing. Councillor Pakeman alluded to it and unlike many councillors tonight, I shall not waste any further time by repeating the same speech. Let's just allow all the one hundred and fifty thousand residents of Gretford the chance to have their say, instead of pretending this rabble of a couple of hundred people speaks for all of them.'

The public gallery erupted.

'Order! Order!' the Mayor squealed, unable to decide what powers he should exercise. If truth be known, the unmoving Chinese to his right unnerved him.

'I order you all to leave!' he shouted to the public gallery.

'Make us!' a male voice shouted back, to loud cheering.

The four caretakers looked at the dais with mounting panic, terror in their eyes at the thought of having to deal with this.

'I will adjourn this meeting for five minutes,' Mayor Joplin said, failing to make his voice heard much passed the front bench 'until the public gallery is cleared.'

'Fuck off with whatever it is you're saying,' a female voice shouted back.

Bane pointed to the caretakers. 'Get that bloody rabble out of here!' he shouted to the caretakers, who walked gingerly to the crowd.

Ignoring the four nervous men and without a common enemy in which to share their animosity, the two factions within the public gallery quickly turned to each other. Cries in support for the town competing with supporters of the countryside. The four caretakers looked on impassively as the eruption continued without abatement.

Both sides stood and squared off against each other, including Martin St John and a very nervous Mr Lafontaine. 'Please don't shout at me,' Mr Lafontaine pleaded. 'I'm just here to support the wife. Anyone with half a brain cell can tell who's in charge of our relationship!'

The Councillors became mere spectators to events, as the public gallery descended into chaos. They looked on in amazement as fists were thrown and insults were traded. 'Better call the police,' Bane said.

'Make sure it's a riot squad,' Swaden added.

All councillors sat in wonder at the riot. All save for Woake, who was staring intently at his iPad, seemingly oblivious to the commotion going on around him. Eventually, he lent towards his microphone.

'Mr Mayor, might I suggest that in consideration that we have now been debating this motion for four hours, that this is now a good time for us to vote on the motion before us. I therefore propose, pursuant to Section 56, Subsection 34 Paragraph G of this Council's Procedural Rules that we move to a vote straight away.' The Mayor looked at Woake, dumbfounded. Woake had rescued him.

'For that, Mr Mayor, I need a seconder. Do I have a seconder?' Woake asked, taking charge.

'I so second!' Swaden cried.

'In which case can all those in favour of the motion please raise their hands?' Bane asked, taking the place of a shell-shocked Mayor Joplin, 'And those against?' Bane counted the hands. 'In which case this motion is passed by forty-one votes to five, with two abstentions.' Only the Labour councillors abstained.

Woake bade his Cabinet colleagues good night as he collected his papers and discreetly left the Chamber, closely followed by Kildare and Swaden.

All three could hear the distant sound of sirens as they reached their respective cars.

Their fellow councillors stayed rooted to their chairs, transfixed by the chaos, as the retired professional middle-class of Gretford descended into riot. They all sat in wonder as the police arrived to break up the brawl.

The Binzhou delegation sat impassively as dozens of campaigners were led out. All except for Sam Tong, whose trademark smile had never left his face throughout the meeting.

Thirty Two

Thursday 25th August 2016

The following morning saw the residents of Gretford wake to the sight of heavy storm clouds lying low in the sky over their town. The humidity of the day before had continued to rise during the night, and as the heat rose into the sky, it met the weather front that had been pushed over South Downs to the south of the district.

Many of the councillors slept fitfully in the clammy heat. The meeting had finally been adjourned by the arrival of the police at eleven thirty, who had responded with the usual heavy-handed approach by closing down the Council Chamber preventing anyone leaving until the fight between the Gretford Guardians and the Gretford Advisory Group had been stopped.

For Ben Jones, this was paradise and he kept his live feed going until he was finally allowed out at half-past midnight.

Fight in the Council Chamber followed *Inflammatory speech by Councillor Swaden sparks upheaval.* Had he bothered to check, Woake would have been comforted by the positive comment posted about him, describing how he had regained control of the meeting from the ineffectual Mayor.

For the Chinese, it was a fascinating demonstration of police powers by another state and provided them with a unique insight into the psyche of the English.

Firstly, Jianjun Li would never have been foolish to start a meeting of the Binzhou City Authority with members of the public present who had not been vetted as full members of the Party. Secondly, Li would never have started a meeting without suitable security personnel present.

Not that any meeting of the Binzhou City Authority would ever have been disturbed by a demonstration like the one last night. Not only does the bulletproof glass partitioning the public gallery from the Council Chamber double up as a sound barrier, no Binzhou resident would dare publicly (and, in many cases, privately) criticise the Binzhou City Authority out of fear of losing Party privileges, such as the right to life.

For the Gretford district councillors, it was an unwelcome reminder of the necessary contact between representative and represented, as well as an uncomfortable reminder of the need to regain election to maintain privilege.

Woake, unlike many councillors, slept peacefully, his brain having the ability to switch off from all stress, emotion and pressure. The army had once described him as a well-functioning psychopath; meaning he lacked the empathy and emotional sensitivity prevalent amongst others. He would never be a killer, but it meant that he was often a poor boyfriend, failing to consider "emotional needs" favoured by modern women.

On occasion, girlfriends have had to send him emojis to remind him how to act in certain circumstances.

Woake was pleasantly surprised to discover that many members of the Bar also suffered from the same condition; otherwise, the stress of seeing clients imprisoned would drive many of them insane.

His alarm woke him at seven thirty. He rose, dressed in his rowing kit, and went out for a run. When he returned, he showered, changed into a tailored suit and sat eating breakfast in his study, reading his case papers for the following morning.

Woake left his house at ten forty-five for the meeting with the Binzhou delegation at eleven thirty. The crematorium was only two miles from his house, but as every Gretford resident knew, it was important to leave plenty of time.

One man who was not quite so calm was Robbie Cole. It was the morning of Anjali Prasad's funeral and he had received an unexpected visit from his manager, Angelina Burbridge, the day before, following a conversation she had with John Todd, checking that everything was in order for the funeral. It was an unnecessary call; ensuring that the crematorium was prepared for Anjali Prasad had taken up most of her time at work. That, and the latest visit from the Council management and leadership, which was scheduled to take place at the same time.

Reminded, and not to say a little alarmed, that she had never received a response from her email to Robbie Cole, she had no choice but to speak to him.

Burbridge phoned him directly on the direct line to the cremator, to little success. It could not be due to the sound, as the cremator was a surprisingly quiet place, even when operating at full capacity. Anyway, the telephone was fitted with a light which flashed when it rang to alert Cole's attention in case he should have trouble hearing it.

Nor could it be the phone would ring off before it could be answered. The phone had an extra-long ring and was also positioned within easy reach, taking into account his short stature.

Looking at her watch, and fearing a visit to the cremator, Burbridge was relieved to work out the reason why. The time was half-past ten, and that meant that all non-administrative staff at the crematorium would be starting their morning break.

Burbridge walked down to the staff canteen. Out of respect to the difference in class between the administrative and non-administrative staff, their morning breaks were set at different times. In deference to the non-administrative staff starting their working day an hour earlier, their twenty-minute break was set at ten thirty.

The admin staff had theirs at eleven.

Burbridge walked into the staff canteen, noticing how the gardeners sat together, separated from the caretakers, who sat away from the cleaners. Robbie Cole sat by himself. His close contact with the clients made him a pariah; none of the other workers wanted to be reminded of their own mortality on a daily basis.

Burbridge noticed him sitting alone in the corner, drinking from a mug of tea.

'Hi Robbie,' she said. 'I was wondering if you had received my email about tomorrow's funeral?' she asked, wanting to keep this conversation as short as possible.

'What email was that?' Cole asked.

'The email about tomorrow's Hindu funeral. You got it, didn't you?' Burbridge persisted.

'Didn't get it,' Cole answered.

'But I sent it on your Council email account,' Burbridge said.

'Doesn't mean that I have a computer on which to read it,' Cole said, taking a sip from his mug.

'Did you or did you not read my email?' Burbridge asked.

'Didn't,' Cole answered.

'In which case, it is little point in asking about how the preparations are coming along.'

'Preparations for what?' Cole asked, finishing his tea.

Closing her eyes and taking a deep breath, Burbridge told him. 'So you have little under twenty-four hours to prepare the cremator for visitors.'

'Not possible,' Cole had responded.

'In what way?'

'Cremator is fit to bursting. It will require double bubble in order to process the latest orders,' Cole had said, using words to deliberately horrify her. 'At the moment, there simply isn't any space for a funeral party. Not to mention that the cremator needs a bloody good clean to make it fit for living clients. We're not used to hosting the living,' he added for good measure, a sly grin accompanying the evil turn in his eye.

'Please, do whatever it takes, and don't worry about overtime. I'll sort it,' Burbridge said, backing away. Little did she realise the enormity of her statement.

Cole watched her leave and laughed to himself, happy that he secured yet more overtime.

He worked manically for the rest of the day, finally clocking off at eleven o'clock that evening. Orders were processed. The viewing area was cleaned with chairs neatly lined out. The exteriors of the cremators were polished, floors were washed and the light bulbs changed. There was just one slight problem.

The capacity of the cremators ensured that only a certain number of orders would be processed on time. There would still be limited space as coffin-laden gurneys would occupy most of the space. Not to mention that being surrounded by other deceased would not be overly edifying for the Prasad family.

Cole stood in front of the gurneys, wondering how he could magically make them disappear. At five thirty, whilst walking around the grounds to help him think, he struck upon the solution. It required him to wait until all the other workers had left for home and with the use of a gurney, the cover of darkness and a little luck, the major problem had been resolved.

The solution would mean overtime for the rest of the week as he would require darkness to help process the backfill caused by Anjali Prasad's funeral. But with luck, no one should ever know.

Especially as he had forged the records for processed clients.

Now, twenty-four hours later, the cremator was spotless, the pride of Gretford. Robbie Cole looked at his work with pride.

All the mourners attending the Prasad funeral met at Vinod and Pippa's house, located in the more salubrious northern end of Gretford. There were few of them. Anjali's grandchildren and a couple of distant relations were the only mourners.

Owing to her advanced age and her general temperament, her few friends had all predeceased her.

By ten thirty, two funeral cars from B Todd & Sons arrived at Vinod's house and collected all twelve attendees.

Anjali Prasad would meet her relatives at Gretford Crematorium.

Vinod Prasad and his relatives were not the only ones making their progress to the crematorium. Oliver Gabriel was in his van, making his way through Whittom village. The self-deluded one-man crime-fighting machine had had a busy couple of weeks.

His advice to a landowner on how to catch a persistent fly-tipper to install CCTV on his land, at the landowner's expense, was a success. The fly-tipper was recorded in the act and duly arrested. A significant achievement for Gabriel, who had especially enjoyed sending the landlord the invoice for removing the waste.

An appeal against a fine for feeding ducks had been dismissed, and he had been touring all the schools in the district, offering advice to each establishment on how to manage the flow of traffic at drop-off and collection.

Traffic flow became a passion for Gabriel, who came to see himself as a saviour of the Gretford commuter against the tyranny of school drop-off and pick-up. By way of justifying the prediction of the police recruitment system of his lack of real-life experience, Gabriel had formulated a genuinely original proposal by reducing the time allowed on the on-road parking spaces outside every school in Gretford from half an hour to only five minutes.

Despite the intransigence of every school, Gabriel was looking forward to witnessing this cutting-edge proposal when school life returned in a couple of weeks.

Especially as he would be on duty in order to penalise any infringers.

Given how busy he had been, it had taken him a surprisingly long time for the otherwise efficient Gabriel to act on Vicky Walsh's instructions and investigate Gretford Crematorium.

Gabriel drove along the crematorium's main driveway, observing the latest funeral party congregating outside the chapel as he parked his van in the main car park. The meagre size of the waiting area could not cope with the size of the present party, in which two hundred mourners were gathered to pay their respects to a popular colleague who had committed suicide.

Thankfully, the storm which the sky promised had so far held off, allowing the mourners to wait outside.

Conscious that his JET uniform and hi-visibility jacket were perhaps not in keeping with the quiet dignity of the 1950s monolith, Gabriel sauntered to the rear of the crematorium.

For once, Gabriel was not sure what he was supposed to be investigating. His instruction manuals to which his training adhered simply did not mention polluting crematoria. Fearful that the limited imagination of public sector service could not provide him with the ability or initiative to conduct this matter properly, Gabriel circled the crematorium, observing the chimney at all times.

To his disappointment, the chimney omitted little smoke.

The time was approaching eleven o'clock in the morning.

With impeccable timing, the Prasad party arrived on the strike of eleven o'clock, just as the large funeral party observed by Gabriel was making its way into the chapel.

Vinod looked on as the previous funeral service left the chapel from the rear door, highlighting the conveyor belt that was the district's own dedication to the business of death.

The Prasad funeral procession parked at the front of the chapel. John Todd exited from the front of the limousine just as the cars pulled up. He stood by Vinod's door, as a fellow undertaker stood by Pippa's.

With near military precision, they opened both doors together.

The same process was repeated at the second car.

Todd waited until all the mourners had abated before addressing Vinod. 'Your mother is waiting for us in the Room of Remembrance,' he said solemnly. 'Would you like me to show you the way?'

Vinod nodded and followed Todd around the side of the chapel. Pippa held his hand, not so much in support but in necessity at the appalling idea that her mother-in-law might have solved the mystery of resurrection.

The crematorium was eerily quiet, the storm clouds appearing to have suppressed all notion of sound. The Prasad family made it to the Room of Remembrance, without ever realising that their walk mirrored Gabriel's.

Todd stood to one side, respectfully holding the door open for the mourners.

Vinod entered the room first.

To Angelina Burbridge's eternal credit, the crematorium's caretakers had done a superb job in organising the room. All of the flowers laid by other mourners had been removed to a shed, to be returned once the funeral had been completed. Had Vinod known it, his mother's funeral had booked the time reserved for four funerals. The legacy left in her will to cover the funeral expenses was more than enough to cover this necessity; not so much to allow her the dignity her wishes required, but to ensure that the technical means of her eventual disposal could be nobly achieved.

Cleared of all its previous furnishings, bouquets of white flowers hung from the wall, cascading down to the floor, temporarily hiding the 1950s beige wall. In the middle of the room was Anjali Prasad, laying in an open casket.

Yet more white flowers surrounded her in the casket.

As per her wishes, she lay totally clad in white. At her head, facing the entering Prasad family, stood an aged pandit. He waited as the mourners surrounded the coffin, all with their heads bowed down to their chests.

At a subtle nod from Todd, the pandit started to chant the first of the Hindu funeral mantras. No one noticed Todd gently closing the door as he left the Prasads to their mourning.

Woake locked his car in the crematorium car park and made his way to the front lawn, opposite the chapel. He noticed the JET van as he walked.

Foster, Overton and Swaden were already in position. Foster and Overton both looked awful, the dark bags under their eyes evidence of their lack of sleep.

Swaden, on the other hand, was dressed as impeccably as Woake.

Woake smiled at Foster and Overton as he arrived.

'Morning chaps,' he said 'good night's sleep?'

'Bloody funny, Sebastian,' Overton answered irritably.

'Turns out these chaps didn't leave Fordhouse until after one,' Swaden said.

'Ouch, should have left when we did, eh, Reg?'

'Sebastian,' Foster said quietly. 'Well done for last night. Thank you for your intervention. Without it, I doubt that the vote would have been taken and we would have had to have rerun the whole bloody fiasco.'

'What time are the Chinese getting here?' Woake asked, deliberately ignoring the praise from Foster. Praise he did not care about.

'Any time now,' Overton answered. 'The police will want to speak to you about last night, as a witness. Thirteen arrests were made, but I'm sure you already know that. By the way Seb, well done for wearing a tie,' Overton added, never one to resist making any aside sound like a criticism.

'Not sure I can help them much,' Woake said, looking away towards the crematorium's entrance, determined to avoid looking at Overton. 'I had my back to the idiots and I ignored most of what was being said. Making the assumption you two have already spoken to the police?'

Both Foster and Overton nodded in unison.

'Here comes a bloke looking as bad as you two,' Woake said, as Bane walked towards him, along with Charlotte Bateup and Peter West.

If Foster and Overton looked awful, then Bane looked positively ill. That he had obviously not shaved that morning and was still wearing the same suit, shirt and tie was evidence enough that he had not even attempted to sleep that night.

Whereas Foster's and Overton's primary concern was to salvage what they could from their political career, for Bane, his primary concern was keeping his job. He knew, when he eventually got home after two o'clock that morning, that he would face questions as to his conduct that evening. Patricia Lafontaine had already said as much, sending out email after email to him through the night demanding an inquiry.

But Bane was also concerned that questions would be asked about his decisions leading to last night, namely the lack of security and the wisdom of the timing of the Chinese delegation.

In regards to this, Bane faced an even bigger problem.

There would be little doubt that the councillor who would lead such an inquiry would be Craig Overton, as Lead Councillor for Governance, albeit as a man already mired by the same controversy. Bane knew full well that Overton would be more than prepared to throw him under the proverbial bus if it would safeguard his own political career.

Bane also knew that at fifty-three years of age, it would be a major doubt that he would ever gain another Managing Director role. The stench of last night would follow him around for the rest of his life.

'Just about on time, Giles,' Overton said. Bane glared at him.

'Just in time to see this,' Swaden said as a convoy of six minibuses arrived outside the chapel.

To the horror of all those present (save for Woake, who stood there looking bemused), ten individuals carrying placards alighted from all six minibuses and took up position opposite the Council delegation.

'Who are these individuals?' Woake asked.

'Representatives of GAG,' Overton answered.

'Surprised they have any members left after last night,' Swaden said.

'How would they know to protest here today?' Woake asked.

'Should imagine one of your loyal colleagues would have tipped them off. I'll go and speak to them, find out what they want,' Bane answered.

'No, don't bother,' Woake interrupted. 'They've already caused enough problems for us. Just ignore them.'

'And the Chinese?' Overton asked.

'Not my fault they're here,' Woake answered deliberately to Overton's annoyance, 'you were the ones so determined to have them over.'

'I meant...' but whatever Overton meant would be lost forever as two taxis bearing half of the Chinese delegation arrived at the crematorium. The representatives from the district looked on as Jianjun Li, Ying Han, Wang Wei and Li Qiang, along with Sam Tong, alighted.

'Why do they need two taxis for only five of them?' Swaden asked. 'Couldn't they have shared one?'

'Show, dear boy. Everything about this lot is a show, namely that they have to have more and have bigger than everyone else,' Woake answered, smiling as Jianjun Li led the Chinese straight towards him.

'Sebastian Woake, Lead Councillor for Finance,' he introduced himself, holding out his hand. 'It's a pleasure to meet you. May I introduce my colleague Reg Swaden, Lead Councillor for Parks, Leisure and Rural Affairs, who I do not believe you have met.

'Thank you for coming here today and I look forward to showing you around our latest project.'

Much to the annoyance and anger of Foster and Overton, the Binzhou delegation followed Woake as he led them away from the protesters and towards the crematorium. Swaden and the directors followed.

The Prasad family mourners continued to stand with their heads bowed in front of them. The pandit sang the funeral chants as the mourners stood transfixed by the solemnity of the prayers. The mystery of the words only added to the beauty of the chants.

The pandit's voice rose in crescendo as he reached his inevitable climax. The mourners continued to stand in silence as the pandit allowed his final words to fall gracefully upon the family.

The family stood transfixed, allowing the gentle beauty of the mantras to fall gracefully onto the serene corpse laying in front of them.

It mattered little that the anglicised family had little idea what had been said for the past half an hour.

None of the mourners noticed as the door was quietly opened by John Todd, who stood silently in the doorway, allowing the family some final quiet moments with their deceased relative.

'Will you please follow me to the chapel?' he said when he judged the time was right.

Quietly, and without a word, the mourners followed Todd as he led them to the chapel. None of them noticed as four undertakers approached the casket.

To say that Oliver Gabriel was disappointed would have been an understatement. He was downright furious with what he found. Or to be more accurate, with what he had not.

During his latest monthly appraisal, Vicky Walsh had intimated that the district was looking to extend the JETs, as they had been such a success in cutting low-level anti-social behaviour. Whilst she had not said so explicitly, the implication was that she would look to Gabriel to lead one of the new sub-teams.

However, in order to get that coveted stripe on his shoulder, Gabriel knew he needed to secure that one big prosecution, the one which would show to all the merits of extending the JETs.

Unfortunately, the possibility of the crematorium providing that much-needed case was rescinding by the minute.

The chimney from the cremator was only omitting a weak pall of white smoke, whilst the lawns and grounds had been beautifully manicured throughout the warm summer months.

As Gabriel walked around the main building complex, there was little to concern even the most precocious of minds. There was very little noise, no litter, and whilst the buildings were more than a little dated, all were safe with little danger to the public.

Not easily dismayed, Gabriel inspected the outbuildings located on the periphery of the site.

Most were locked, and Gabriel knew he lacked the authority to enter private property without a warrant.

Not that he even had the authority to apply for one.

The ones that were open contained nothing more dangerous than garden machinery or were used as nothing more offensive than as storerooms.

Disappointed, Gabriel walked towards his van. As he was halfway to the car park, his attention was taken by a small, dilapidated caretaker's hut located towards the boundary of the estate but half-hidden by a line of trees which shielded the crematorium from the neighbouring houses.

With little else to be doing, Gabriel took a detour towards the hut.

The twelve mourners gathered in the chapel, rather embarrassingly spreading themselves out along the two front pews.

As with the Room of Remembrance, the crematorium staff had done a fantastic job in transforming the chapel in the half hour between the previous funeral service and Anjali Prasad's.

White flowers cascaded down the walls and bouquets of flowers had subtly hidden the crucifixes on all four walls.

The pandit took up position in the pulpit, waiting for the signal from John Todd, who was standing beside the dais at the far end of the nave. Presently, the casket carrying Anjali Prasad was carried in by the four undertakers, who placed it on top of the dais. Todd opened the casket to reveal Anjali inside.

At the silent nod from Todd, the pandit began the second round of chanting, as the body of Anjali Prasad was carried into the chapel.

Her casket was laid to rest on the raised dais. Behind the dais, in the corner of the chapel, was a large white door.

Working in the cremator, behind the chapel, Robbie Cole could hear the strange sounds emanating from the chapel. Standing on his beer crate, Cole slid the coffin belonging to the tragic suicide case into a furnace.

He moved over to the control panel and, still standing on his beer crate, he activated the burning process which would destroy the remains of his latest customer. Cole peered through the viewing hatch and saw the coffin begin to catch fire.

Thirty Three

Oliver Gabriel approached the hut, which, at closer inspection, was in an even more dilapidated state than it had first appeared. Its roof was caving in, whilst the wooden walls were already rotted through.

The surrounding trees had grown sufficiently large enough that the hut itself appeared to be disappearing into a wilderness, as if it had been forgotten about by the crematorium.

Gabriel tentatively opened the rotting door, its lock had long since rusted through. Inside it was pitch black. Gabriel did not even bother trying to find a light switch, instead grabbing his torch from his utility belt and illuminating the room with artificial light.

Gabriel walked through the door, shining his torch on long-abandoned lawnmowers, empty gas canisters, rusting gardening tools and, in the far corner, a large rectangular object covered by a dust sheet.

'The importance of this project to our residents is twofold,' Woake told the Binzhou delegation, through Sam Tong. 'This facility is a major source of income for the Council, although it is somewhat frustrating that this facility currently cannot operate at full capacity.'

'Why is that?' Jianjun Li asked.

'The age of the building,' Woake answered, not bothering to expand his answer. 'Which leads onto the second part. Taking the emotion into account, it is important that we provide a service with a greater degree of dignity to the deceased and to the mourners.'

'In what way?' Ying Han asked.

'At the moment, multiple services can interact amongst themselves, which I think you'll agree is far from ideal. We will shortly enter the facility itself, so you can see the architectural designs and our exciting plans for the crem.'

'What is that group doing?' Jianjun Li asked, referring to the small group of protesters, who stalked the group as Woake led them across the grounds.

'Oh, I wouldn't worry about them,' Woake answered. 'They're just the leftovers from last night.'

'Are you always surrounded by these people?' Jianjun Li asked.

'By what people?'

'By people who are constantly protesting against you, constantly questioning you, constantly fighting your plans?'

'Oh, yes,' Woake answered, smiling, 'but they tend to be backbench councillors.'

Cole finished straightening the chairs in the public viewing room. Content that the cremator was as clean and tidy as he could get it, he positioned a gurney by the chapel door, ready to receive Anjali Prasad's casket.

Oliver Gabriel walked tentatively through the former caretaker's hut, squeezing his thin frame between an old tractor and a shelf full of old paint tins.

He jumped as he accidentally knocked an open paint tin onto the ground. The remains of 1950s beige paint trickled through the rotting floorboards through to the ground below.

Gabriel made it to the far corner, where the long rectangular object lay covered up by the dust sheet. He stroked the dust sheet, feeling the object underneath, as hard and as solid as a chest of drawers. However, there was something about its shape which held his attention. Whilst long, the object underneath appeared to be conical in shape.

And unless he was much mistaken, there appeared to be two objects, one on top of the other.

Taking a deep breath, Gabriel pulled back the dust sheet.

He peered down as his torch illuminated the shiny veneer of a coffin. A brass plaque with the name *Emma Guest* stared straight back at him. To his horror, Gabriel saw another coffin laid next to it, meaning that four had been stored in the hut.

However, unlike the rest of the shed's contents, the coffin was shining new and, as Gabriel noticed, the date on the coffin read 22nd August, meaning that the funeral would have taken place three days previously. Therefore, the coffin should have been burnt.

Which, as Gabriel's methodical investigative brain worked out, if the coffin had not been through the cremator from a couple of days ago, where was poor Ms Guest? Or was this part of the pollutant conspiracy at the crematorium; that the bodies were burnt but that the coffins were not?

Determined to solve the mystery, Gabriel shone his torch along the coffin lid. He found the screws holding the lid in place and began to turn them.

Not that last night helped; while many of those arrested were Gretford Guardians, the previous late night effectively rendered all but the hardcore of the Gretford Advisory Group unfit for duty. As it was, only sixty had arrived outside his house that morning.

Determined to make a stand, his small band of supporters doggedly stayed with the Chinese and district councillors as they toured the crematorium.

However, out of respect for the purpose of the crematorium, Martin St John had been persuaded by Peter Murray not to use a microphone that day.

It was to St John's initial annoyance which later turned into anger that his protest was being totally ignored by the councillors.

Gabriel finished turning the final screw and felt the lid rest loosely on the casket. Holding his torch in his mouth, he lifted the lid and twisted it around in order to expose the top half of the casket.

Taking his torch in his right hand, Gabriel peered down into the darkened casket.

The quickness of the flash reflecting off the grey geriatric lying in peace below him. Letting out a weak gasp of shock, Gabriel staggered backwards, disgusted by how the artificial light emphasised Ms Guest's shiny whitened skin and hair, juxtaposed by her red lips shining in magnificent vulgarity; a funeral director's poor attempt at applying make-up.

The shining corpse haunted Gabriel as he staggered backwards in horror, tripping over a stepladder which had been placed on the rotting floor.

Falling backwards, Gabriel hit his back against an old shelving unit used to hold abandoned paint tins.

Gabriel fell onto the floor, the last image in his mind before a paint tin struck him on the head was the image of Emma Guest smirking at him from her coffin.

The paint tin hit him squarely in the middle of his forehead, knocking him out instantly. Gabriel lay unconscious on the rotting floor, covered in beige paint which soaked his otherwise pristine uniform.

'Apart from dignity, the key part to this development is creating an environment which reflects our religiously diverse society,' Woake told his tour, surprising himself at how fluent he was becoming in the language which is public authority speech.

'As you can no doubt see, this crematorium was built at a time when Christianity was the pre-dominant religious belief. Now, Gretford is like any other large town, it is multi-cultural and we on the Council must provide services reflective of this.' Woake led them towards the door of the management area.

'You will see shortly the design for a new building complex, which has been specially designed to be religiously neutral, allowing those of all faiths and those of no faith to partake in the services provided.'

The chants were finished. The hymns had been sung, and Vinod Prasad had even made a short tribute to his mother.

It was now time to send Anjali Prasad on her last journey.

At the invitation of the pandit, Vinod led the mourners to his mother's casket, shadowed by John Todd, who stood silently to one side, overseeing the proceedings.

The family stood around the casket, with the pandit standing at the head.

***

Oliver Gabriel woke groggily, his body aching. He was unable to open his eyes, which were stuck shut.

Gabriel raised his right hand to his head, feeling the sticky liquid on his forehead and in his eyes. Fearing it was blood, he brought his hand down to his nose, relieved but somewhat disappointed to smell only paint.

Relieved that it was not his blood, meaning that his injuries were only light, though disappointed that his injuries would not be significant enough to guarantee a healthy pay out from the owners of the crematorium.

This thought brought him back to his present problem. Feeling dizzy and nauseous, Gabriel rose shakily to his feet, wiping the paint from his stinging eyes.

He was about to leave the hut when realisation of the open coffin stopped him. He had to make his report and find whoever was in charge of the crematorium. But he could not leave Ms Guest open in such a way. Besides, he was worried that he himself had broken some law by opening the coffin.

Steeling himself for what he would see, he walked towards the open coffin, this time without the aid of the torch.

Closing his eyes so he would not have to peer down towards the cadaver, Gabriel closed the lid, using his fingers to check that the lid was in position. Only then did he use his torch to screw the lid shut.

Walking back through the hut, Gabriel emerged, blinking and bleary-eyed into the dark summer's day, immediately realising that his once immaculate uniform and hi-vis were now, like his head, covered in beige paint.

Gabriel looked around him, trying to get his bearings. He was at the rear end of the complex, and previous experience had told him that the management area of such a complex was always to the rear, away from public viewing.

He could see a large door with windows on either side, and through the windows there were people working on computers.

That had to be the management. Gabriel walked towards the door just as Woake appeared from around the corner, leading his tour.

***

In the chapel, the pandit chanted his final verse, a prayer that would send Anjali Prasad's soul travelling with many blessings into the heavens above.

The start of the chanting was the sign that John Todd needed, who silently walked towards the large white door. He knocked once.

The door was opened immediately by Robbie Cole, who walked forwards with as much dignity as a vertically challenged cremator technician in an oversized boiler suit could muster.

He pushed an empty gurney which dwarfed him towards the casket, stopping it as he reached the dais.

Unused to dealing with the living, Cole was unsure as to what he should say, and it was with some trepidation that he walked towards Vinod.

Vinod himself was unsure as to what to make of Cole, in his rolled-up boiler suit.

'I'm very sorry for your loss,' the strange creature growled at him.

'Thank you,' was all Vinod could say in return.

'Could you please follow my directions?' Cole asked, caught between the knowledge that he would have to say something, but not wanting to disturb the chants. Although he had hoped he had whispered to Vinod, he had in fact sounded like a large dog growling.

'Only the men are permitted to touch the casket,' Cole said. 'When you are ready, could you please push mum onto the gurney?'

Vinod motioned for his three male relatives to advance with him to the dais. Together, they pushed the casket onto the gurney.

It was to Vinod's great surprise that the casket was heavier than he expected.

'Could you please follow me?' Cole growled as he pushed the gurney into the cremator.

The mourners followed, with the pandit walking in last, still chanting the final prayer.

John Todd stood in the chapel, closing the doors behind the mourners, relieved that his part of the service was now complete.

He would congratulate Angelina Burbridge on an excellent job before notifying her that the service was finished. Todd would meet the Prasads for one last time outside, and with any luck he would be back at his desk within the hour.

***

'Can the women please wait here?' Cole asked as he walked past the viewing area.

Pippa led the female mourners onto the public seats and watched as the men surrounded the gurney.

Cole pushed the gurney into position, so it laid head onto the door of the left-hand furnace, next to the furnace which was currently processing the unfortunate suicide. He checked the controls, making sure that the furnace had reached its optimum heat level.

Cole waited for the chants to finish before addressing Vinod.

Presently the chants died down.

'We are now ready to send mum onto her last journey,' Cole growled, still wanting to sound solemn. 'When you are ready, I will open the door into the furnace and if you could push mum in immediately?'

Vinod nodded to Cole.

Cole walked towards the furnace door, picking up a black bucket as he went. Cole placed the bucket on the ground and stood on it as he opened the door.

He had changed the beer crate for a bucket, hoping that a bucket would add more dignity than a beer crate.

As the door opened, Vinod and his relatives pushed forward the gurney, and as it stopped on the edge of the furnace, pushed the casket into the fiery oblivion.

The only sound was the gentle murmurings from the pandit.

Vinod pulled back the gurney, allowing Cole to close the door. Still standing on his bucket, Cole pushed the buttons which activated the fire.

Soon, Anjali Prasad was lost in fire as her spirit rose towards the heavens, in what was hoped would be her final journey.

Thirty Four

Oliver Gabriel walked towards the group, recognising Woake, Foster and Overton. He had a vague recognition of Bane and the other directors; his positions at the Council had always been sufficiently junior enough to never be invited to a senior management meeting.

He failed to recognise the Chinese.

As he walked towards the group and the crematorium, Gabriel's attention was struck by the chimney, which rose fifty metres from the furnace below. To his horror, the chimney emitted a thick white smoke, followed by thick white ash which settled like snow on the crematorium's roof.

Gabriel marched straight up to the group, his emotion overtaking his otherwise cool composure.

'Is this fucking disgrace anything to do with you?' he shouted at Woake. Woake and the rest of the group turned to face him; a giant beanpole in an ill-fitting officious uniform whose absurdity of his own self-importance had been diluted by the giant egg-shaped bruise on the centre of his forehead and that one side of his head and body was covered in paint. 'There are fucking dead bodies here!' Gabriel screamed.

'Of course there are dead bodies here, it's a crematorium,' Woake said, somewhat confused.

'Apparently he's been fucking dead bodies,' Tong translated for the Binzhou delegation.

'What seems to be your problem?' Woake asked, remaining calm before the Chinese.

'Who is this fucking lunatic?' Jianjun Li asked Sam Tong, in Mandarin.

'I'll tell you what my problem is!' Gabriel shouted. 'Dead bodies due for burning dumped in that shed behind me, not to mention the smoke and ashes coming out of that chimney!'

'Apparently, once he's fucked the bodies, he dumps them in that shed over there,' Tong said.

'I think they've got a bigger problem here than that fucking degenerate. Looks like they might have a problem with their ovens,' Jianjun Li said, looking cautiously at the chimney. 'I'd say that they've got most of the remains of the bodies settling on the roof than they have anywhere else,' Jianjun Li added, now looking at the roof.

'What are you talking about, man?' Bane said to Gabriel 'and keep your voice down.'

'There are coffins, full of bodies in that shed, that should have been cremated days ago,' Gabriel answered.

'Apparently he's keeping four bodies in that shed over there and hasn't burnt them yet,' Tong told his fellow Chinamen.

'Can't be any worse than what these idiots are trying to do here,' Jianjun Li said.

'How do you know that?' Bane asked.

'Because I've fucking seen them!' Gabriel shouted back.

'Was that before or after you got concussed?' Woake asked.

'I got hit on the head by a paint tin,' Gabriel said.

'Apparently one of the dead bodies hit him on the head with a tin of paint,' Tong said dubiously.

'Who are you?' Jianjun Li asked Gabriel in English.

'He's a member of the Council's Joint Enforcement Team,' Bane answered.

'Ask him what that means,' Jianjun Li told Tong, the mention of an enforcement team having piqued his interest.

'It means that I have little choice but to report the owner of this establishment to the police,' Gabriel answered.

'But we own the crematorium,' Overton said, unwisely.

'In which case I will report the Council and I will write up my report into this disgusting behaviour.'

The emergence of a loud humming sound, which appeared to come from the sky, interrupted Bane in his answer, growing louder as it approached the crematorium, drowning out all conversation.

As the group looked up to the sky, they saw a helicopter fly low under the heavy cloud and hover directly above them.

Vinod Prasad and the other three male mourners stood silently in front of the furnace door as Robbie Cole dismounted from his bucket.

'It is now done,' Cole said. 'I wish you the very best in your time of grief,' he added.

The female mourners stirred in the public viewing area, and Vinod turned his back on his mother after one final bow towards the furnace.

He began walking back towards his wife, followed by the other three men, and the pandit.

Vinod was halfway back to Pippa when a loud alarm stopped him, sending crescendos of pain through all their eardrums.

All, save for Cole, who sprinted back to the control panel, his bucket in his hand, oblivious to the wailing siren.

With mounting panic, Cole stepped up to the furnace consuming Anjali Prasad, his eyes level with the control panel.

To his horror, he saw that the pressure gauges were at maximum capacity. In his efforts to ensure that each order could be processed as expeditiously as they could, Cole had taken the somewhat unwise decision to operate both furnaces at near enough full pressure.

The alarm was still ringing in everyone's ears as the furnace door blew off its hinges and smashed into the panel just inches above Cole's head.

For the first time in years, Cole blessed his diminutive height.

A tongue of flame spurted straight out of the furnace, singeing the wall opposite.

A second later, Anjali Prasad's flaming casket was spat out from the furnace, finally embarking upon its last journey.

The casket flew straight into the wall opposite, where it crashed straight onto the floor, separating Cole from the rest of the mourners.

Another tongue of flame erupted out of the furnace, setting off the fire alarm, activating the sprinklers above, saturating Cole and the mourners alike within seconds.

More out of habit rather than necessity, Cole pressed the shut-down button and stood back in mounting terror at the displays in front of him.

Vinod needed no further encouragement. Shepherding his family, and under the guardianship of John Todd who had entered the cremator at the first sign of alarm, Vinod led his family and the pandit through the chapel and out onto the main lawn, where they were quickly deafened by the sound of the hovering helicopter.

Cole remained standing in terror. The dials in front of him told him that the pressure in the second furnace was still rising dangerously high.

With water washing down his eyes, Cole was temporarily blinded. Wiping the water away, he tried in vain to press every button on the control panel, in a pathetic attempt to shut the machinery down, from which loud banging noises could now be heard.

Cole stepped away from the panel and looked through the observation window as the remains of the coffin inside were hurled against the furnace door.

Unable to penetrate the reinforced steel door, the internal pressure from the combustion sought the next available exit.

His eyes stinging from the sprinklers, Cole took one last look at the furnace door.

As he did so, the gasses created inside the furnace became too great for the chimney. An invisible hand swept Cole off his feet, and he landed next to Anjali Prasad's smouldering coffin.

A split second later, his eardrums were perforated by an explosion, which rocked the crematorium's main building. Tremors were sent out across Gretford, as if the market town had, for the first time in its uneventful history, been rocked by an earthquake.

As he recovered, Cole looked up to the open sky, seeing the heavy storm clouds exposed through what had once been the crematorium's main chimney. He could see the ashes accumulated by years of overwork from both furnaces settle around the crematorium.

For the second "first" in as many minutes, Gretford seemed to be suffering from the meteorological phenomena known as summer snow.

Charles Williams was a troubled man.

The storm clouds which hung low over Gretford ensured he had to maintain the helicopter at just over the legal flight limit of 250ft. The turbulence combined with his apprehension of the weather forecast added to his unease as he struggled to maintain a level flight. Not that Williams's unease was helped by the presence of his passengers.

If it could be said that the senior half of the Chinese delegation were in uninterested competition with each other over the development plans of which Gretford District Council was so proud, then the junior half were just downright oblivious.

As Williams repeated the same tour as the day before, except that the second tour started in the south of the district rather than the north, his Chinese passengers sat back and relaxed in tedium ignorance of what was being said in a language of which they understood little.

Not that it stopped Williams. Out of need to remain fully focused, Williams continued with his full commentary of the district, fully knowing that his passengers understood little and cared even less.

For what Williams, and indeed the rest of ManCab, failed to understand was that any decision made by the Binzhou City Authority would be made by its own leadership following the visit, based on the advice drafted by the more senior half of the delegation.

The purpose of Zhang Yong and his fellow junior colleagues was purely to add to numbers, to emphasise the importance of their own city rather than help formulate policy. Such policy would be made by Jianjun Li, and Zhang Yong would be in full agreement.

Such loyalty was demanded rather than expected.

'Below us is Gretford Crematorium,' Williams said, bringing the helicopter to hover just above the complex, 'which I have brought you to as it's a fine example of the type of major project which we are proudly undertaking. At a cost of approximately £8 million, we are providing our residents with a first-class asset,' he told his oblivious audience.

'Unless I am much mistaken,' Williams continued, 'we can see your colleagues down there, and what appears to be another crowd following them.' For the next five minutes, Williams spoke about the merits of the new project, paying particular attention to the level of investment, the rate of return and the level of income generated.

'You wouldn't believe this, and I certainly didn't, but this crematorium is one of our biggest money-earners. Not that it should be much of a surprise. The reality is that we all have to die at some point, so it's inevitable that for a large town like Gretford that it would provide the owner with such a lucrative, Jesus Christ!' Williams shouted, as the helicopter was rocked by a large explosion, which seemed to come from directly below them.

The Chinese panicked, shouting at Williams and at each other as they were thrown straight back into their seats by the force of the explosion. Williams, for his part, hoped his face did not give away the abject terror he felt. More out of reflex rather than cool thought (this was the first major emergency as a pilot he had ever experienced), he increased the throttle to raise the helicopter above the blast whilst pulling back on the joystick in order to allow the machine to travel with the blast rather than fight it.

Unintentionally, Williams had created a giant fan in the sky, oblivious to the effects it had on the ground.

As the smoke cleared from the crater in the crematorium's roof, Williams manoeuvred the helicopter away from the building, providing himself and the passengers the perfect opportunity to record the incident on their phones.

Woake and the others stood around the management doors as the crematorium's staff evacuated the building. Woake could only look on in admiration as some members of staff had already donned high-visibility jackets and were marshalling the funeral parties and the employees.

An alarm could be heard ringing from within the open doors.

'What's going on?' Bane asked a harassed-looking Angelina Burbridge, having to shout over the din of the hovering helicopter.

'No idea!' Burbridge shouted back. 'The fire alarm has just gone off in the cremator and some members of the latest funeral party have apparently shouted that there was a fire. The fire service will have been called automatically. I'm just on my way to the cremator now.'

'We'll come with you,' Woake shouted as he, Bane, West and Gabriel followed Burbridge to the cremator's rear door.

As they were following Burbridge, the group and all those around them were knocked off their feet by a sudden explosion. Councillors, demonstrators, staff and public alike all cowered on the ground, hiding as much as they could from falling masonry.

Woake, thanks to the policy of successive governments, had

undergone similar experiences in Afghanistan and so was the first to recover.

He stood and stared in wonder as the helicopter, which had been veered backwards by the explosion, fanned everyone with warm ash.

Woake turned to Gabriel. 'At least now, you're not the only one covered in crap,' he said.

Gabriel was unable to answer. It had become apparent that he had now gone into shock.

Robbie Cole continued to stand in the remains of the cremator, thankful that he had somehow survived.

However, the full enormity of his predicament slowly dawned on him.

No one could ever blame him for the explosion; local authority's obsession with records and note-keeping would prove that it was he who had originally raised concerns about the state of the cremator after the first alarm weeks previously.

What concerned Cole was that there were four coffins which had not been processed, and judging from the damage, would not be for the foreseeable future. However, his forged records would show that all four had been actually burnt on the day of service.

In short, Cole was now the proud owner of four coffins, complete with cadavers, which legally no longer existed.

However, the families would, quite understandably, want their relatives' mortal remains.

He faced a stark choice. To leave the coffins where they were was out of the question. Firstly, the well-publicised development would mean that someone would go into the shed eventually and it would only be a matter time before the coffins were discovered. Secondly, given recent events, it was more than likely that someone would investigate it immediately.

He had to destroy the evidence. Immediately.

The entire plan came to Cole as he continued looking up into the sky. Fully in the knowledge of everything he had to do, Cole rushed straight out of the cremator and towards the hut.

For the second time that day, Cole made a silent prayer of gratitude for his limited height.

Cole ran past his colleagues, who were all seemingly oblivious of a silver-haired dwarf running amongst them, such was their combined panic and excitement following the explosion.

Cole reached the rotting door and knelt down in front of it, checking to see if he had been noticed, relieved to see that everyone else was too preoccupied with their immediate surroundings to have noticed him.

Slowly, and not to draw attention to himself, Cole crept into the hut. He found what he was looking for without too much difficulty.

Unscrewing the petrol tank to the old ride-on lawnmower, Cole stuffed some tissues into its funnel and lit it with a cigarette lighter.

He moved over to the coffins and poured the contents of an old petrol can onto them. Satisfied that the top two had received a generous coating, Cole walked to the rear wall of the hut and threw the lighter onto the coffin and watched as the fire consumed the coffins.

He escaped through the rotten wall and made his way back to the congregating crematorium employees.

To the dismay of his supervisor, he registered his existence just as the petrol tank of the old lawnmower finally caught fire, causing the final explosion at Gretford Crematorium.

All three fire engines from Gretford Fire Station attended the scene. Within minutes of their arrival, the remains of the cremator had been cordoned off and the dilapidated gardener's hut had been reduced to nothing more than a pile of smouldering ash exposing the skeletons of what had been in a past life garden machinery.

Soon, Gretford's firemen had joined their fellow Gretfordians in standing casually outside the crematorium, waiting on the arrival of the fire investigators.

The rain began spitting at one o'clock, with the perceptive amongst those present quickly moving inside. Within minutes, Gretford was deluged by the storm which had been promised all day.

Those stuck at the crematorium were forced to take shelter in the chapel, where firemen mingled with councillors who in turned stood beside two funeral parties and the crematorium's employees.

The Chinese remained standing in their group, ignored by the district representatives who were too embarrassed to approach them.

All witnesses to the explosion were duly separated from the rest of the group, including Vinod Prasad and his family. Special attention was paid to Robbie Cole and Angelina Burbridge, who found the interview a welcome relief from her painful duty of contacting all the funeral directors in the area and cancelling every funeral for the foreseeable future.

For the second time in two days, Gretford district councillors had to suffer the indignity of being interviewed as witnesses to the events which fate had dealt.

For the second time in two days, the Chinese found themselves as spectators to a town whose leaders fought desperately and not over successfully in trying to modernise.

Unable to leave the crematorium, the Binzhou delegation was forced to remain on the premises, until all those present were allowed to leave in the late afternoon.

Unfortunately for the Chinese, it meant that they missed the Sir John Gielgud Theatre's production of The Cherry Orchard. Or fortunately, depending upon one's viewpoint.

Woake's phone vibrated as he was waiting to be interviewed as a witness to the explosion. It was a message from Richard Myers. *Our girl has just received a six-month sentence suspended for two years. Judge took pity on the impact on the children.*

By nightfall, the areas around the cremator and the remains of the hut had been taped off. The darkness had ensured that the investigators would have to wait until the following morning to continue with their investigations.

A restful peace descended upon the crematorium and its grounds, deserted save for foxes which scented their way around the premises. The storm had passed, allowing the light of the moon to shine down upon Gretford.

And for a small, lone figure weaving its way through the forest towards the burnt-out remains of the hut.

Fully aware of fire's limitations when disposing of a body, there was one last job Robbie Cole had to complete.

Not wanting to draw attention to himself, Cole used the light of the moon to find the location of the hut.

It was not difficult for him to find.

Cole crept to the edge of the smouldering ruins, taking a moment to admire his handiwork whilst checking that he was alone.

Creeping forward, so as to disturb as little of the rubble as possible, Cole found the remains of the coffins.

Risking the use of a Maglite, Cole found exactly what he expected to see.

Staring up at him were all that remained of the four bodies. It was impossible to tell them apart. Skulls were mingled with femurs. Tibias lay disjointed next to hips.

Fully aware that the fluids used in the embalming process to preserve the cadaver were, ironically, highly flammable, Cole knew the fire in the hut would be sufficient to deal with the caskets he had stored there.

Not being of a squeamish disposition, Cole picked up all the bones and the name plaques and placed them in a rucksack he had brought with him specifically for this job, until all that remained was ash.

Satisfied that no one could ever say that bodies had been stored in the hut, Cole raked over the marks his boots had left in the ash.

An hour later, Cole was safely snoring in his bed, his rucksack beside his bed.

No one ever knew that Cole had visited the hut that evening.

Thirty Five

September 2016

Once the storm had passed, Gretford bathed under an Indian summer in the weeks immediately after the disaster at the crematorium.

Acting with a hitherto unknown ability to cut through administrative red tape with the speed that only a local authority can act when a prime asset is knocked out of action, it was only a couple of weeks until a temporary cremator had been installed at the crematorium.

'It really is quite amazing,' Overton told a bored Woake during that September's Cabinet meeting. 'We have been able to source a new cremator which we were going to have to buy anyway as part of the new development. The chapel is still good for use, and we have placed the new cremator where it was going to go anyway, so we will build around it. The new cremator is attached to the current chapel by a temporary tunnel and it also has a temporary chimney. At least the explosion has now guaranteed that the new building will have to be built, as everyone agrees that the town now needs one.'

So with only a month's loss of income to accompany the Council's embarrassment, Gretford had a working crematorium, admittedly one not working at full capacity.

Angelina Burbridge had the uneasy task of having to talk to Robbie Cole.

It was proving to be a rather uncomfortable month for Burbridge, as councillors and local press (not to mention local solicitors) had been trying to find someone to blame. As manager, focus had, not unreasonably, fallen on her.

The preliminary hearing had concluded that faulty installation and not maintenance was to blame, and emails from Burbridge urging Cole to only use the cremator to the safe level dictated by the external technician back in July had exonerated her.

That Cole had never read the email was a minor detail of little importance to anyone.

The Council investigation, not to mention internal reports, would take months to conclude, by which time Burbridge would have been tipped off as to their contents and suitably briefed by her supporters higher up the management chain.

If September was proving to be rather uncomfortable for Burbridge, the same could not be said for Cole, who realised that his job was safe no matter what.

Simply put, Cole knew that no local authority would dare sack a fifty-five-year-old dwarf whose physical impairment impeded his safe operation of the machinery to which he was ordered to use.

As he knew full well, if any potential claim for unfair dismissal based upon his physical disability would not do for the Council, then his claim for ageism certainly would.

So it was that by the end of September, both parties returned to full-time work, secure in the knowledge that their jobs were safe.

There was one burning detail between them though, which was outstanding.

With the usual trepidation Burbridge reserved only for her encounters with Cole, she entered the crematorium's new cremator at midday.

It was Cole's first day back to work following the explosion, and Cole was already halfway through processing that morning's orders.

Unfortunately for Cole, whilst the equipment was new, the design was not.

Upon noticing the entrance of Burbridge into his domain, Cole stepped down from his beer crate, a much-missed object which Cole was relieved to find had survived the explosion.

'Robbie, may I have a word?' Burbridge said as Cole marched towards her.

'Yep,' Cole responded.

'Robbie,' Burbridge said nervously, fully aware that she was about to broach a rather sensitive topic. 'We have a problem.'

'Not here you don't, machinery's all working like a dream. I'm currently on top of the orders, which is the first time I have been able to say that for many a long year.'

'It's not that. We have had a rather serious complaint and I am afraid that the evidence from the initial investigation into the explosion sort of verifies it.'

'What's that?' Cole asked, limiting his answers to only a few words. He had an uncomfortable feeling about what this complaint would be about.

'Well,' continued Burbridge, 'we have had a report from a JET.'

'From a what?' Cole interrupted.

'From a JET.'

'Never heard of them,' Cole said dismissively, folding his arms.

'They're part of the district's own criminal enforcement team.'

'So the police?' Cole asked, obstructing Burbridge's train of thought.

'No, not the police,' she answered, although that had not stopped her hearing from a friend at Fordhouse that it did not stop this particular JET from acting like one. 'The complaint has come from an enforcement officer.'

'I thought you said he wasn't a police officer?' Cole asked.

'Forget the bloody police,' Burbridge said, momentarily losing her cool. 'This particular individual in question received a tip-off about the crematorium, who knows from where. Unfortunately for us, this said individual decided to investigate on exactly the same day as the explosion.

'Whilst inspecting the crem, he came across the gardener's hut which caught fire. Guess what he found inside?'

'Gardening tools?' Cole asked.

'He alleges that he found four coffins. New coffins. He inspected one and saw that the brass plaque bore the name *Emma Guest*. You wouldn't know anything about that, would you?' Burbridge asked.

Cole shook his head. Burbridge continued. 'Emma Guest's funeral service was held on 22nd August, three days before the explosion. Once the curtains had been drawn at the end of the service, you became the last person to have contact with her.'

'Doesn't mean that I know what this police officer is talking about,' Cole answered, not necessarily obtusely; like many, he struggled to know the difference between a police officer and a criminal enforcement officer.

'So you wouldn't know how her coffin got to be inside the

gardener's shed?'

'I thought you said it was a hut?'

'Bloody hell, Robbie, can't you just answer the bloody question?' Burbridge shouted.

'I burnt it.' Cole said truthfully.

'You what?' Burbridge said.

'I said I burnt it. The coffin,' Cole added by way of explanation. 'I would have written it in the records,' he added, walking over to a filing cabinet located in the corner of the cremator. To his eternal gratitude, the filing cabinet had also survived the explosion.

Opening the top draw, Cole took out a lever arch file and walked back towards Burbridge. With the aid of his beer crate, Cole used an empty gurney as a temporary desk. He took out a piece of paper.

'As you can see, it says quite clearly that Emma Guest was processed two hours after her service,' he said, blessing the foresight to forge the entries for all four of the coffins. He went into a side room of the cremator, reserved for processing the ashes.

'And as you can see, here are her mortal remains,' he said, holding up an urn. Burbridge flinched as she read *Emma Guest* on the side. 'Would you like to see inside?' he asked, beginning to remove the top. Burbridge held out her hand.

'No, don't!' she shouted in disgusted panic. 'Why aren't they at the reception waiting to be collected?'

'It's my first day back. You mentioned corroborating evidence?' Cole said, gaining the initiative.

'Apparently the fire service discovered what could be the remains of at least one coffin. Unfortunately, they were so badly damaged by the fire and the subsequent explosion that it's impossible to say for sure how long they've been there, or indeed how many there were.'

'Did they discover any bodies?'

'I don't believe so,' Burbridge answered.

'Couldn't have been Emma Guest's coffin then.' Cole saw the questioning look in her eyes. 'Takes a lot to burn a body, as recent events have proved. Had there been a body in any one of the coffins, then there would have been remains, bones for example.'

'I believe all they found was ash,' Burbridge said.

'Can't be anything to do with me, my records date back years.'

'They think someone started it intentionally. In fact, they're certain that it was intentional.'

'How?' Cole asked, beginning to worry.

'Petrol.'

'Doesn't mean much. That bloody helicopter could have sprayed the area with burning ashes. If the building was as old as they say it was, then there could have been leaking petrol from some old machine. Why don't you ask the gardeners what they think?'

'I have already done that,' Burbridge answered. 'They all deny all knowledge of it. Say they hadn't been in it for years.'

'They would, wouldn't they? And how would I be able to move a coffin that far?'

Burbridge looked him up and down. Not a particularly strenuous job. 'I see your point.'

Emma Guest's family took possession of her ashes, totally unaware that as they threw the World War II veteran's ashes off the White Cliffs of Dover, that they were in fact honouring the remains of a bonfire from Cole's garden, burnt during his enforced period of leave.

During which, the bones of the four unfortunates were buried in his garden.

Cole returned to work, Burbridge returned to managing the income expectancy of a needy Council and the dignity of death.

The following week saw another meeting between a junior staff member and his manager.

Oliver Gabriel sat in front of Walsh, wearing his most immaculate JET uniform.

'Ollie, we have a problem,' Walsh started the meeting.

'I'd say that we have a problem. We have four unaccounted bodies out there and relatives totally unaware that their relatives have been treated in such a disgraceful way.'

'That is precisely the point, we don't.'

'What?' Gabriel asked incredulously. 'I saw the name on the coffin. Emma Guest. An elderly white-haired lady in her nineties.'

'You were also hit on the head by an old paint tin, concussed and partially blinded by beige paint,' Walsh said.

'That was after I saw the body and the name on the coffin,'

Gabriel replied, not quite believing what he was hearing.

'Emma Guest?' Walsh asked.

'Yes, Emma Guest.'

'This is a copy of the crem's logbook, which shows quite clearly that Emma Guest's coffin was burnt on the same day as her funeral,' Walsh said, handing him a copy of the logbook. 'And this copy shows quite clearly that her daughter-in-law collected the ashes yesterday morning.'

Gabriel stared in horror at the two pieces of paper, the most important investigation of his professional life collapsing before his eyes. 'But it's not true. I know what I saw. And the firemen found four coffins,' he said desperately.

'No, Ollie,' Walsh answered. 'They found at least one coffin, but the remains are so badly destroyed by the fire that they're no use to anyone.'

'But surely there are remains of the bodies?'

'All that was found,' Walsh said, 'was ash. Nothing to suggest that a body had ever been near the hut.'

Gabriel sat there, staring ahead but seeing little, a man whose confidence in everything he believed in, shattered.

'Which brings us onto the second problem,' Walsh said.

'Oh yes,' Gabriel mumbled.

'You shouting and swearing at the Managing Director and senior councillors in front of a foreign delegation.'

'You would have been had you seen what I had seen,' Gabriel muttered. Walsh sat there, saying nothing. 'And I was concussed.'

'Were you?'

'You know I was,' Gabriel said aggressively.

'But you claim to have seen the bodies whilst fully aware of your surroundings, but then claim that you only acted in such a deplorable way once you were concussed. You can't have it both ways.'

'But it's the truth,' Gabriel muttered, simultaneously appalled at the unfairness and the irony of life.

'Unfortunately, it has called your conduct as a JET into question. Whilst no one can doubt your fastidious nature in combating anti-social behaviour, and I am sure that the Finance team are grateful for your own efforts in denting this Council's budget gap, we have received complaints about your perhaps overzealous efforts.'

'But these people are criminals,' Gabriel said with all the conviction of the ignorant failing to understand the difference between unlawful and illegal.

'Not always, they are our residents who we need to serve,' Walsh said, aware that she was a hypocrite; having done nothing but praise Gabriel and having even encouraged his efforts, Walsh now knew that the only way of saving her job (and therefore the JETs) was by relieving a man of his.

'I am afraid that your time on the JETs is now over,' Walsh said.

Gabriel sat pathetically, unable to say anything.

Within ten minutes, Gabriel left Fordhouse one last time dressed as a JET. Not even the Council would have had Gabriel suffer the indignity of walking out of the offices in just his Y-fronts.

Gabriel was not to be the only casualty to be lost because of the explosion.

At the same Cabinet meeting to which Overton was extolling the benefits of the new cremator, Leader of the Council William Foster was forced into providing a humiliating update to the Cabinet.

Unfortunately for Gretford, it could not be said that its political leaders had made a favourable impression on their colleagues from Binzhou, who had left Gretford as soon as they were allowed to leave the crematorium.

A meagre letter of thanks for the hospitality had been sent through Sam Tong.

'If the recent articles in *The Gretford Gazette* are to be believed,' Foster said depressingly, 'then it looks like Binzhou is now looking at Woking as a potential partner, so impressed were they with what they perceived to be Woking's future plans.'

In fact, the news had been confirmed by the councillor-loathing chief executive of the University of South-East England, Nick Churchouse, who could barely keep his glee from his voice when he told Foster.

As a result, the work of the Major Projects team was to be suspended until alternative investment streams could be identified.

The depression continued.

Due to the public outcry and the fallout of the forty-eight-hour delegation, the Council was to launch its own inquiry, to be led by the Overview and Scrutiny Committee, chaired by the Lib Dem leader Barbara Mason.

Mason had asked Bane, and had been granted, a brand-new committee structure, with its own budget and team of officers, led by a newly created position of Secretary to the Overview and Scrutiny Committee.

'We do not know yet who this person will be,' Foster said, 'but I think we can all expect to be called to give evidence.'

Which led Foster to explain the level of compensation to be handed to those affected by the explosion.

Whilst those who saw their services cancelled just received the paid fee, those who were there that day and were sufficiently traumatised would each receive compensation of up to £10,000 each.

At least, Woake thought, as he signed off each claim, that the Council's insurance company was footing the bill. Otherwise the financial stability of the Council would be even more precarious than it was previously.

'Which leads us onto the next problem, what do we do with the family of Stephen Roe? In case some of you don't know, his was the service before Prasad's, which started this entire sorry affair.'

'What's the problem?' Woake asked.

'It was his ashes which covered the roof, and us,' Foster answered.

'Can't we just tell his family to climb the scaffolding supporting the crem with a bucket and salvage what they can?' Swaden asked.

Swaden, ever a man of his time, had forgotten that all minutes of Cabinet meetings were now to be published to the Conservative Group, a leadership pledge made to his Group which Foster had been forced to honour.

It was not long until *The Gretford Gazette* was tipped off and the line was quoted. Like all scandals, the quote was taken completely out of context and given an interpretation which was never intended to be there.

Coming so soon after his other inflammatory comment at Full Council, it was quickly decided that Swaden would retire from the Cabinet with immediate effect. In gratitude for his long service, Swaden was made Deputy Mayor, to be made full Mayor when Mayor Joplin's term of office would end in May the following year.

In the end, Woake's advice was followed, that the families of the unfortunate Stephen Roe and Anjali Prasad received a higher level of compensation.

Pippa Prasad was far from upset. The compensation they had received for the explosion not only financed a five-star luxury break to the Seychelles, it also paid for a pair of diamond earrings.

Thirty Six

Reg Swaden was not the last political casualty of the Crematorium Incident, as *The Gretford Gazette* had christened it.

On the first Monday of October, Foster was called into a meeting with Giles Bane. He entered the leadership suite and greeted the PAs with a curt "good morning," receiving an equally curt "good morning" back.

Bane was waiting for Foster in the doorway of his office, deliberately catching Foster off guard, who was hoping to have a few minutes alone in the leadership suite to compose himself.

'Hiya Will, how are you?' Bane asked, all smiling.

'Fine,' Foster answered, despite feeling anything but. The past month had seen the forced abandonment of his hopes and dreams, caused by a scandal which had little chance of abating.

Bane held the door open for Foster as he walked into Bane's office, winking at the PAs as he closed the door.

Bane stopped smiling as soon as the door was closed.

Foster was already sitting down as Bane returned to his desk.

'Thank you for seeing me this morning, Will. Good weekend?'

'Fine, thanks,' Foster answered.

'So Reg has left the Cabinet.'

'Yes, sad news. He'll be sorely missed, although it was particularly stupid to say such a thing, especially as every comment is now recorded.'

'Interesting developments re the Council inquiry. Apparently, Barbara Mason is close to announcing her new Committee Secretary. Rumour has it he or she will be her attack dog.'

'Your position should become interesting then,' Foster quipped.

'Quite, though not as interesting as yours.'

'I'm sorry?' Foster asked, with a growing sense of foreboding.

'You'll be on quite a sticky wicket,' Bane said 'after all, who invited the Chinese over? Who insisted on showcasing the Full Council on a meeting we all knew was going to be fractious?'

'You're not possibly blaming me? It wasn't me who insulted the public, or who incited the fight, or who was responsible for the crematorium blowing up.'

'No, you weren't,' Bane agreed, 'but it was your idea to invite them, and thankfully records show that.'

'So what do you want?' Foster asked.

'Not you, that's for sure,' Bane said grinning, 'but the public outrage is such that an example should probably be made.'

'Who? Woake? He's responsible for the finance of the crematorium.'

'No, I don't think that Sebastian should be the one to carry the can. Nor would it be fair for Cathy, Serena or even Charles to suffer.'

'You can't be saying that Mark should resign?'

'No Will I'm not, although any right-minded individual would argue that his pet JETs acting like Gretford's own black shirts should be investigated.'

'Not Craig?' Foster asked.

'As Lead for Sustainable Projects, the management of the crematorium development fell directly into his remit. Combined with the Governance brief, questions are bound to be asked about the advisability of bestowing the responsibility of waste collection, roads, assets, governance and major projects in one so young. I do believe that he is yet to turn thirty.

'Not to mention that there appears to be a severe conflict of interest. As Lead for Governance, he would be directly responsible for investigating his actions as Lead for Sustainable Projects. Doesn't seem right, does it?'

'No,' Foster said 'no it doesn't. So what do you want? For him to lose Sustainable Projects?'

'No, I do not,' Bane said with mounting panic. The idea of a bitter Overton investigating Bane's own actions would have been a fate worse than maintaining the status quo. 'But I do think that it is a good idea for someone to take over Governance from him. One who has more professional experience of the challenges that will be facing the Governance portfolio in the months to come.'

'And if I refuse?' Foster asked, hoping to sound more confident than he felt.

'Then I am sure that the minutes of meetings describing your enthusiasm for the deal in the face of Cabinet reluctance will end up in the possession of *The Gretford Gazette*. Perhaps certain ambitious members of your Group might see an opportunity to wield the knife. Pakeman for example. Or Williams, or even Woake.'

So like Oliver Gabriel, Craig Overton was set to lose a job so that someone more senior could keep his.

The following day, Gretford District Council issued a press release announcing that Councillor Craig Overton was to step down as Lead for Governance in order to concentrate more time on his challenging role as Lead for Sustainable Projects.

Not that Oliver Gabriel would have known that as he walked up the steps into Fordhouse that morning.

It had been a month since he last walked out of Fordhouse, a month he had spent searching through all the local authorities in the south-east of England, hoping to apply for a role similar to that of a JET.

It was unfortunate for Gabriel, that most other local authorities had the good sense not to introduce such a scheme, and those that had were more than happy with their own small teams of income generators that at the moment they had no plans to expand.

It had dawned on him that he would have to cast his search further afield. No doubt there would be areas of Leeds with their own anti-social behaviour issues that he could apply for?

Gabriel was despairing at such a thought when, totally unexpectedly, his mobile phone rang with a withheld number, calling him in for a meeting at Fordhouse.

Gabriel walked into the appointed meeting room at exactly ten o'clock. Barbara Mason, the Leader of the Liberal Democrats Group and Leader of the Opposition at GDC, was already sitting at a desk.

'Good morning, Ollie, thank you for agreeing to see me this morning,' she said, welcoming him.

'Thank you for the invitation, Barbara,' Gabriel said, equally serious as he took his place opposite her. A large woman in her late fifties, with grey hair, the unmarried Barbara Mason had always been one of Gabriel's favourite councillors.

In his opinion, her serious and sincere demeanour was the perfect combination for which all councillors had to strive. Not for Gabriel the jovial banter between councillors which he had witnessed in some committee meetings, nor should councillors trade childish insults for political gain, which he often read about in *The Gretford Gazette*.

Council was a serious business of public service, which Mason embodied perfectly.

'I was sorry to hear that you lost your job,' Mason said earnestly. For her part, she always respected Gabriel's efficiency as Secretary of the Planning Committee and his commitment to his subsequent role on the Council.

Giving credence to the claim that the Liberal Democrats are perhaps the most enthusiastic proponents of quashing civil liberties for the public good, Mason respected the zealous way in which Gabriel went about tackling anti-social behaviour. 'How is the job hunt going?' she asked.

'I have a few leads,' Gabriel said, not wanting to sound too desperate. 'But the main issue is that in this age of austerity, many public authorities are not recruiting.'

'I appreciate that,' Mason said sadly. She always believed in the big state. 'Which is why I have called you in today. As you may or may not be aware, the fiascos which are the Local Plan and the crematorium, combined with the now-defunct Binzhou partnership, have put the overview and scrutiny of this Council into greater focus. I have recently started an inquiry into recent events, as per my role as Chair of Overview and Scrutiny.

'I have received agreement from senior officers for a total overhaul of Council scrutiny, which I will implement in the coming weeks. Overton has lost Governance,' Mason said with a smile, 'but I understand that his replacement, who will be announced shortly, has a legal background. It is therefore vital that someone who shares my commitment to holding this Council to account manages the new committee. I have read your account of the explosion at the crem.'

'I can assure you that my account is totally accurate,' Gabriel replied.

'I know, and I believe you. What happened to you must have been deeply distressing.' Gabriel nodded. 'Which is why you are here. The new Overview and Scrutiny Committee will have a new team of officers serving it, but I need someone I can trust to lead the team, who, whilst ostensibly will be serving the Council, will also be someone who appreciates that they owe their new position to me.'

'I understand,' Gabriel said.

'I believe that your efficiency, commitment and investigative mind will be perfect as the team leader. Officially, your position will be Secretary to the Overview and Scrutiny Committee. I have an employment contract drafted by the HR department for your perusal. You can start on Monday,' she concluded.

Gabriel left Fordhouse an hour later, fully briefed in his new role as Councillor Barbara Mason's attack dog against the Tory leadership.

EPILOGUE

Early October 2016

It was a week later and Woake was sitting in courtroom 3 of the City of London County Court. The balmy Indian summer had given way to the first onslaught of autumn. Woake could see through the courtroom's window that the leaves were beginning to turn brown.

Woake was sitting next to his client, a woman in her twenties who had brought a claim against a seventy-two-year-old taxi driver of Middle Eastern descent. Or to be more accurate, her insurance company had.

Woake's client maintained that the defendant had pulled out in front of her unexpectedly at a junction rather than giving way. The defendant, however, maintained that the claimant had signalled for him to pull out, and had issued a counterclaim.

The claimant was merely asking for damages to cover the repairs to the car. The defendant was asking for damages for whiplash and travel anxiety.

Woake was halfway through his cross-examination of the defendant. As a civil case, the rules around cross-examination were stricter than in criminal matters. Simply put, Woake was not permitted to be as dominating, nor as aggressive, as he could be in a criminal trial.

'Mr Ahmed, I understand that you have been a taxi driver since 1995, is that correct?'

'Yes it is,' the defendant replied.

'I am looking at your medical report. Could you please turn to page 35 in the file in front of you?' Woake waited until Ahmed had found the correct page. 'This page is the part of your medical report detailing your past medical history. It says that you were involved in a road traffic accident in 1997, 1999, 2002, 2005, 2007, 2011, 2012 and 2015, as well as the accident of this year. In each case, you have claimed to have suffered from whiplash and travel anxiety.'

'Yes, that is correct,' Ahmed said aggressively.

Woake ignored him. 'And on all these occasions, it was never your fault?'

'No, never.'

'You've been terribly unlucky then, haven't you, Mr Ahmed?'

'I'm not sure where my learned friend is going with this,' Woake's opponent interrupted.

'I think I do,' the deputy district judge hearing the case said wearily. It was the second such civil action he had heard that day, and he had another to do afterwards.

Woake won the case. Full damages were awarded to his client.

Woake was in his car, driving back to Gretford. It had just gone two o'clock in the afternoon, and whilst he had plenty of time to drive to Inner Temple and endure the tedium of Chambers' afternoon tea, an appointment at Fordhouse saved him from that particular pleasure.

It was a Friday afternoon, and he had plans for the forthcoming weekend.

There were, however, two calls he had to make, having missed both earlier that morning.

The first was to Richard Myers, his Head of Chambers.

'Ah, Woake,' Myers answered the phone 'good of you to call me back.'

'Hi Richard, how are you?'

'Fine, thanks. How was your foray into the world of civil litigation?'

'Fine, although the judge had little option but to grant me the win when I highlighted the defendant's previous claims. All told, the lying bastard has made nine such claims, including today's, since 1997.'

'Well done. I have some news for you. The DWP phoned. They're going to be sending us more cases in the coming days. I'll send some over to you.'

'Thanks,' Woake replied as he weaved his way through the London traffic.

'I'm also sending you off to become a pupil-master.'

'I thought the new name is pupil-supervisor?' Woake responded.

'Bollocks to that. Whilst I'm Head of Chambers, we'll use the traditional terminology.'

'So why pupil-master?'

'Thought the influence of a younger more sensitive colleague would rub off well on you.'

'Worked on you.'

'Plus, it's the next step up on your ascent to a more senior position at Chambers.'

'Thinking of retirement?' Woake asked.

'Must always think of your future development, Woake. Coming to Chambers?' Myers asked.

'Can't. I have a meeting to attend at Gretford.'

'Council?'

'Afraid so.'

'Still involved with that?'

'Just been promoted. I'm now Lead Councillor for Finance and Governance.'

'Which means?'

'Which means that I am now in charge of ensuring that the Council adheres to all legislation and guidelines, as well as good conduct and discipline.'

'Could have guessed that two visits to Chambers in a week was pushing it. What's your meeting about?'

'I have to open a pedestrian crossing in the centre of town, which has been redecorated to match the flag of Stonewall.'

'Of what?' Myers asked.

'Stonewall, it's the leading gay rights charity. Apparently there's some Pride in Sussex event this weekend and Gretford has decided to show solidarity by painting a pedestrian crossing the colours of the rainbow.'

'A crossing of many colours?' Myers asked.

'Quite.'

'How the hell is anyone who is colour-blind supposed to see it?'

'You know, I do believe the impact that a multi-coloured pedestrian crossing would have on the visually impaired was never considered,' Woake answered.

'And why should someone who doesn't agree with the political agenda set out by Stonewall be forced to use a pedestrian crossing dedicated to its agenda?'

'It's all down to recognition,' Woake answered.

'Should imagine anyone would get plenty of recognition walking on that monstrosity. I'm making the assumption that it will be permanent?'

'Should imagine so. It will no doubt become a permanent fixture to mark the permanent fight being fought for the perception of what is normal,' Woake answered.

'We fought a fucking world war in order to allow everyone to have the right to have a perception of what is normal, even if it differs from everyone else.'

Woake sighed, said his farewells and rang off.

The second call was to Giles Bane, who answered on the third ring.

'Hiya Sebastian, how are you?'

'Fine Giles. I missed a call from you but appreciate that I'm seeing you shortly, so this call's probably a waste of time.'

'Not at all Seb, just wanted to phone up to say congratulations on your new appointment. And to let you know a bit of news.'

'Oh yes?' Woake asked with half-interest.

'I thought you might like to know that Oliver Gabriel has just been appointed Secretary to the Overview and Scrutiny Committee.'

'Who?'

'Oliver Gabriel, he was that JET who caused all those problems at the crem.'

'That deranged lunatic? Why should I be worried?'

'Rumour has it he has been appointed with the sole intention of helping Barbara Mason and her Lib Dems bring down the Tory administration. As the new Lead Councillor, you'll be directly responsible for overseeing how the inquiry unfolds and limiting any damage to the leadership and directors.'

'What you mean is, you want me to help you out of the mire?'

'I wouldn't say that,' Bane said in mock astonishment. 'I just thought it would be useful for you to have a meeting with your new officers to discuss a forward strategy.'

'Thanks Giles, and when is this meeting?'

'Next week.'

'Thanks Giles, see you shortly.'

***

Two hours later, Woake was standing at the pedestrian crossing straddling the main road separating Fordhouse from Gretford High Street. A small crowd had gathered in the failing light of the late afternoon, looking down on the new crossing in all its multi-coloured glory.

The traffic had been temporarily stopped.

Serena Kildare accompanied Woake. As Lead Councillor for Health and Community, the Pride event fell into her portfolio.

In all honesty, Woake had little idea why he had been asked to do it.

Not that he cared. Later that afternoon, Woake would be checking them into a boutique hotel in the New Forest which he had booked for that weekend.

A quick look at the officers gathered around the crossing answered the question. Along with Giles Bane and a couple of officers who he did not recognise, stood Vicky Walsh.

'Hello Councillor,' she greeted Woake. 'I thought that as you have only recently undertaken our equality and diversity training scheme, that you would welcome the opportunity to highlight how at one you are with all those still campaigning for equality in their lives.'

'It's very kind of you to have thought of me,' Woake answered.

Bane greeted Woake like a long-lost friend, their recent telephone conversation conveniently forgotten.

Woake addressed the one reporter from *The Gretford Gazette*, the only representative from the media.

'It is my greatest pleasure,' Woake said as he addressed the lone reporter, 'to open this new crossing as the perfect symbol of unity the Council shares with all those who strive for a better future for not only themselves but for others as well.'

Woake stood back, towards the group of Gretford District Council representatives, taking his place next to Kildare.

All eyes looked down at the crossing.

No one noticed Kildare's hand stroking the little finger on Woake's left hand, her middle finger following the edge of his signet ring.

Evening had begun, casting the multi-coloured crossing into shadows, turning the bright colours of the rainbow into different shades of black, grey and white.

In front of them, the Gretford rush hour traffic resumed. All the motorists oblivious not only to the recently repainted crossing but also to the politicians and civil servants standing to one side.

Printed in Great Britain
by Amazon